A BABY
for the
HOME FRONT GIRLS

BOOKS BY SUSANNA BAVIN

A BABY
for the
HOME FRONT GIRLS

SUSANNA BAVIN

bookouture

Published by Bookouture in 2025

An imprint of Storyfire Ltd.
Carmelite House
50 Victoria Embankment
London EC4Y 0DZ

www.bookouture.com

The authorised representative in the EEA is Hachette Ireland
8 Castlecourt Centre
Dublin 15 D15 XTP3
Ireland
(email: info@hbgi.ie)

ISBN: 978-1-83618-374-7
eBook ISBN: 978-1-83618-373-0

*Dedicated to the wartime Brownies,
who, nationwide, salvaged enough jam jars
to finance an aircraft and a lifeboat*

ONE

JANUARY 1942

While George paid the taxi driver, Lorna stood on the pavement and peered into the darkness. This was the gracious London square that was now her home.

Even though there was a vast mound of rubble in the centre of the line of tall, elegant townhouses on the opposite side, and even though the garden in the middle of the square had been given over to vegetable gardening for the duration of the war, it was certainly gracious. A sliver of moonlight fell on the cold frames edging the area, making the glass reflect like puddles.

Aside from the small quantity of light that came from the sky, there was no other brightness. Even though there had been blackouts every single night for three years now, and everybody was used to them, and indeed small children couldn't even remember when it had been different, there was a little part of Lorna that would never be fully accustomed to the sheer depth of the darkness without street-lamps, or light spilling from houses. Even motorcar headlamps were fitted with metal filters to minimise the spread of their beams. Just like everyone else, Lorna had at one time or another stumbled when she'd misjudged where the kerb was, and had bumped into someone and apologised, only to realise that she'd just said sorry to a pillarbox or a lamp-post.

Tonight, there was a sharp nip in the wintry air, and she pulled her velvet evening cloak more snugly around herself, tilting back her head to look up at the stars.

'Stargazing?' George asked, coming to stand beside her as the motor pulled away. A narrow shaft of moonlight fell on his lean features, sharpening his cheekbones. A handsome man, he probably appeared severe to those who didn't know him, and it was true that he was generally serious, but Lorna knew him for the loving, generous, steadfast man he was.

'It's a clear night,' she observed, 'but at least there isn't a full moon, or Jerry might get ideas about an air raid.'

George laughed. 'I thought you were going to say how beautiful the stars are.'

'Oh, are we supposed to carry on saying romantic things now we're married?' Lorna asked innocently. She stepped closer to George and entwined her gloved fingers in his. 'Are you telling me you're not averse to a spot of lovey-dovey talk?'

Lorna was tall, but George was taller. He looked down into her face, his grey-blue eyes very dark. 'Are you *flirting* with me, Mrs Broughton?'

'Who, me? I'll have you know I'm a respectable married lady.'

'And don't you forget it.' George dropped a kiss on her nose.

A happy sigh escaped Lorna. 'Seriously, though, the stars are beautiful. All the special things are more beautiful in wartime. Flowers, the stars, the sound of children's laughter...'

'Wives,' George added.

'Really? All wives or just one wife in particular?'

'There might be a certain dark-haired, green-eyed wife with a lovely, slender body,' George murmured. 'Shall we go inside and switch on the light so I can make sure I've brought the right one home with me?'

He ushered her up the steps to the front door of his family's London townhouse, where he and Lorna had now taken up residence. Previously, George had had a suite of rooms in a building that accommodated men only, but he'd had to give that up when he married. Lorna thought it was a shame. She would have liked them to share a cosy flat, where they could shut the front door and be alone in their own little world. That would have been perfect.

They had married in the middle of November in Manchester, a place that was dear to both their hearts. They'd had a blissful two-night honeymoon – which, let's face it, was one night longer than many couples in these days of wartime – after which they had immediately headed down to London, where George worked for the War Office. That was something else to be grateful for – not being separated from one another. Lorna had been given permission to resign from her war work in the salvage depot in Chorlton-cum-Hardy.

She and George entered the Broughtons' townhouse. The ground floor now housed the local ARP station and the office belonging to George's father, Sir Jolyon. Lady Broughton's former morning room was filled with racks of clothing belonging to the WVS's clothing exchange, and the grand drawing room and the library were a supplies depot. The books from the library had survived by the skin of their teeth. In common with many books, they had been donated as salvage, but an exemption had been made for rare and historically valuable books, so they had been put into storage instead.

'Samuel would be pleased,' Lorna had said with a smile when she was told.

Samuel Atkinson was a bookseller in Manchester, a quiet, decent chap who was married to Lorna's dear friend, Betty. They had been colleagues at the salvage depot in the south of Manchester, where Lorna had done her war work before marrying George and moving to London.

She and George climbed the splendid staircase. Its bottom step was wider and curved around the newel post in a graceful flourish. Beneath the smooth wooden banister were ornamental balusters of cast iron. Upstairs, one of the bedrooms had been transformed into a drawing room, using furniture from the former morning room. George had set up the mandatory blackout before they went out for the evening and now, as they walked in, he switched on the light.

Lorna turned so George could help her with her cloak, beneath which she wore her dusty-pink evening gown with its skirt of sunray pleats. George laid her cloak over a wing-backed armchair before throwing his wool overcoat on top, followed by his gloves, silk scarf and hat.

Lorna peeled off her elbow-length gloves and sat on the sofa. George picked up the silver box from the table, opened it and offered it to her. She shook her head, and George took out a cigarette for himself.

'I'll be glad when the cigarette shortage is over,' he remarked. 'I'm getting heartily tired of seeing "No cigarettes" and "No tobacco" notices in the tobacconists' windows.' He joined Lorna on the sofa, lifting his arm for her to snuggle close. 'Best part of the day,' he murmured, 'having you all to myself.'

He inhaled, then blew out smoke before dangling the hand that held the cigarette over the arm of the sofa. Lorna shut her eyes for a moment. He smelled of sandalwood and, very faintly, of the starch that kept his shirts so smart.

'How long do you think people will keep spying on us?' Lorna spoke lightly, wanting to hide how deeply this hurt her.

'Spying? That's a strong word.'

'That's how it seems sometimes. Wherever we go, I can feel all those eyes on us. People are just waiting for us to betray the fact that we know getting married was a mistake.'

'Oh, Lorna,' George said indulgently.

'No, that's not true,' she corrected herself. 'They're not

waiting for *us*. They're waiting for *you* to realise *you've* made a mistake.'

'They'll wait a deuce of a long time, then,' George said drily.

'You know what I mean,' pushed Lorna.

'Yes, I do,' he replied. 'You have to admit that, with the way our first engagement ended, with us going to court—'

'Thanks to my father,' Lorna put in.

'—our second engagement certainly stirred up national interest. Now that we're man and wife, there will always be somebody who's looking for the cracks in our marriage.'

'You don't sound bothered about it,' Lorna observed.

George inhaled on his cigarette. 'It was bound to happen. If other people have nothing better to do, more fool them. Just you wait. When we celebrate our golden wedding, there'll be someone who can't resist making a joke out of our first engagement having gone so wrong. But the real joke, my lovely wife,' he added, pressing a kiss into her hair, 'will be on *them*, because we'll have had fifty wonderful years together with many more ahead of us.'

Fifty years! Lorna was too thrilled at being a bride to imagine herself as an older woman with five decades of marriage behind her. Still, after everything she and George had gone through to bring them to the point of being newly-weds, it was exciting, reassuring and deeply romantic to hear him speaking with such confidence about their future. Although it irritated Lorna to know they were under scrutiny by people who would be highly entertained if they tripped up and seemed to regret their marriage, all that truly mattered to her was the certainty of the love she and George shared. No one else knew what they'd gone through to bring them back together after their separation.

Maybe George was thinking something similar, because he said, 'This time last year, we'd not long since met up again, and I was impressed and intrigued by your courage and determination, not to mention that I was desperate to see you again. I know the Christmas Blitz was a terrible thing for Manchester to go through, but it was instrumental in reuniting us. Working together on those rescues opened my eyes to the *real* you.'

'This Christmas couldn't have been more different,' said Lorna.

Together with Sir Jolyon, they had travelled up to Yorkshire for a fleeting but highly enjoyable visit to the family seat, Platt House. It had been Lorna's first time there as a member of the family. Times were when she would have dreaded being Lady Broughton's guest, because her ladyship used to regard her as a gold-digger who was simply after George's inheritance, including his future title. But last year, Lorna's conduct while staying at Platt House had shown Lady Broughton that she was a decent, capable sort of woman and would one day make a worthwhile lady of the manor. Since then, the two of them had become firm allies.

'I'll tell you what made this Christmas feel different,' said Lorna.

'Being hopelessly in love with your devoted husband?' George suggested.

'Maybe that came into it,' teased Lorna, 'but what I was thinking of was the feeling of hope now that America is in the war.'

'That's true,' George agreed.

Last month, following the attack on Pearl Harbor that had shocked the world, America had declared war on Japan and then, a few days later, on Italy and Germany. At about the same time, the British had retaken Benghazi, and the Russians had retaken Kalinin. All in all, there was now a general and growing belief that the Allies would eventually win the war – though 'eventually' was still a very long way off.

Lady Broughton's Christmas gift to Lorna had been a copy of the sheet music of the popular song 'The King is Still in

London'. Whenever Lorna sang it as she accompanied herself on the piano, she had to miss out the final words because of the lump in her throat. The song's title said it all, really. The King and Queen, instead of retreating to safety – and no one would have thought any the worse of them if they had – had stayed put in London, making the nation proud and determined, and adding to the feeling of resolve.

Now, at long last, with America in the war, that resolve was finally paying off.

'My main wish now,' said Lorna, 'apart from the usual wish about my loved ones staying safe, is that your work keeps you in London and you don't have to go off overseas again. Having you here is all that matters.'

George stubbed out his cigarette in the ashtray on the small table beside him. Cupping her cheek in his palm, he lifted her face. Bending his head, he covered her mouth with his.

'No, *this* is all that matters,' he murmured, and kissed her.

TWO

Since marrying her lovely Samuel last April, Betty had settled into a routine that enabled her to combine her domestic responsibilities with her war work in the salvage depot.

This involved her getting up early to hurry to the butcher's and the grocer's as soon as they opened at half past seven and eight o'clock respectively to get her shopping done, before coming home to make breakfast. It had been easy to do this through the warm, light summer mornings, but as autumn had turned to winter it had become harder. But now it was January and there were longer days to look forward to in the coming weeks.

Betty walked home briskly through the blacked-out streets at the end of her working day. It was jolly cold. 'Proper parky,' her darling mum would have said. She'd been gone for several years now, but Betty still missed her, and knew she always would.

'But that's a good thing in its own way,' Mrs Beaumont, her former landlady, had suggested back in the days when Betty had lodged at Star House. 'It shows what a good mother she was and how much you loved one another.'

One of the great sorrows of Betty's life was that her mother had never met Samuel. Instead, Samuel's mother-in-law was Grace, Dad's second wife. Grace hadn't always been nice to Betty and, to be fair, Betty had felt iffy about Grace, too. When Mum had still been around, Grace had had a reputation locally for being a widow who was on the lookout for husband number two. Then poor Mum had died unexpectedly, and it hadn't been long before Grace had got her hooks into Dad.

Betty reached the bookshop. The blackout blinds had been pulled down to cover the big window and the door, which had glass panels in it. Standing on the step in the porch, she knocked on the door's upper pane, knowing that Samuel would be there, listening out for her.

She could see herself in the glass, the blackout backdrop almost making her look like she was in a black-and-white film on the silver screen. That made her smile because today she was wearing what she called her film-star hat, with its stylish asymmetrical brim. Mind you, that was the only film-starry thing about her, as far as she was concerned. The rest of her seemed fairly ordinary in a fresh-faced, natural sort of way. It was more important to have a friendly expression than fabulous looks. That was what Mum used to say. But Samuel thought Betty was the prettiest girl in the world. His admiration made her *feel* pretty. And she had good skin. She knew that because Radiance, the face cream people, had actually used her photograph in not one, but *two* of their advertisements last year.

The door opened a crack and Betty slid through it and into Samuel's arms almost before he could shut the door behind her. A rush of love coursed through her. Samuel's embrace always made her feel that way. There was something endearingly gangly about his limbs even though he wasn't especially tall. In fact, he was of medium height for a man, and he had a serious, unassuming manner, though Betty knew how strong and dependable his character was. He had believed in her and stood by her during that frightening time when she had been held by the police under suspicion of large-scale theft and the selling-on of stolen goods.

'You s-smell of fresh, c-cold air,' he said, holding her close.

Betty tilted her head so her hat didn't get knocked off. 'You smell of tobacco and books.'

'Not books but *old* books,' Samuel replied. 'I've been looking through boxes of antiquarian titles to pick out the volumes that have to be k-kept because they're important.'

As well as being a bookseller, Samuel did war work that involved books. His shop was a receiving point for second-hand books that he and Betty sorted through to send either to bombed-out libraries or to the troops overseas. Samuel also singled out anything that would fetch a good price that would be donated to the war effort as well as, like just now, ensuring that the right books were kept safe for future generations.

'I've got the f-fire going in the parlour,' he said. 'C-come and warm up.'

They walked between the bookcases, their feet striking the bare floorboards, and through the door in the back of the shop into what had been, when Betty had first seen it, a cross between a storeroom, an office and a parlour – the parlour part being the least in evidence of the three.

But after Samuel had started going out with her, he had gradually turned the room into a proper parlour. Almost all the bookcases had been squeezed onto the shop floor and, each time Betty had visited, more pieces of furniture had been added. Over by the fireplace, a pair of comfy armchairs had a handy table in between them. On the other side of the room stood a sideboard and a gateleg table with a pair of dining chairs. Other pieces of furniture – an upright piano, a wireless, a standard lamp, a green-baize-covered card table – added to the cosiness, as did a selection of ornaments on the mantelpiece. It was even possible these days to enjoy the sight of the wallpaper, with its pattern of cabbage roses.

Betty hung up her outdoor things in the cupboard next to the kitchen door and sat in one of the armchairs, leaning forward to hold out her hands to the cheerful fire. Samuel sat in the other armchair. He had already removed the tweed jacket with elbow-patches that he wore in the shop and had put on the V-necked sweater Betty had knitted for him. It was in a deep shade of maroon that she had taken a bit of a gamble on, since Samuel generally wore browns and fawns, but she had known as soon as she saw the colour that it would be perfect on him. There hadn't been time to take him to the wool shop to check. If she'd done that, someone else would have snapped it up.

'It really shouldn't suit him at all,' Grace had said the first time she saw him in it, 'with his hazel eyes and that nondescript brown hair.'

'*Nondescript?*' Betty had repeated indignantly.

'Well, what else would you call it?' Grace had touched her own conker-brown locks self-consciously. 'It's just a middling sort of brown. Anyroad, what matters is that the maroon suits him. You made a good choice there, Betty.'

That was how things were now with Grace. In former days, she had connived to shunt Betty out of the home where she had grown up. Having succeeded in that, she had then done her level best to ration Betty's time with her beloved dad. Things had changed when Dad had discovered the truth. He had given Grace a dressing-down in front of Betty, and since then Grace had changed her attitude.

Now, Betty looked lovingly at her husband. He wore his hair slicked back with Brilliantine, as all the men did these days, but even so the natural curl showed here and there, as if he'd just run his hand through his hair. The firelight lent a dash of shine to the lenses of his glasses, behind which his characteristic kindness was evident in his hazel eyes, making his scholarly face appear gentle.

'Good day?' he asked.

'Fine,' Betty answered, 'but I'll be glad when the days draw out. The depot can be a pretty dreary place in the winter.'

She looked at the clock on the mantelpiece. Their old-fashioned mantel had three shelves above the fireplace, and Betty had enjoyed filling it with keepsakes, including her two favourite wedding photographs, one of her with her new husband, the other of her with Sally and Lorna, her two bridesmaids, as well as Mrs Beaumont, their landlady. She'd had an extra copy of that one printed especially for Mrs Beaumont, whom all the girls were very fond of.

'I'd best get cooking,' she said, standing up.

'W-what are we having?' Samuel asked.

'The wartime equivalent of steak-and-kidney pie,' she told him. 'Butter-bean-and-kidney pie; and we can finish the ginger pudding for afters.'

'I'll polish our sh-shoes while you make a start,' said Samuel.

'Did you have a chance to pop in on the Kendalls?' Betty asked, removing her apron from the back of the kitchen door.

'Just for half an hour w-while the shop was c-closed for dinner.'

'Are they all right for coal? It's so cold at the moment...'

'I'll arrange a delivery f-for them when I book our next one,' said Samuel.

Mr and Mrs Kendall were an elderly couple who lived over the road in a small but spotless upstairs flat. They were both infirm, especially Mrs Kendall. She was a dainty, kind-eyed lady, who had obviously been pretty when she was young. She had suffered from rheumatoid arthritis for some years, which had left her with restricted mobility. Samuel had taken the Kendalls under his wing before Betty came into his life, and now Betty was happy to care for them, too. She'd become even more fond of Mrs Kendall when the dear lady had given her close friend Lorna the beautiful fabric that should have been made into Tilly Kendall's wedding dress years ago, except that Tilly had died.

Betty and Samuel dropped in to see the Kendalls during the evenings when they weren't going out to their voluntary war work. Tonight, they were both due to be out on duty – Betty was a fire-watcher, Samuel an ARP warden – and so they were going to stay at home together until it was time to head out.

After their meal, Betty washed up while the kettle boiled. Presently, she brought two cups of tea through to the parlour. She put them down before settling herself on the hearthrug to lean comfortably against Samuel's legs. She angled herself so that she could either gaze into the flames or look up at her husband.

They listened to the news on the wireless, which included information about the stream of new arrivals in the country.

'It's extraordinary to think of having hundreds of thousands of American soldiers here,' Betty remarked. 'Where on earth are we going to put them all?'

At the end of the news, they chatted for a while and made a list of errands for the week.

'I can get some things done on Saturday,' said Betty. 'No, wait, I can't. It's my Saturday for the depot.'

'Wh-when is S-Sally going to get a new girl to replace Lorna?' Samuel asked. 'The two of you are w-working alternate Saturdays now instead of one in three.'

'Says the man who works every single Saturday in his book-shop,' Betty answered teasingly.

'Don't mind me,' he replied. 'I'm being s-selfish. I like having you at home even when I'm w-working.'

'You could never be selfish,' Betty said loyally – and truthfully. 'You're the most caring man I've ever met.'

'Do I get a k-kiss for that?'

'Since you ask nicely,' Betty said demurely.

THREE

Betty always did her fire-watching duty with Sally.

The two of them were great chums and before Betty's wedding they had both lived in Star House. They worked together in the salvage depot, where Sally was the manager. Betty was proud of her friend for making such a success of the job.

Not for the first time that night, Betty climbed up the ladder, eased her way through the open skylight and emerged onto the salvage depot's flat roof, where the chilly night air immediately nipped at her cheeks. Beneath the ink-dark sky studded with stars, she went to join Sally, who was stamping her feet and energetically swinging her arms across her body. She had a slim figure and a good-looking, heart-shaped face, with hazel eyes and a friendly smile.

Betty stopped beside her friend. An elaborate shiver that was partly for dramatic effect but partly completely real shuddered through her well-wrapped body.

'That's one thing about fire-watching in winter,' Betty said. 'It keeps you fit. The number of times you go all the way downstairs to put the kettle on, then the number of times you have to rush back down because you're bursting for the privy.'

As fire-watchers, their job was to report the location of any flames they saw during air raids as well as to respond to anything that happened to the depot. They were also responsible for the stretch of Beech Road where the depot was. Usually, this meant tackling incendiaries. Like many civilians, they were so accustomed to this now that they didn't think twice about the danger.

The number of air raids had dwindled during November and December, but there had been one early in January. The most important thing was to maintain vigilance and not be lulled into a false sense of security.

Back at the start of this viciously cold snap, the girls had tried taking turns, one acting as the lookout on the roof while the other stayed inside, supposedly to keep warm, but without a fire to huddle over that hadn't worked. They couldn't afford to have even a tiny fire during the night. What little coal they had was needed in daytime.

Remembering the conversation she'd had with Samuel earlier on, Betty asked Sally, 'Now we're into the new year, are you going to see about getting a new girl to join us? Not that I don't enjoy it being just us. It's been like old times, when we first came here.'

'I didn't want to ask for a new girl as soon as Lorna left,' Sally explained. 'I wanted to leave a gap so that Mrs Lockwood wouldn't get any ideas. I didn't like being beholden to her for opening the depot on Lorna's wedding day so that I didn't have to.'

'Oh, but if you hadn't asked her,' Betty answered at once, 'you couldn't have been the other matron of honour!'

'I know,' said Sally, 'and I'm glad Mrs Lockwood stepped in – but I did have this feeling we might be reawakening the monster...'

Betty chuckled. That was a good description. Mrs Lockwood was a fearsome lady who belonged to the Women's Voluntary Service. Because she had tried to muscle in and take over the local branch, Mrs Callaghan, the branch organiser, had made her the salvage officer. While this had effectively diverted Mrs Lockwood's attention from the Chorlton WVS, it had thrust it squarely onto the salvage depot. After Sally had become the depot manager, she and Mrs Lockwood had spent some months locked in combat before Mr Merivale and Mr Pratt from the Town Hall had finally seen sense and made it clear that the authority lay in Sally's capable hands.

Lorna's wedding day had been a Saturday and Sally had been rostered to open the depot. It hadn't been easy for her to seek Mrs Lockwood's help, but, as much as her feud with that imperious lady mattered, Lorna's wedding had mattered more. But Betty could quite understand why Sally had wanted to let some time pass before she replaced Lorna. It would have been just frightful if Mrs Lockwood had barged in on the act.

'Anyway,' Sally added, 'it's been all right with just the two of us, hasn't it? We've managed. But it'll be better to have three again.'

'Not so many Saturdays!' Betty said cheerfully. 'And more fun.'

'Yes, it was fun with Lorna here, wasn't it?' Sally agreed. 'I miss her, but I'm glad she's able to be with George. So many married couples are separated at present – and I don't just mean the men who are away fighting.'

Betty squeezed Sally's hand. 'I know how you hate being apart from Andrew.'

Sally nodded and sniffed. 'I do. We *both* do.' She stood up straight and her shoulders went back. 'But at least he's still here in England, putting his carpentry skills to good use in the army. If he can't be at home with me, then I'll gladly, *gratefully* settle for knowing he's down south.'

'We're all glad he hasn't been deployed abroad,' Betty assured her warmly.

'And I'm glad for Lorna, that she was allowed to resign from her war work here so she could be with George,' Sally added.

'I feel fortunate every single day because of being with Samuel,' Betty said, her voice rich with emotion.

'Oh, I've had a letter from Andrew,' Sally told her. 'He's got some leave coming up.'

'That's wonderful!' Betty exclaimed, delighted for her friend.

Sally tilted her chin. 'The thing is, it's embarkation leave.'

'But he's a carpenter, not a soldier!'

'Everyone in the army is a soldier, no matter what job they have in civilian life. Andrew's carpentry has kept him on home soil since he joined up, and that's something to be grateful for.'

Betty recognised Sally's sensible voice when she heard it, and understood that Sally wouldn't want her to make a fuss, so she merely asked, 'Do you know where he's being shipped to?'

'No, but I hope he'll be able to tell me when he comes home.'

'When is his leave?'

'Mid-January.' Excitement rang in Sally's voice as she added, 'I can't wait to see him. Being together again will get my year off to the best possible start. I wonder what 1942 will bring for you and Lorna? Who knows, maybe Lorna and George will start a family? Can you imagine how *beautiful* their children will be? They're such a good-looking couple. And... what about you and Samuel?' she asked quietly.

'Us having a family, you mean?'

'That's exactly what I mean.' Sally's voice was steady. 'Do you think you can't talk to me about babies because I lost mine?'

Betty felt a deep pang of sympathy for her friend. 'I'm so sorry that happened to you.'

'I don't remember all that much about it, to be honest,' Sally admitted. 'I was in so much pain I was halfway delirious. I have vague memories of being in the back of the motor and seeing the brilliant lights of strings of incendiaries dropping to earth, but I don't know if they're real memories or something I made up afterwards…'

'Lorna was so brave to drive you to hospital through that air raid,' said Betty.

'That was the worst raid since the Christmas Blitz,' said Sally. 'When other people remember it, they talk about the police headquarters, the Theatre Royal and the College of Technology being badly damaged, but to me all it means is that I lost my baby.' She went very still for a moment, then seemed to come back to life. 'But that's no reason for other people, for my *friends*, to avoid baby talk. I mean it, Betty.'

Betty drew a breath. How brave Sally was. Sensible, too. No matter what happened, she always took it on the chin, and Betty knew it was important to take her at her word.

'Well… yes, we want a family, of course. I want to have the same kind of loving relationship with my children that I had with my mum.' Betty gave a little shrug that belied the importance of her sentiments. 'That's my dream.'

'I think that's perfect,' Sally whispered. 'I know how much you loved your mum and how dearly you still miss her.'

Tears sprang into Betty's eyes. 'It means a lot hearing you say that. As a matter of fact, I had hoped – *we* had hoped that I'd be in the family way by now, but it just hasn't happened yet.' She paused a moment before she added with a twinkle, 'But it's been fun trying.'

She and Sally exchanged a look and giggled.

'Thanks,' Sally said sincerely. 'I'm glad you felt able to tell me about wanting a baby. I wouldn't want you thinking you have to pussyfoot around the subject because of… well, you know.'

'I know,' Betty murmured, deeply touched by her friend's courage.

Sally hugged her. 'You and Samuel will be wonderful parents, and I hope it happens for you soon.' Stepping back a little, she held Betty by her arms and looked into her face, her own eyes serious. 'One more thing, Betty. You can always, *always* talk to me. Remember that.'

Quarter to six came. As had long been their routine, Betty cleared up the folding chairs, blankets and mugs and took them down through the skylight to put them away while Sally remained on duty, binoculars at the ready.

Betty returned to the roof for the final few minutes. At six o'clock on the dot, the girls climbed back down the ladder and headed down to the ground floor, ready for a prompt getaway. All they needed to do was lock up the building and the big front gates, which had stood wide open all night so that anyone could get in or out in an emergency. After that, they would leave via the wooden door in the fence at the front of the yard.

Still chatting, they hauled the gates closed and bolted them. Just when they were about to walk to the door, Betty thought she caught a tiny sound.

'Did you hear that? Was it a cat?'

Sally shook her head.

'It sounded like a faint mewing sound,' Betty added.

'If it's a cat, it can stay here until we open up at eight,' said Sally. 'It won't come to any harm.'

'There it is again.' Betty looked round, trying to home in on the sound. 'If it's got itself trapped in one of the crates, we'd better let it out.'

'You're such a softy.' Sally smiled, her hazel eyes softening.

'And you're not?' Betty replied with a grin.

They walked across to the crates, which held various types

of salvage like rubber and small pieces of metal or wood. Sally started at one end, peering in each one, but Betty felt drawn to the far end. She gazed inside – and gasped, the intake of breath almost burning her throat.

On top of a pile of deflated bicycle tyres, wrapped up in a blanket, was a baby.

FOUR

Sally appeared at Betty's side. 'Have you found the cat? I hope it isn't injured – *oh!*'

Betty couldn't tear her eyes away from the baby. It was tiny, not a bonny child of a few months or even a few weeks. Betty didn't know much about babies, but she could tell that this one's age could be reckoned in days, at the most. Maybe even *hours*...

Next to her, Sally began to extend her arms. Acting purely on instinct, Betty took a step forward, bringing her toes sharply into contact with the crate, and leaned over to lift the infant out. It seemed to be warmly wrapped, but that was the only good thing about this situation. Betty cuddled the child, hardly breathing as she gazed at the eyelashes fanned out on the soft cheeks. Had the little one dropped off to sleep? Fainted away in the cold temperature? Then the baby's eyes opened, and Betty's breath hitched.

After a long moment, she looked at Sally. 'How could we possibly not have noticed someone sneaking into the yard during the night?' she asked, shocked at their lack of vigilance.

'We were looking into the distance, not straight down into the yard,' Sally pointed out.

'What do we do?' Betty asked. 'Go to the police station?'

Even as she said it, she was consumed by reluctance.

'Let's take him – her – to Star House,' said Sally, decisive as always. 'Mrs Beaumont knows everybody in Wilton Road. She'll be able to get her hands on baby things. Then we'll go to the police.'

Betty nodded. Sally was right. But was she perhaps being a bit *too* sensible?

'Are you all right, Sally?' Betty asked quietly.

'Me? Of course. It's the baby that matters.'

'True,' Betty agreed, 'but you matter too. If – if this is too much for you, I can manage, honestly.'

Sally's expression softened and she smiled sadly. 'You always have my welfare at heart, don't you?'

'You should have had your own baby in your arms now,' Betty said softly. 'Stumbling across this one must...' She let her words trail away. No words could possibly do justice to what was in her heart just then. In any case, Sally knew what she meant.

'Thanks for understanding,' said Sally. 'Now let's get this little one back to Star House.'

She held open the door in the fence and Betty took extra care when lifting her feet clear of the plank across the bottom of the opening as she carried her precious bundle through. Precious – yes. How could anybody leave a baby behind at night?

Sally had been right about Mrs Beaumont. After the initial astonishment, she wasted no time wondering or exclaiming. Leaving instructions for Sally to line a drawer with a blanket, she put on her hat and coat and off she went.

While Betty cradled the tiny bundle, Sally got a fire going and fixed up the impromptu cot, which she put on the hearthrug.

Sitting back on her heels, she said, 'There. Baby's new bed.'

She gave Betty an expectant look, but Betty felt a powerful urge to keep the child in her arms.

'He or she seems quite comfy here with me.'

She snuggled the baby closer. It was all she could do to hold back from dropping a kiss on the little forehead. Although she was looking forward to starting a family with Samuel, she had never felt anxious about it, being happy to assume that nature would take its course and a baby would come before long. But now, with this button-nosed little poppet in her arms, she felt a jolt of emotion. Of all the silly things to remember, it reminded her of Lorna making jokes about crashing the gears when she was learning to drive. That was how Betty felt now – as if her wish for a child, which had been happily bobbing along in low gear, had all at once thrust its way into the highest gear. Suddenly she didn't simply *want* a baby. She *longed* for one.

The child opened its eyes, wriggled its limbs and started to cry. Fortunately, Mrs Beaumont arrived home just then, along with Mrs Dawson from up the road. She was still in her hairnet and curlers. She wouldn't remove them until just before she went shopping later.

From a cloth bag she produced a baby's bottle with milk in it.

'Someone's hungry,' she commented. 'Here, I know what I'm doing. I'll do the feeding.'

She took the baby from Betty and settled down, gently nudging the teat into the infant's mouth. The yelling stopped and the baby suckled energetically.

'My, you're *tiny*, aren't you?' said Mrs Dawson, bending her head over the child. 'You don't look very old, poor lamb. Is that better? You're hungry, aren't you? Never mind. A bit of formula will sort you out.' Lifting her head, she looked at the girls and Mrs Beaumont. 'Guard this with your lives – and I don't mean the formula. I mean the bottle and the teat. They're like gold-dust now. I want them back as soon as you get the baby sorted out.'

'Speaking of which,' said Mrs Beaumont, 'I must go and report this to the police.'

Sally stood up. 'I'll come with you.'

'I'll stop here.' The words popped out of Betty's mouth before she had time to think. All she knew was that she couldn't bear to leave this baby. A flutter of panic rippled through her. What would the police do? Take the baby away?

A few minutes later, Mrs Beaumont returned along with Sergeant Robbins, a middle-aged man whose upright figure made him look as if he kept his shoulders pushed back at all times. He looked stern when he walked into the sitting room, but his brown eyes softened at the sight of the baby.

'This takes me back a few years,' he remarked. Then his eyes hardened. 'And you say the baby was abandoned? Left during the night to be found in the morning?'

Betty nodded. 'It doesn't bear thinking about...'

'Some women need stringing up, they really do,' said the policeman.

'Where's Sally?' Betty asked.

'She's gone to fetch the doctor,' Mrs Beaumont answered.

By the time Mrs Dawson had winded the baby, Sally had arrived, accompanied by Dr Mullen.

'What's this I hear about a foundling?' he asked. 'Let's have a look at you, little one.'

A tiny crack appeared in Betty's heart. 'A foundling?' she repeated softly.

'It means the baby has been abandoned,' said Dr Mullen. 'A deserted infant, mother unknown.'

'Mother unknown.' This time it was Sally who repeated him. 'Imagine abandoning your baby...' Her complexion paled and she looked stricken.

The doctor lifted away the edges of the blanket. 'Hm. Inside the blanket, Baby is wrapped in a knitted shawl.'

'*Crocheted,*' Mrs Beaumont corrected him, looking over his shoulder.

It was white with light-green edges.

Sergeant Robbins said in a stern voice, 'We in this room are the only ones who know the details of this shawl – apart from the mother. You aren't allowed to tell anyone about it. If a woman comes forward claiming to be the mother, she'll have to describe the shawl before the authorities will take her seriously, so the details are our secret. Understand?'

The women all nodded as they murmured their agreement, but Betty's emotions seemed to churn together. Might the mother really return? Betty wanted the baby to be reunited with its mother, of course she did; she wanted the mother to come to her senses... but, oh, what a wrench it would be to say goodbye if the tiny foundling was taken away.

'A little foundling girl,' said Dr Mullen, looking up from his examination. 'She needs changing but otherwise looks to be in good health and none the worse for her night out in the open.'

'How old is she?' Mrs Beaumont asked.

'Twenty-four hours at the most, probably less.'

'*Twenty-four hours!*' Sally exclaimed, her hazel eyes widening. 'Then the mother must be in need of attention herself.'

'She doesn't deserve it after what she's done,' Mrs Dawson declared, a harsh note in her voice.

'I need to get back to the station,' said Sergeant Robbins. 'I'll attend to the formalities, Doctor. I'll telephone the Town Hall and report this to the Welfare Department, so you can expect a visit shortly, Mrs Beaumont. Before I do that, we need to settle on the name. This won't be the baby's real, permanent name. Foundlings are given a temporary name to tide them over. Traditionally, they're named after the person who found them and the place where they were found.'

'Betty found her.' Sally beamed at her. 'You're going to have a baby named after you, even if it isn't a permanent name. Betty and baby Betty.'

'Not baby Betty,' said Mrs Beaumont. 'What about another version of Elizabeth instead, so we always know who we're talking about?'

'Always?' queried Sergeant Robbins. 'You do understand, don't you, that the baby will only stay here until the welfare lady takes her away?'

But Mrs Beaumont wasn't about to be put off. '*Bessie*,' she said, sounding pleased. 'That's a sweet name. You don't mind, do you, Betty? It's nearly the same as your name.'

'Bessie,' Betty murmured, feeling the name creep into her heart.

'And you say she was found at the salvage depot?' said Dr Mullen. 'You can't call her Bessie Depot. Whereabouts was she left? On the doorstep?'

'In a crate,' said Sally.

There was a moment's silence as everyone pondered the thought of Bessie Crate.

'I know,' said Sergeant Robbins. 'The depot is on Beech Road, so how about Bessie Beech?'

'Oh *yes*,' said Betty. 'That's perfect.'

The sergeant nodded. 'It'll do for the time being. I'll tell the Welfare Department that little Bessie Beech is here, and they'll be along to take her off your hands as soon as they can.'

'I'll see you out, Sergeant,' said Mrs Beaumont.

'I must go as well,' the doctor added. 'Get in touch if you need me.'

Mrs Beaumont ushered the two men out. When she returned, she asked, 'Aren't you going to go home, Betty?' In an indulgent voice, she added to Sally, 'She doesn't want to leave the baby. Don't start getting attached, girls. Bessie Beech is a little darling and we all feel sorry for her, but she'll be gone by the time you close the depot this evening.'

'Gone?' Betty exclaimed, unable to suppress an inner tug of distress.

Sally looked at her. Betty sensed she was upset too, but her good sense came to the fore.

'Mrs Beaumont is right,' Sally stated. 'We've done our part. We have to be grateful you heard her. If you hadn't, we wouldn't have found her until after we opened the depot at eight o'clock and she'd have been alone and hungry for even longer, poor little mite.'

Betty nodded. It was time to stop feeling emotional and put her sensible hat on.

'Samuel will be wondering where I am,' she said.

Deborah walked into the room in her dressing gown. She had moved into Betty's old bedroom after Betty had got married and gone to live at the bookshop. With bright-blue eyes in a heart-shaped face, and a friendly smile, Deborah was an attractive girl. She and Sally had been pals all their lives and Betty was glad they now had the chance to live together.

'Did all the voices wake you?' Mrs Beaumont greeted Deborah.

Deborah looked at their faces. 'Has something happened?'

Betty was about to explain but Mrs Beaumont intervened.

'You go on home, Betty,' she urged. 'Sally and I will tell Deborah everything.'

Foiled in her attempt to linger, Betty hurried home. She had wanted to stay, but the moment she was on her way she couldn't wait to tell Samuel all about little Bessie Beech.

Samuel was as disturbed as she was to think of the baby being left at the depot. Behind his glasses, his kindly hazel eyes were troubled.

'A newborn too,' he said.

'How could a mother do such a thing?' Betty asked.

She prepared breakfast, her thoughts lingering with little Bessie Beech.

'I know I'm never going to see her again,' she said, knowing she somehow had to come to terms with this, 'but there's something special about having a baby named after me.'

Was it silly to fancy that it gave her a connection with the abandoned child? Of course it was. She was just caught up in the emotion of the situation, which was completely understandable. Anyone would feel the same. She was sure Sally did.

Indeed, Sally confirmed it while they did the daily sacks together a little later on. Bags of assorted salvage – metal, rubber, string, paper, wool, cardboard boxes – were delivered to the depot first thing every morning and their contents had to be sorted out.

'I'm still amazed that somebody crept into the yard in the dead of night, and we had no idea,' said Sally, her voice full of wonderment.

'Night-time in the blackout,' said Betty. 'It doesn't get any darker than that. The only way we'd have known would have been if she'd made a noise. Even then, it would have had to be quite loud.'

Sally was holding a sack in one hand and leaning down to take something from the bottom of it with the other, but she straightened up without removing anything. She pressed her lips together, her eyes shining with tears.

'How could...?' She had to stop talking for a minute. 'How could a mother do that? A *mother*? Didn't she know how *lucky* she is?'

Wishing she could lessen Sally's distress, Betty swallowed before she spoke. 'Oh, Sally.' She knew her friend was remembering losing her own much-wanted baby.

Sally delved inside her sack again. 'I just can't understand it. It's beyond me.'

They finished attending to the sacks. Sally went into her

office to compile some statistics – or possibly just needing to be alone – while Betty tied bundles of waste paper.

'It's strange,' Sally said when they stopped for their tea break. 'The day is carrying on as normal, but that doesn't feel right after what happened first thing.'

'I know,' Betty agreed. 'I keep thinking about her an' all.' Her nerve ends jangled with yearning. 'I wonder what's happening at Star House.'

They found out soon enough. Louise appeared in the yard. She looked tired but her eyes were bright. She had moved into Star House last spring at the same time as Deborah. A good-looking girl with brown eyes and light-brown hair, she was a munitions worker in one of the factories in Trafford Park. She was in her mid-twenties, a handful of years older than the other girls.

'I arrived home from my shift to hear all about little Bessie Beech,' she said. 'The lady from the Welfare Department is at Star House now. She's asked if you two can go home. I'll stay here, if you like, so you don't have to lock up.'

Betty and Sally hastily put on their coats over their dungarees and headed for Wilton Road.

The lady from Welfare introduced herself as Mrs Fitch. She was older than they were, probably in her thirties, with nicely waved dark hair.

'I've already heard the story from Mrs Beaumont and Sergeant Robbins,' she said, 'but I'd like to hear it from you too.'

It didn't take them long to tell what had happened. Once again, Sally praised Betty for her keen hearing.

'And you heard nothing at all while you were up on the roof?' Mrs Fitch asked. 'There's no need to feel guilty if you didn't. The guilt rests with the mother who abandoned her baby.'

'What will happen to Bessie Beech now?' Sally asked.

'Strictly speaking,' said Mrs Fitch, 'I ought to take her to the Foundling Hospital in town.'

'Hospital?' Betty asked, immediately concerned. 'I thought Dr Mullen said she was healthy.'

'Orphanages for foundlings are generally known as hospitals,' Mrs Fitch explained. 'It sounds old-fashioned, but there you are. Unfortunately, the one in town has a tummy bug going around at present, so Bessie Beech can't go there quite yet. The local orphanage here in Chorlton, St Nicholas's on Church Road, was evacuated at the beginning of the war, so she can't go there either. Therefore, I have asked Mrs Beaumont if she will continue to have Bessie Beech here, just for the time being, and she has kindly agreed.' Mrs Fitch glanced at her notes. 'Miss Louise Dayton has already agreed to help with Bessie.'

'So will I, of course,' Sally said immediately, 'and I'm sure Deborah will as well.'

'I don't live here,' said Betty, fervently wishing in that moment that she still did, 'but I'll come round and help as much as I can.'

Mrs Fitch smiled. 'It looks like little Bessie Beech is in good hands. I brought a batch of formula with me, and I've given Mrs Beaumont the standard thirty coupons for the baby's layette.'

'That sounds quite good,' said Betty, pleased on Bessie Beech's behalf, 'when you consider an adult gets sixty-six.'

'See if you still think so after you've been shopping,' Mrs Fitch said drily. 'A nappy requires one coupon. The normal number in peacetime was three dozen, though mothers often make do with a smaller number now – well, they have to. The coupons soon get eaten up, I can tell you.'

Sally smiled. 'I foresee plenty of make-do-and-mend.'

'Worn-out towels can be cut down and made into bibs,' said Mrs Fitch, 'and knitted garments can be unravelled and made into baby clothes. There's a Board of Trade leaflet that would have you believe that babies don't need nearly as many clothes as we used to think, but I can only conclude it was written by men.'

'Don't fret over little Bessie Beech,' said Sally. 'She's in the right place. We'll all take great care of her.'

'Just for the time being,' Mrs Fitch said firmly.

FIVE

Betty took Samuel to Star House to see little Bessie Beech. His hazel eyes softened as he admired her. She was asleep in her drawer in front of the fire.

'She has two drawers now,' said Louise. 'This one, and another one in Mrs Beaumont's bedroom.'

'Sh-she's so tiny!' Samuel marvelled.

'But she has a good appetite,' said Sally, 'and Dr Mullen says it won't be long before we see her growing.'

'Has he been back?' Betty asked, feeling she'd missed out.

'Yes,' said Mrs Beaumont, 'and he's pleased with how she's doing.'

Samuel smiled at Betty. Was that a glimmer of a tear behind his spectacles? 'I'm proud of you f-for finding her.'

'Little Bessie Beech has every reason to be grateful to Betty,' Sally said warmly.

Betty felt a glow inside. She was sure there was a bond between her and little Bessie Beech, and it made it even more special to think that others were aware of it, too.

But that idea was soon dashed when Mrs White, Sally's mother, appeared. She'd come on the bus from Withington to spend the evening with Sally. She had the same hazel eyes as her daughter but, whereas Sally was a dark-blonde, Mrs White had clearly once been brown-haired, as the salt-and-pepper showed. Betty liked Mrs White, though she found it odd that she was old enough to be Sally's gran. Mrs White was a lot older than Betty's darling mum would have been if she'd still been here.

Mrs White knew nothing of little Bessie Beech, and so the story had to be told all over again.

'Well, I never! she said.

'It's shocking, isn't it?' said Mrs Beaumont. 'A helpless baby being dumped like that.'

'It's wicked, that's what it is,' Mrs White replied indignantly.

'But the main thing is that sh-she was saved,' said Samuel.

'Why is she living here?' Mrs White asked.

'We're waiting for a place at the Foundling Hospital,' Louise answered.

'But that could take for ever,' said Mrs White.

'It's not that they haven't got a space available,' Mrs Beaumont told her. 'It's because there's been a sickness bug. Mrs Fitch from the Welfare Department popped in today to see me. Apparently, most of the children have recovered, so it shouldn't be too long now.'

'I don't like to think of her being taken away,' said Louise. 'She's such a little sweetheart.'

'I'm sure she's better off here with us than she would be in the Foundling Hospital,' Sally said with a note of longing in her voice.

'Whatever that mother was thinking when she abandoned her baby,' Mrs White declared, 'she did the right thing when she left little Bessie in the depot yard. I know it happened out of luck, not out of judgement, but it turned out to be the best thing that could have happened.'

Louise stood up. 'Excuse me. I must get ready.'

'Are you going out on duty?' Betty asked her.

Louise nodded and left the room. As many people did, she was now going straight from her paid war work to her voluntary war work. She wasn't a fire-watcher like Betty and Sally, or in the WVS like Deborah. In fact, she wasn't part of an official service as such, but was a member of one of many teams who assisted the fire brigade by repairing hoses that had been burned through by flying embers in air raids.

Louise left the house. Deborah was already out on WVS duty. Samuel offered to oil the garden gate and the door to the Anderson shelter, and Mrs Beaumont went with him, leaving Betty with Sally and her mother.

And that was when Mrs White dropped her bombshell. She went to sit beside Sally and took her hand.

'Now then,' Mrs White began.

Betty stood up. This was obviously private.

'That's all right, Betty,' said Mrs White. 'You stay put. I know I can say this in front of you, because you and my Sally are such good friends.' She sighed, then pulled in her chin and looked thoughtfully at her daughter. 'Sally, I really think this was meant to be.'

Sally frowned. 'What was?'

'Little Bessie Beech,' said her mother. 'It broke my heart when you lost your baby last summer, and I know it broke yours, too.' A catch in her voice forced her to stop speaking for a moment. 'We've talked about how you might never be able to have a child of your own, but, oh Sally, just look at little Bessie Beech.' Mrs White's eyes shone with tears. 'She was left in *your* salvage depot and now she's living under *your* roof. Doesn't that tell you something?' The tears spilled over and she had to swipe them away. 'This was meant to be.'

. . .

'... So w-what do you think, Betty?'

'Sorry? What?'

Betty and Samuel were walking home from Star House a short while after Mrs White had stunned Betty with her suggestion for little Bessie Beech's future. Betty's hand was nestled in the crook of her husband's arm. Her heart thumped and she had the oddest feeling that she was watching herself and Samuel. It was a bit like being in a dream.

'You haven't taken in a w-word I've s-said, have you?' Samuel asked, but he wasn't annoyed, not her Samuel. He was much too patient and gentle for that. It was obvious from his tone that all he felt was concern. 'W-what is it, Betty? Don't tell me. It's little Bessie Beech, isn't it?'

'Please don't let's talk about it out here,' Betty answered. 'It's too important. Let's wait until we get home.'

When they went into the shop, Samuel lingered to put the blackout in place while Betty went through to their parlour. She removed her outdoor things and opened the built-in cupboard in between the kitchen door and the door to the stairs. She hung up her coat and put her hat on the shelf above.

In the kitchen, she shook the kettle to see if there was enough water in it before putting it on the gas. Then she fetched Samuel's carpet slippers for him to change into.

Usually they sat in the armchairs, with Betty often moving to sit on the hearthrug, leaning against her husband's legs, both of them loving the nearness. This evening, however, Samuel didn't sit in his chair but on the sofa.

He patted the place beside him. 'C-come and sit next to me.'

There was a small table at either end. Betty put down their cups of tea and sat.

'W-what's this about?' Samuel asked her, taking her hand, his face softening as it always did when he looked at her. 'I could see how taken you were with little Bessie Beech.'

'Do you mind?'

'Mind? She's a lovely little dot.'

'I love that,' Betty said warmly. 'A little *dot* – because she's so tiny. Of course she is: she's nearly brand new.' She drew in a breath. 'When you were outside doing the oiling, Mrs White said – well, she didn't say it in so many words, but what she meant was that... that Sally should adopt Bessie. And... oh, Samuel, I don't want that. I love Sally and I know what a wonderful mother she'd be, but... but I don't want her to have little Bessie Beech, because... because I want *us* to care for her.'

SIX

The next morning at the depot, Betty's pulse sped up painfully as she prepared to talk it over. Samuel had said last night that it was important to discuss the matter with Sally, and Betty knew he was right. She simply had to know what was in her friend's mind.

'The bookshop is always quiet f-first thing,' Samuel had said, 'so I'll telephone the lady from the Town Hall.'

Normally, if Betty had something she specially wanted to share with Sally, she would do it while they emptied and sorted the daily sacks, but this felt altogether too important for that. Betty felt herself to be on the brink of something life-changing. Her thoughts were all over the place as she waited for their tea break. They took this together, sitting at the table in the staffroom, in front of the window so they could see if anyone came into the yard below.

'How did you sleep?' Betty asked. 'I bet you couldn't stop thinking about your mum's idea.'

'It certainly kept me awake,' Sally agreed.

'Have you... *decided* anything?' Betty bit her lip, then rushed on. 'I'm sorry. This feels all wrong. I need to know what you think,' she added urgently, 'but I shouldn't be doing it without telling you my side. It feels sneaky.'

'You could never be sneaky,' Sally answered her. 'Little Bessie Beech is adorable, but if I ever adopt a child, it'll be because Andrew and I have discussed it – and not just discussed it but built up to it. It isn't something you do on a whim. It's an idea and a feeling and a belief that grows inside you. That's what I think, anyway.' She gave a little chuckle. 'I certainly wouldn't rush into an adoption just because my mother thinks it's a good idea.'

'I'm so relieved to hear you say that,' Betty replied, blinking away a tear.

'Because *you* want to adopt little Bessie Beech yourself.'

Betty's mouth dropped open so fast she almost expected to hear the clunk as it hit the table. 'How do you know that?'

'Because I know you so well,' Sally told her warmly, 'and I've watched you with her. That's why you brought Samuel to see her, isn't it? You can kid other people you brought him because you were the one who found her. You can even kid yourself if you want to, but you can't kid me.'

'Well... yes.' Betty uttered a little laugh in which relief mingled with joy. 'You're right.'

Sally leaned forward. 'So, you and Samuel are interested in adopting little Bessie Beech? That's wonderful!'

'Yes, it is – or it will be if we're allowed to do it.' Betty tried hard not to get carried away.

'I can't think of any couple who'd make more loving parents,' Sally declared. 'I imagine it'll go in your favour that Samuel is here at home and not away fighting. Little Bessie Beech will be a lucky girl if she has her daddy living at home with her.'

'Samuel is telephoning Mrs Fitch this morning,' said Betty. In fact, given that she had waited until their tea break to speak to Sally, he might well have already done it. Excitement trembled inside her.

'I hope it all goes well for you,' Sally said, her voice ringing with sincerity. 'Thank you for confiding in me – and thank you for caring about not upsetting me. I promise that I'm happy for you – and I hope little Bessie Beech becomes my niece very soon.'

Mrs Fitch came to the bookshop on Friday afternoon to meet with Samuel and Betty. Sally had gladly given Betty the time off from the depot and had sent her on her way with a kiss on the cheek.

To Betty's surprise and distress, Mrs Fitch seemed inclined to take their interest in little Bessie Beech with a pinch of salt.

'It's understandable,' she said matter-of-factly. 'Mrs Atkinson was the one who found the baby and now you're both caught up in the emotion of the moment.' She looked at Samuel, raising an eyebrow as she did so. It made her appear sceptical. 'Are you simply following your wife's lead in this, Mr Atkinson?'

'Adopting a baby isn't s-something I would d-do just to please my wife, no matter how much I love her.'

'Do the two of you already have a family?' Mrs Fitch asked bluntly.

'No,' said Samuel.

'Not *yet*,' Betty added.

'How long have you been married?' was the next question.

'Since last Easter,' Betty answered.

Mrs Fitch made a sound that was almost a laugh. 'No time at all,' she declared. 'It's much too soon for you to have given up on having children of your own.'

'We haven't!' Betty exclaimed, alarmed and disappointed at

the way this conversation was going. 'We want little Bessie Beech for her own sake, not because we're... desperate.'

Mrs Fitch narrowed her eyes. 'And if your own children follow?'

'Then Bessie will be our oldest,' Samuel stated in his quiet way. 'W-we won't love her any less.'

Mrs Fitch shook her head on a small sigh. 'Well, it's early days yet and you may change your minds once the immediate allure has worn off.'

'No, we *won't!*' Betty exclaimed. Feeling she had come on too strong, she added in a moderate tone, 'We've made up our minds.'

Mrs Fitch raised her eyebrows and tilted her head before saying, 'In any case, there's a process to go through – if indeed you do decide to go ahead. You will have to convince both the Welfare Department and the Foundling Hospital that you'll make good parents, able to provide a stable home.'

'W-why the Foundling Hospital?' Samuel asked.

'Because that's where Bessie Beech is *meant* to be,' said Mrs Fitch. 'The only reason she isn't there is because of that tummy bug – which, incidentally, has now gone away. I will arrange for her to be taken there.'

'C-can't she stay at Star House?' Samuel asked.

'So that you can *pretend* she's yours? That really wouldn't be wise,' Mrs Fitch said crisply. Then a kindly note entered her voice. 'I suggest your next step should be to visit the Foundling Hospital yourselves. You'll see that little Bessie Beech will be in good hands, and you'll be able to meet Warden Everett informally. His opinion will be crucial if you are to be granted permission to adopt. If I might use the telephone in your shop, Mr Atkinson, I can ring him now and make the introduction.'

'Thank you,' said Samuel. 'It d-doesn't matter when the appointment is. I'll c-close the shop.'

'And I'm sure I can take time off work,' Betty added.

Mrs Fitch made her telephone call, then shared the arrangements.

'Tomorrow morning,' she said. 'Warden Everett and Mrs Warden will be pleased to show you round.'

'Mrs Warden?' Betty asked. 'Not Mrs Everett?'

'It's old-fashioned,' said Mrs Fitch, 'but that's the custom at the Foundling Hospital.'

They thanked her for her help and saw her out, then they turned to look at one another before moving into each other's arms and holding on tight. Betty shut her eyes. She had expected Mrs Fitch to be delighted that they wanted to adopt little Bessie Beech, but that hadn't been the case at all.

Did this mean their dream might not come true?

Warden Everett was a skinny man with dark eyes and a long nose. His hair had been slicked into submission by Brilliantine and had a dead-straight parting in what seemed to Betty to be the wrong place. Most men had a side-parting, but Warden Everett wore his closer to the middle, though not actually in the centre. It looked like he'd been so busy getting the parting straight that he hadn't paid attention to where it was.

At first sight, Mrs Warden appeared plain, with large facial features, but then Betty noticed the kindly intelligence in her eyes. It was those eyes that told Betty that, no matter how cordial this meeting was, she and Samuel were under scrutiny.

Warden Everett led the conversation, with Mrs Warden for the most part nodding along as she listened with great attention, though Betty felt sure she must be every bit as knowledgeable as her husband. She couldn't imagine Samuel expecting her to sit by and let him take the lead in that way. She always treated him with respect, of course, and he treated her with respect too, and being with the Everetts underlined that for her.

To start with, the conversation was similar to the one they'd had with Mrs Fitch the previous day, then it took a different turn that was both unexpected and rather unsettling.

'What about the way Bessie Beech might turn out when she's older?' the warden asked.

'W-what d'you mean?' Samuel asked, evidently as baffled as Betty by the question.

'What if she inherits her mother's morals, or lack thereof?'

'You don't know anything about her mother!' Betty protested. 'Nobody does.'

Warden Everett looked at her. 'I cannot imagine any set of circumstances in which the mother who abandons her baby is a decent, upstanding member of the community. I can see you think I'm being harsh, but that is a serious consideration where a foundling is concerned.'

Samuel turned his head to give Betty a reassuring smile, then he addressed the warden. 'My w-wife and I don't have your extensive knowledge on s-such things, Warden. All we can promise is to love little Bessie Beech and bring her up to the best of our ability.'

Mrs Warden gave Betty an approving glance, though she said nothing.

Warden Everett nodded. 'Well said, Mr Atkinson. I applaud your optimism. Now then, would you care to look round the hospital? This is where the child is going to live until her adoption – if there is an adoption.'

Betty and Samuel were shown the dormitories and what was referred to as the sluice rooms – long, narrow rooms, each with a row of basins. Then they came downstairs to see the refectory, the name of which made it sound a great deal grander than it was, separate common rooms for the boys and the girls, and lastly the assembly hall.

'A photograph is being taken in the hall at the moment,' said

Warden Everett, 'but we can creep in and watch, if you would care to.'

'Yes, please,' said Betty.

The warden held the door for them. In the middle of the floor was a circle of kneeling children, all facing towards the middle, where there was a pile of toys and games. Over to one side, three women watched.

'Hold still, everyone,' said the photographer, a tall, thin man with a hooked nose. 'Keep your eyes on the toys. Think how wonderful they are.'

Betty's heart swelled with happiness at the sight of the donations of toys. She squeezed Samuel's hand, and he squeezed back.

A flashbulb went off and everyone blinked.

'All done,' the photographer announced. 'Thanks, kids.'

The children rose quietly to their feet and moved into an orderly line. One of the women came forward and led them from the room. The other two began gathering the toys and piling them in large cardboard boxes.

'W-what's happening?' Samuel asked. 'W-why are the toys being boxed up?'

'We borrowed them for the photograph,' Warden Everett explained. 'The publication of the picture will show the gratitude in the children's faces and that will encourage the public to make donations of money.'

'So, the toys aren't really for the children?' Betty asked, unable to believe it.

'That's correct,' the warden confirmed. 'As I say, this is a way of encouraging donations. Now then, if you'd care to come this way...'

The tour didn't last much longer. As soon as they had shaken hands, said their thank-yous and goodbyes and were once more outside in the street, Betty and Samuel turned to one another.

'That s-settles it,' Samuel declared, the light of determination shining in his gentle eyes. 'We're going to adopt little Bessie Beech, w-whatever it takes.'

Betty's heart melted. She had never loved him more.

SEVEN

The next day was Saturday, and it was Betty's turn to open the depot. Even before she was awake, instinct sent her burrowing down again beneath the bedclothes, not because she was reluctant to get up but because the bedroom was unusually cold. After a few moments, she sat up and blinked. Had they left the window open last night? No, of course not. She sat up and swung her legs out of bed, but when she placed her feet on the mat, instead of providing comfort it felt chilled.

She pushed her feet inside her slippers and, without switching on the bedside lamp, went to the window. She pulled one of the heavy blackout curtains a little way open, followed by the real curtain, and a deep coldness immediately reached out and enveloped her. Betty was used to seeing a lacy pattern of frost on the inside of the window in the depths of winter, but this was more than that. It was a layer of ice. Her breath fogged and she let the curtains fall back into place.

Samuel was awake now.

'There's ice on the inside of the window,' Betty told him. 'Not just frost – *ice*! Stay there. I'll fetch you a cup of tea.'

But when she returned Samuel was already dressed, with a thick sweater under his tweed jacket.

'There's too much to do to hang about in bed,' he said. 'There was a blizzard last night.'

'Was there?'

He smiled and his eyes crinkled. 'You s-slept through it. Get d-dressed, then I'll go and s-see the Kendalls while you do the shopping.'

'Should we tell them about our hope of adopting little Bessie Beech?' Betty asked, excitement tingling beneath her skin and making her nerve ends sing with joy.

Samuel's hazel eyes were tender. 'W-would you like to?'

Betty thought about it. She loved the Kendalls, especially dear Mrs Kendall, and was eager to share the news, but then she drew back from the idea.

'No, we need to tell my dad first – and Grace,' she added.

Samuel's smile was warm as he took her in his arms. 'W-we'll go over to S-Salford tomorrow,' he promised.

'Dad's going to be chuffed to bits at being a grandfather,' Betty said happily. 'And a baby will bring Grace and me closer. I'll make it clear to her that she's going to be a *grandmother*, not a *step*-grandmother.'

'That's generous of you,' Samuel murmured, 'after everything she did.'

Betty shrugged lightly. 'It's the right thing to do. I want little Bessie Beech to have the best family we can give her, and that means letting go of any lingering bad feeling. But she'll always know about her *real* gran,' she added, feeling a swell of love for Mum together with a deep pang of loss.

Samuel held her closely. 'Yes, sh-she will. W-we'll make sure of that.'

'And we'll tell her all about your parents as well,' Betty added, cuddling up. In Samuel's arms was such a safe and loving place to be.

'She'll have the very best upbringing possible.' He kissed the top of Betty's head, then eased his embrace. 'We'll talk about this later. Time to get moving.'

Betty soon joined him downstairs. He had got the parlour fire going and she went straight to it.

'I'm not sure I'll be able to tear myself away,' she said ruefully.

Samuel held her coat open to the flames, then she slipped into it, holding it snugly round herself for a few moments before fastening the buttons. She wrapped a scarf round her neck and tucked it in before putting on her gloves and pulling her hat down over her ears. With Samuel also wrapped up, they walked through the shop.

Samuel raised the big blackout blind on the display window. As with the window upstairs, it wasn't possible to see through it clearly because of the coating of ice.

Samuel reached for a couple of books in the window display. 'All the books will have to come into the shop. The pages are already starting to warp. But that's a job for later.'

Betty raised the blind on the door and Samuel unlocked and unbolted it. He pulled it open, setting the little brass bell above jingling, and finally they were able to see the world outside – or rather, they couldn't see it. There was a foot of snow and flakes were still falling thickly, being raced along by a stiff breeze.

'Oh my goodness,' Betty breathed.

'W-wellingtons,' said Samuel.

He shut the door, and they exchanged their stout shoes for thick socks and wellies before trying again.

Bracing herself, Betty left the shop's porch and stepped down onto the pavement. Snow crunched and for a moment she expected to walk on top of it, but instead her feet sank right in.

'Be c-careful,' said Samuel. 'Take your time.'

'You too,' said Betty.

She set off, needing to lift each foot clear of the snow with every laborious step as the flakes swirled around her. This was no powdery tickle dusting her cheeks. Instead, the flakes were tiny darts of bitter chill.

Normally, the butcher's queue was relaxed, with friends and neighbours standing beside one another to chat, but today everyone hugged the wall, wanting as much shelter as they could get.

In each shop, the shopkeepers had set limits above and beyond rationing and the points system on what anybody was allowed to buy.

'I was due a delivery today,' said Mr Osband, the grocer, 'but who can say if it'll get through in these conditions, so I've got to make my stock last.'

When it was Betty's turn to make her choices, a woman behind her, whom she didn't know, spoke up.

'How come she's getting extra?'

Mr Osband eyed the woman over Betty's shoulder. 'Mrs Atkinson shops for an elderly customer who is housebound,' he said in a carrying voice, 'so don't be trying to stir up trouble, Mrs Crawley. You know full well I don't play favourites in my shop.'

Carrying her bag carefully, Betty set off for the Kendalls' home. It wasn't far but the depth of the snow made it a real slog. She climbed the steps and Samuel let her in.

The Kendalls were in front of the fire, drinking tea. Samuel had pushed their armchairs close to the hearth.

Mr Kendall made as if to rise when Betty walked in. 'Come and sit by the fire.'

'No, don't move,' Betty insisted. 'Believe me, you're in the right place. It's ever so nippy out there. Anyroad, I can't stop long. I'll quickly peel you some spuds and an onion and open a tin of corned beef,' she said to Mrs Kendall, knowing that her friend's arthritic fingers couldn't manage those little jobs, 'and you can put together a corned beef hash later.'

'You're a good girl,' Mrs Kendall said appreciatively.

Betty draped her coat over the back of a chair and went into the tiny kitchen. Usually, she would leave the door open so they could chat to one another, but today it was important not to let the warmth out of the parlour.

She put the chopped onion in a small bowl with a saucer over the top to contain the smell, before she peeled the potatoes, cut them into chunks and left them in a pan of water on the stove. As she did the little jobs, she smiled at the thought of how happy the Kendalls were going to be when, in due course, they were told about little Bessie Beech's future.

After that, Betty and Samuel trudged across the road to the shop, stamping their feet in the porch to get the snow off their wellies before they went indoors.

'W-would you like me to w-walk you to the d-depot?' Samuel offered as they had breakfast. 'It's going to be a heck of a s-slog getting there.'

'All the more reason for you to stop here,' said Betty. 'You need to open the shop.'

'I d-don't imagine I'll be overrun with c-customers on a day like this.'

Before Betty set off, Samuel produced an empty hot-water bottle.

'Don't be silly,' she said, surprised and amused, but she took it to please him, and she hadn't plodded even halfway to the depot before she was anxiously looking forward to filling the bottle and hugging it to her.

Normally, it took her about fifteen or twenty minutes to walk to the salvage depot on Beech Road, but today it took the best part of an hour, with snow falling heavily the whole time. The depot yard had a six-foot wooden fence at the front, with a pair of large gates that stood open during the day for the vans that collected the salvage, and a door that the girls used to gain entry before the depot opened.

Her fingers shaking with cold despite her gloves, Betty

fumbled to get the key into the lock and turn it. Then she pushed the door – and nothing happened. It made her think she hadn't turned the key properly, but she knew she had, though she checked all the same.

She gave the door another push. It gave slightly and she realised that it was the weight of the snow on the other side that was holding it shut. A hefty shove made it give way a bit more and she squeezed through the gap, stopping dead at the sight of the depot under a deep covering of white. As well as at least eighteen inches on the ground, there were huge, indistinct white shapes where the snow had buried the pile of old tyres and the heap of wood. The other side of the yard was protected by a frame with tarpaulins along the top, but the tarpaulins now hung heavily, weighed down by snow.

Betty made her way to the building and let herself in, finding the air inside as cold as that outside.

'First things first,' she murmured to herself while she rubbed her hands up and down her arms. 'A cup of tea, and get that hot-water bottle filled before you turn into an icicle, Betty Atkinson.'

She gazed through the window at the yard deep in snow. What were the chances of the snow melting by this time tomorrow? Would she and Samuel have to postpone sharing their happy news with Dad and Grace?

EIGHT

Deborah woke with a jolt.

Her head felt thick and muzzy, but she forced herself to sit up at once for fear of dropping off again. She scrubbed her face with her palms, taking care not to touch her hair and disturb her rollers. Your scalp could get a nasty little nip from a roller if you rubbed it. She hated wearing curlers to bed. She had very dark, glossy hair that garnered lots of admiration, but its fineness was the bane of her life. She would have given anything to have thick hair.

She thrust a hand under her pillow and scrabbled for the alarm clock, pushing down the button on top to stop its clamour before it started and disturbed anyone else. It was coming up to two in the morning and it was her turn for tap duty.

She wriggled out of her bedding. She was wearing a jumper and dressing gown on top of her night things, as well as two pairs of socks, which made it difficult to stuff her feet into her slippers. Being careful where she placed her feet, she made her way to the door. All of them were sleeping in the sitting room because of the extreme cold – Mrs Beaumont, Sally, Louise and Deborah herself. They had struggled downstairs with their mattresses and had shoved the furniture aside to make enough space, and they kept the coal fire burning very low all night to ward off the chill. They always made sure that little Bessie Beech's drawer was closest to the fireplace.

Before she could open the door, Deborah had to move the rolled-up rug away from the gap at the bottom that stopped cold air getting into the room from the hallway. She pulled the door to behind her before she switched on the light and pattered upstairs to run the taps in the bath and the basin, and pull the chain. Then she came downstairs to run the water in the kitchen and the scullery. This had to be done regularly day and night to ensure the pipes didn't freeze. Wherever you went, you heard stories of burst pipes, and the residents of Star House were determined not to let such a calamity happen to them.

This was the second week of the snow and the whole country was suffering. The snow was deep, the temperatures biting. Food deliveries to the shops were few and far between, and the RAF were doing food-drops to villages that were cut off and to trains that were stuck in vast drifts. Even the snow-ploughs were stranded, and there was no birdsong because the birds had perished in the cold. Homes and businesses alike were plagued by power cuts and everybody was eking out their limited supplies of coal. In the coalbunker near Star House's back door, what fuel they still possessed was frozen solid and had to be bashed with a hammer and chisel to separate the pieces.

Deborah's journeys to and from town to go to work took simply ages as the buses struggled on dangerously slippery roads, negotiating corners with extreme care for fear of slowly spinning in a circle. Deborah was sure she couldn't be the only passenger who cuddled a hot-water bottle beneath her coat. One of the first things she did each day when she arrived at work was to queue up for the kettle – when there wasn't a power cut – so she could refresh her bottle. Many of the clerks had brought blankets or even sleeping bags to the office, so they could be snugly wrapped from the waist down, for all the good it did.

'I don't think I've ever been so cold in my life,' Deborah remarked to Miss Rushton, her colleague in the Food Office.

Miss Rushton was a pretty redhead with freckles across the bridge of her nose. Her slender figure and fair-skinned complexion gave her a porcelain loveliness and an air of fragility that was emphasised by the thick jumpers she wore at present, though there was nothing fragile about the way she helped to heave her desk and Deborah's close to the hot-water pipes and the clunky old radiator.

Deborah liked Miss Rosalind Rushton, but she wasn't a patch on Sally, who had worked here before she had gone to the salvage depot. Sally and Deborah had been friends all their lives and Deborah loved living under the same roof as her chum.

Typical Sally. At the salvage depot, she had moved her desk out of her office and opened up the room to the locals. She kept a small fire burning in there during the day.

'It's a lifeline for some elderly people,' Sally had said at home when the five of them were huddled around the fireplace. 'It saves them having to use up their own coal allowance.'

'What about the depot's coal?' Mrs Beaumont had asked.

'Betty and I have been chopping up salvaged wood for the fire,' Sally explained. 'I don't think anybody could reasonably expect us to keep it for salvage in the present circumstances.'

Sally had arranged with the Chorlton WVS that they would send a first aider along to the depot for an hour each day to tend to any sprains and strains that folk had acquired thanks to the snow.

'You're providing a real public service there, Sally,' Louise said admiringly.

'Sally always finds ways to do a bit extra at work,' Deborah replied, pleased to have the chance to praise her friend. 'When she worked with me at the Food Office, she was always collecting new recipes to hand out to housewives.'

'That's a good idea,' said Mrs Beaumont.

'The housewives thought so,' Deborah said with a grin, 'but Mr Morland, our boss, didn't like it. He thought we should stick to our official duties. I say "we". I mean Sally, of course.'

'And now she's doing what she can for the community in Chorlton,' said Mrs Beaumont.

'It isn't just me,' Sally said. 'Everyone is. We're all trying to help one another – clearing pathways along the pavements, shopping for the housebound, distributing blankets, all sorts of things.'

'It's all we can do,' said Mrs Beaumont, 'for as long as this snow lasts.'

As much as Deborah wanted to rush along Beech Road to get home, she was forced to take it with extreme care. One false move, and she would go flying head over heels. 'Arse over tit,' said her brother Rod's voice in her head. She'd heard him say that once to one of his mates when he didn't know she was listening. At the time, the young Deborah had giggled to herself at the coarseness while knowing she could never tell anybody because of getting Rod into trouble. Looking back, she remembered times when Mum or Dad had said, 'Boys will be boys,' whenever Rod had done something rowdy, though 'exuberant' was the word Mum liked to use.

There was a bank of snow on each side of the pavement, with a channel down the middle where people had dug a path. Re-digging the pathways had to be done after every fresh fall of snow and it was important to dig right down to the paving stones. But you still had to watch your step. Even newly cleared paths were slippery, and everyone knew someone suffering from a bad sprain or even a fracture.

It was Saturday and Deborah had worked until one o'clock in the Food Office. Normally, she would have been back at Star House well before two, but this never-ending snow had made mincemeat of timetables and routines. Punctuality felt like a distant memory.

Deborah made her way alongside the old recreation ground, which had been turned into allotments for the duration of the war. It was an odd thing to miss, but she missed seeing the privet hedge that surrounded the rec. It was now a long lump of white.

She turned the corner into Wilton Road and walked as steadily as she could to Star House. The garden gate had had to be left open since the snow started. If they'd managed to shut it, it would just have been another thing in need of being dug out.

Letting herself into the house, she called, 'I'm back!'

Mrs Beaumont appeared from the sitting room. 'Leave your wellies by the door and come and sit beside the fire. I'll fetch your dinner.'

'Thanks,' Deborah said gratefully. 'I'm famished.'

They were living entirely in the sitting room now. Deborah picked her way carefully towards the fireplace, stepping between the mattresses and pillows. She perched on the sofa and Mrs Beaumont brought her a plate of stew on a tray.

'There's not much meat, unfortunately,' said the landlady, 'but I've done my special herby dumplings.'

Deborah didn't much care what it was as long as it was hot and filling. And, as with all Mrs Beaumont's catering, it was very tasty. Before the war, Star House had been a boarding house for music hall artistes – hence its name – and Mrs Beaumont prided herself on offering a high standard of hospitality.

Deborah cleaned her plate with a slice of bread, aware of Mrs Beaumont watching in quiet satisfaction. Then the land-lady whisked away the empty plate to take it to the kitchen, before reappearing a few moments later with a bowl of sponge pudding and custard.

'Better?' she asked as Deborah finished.

Deborah smiled. 'Much, thanks. That was delicious.' She looked at the clock.

'A cup of tea and a ciggie first,' Mrs Beaumont told her firmly, 'and then you can go out.'

'I'm already late!' Deborah protested.

'Everyone's late at the moment,' Mrs Beaumont replied. 'It's no use setting off without plenty of hot food and drink inside you, or you'll start to flag, and then you'll be no use to anyone.'

'Yes, *Mum*,' Deborah said cheekily.

Like the other girls, she was very fond of their landlady. She might look idiosyncratic, with her dyed hair of glossy black, her jewel-coloured clothes and her ten-inch, 'theatre-length' cigarette-holder, but she was highly professional as well as being a genuinely caring person who had the girls' welfare at heart.

Presently, Deborah was all set to go on WVS duty. Mrs Beaumont left the house at the same time to go to her knitting circle. Both of them were wrapped up warm. Deborah had put on her green WVS jumper on top of the woolly she'd worn this morning and could barely fasten her coat. She knew the feeling wouldn't last but she felt toasty as she walked along Beech Road heading for MacFadyen's – or to give it its full title, MacFadyen's Memorial Congregational Church – where the Chorlton WVS was based.

Deborah knew she could be required to do one of any number of snow-related jobs, from making sandwiches for the workmen doing repairs to checking people's attics to see if their skylights had caved in under the weight of the snow, from distributing blankets, paper towels and cardboard cups to collecting samples from doctors' surgeries and delivering them to hospital.

Today she was assigned a job she hadn't been given before.

It was explained to her by Mrs Callaghan, the branch organiser. Tall, though not willowy, she was a dark-eyed, pale-complexioned woman with strong features.

'Your task this afternoon, Miss Grant, is to deliver a gallon cannister of soup to Longford Hall.'

'Isn't that in Stretford?' Deborah asked.

One of Mrs Callaghan's eyebrows climbed up her forehead. 'I was expecting you to ask how you're going to transport it, not to object to going over the border.'

Heat flooded Deborah's face. 'I'm not objecting. It just seems odd, that's all. Stretford have their own WVS, don't they?'

'Indeed they do,' said Mrs Callaghan, 'and they have requested our assistance. They've set up a temporary dining room in Longford Hall for as long as the snow lasts. We sent over several hundred sandwiches and ten gallons of soup this morning – or at least, we meant to, but one cannister was left behind, and you're to deliver it, if you please.'

Deborah made a point of smiling to make up for her earlier blunder. 'How?'

'In a pram. Word of warning: if you feel your feet going from under you, don't hang on to the pram's handle for support or you'll bring it crashing over, and we don't want that.'

'Thanks for your concern,' Deborah answered with a smile.

Mrs Callaghan returned the smile, her voice dry as she replied, 'It wasn't you I was thinking of, Miss Grant. After all, we can't afford to waste good food.'

NINE

It wasn't all that far to Longford Hall. Under normal circumstances, the walk would have taken perhaps half an hour, maybe a little less, but it was going to take considerably longer today, even without taking the pram into account.

Deborah maintained as steady a pace as she could. It wasn't long before her hands felt frozen despite the woolly mittens on top of her gloves. She stopped for a minute to bash her hands together to get the blood flowing, but her feet immediately got cold, so she started pushing the pram again.

She walked along High Lane past the two churches to where the road became Edge Lane and the houses were Victorian villas, handsome buildings with bay windows and tall chimneys, the red brickwork that was part and parcel of Manchester's identity decorated with white stonework. Today icicles hung from the eaves. Sally had told her that Mrs Lockwood lived down here somewhere. Deborah went as far as Limits Lane, so called because it was at the limit of both Chorlton and Stretford. In fact, each side of the road lay in a different suburb.

Here, she looked round for a dug-out channel to take her

over the road to Longford Park. She had to walk on a short way to find one. Once she was across, she steered the pram awkwardly through the grounds to the hall itself. Here, she was drawn indoors by a Stretford WVS lady, who made her a cup of tea, which Deborah was less interested in drinking than in wrapping her hands round so her fingers could thaw out, tingling as they did.

'You'd do better to drink it,' said the WVS woman, who had introduced herself as Mrs Carter. She was a rather beautiful young woman with dancing eyes and a rosebud mouth. 'Get yourself warmed up inside.'

Deborah took a sip. 'I'm glad to be here in one piece.'

'The pavements are treacherous,' Mrs Carter agreed, 'and it can't have been easy having to shove the pram along.' She smiled and her eyes twinkled. 'We're grateful that you did, though. That gallon of soup will go in no time.'

'I'll have to head back soon...' Deborah said somewhat reluctantly.

'Make sure you're properly warmed through before you set off,' Mrs Carter insisted.

'No fear,' Deborah replied with a smile. 'It isn't that far but I wouldn't mind a spot of sunshine to cheer things up. Just imagine the snow sparkling and all the frost crystals glittering. That would be quite something to see, wouldn't it? We'd have a real winter wonderland.'

'Unfortunately,' said a new voice – a man's, 'when the sun comes out, that won't be a wonderland. It'll be the start of the thaw, and it won't be at all pretty. After three weeks of snow, the thaw will bring a whole new set of problems.'

Deborah turned to the speaker, her glance noting his policeman's uniform – and then she froze. Even her breathing stopped. It was the young man who had made a fool out of her last year. Twice. In fairness – not that Deborah altogether felt like being fair – but in fairness he hadn't intended to, though that didn't make the end result any different. The first time, they'd both been part of a group making a row of bomb-damaged cottages habitable. Deborah had – very sensibly, she thought – opted to borrow Betty's dungarees, and this young man, this idiot, this oaf, had glanced her way without looking properly and mistaken her for a *man*. She had nearly died of embarrassment.

But that was nothing compared to their second meeting. That had taken place immediately after Deborah had been involved in a rescue during an air raid. An elderly gentleman had been trapped beneath rubble in his downstairs front room and the only way to free him had been to go in via the next-door house. The heavy rescue men had removed next door's fireplace and cut their way through the party wall to reach the room where the man lay pinned down. He was injured and in pain, but the hole wasn't yet big enough for them to get through to him – though it was big enough, just about, for Deborah to squeeze through to administer an injection of morphine. When she had emerged back where she'd started from, she'd been amazed at her own courage, not to mention deeply proud. Then the damped-down fire had shown signs of flaring back to life and a couple of young men had seized buckets of water to chuck on it. One of them had succeeded in 'extinguishing' Deborah by mistake... And guess who he had been?

Now he'd done it again. Well, all right, maybe he hadn't made a twit of her to the same degree this time in so far as they weren't surrounded by other people. All the same, he'd just had to stick his oar in and correct her. All she had done was make a fanciful remark, possibly even a poetic remark, and he'd had to jump in and set her straight. She wanted to tell him in no uncertain terms to mind his own flaming business, but mainly she hoped against hope that he wouldn't recognise her.

His brows drew together above his dark eyes. 'I say – do we know one another?'

Deborah breathed in so sharply her cheeks practically turned inside out. 'No.'

'Wait,' he said. 'I remember now—'

Deborah spoke over him, addressing Mrs Carter, who was, to her chagrin, watching with bright-eyed interest.

'I have to go now, Mrs Carter.'

'If you say so.' Mrs Carter didn't even try to hide the sparkle in her eyes.

Deborah swept past the young policeman as if he didn't exist. When she'd told her chums at work about her two unfortunate encounters with him, she'd laughed at herself and enjoyed the attention, but she didn't feel like laughing today. Seeing him again, and especially being corrected by him, brought back the humiliation of their first two meetings. She couldn't get out of Longford Hall fast enough.

She grabbed the pram handle and tried to march away, but all it took was for one of her heels to skid to bring her to her senses and make her moderate her pace. The deep snow-silence settled all around her, but her feelings were still fizzing. That man! He was a copper, too. Policemen were supposed to look after the public, not make fools of them. And how *dare* he barge in on her conversation with his dire warnings about the dangers of the thaw? As if she was some kind of idiot.

'Miss! Miss! Excuse me, miss!'

Oh no. Not him again. Why was he coming after her? That was the very last thing she needed. Deborah pretended not to hear. She stuck her chin in the air and carried on walking.

A massive explosion filled the air, its boom all the louder because of the deep quiet and stillness the snow had laid everywhere. The ground trembled and the snow moved in ripples. Deborah found herself standing in a snowstorm as massive flakes – no, not flakes, whole chunks of snow bombarded her from above. Instinctively she raised her arms to protect herself. It took her a few moments to realise this wasn't a fresh fall of snow. It was snow that had been hurled up into the air by the explosion.

She pulled herself together, all her wartime training and experience springing to the fore. Abandoning the pram, she headed as briskly as she could for the gateway out of the park. She could hear voices behind her, shouting to one another. Just as she came to the exit, a figure went past her at speed. It was the young copper.

But when he emerged onto the pavement, he stopped dead. Joining him seconds later, Deborah understood why. Her own feet halted of their own accord as well. Over the road, a short way along from the top of Limits Lane, in the middle of a row of semi-detached houses, one pair of homes was missing. Gone. The lines of houses on either side had shaken off their coating of snow and looked stark against the all-pervading white. Where the missing semis had been, there was now a vast heap of rubble. Roof-tiles lay scattered in the snow, along with lengths of wood, jagged pieces of glass, a door. A curtain had got caught in the skeletal branches of a tree, and half an upright piano protruded at a wonky angle from the snow on the road.

Deborah realised she and the copper weren't alone. Several others were also standing staring. Then, as if a starting pistol had been fired, all of them headed over the road, slipping and stumbling in the snow. It felt like being in a dream – one of those dreams where you're desperate to reach somewhere but somehow, no matter how hard you try, you never get any closer.

'What was it?' somebody asked in a breathless voice. 'A gas explosion?'

But everyone else was working too hard to get through the snow to form a reply.

As the group – a mixture of WVS, workmen and civilians – approached the site of the explosion, it was the young copper who took charge. Raising his voice, he called for everyone's attention.

'I'm Constable Timms. Right, we've all been in situations like this before. Don't forget that, as well as searching for casualties, we have to keep ourselves safe. I need some of you to check with the neighbours how many casualties we're looking for. You, you and you, that's your job. You lot over there, get back to Longford Hall and gather as much equipment as you can lay your hands on – shovels, ropes, pickaxes if there are any. You two ladies.' He indicated Mrs Carter and another WVS woman. 'Blankets and bandages, please.' To an elderly chap wearing an ARP armband, he said, 'I can't smell gas, but can you telephone the gas board just in case? The rest of you, we need to start moving rubble. Form a chain, please.'

Deborah willingly joined the human chain, passing chunks of brickwork, lengths of timber and pieces of broken furniture out of the way. She kept an eye on Constable Timms, reluctantly impressed by his efficiency and calm. Together with the ARP warden, he climbed carefully up the rubble, stopping now and then to lie down and listen.

'*Quiet!*' the ARP man shouted each time.

The people in the chain froze and held their breath as Constable Timms listened hard, his ear pressed to the rubble. Hope and willpower seemed to hang in the air, but each time the copper stood up again he shook his head, and a ripple of dismay passed through the chain, before everybody carried on with their work.

One more time the ARP warden called for hush so that Constable Timms could listen. He pressed the side of his face to the rubble. Then he flattened himself as if trying to make himself one with the destruction. Raising himself slightly, he beckoned to the ARP man, and they both lay down and listened while the human chain stood like statues. Deborah was holding a hefty piece of rubble that felt likely to yank her shoulders out of their sockets if she had to hold it for much longer, but not on any account would she put it down in case it made a noise.

Constable Timms sat back on his heels and the ARP warden stood up.

'*Voices!*' he declared.

A feeling of energy sizzled in the air. Everyone worked harder than ever to clear the debris out of the way while Constable Timms, the ARP warden and a couple of other men discussed the safest way to dig down.

Constable Timms came to stand in front of the human chain.

'As far as we know, there was nobody at home in the other house, but a young mum is trapped under this one with a baby and a toddler. They're all alive.' He paused to allow a moment for relieved murmurs and glances. 'It's going to take a while to reach them, but we won't stop until they are all safely out.'

It took more than two hours to dig down far enough, removing the rubble and debris bit by bit, ensuring that each piece could be safely removed with no danger of causing a collapse that would entomb the family.

At last Constable Timms climbed down into the hole. Everyone watched in motionless silence until he reappeared and passed a howling little boy up through the gap into Mrs Carter's waiting arms. She wrapped the little one in a blanket and held him close to her as she made her way down the heap. At the bottom, she stood rocking him and murmuring soothingly.

'There, there, little one. Mummy will be here soon...'

Next, Constable Timms lifted out the baby, who was plucked from his arms by another WVS lady before he disappeared again. After another tense five minutes, a young woman's head, plastered in thick dust, popped from the hole. She was helped out, and then willing hands reached down to haul the copper out. The mother skidded and slid down the rubble to gather her children to her before turning to gaze with shining eyes at their rescuer.

'Thank you, thank you,' she uttered in a choked voice.

Constable Timms gave her a surprisingly boyish grin. 'Don't go away,' he said. 'I've got one more rescue to perform.'

He disappeared once more down the hole, returning a minute later with a teddy bear. The little boy promptly stopped bawling and stared in wonder.

'Yours, I believe,' said Constable Timms, coming down the heap to hold out the beloved toy to the child. The toddler grabbed it and held it tight to his small body with one arm while, with the other arm, he clamped himself to the constable's leg, making everyone in the human chain, Deborah included, sigh out a happy, '*Ahhhh*' sound and exchange smiling glances.

'Talk about happy endings,' said a man in the human chain. 'That could have been so much worse.'

Yes – it could. Deborah's mind filled with images of the results of aerial bombardment – mountains of rubble, jagged-edged craters, the rotten-egg stench of gas from ruptured mains. She had seen corpses. She had even – oh glory, she had even seen *body* parts.

It was sobering to know that where you lived, the place where you'd grown up and where you ought to have been safe, had a bull's-eye on it that made it a target for bombs; and it was positively chilling to think that, if you lived that way for long enough, you got used to it.

But here, now, today, this group of people, working together, had turned a potential tragedy into a small victory. It was what war work was all about.

Deborah's eyes filled with tears, something that had happened numerous times in the recent bitter temperatures, but this time it wasn't the cold but a rush of simple pride and a sense of resolve. A tear slid onto her cold cheek and stopped moving.

'Well done... Good show... Thank you for your efforts.'

It was Constable Timms. He was walking along the human

chain, taking the time to appreciate the physical graft that had supported the rescue and enabled it to take place. Several men clapped him on the shoulder and said, 'Well done to you too, mate.'

Deborah turned away. She was glad Constable Timms had led a successful rescue, and she couldn't do anything but admire how he had handled it, but he was still in her bad books and she didn't want anything to do with him. His footsteps crunched along behind her and she waited for them to pass by, but they stopped. Her stomach executed a little flip of disquiet.

'Miss...?'

Oh drat. She turned round. She had to. She put a surprised expression on her face, as if she'd had no idea he was anywhere nearby. Her stomach gave another flip, this time of – she wasn't sure what. She hadn't expected him to be standing so close.

'Thanks for your help today,' he said.

Before this she had known his eyes were dark, but now she felt the darkness as a warmth directed at her. Just at her. At least, that was what she hoped – no, wait. What was she thinking? This was ridiculous. *She* was ridiculous.

'You, um...' she answered, thereby proving to anyone within hearing distance just how ridiculous she was. 'That is, you did a good job.'

'Thanks.' He gave her a crisp nod. Then – oh my – he leaned closer. 'Excuse me, but may I...?'

Deborah's heart all but stopped as he lifted a fingertip to her cheek and gently flicked something away.

'A tear had frozen on your cheek,' he explained.

He walked on, but it was several moments before Deborah's heart remembered to start beating again.

TEN

The snow lasted for three weeks.

Three weeks! Sally had never known cold like it. It made her bones ache, and it seemed she would never feel her feet again, no matter how many pairs of socks she wore crammed into her boots.

She used up every crumb of coal and every sliver of wood the salvage depot possessed keeping the office warm during the day for the benefit of local people. Having to dry out fuel before it could be used added to everyone's problems. Several times, Sally and Betty trudged to a nearby bomb site and dug their way through three feet of snow in search of bricks to give out to folk to put inside their fireplaces, one on each side and one at the back, to store the heat and save on the need for fuel.

One time, just before they arrived at the bomb site, there was a cloudburst, not of rain but of *snow*. They waited it out in a bus shelter, stamping their feet.

'Remind me never to complain about rain again,' said Betty. Normally her complexion was pure peaches-and-cream, but the cold had added dashes of red to her cheeks and her nose, making her eyes appear even bluer.

'Likewise,' Sally agreed, tucking her hands into her armpits. 'I never want to see snow again after this is over. It feels like it's going to go on for ever.'

The snow fell heavily, coating the shelter and dulling all sound.

Peering out, Betty said, 'It's almost thick enough to be taken for fog.'

'It's bad today,' Sally observed. 'Well, it's been bad every day, of course, but it seems worse today. Perhaps you should forgo coming round to see little Bessie Beech.'

'No,' Betty said, not loudly but with determination.

Sally nodded, understanding. In spite of the hard slog involved in getting anywhere these days, Betty had called every single day to visit little Bessie Beech at Star House. It melted Sally's heart to witness the love in her friend's eyes as she gazed at the infant or dropped a kiss on her head with its wisps of hair. Betty looked so natural with a baby in her arms.

Sally took care to hide the times when her generous happiness for Betty suddenly transformed into a stabbing pain. *It should have been me.* It was impossible not to ache for what she had lost, for everything that she had looked forward to so very much, but not for worlds would she have spoiled Betty's precious moments with the tiny foundling.

'It must be hard for you, not having been able to see your dad yet to tell him all about little Bessie Beech,' Sally said warmly.

Tears glittered in Betty's blue eyes for a moment before she blinked them away. 'We're all having to live in our own little worlds, aren't we? Everybody is cut off from everybody else.'

'We've had bad winters before,' Sally acknowledged, 'but this is the worst one I can remember.'

Betty gave her a rueful smile. 'At least it means Hitler can't invade.'

When the snowfall ended, they stomped their way onto the bomb site and started digging.

'Coming here makes me think of that explosion,' Betty said when they stopped for breath.

Sally didn't have to ask what she meant: the incident that had occurred after Deborah had delivered soup to Longford Hall.

'I meant to tell you,' she said. 'They're now sure of what happened. It was an unexploded bomb in the shrubbery. Goodness knows how long it had been there.'

'I wonder what triggered it?' said Betty.

Sally shrugged. 'We'll never know. My dad says there must be lots of UXBs and we'll be finding them for years to come.'

Her darling dad was an ARP warden over in Withington. One of the jobs of the ARP was to account for every bomb that was dropped and record them all on hand-drawn maps known as tracings, because the wardens used tracing paper on official maps. But some UXBs weren't known about and didn't get recorded.

After they had found two dozen or so bricks, they heaped them onto a little cart that Mr Brown from the stationer's had made for them out of an orange box and the wheels off an old tricycle. Two dozen bricks wasn't many compared to the number that was needed, but it was as much as the trolley could carry without falling to bits.

Betty tugged on the rope. Even though the cart was small, it was a devil of a job pulling it through the snow, especially as the channel that had been relatively easy to walk through earlier now contained a fresh layer.

They arrived back at the depot at the same time as old Mr and Mrs Tunstall, who had come along to take advantage of the warm office, bringing a twist of tea with them. Betty settled them by the fire while Sally unloaded the bricks.

When she emerged from the office, Betty was smiling. 'Mrs Tunstall says she'll never forget what you've done for everyone.'

'Just helping out,' said Sally.

'Don't be so modest,' said Betty. 'You've made a huge difference.'

'So have you,' said Sally. 'Teamwork!'

'But the ideas are all yours,' said Betty. She smiled brightly, which made her dimple appear, as she wagged a finger at Sally. 'I'm determined to pay you a compliment, so you'd better accept it.'

Sally bobbed a curtsey. 'Thank you.'

'And don't think I don't know,' Betty added.

'Know what?'

'That helping others is good for you too, because it's kept your mind off Andrew being unable to have his embarkation leave.'

'Things are the way they are,' Sally said in her usual sensible fashion. 'There's nothing to be gained by showing how hard it is.'

'Maybe not,' Betty answered, 'but there might be something to be gained from a hug from a friend.'

And she took Sally in her arms.

The snow lasted into February, and then came the thaw, which involved a whole new set of challenges. As the snow melted, the drains overflowed and it was impossible to cross the road without walking ankle-deep.

'That's what Constable Timms said would happen,' Deborah remarked to Sally.

'The policeman who was in charge of the rescue outside Longford Park,' Sally said, remembering.

Her friend nodded. 'He said the thaw would bring new problems, and it has.'

'Getting through the snow was bad enough,' said Betty, 'but this is worse. I pity anyone who hasn't got wellies.'

There were mountains of slush everywhere. Although they shrivelled day by day, they also grew dirtier. On top of this, folk fell ill and there was a lot of influenza about. Sally worried about her parents and, now that it was possible to get about again at last, she visited them regularly.

'I'm not suggesting you aren't concerned about your mum and dad,' she said to Deborah, whose parents lived a few doors down from hers, 'but my parents are so much older.'

'Of course,' Deborah said sympathetically.

Sally's parents had had her at the time when their contemporaries were starting to become grandparents. Sally loved them dearly. She had always thought the world of her dad, but it was only last year, following her miscarriage, that she had truly grown close to her mother. Before that, Mum had been a prickly person with, at times, rather a sullen temper. She still had her moments, but now Sally wasn't in the firing line the way she used to be.

'How did you cope in the snow?' Sally asked her parents. 'How did you manage, going out and about?'

'Same as everyone else – *carefully*!' Dad answered cheerfully.

Bald on top with the thinnest layer of hair around the sides and at the back, he had bushy eyebrows, in between which were two deep vertical lines. Sally could remember when he used to be full-faced. For some years now, his cheeks had been rather sunken, a sign of his age. He was closer to seventy than sixty. Sally had always worshipped him and now she carried a secret fear that this damnable war might prove too much for him. She ached, too, with sorrow to think that the father who was old enough to be her grandfather might never have the chance to be a real grandfather. Her miscarriage last summer hadn't just been a terrible loss for her and Andrew. It had been devastating for her parents.

But just now Dad's blue eyes were bright with pleasure at seeing her again. For Sally to have been apart from Mum and Dad for three whole weeks was unprecedented. She had thought about them constantly and prayed that all was well, knowing that they were every bit as concerned for her.

She enjoyed a special hug with her mother, and they both shed a few tears, grateful to be reunited.

'I know you don't want to live in my pocket, Sally,' Mum whispered, 'but I'd have given *anything* to have you here in Withington through the snowstorm.'

'I missed you too,' Sally whispered back. 'I know it's sometimes hard for you that I choose to live in Star House, but I love having easy access to you and Dad, and these three weeks have been hard.'

It was a huge relief to find that Mum and Dad were both in good health, as was Sally's mother-in-law, Mrs Henshaw, who lived with her sister and brother-in-law in Seymour Grove, up the road from Chorlton. Sally and Andrew had started off their married life living with his mother and the three of them had got along beautifully, first in the Henshaws' house and then, after they had been bombed out, as guests of Mrs Beaumont in Star House. After Andrew had joined up last April, Mrs Henshaw had gone to live with Auntie Vera and Uncle Mick. This had led to a distinct cooling between her and Sally, because she had expected Sally to go with her, but Sally had elected to stay put. Any ill-feeling, however, had been swept aside by Sally's miscarriage.

'I'm perfectly well, Sally dear,' said Mrs Henshaw when Sally went round to see her at Auntie Vera's, 'and I'm glad to see you are too.' She sighed heavily, which wasn't like her. She tended to be a no-nonsense sort of person. 'I know the snow and the thaw have been dreadful. But for me the worst thing was not being able to see Andrew.'

'I know,' agreed Sally. 'I feel the same. I'm desperate to hear from him. I have this horrible feeling that the moment the thaw started he might have been shipped out.'

It wasn't long before letters arrived from Andrew – several all at once. He was still in England.

'He says he spent most of the snowstorm helping to dig out trains,' Sally told Mrs Beaumont, Louise and Deborah as they sat in front of the fire in Star House. 'Each train took days to dig out, but then they couldn't move because all the points on the tracks were frozen solid.'

'It'll be March this Sunday,' said Louise. 'It's astonishing to think that half of January and much of February were taken up with the snow and now the thaw.'

'All those weeks,' said Sally. She couldn't suppress a sigh. 'I suppose all the postponed embarkations will take place at top speed now.'

'Does Andrew not say anything about leave in his letters?' Deborah asked sympathetically.

'Not a word,' Sally answered. Was she not going to have the chance to see her husband before he was shipped off to wherever he was being sent?

But the following week, Mrs Beaumont came hurrying into the depot yard, flourishing a telegram.

EMBARKATION LEAVE STOP SEVENTY TWO
HOURS STOP HOME TOMORROW STOP ANDREW

ELEVEN

Sally's jubilation was short-lived.

That evening when she arrived home, it was to find that little Bessie Beech had left Star House. The others were talking about it, but Sally couldn't form a single word. She felt as if all the breath had been sucked out of her body.

'She was only tiny,' said Louise, 'but she made a big difference to all our lives.' She turned to Mrs Beaumont. 'It must be hardest on you. You were here with her all the time and did nearly everything for her.'

'And she's been here such a long time too,' Deborah added. 'Did you know she was going to be taken away today?' she asked Sally. 'I expect Betty told you.'

'If she'd known it was going to be today, she'd have said something.' Sally felt all churned up. 'Poor Betty. I'm going to have to tell her tomorrow. In fact, I think I'll pop round there and tell her this evening.'

'That would be for the best, dear,' said Mrs Beaumont.

'Shall I come with you?' Deborah suggested, concerned. 'You know, to give Betty some extra support – and, well, in case you need a sympathetic ear on the way home afterwards too? Perhaps Louise could come as well?'

'Happy to,' said Louise, 'if it's the right thing. If we turn up mob-handed, it might be a bit overwhelming...'

In the event, they didn't have to make the decision, because Betty came to Star House.

'Samuel's gone to an ARP meeting this evening,' she said as she entered the sitting room, 'so I thought I'd pop round and have a cuddle— *oh.*'

She stopped dead just inside the doorway, her gaze fixed on the empty space in front of the fireplace.

'Mrs Fitch and another lady came for her this afternoon,' Mrs Beaumont explained. 'Come and sit down, Betty dear, and I'll put the kettle on.'

Deborah was beside Sally on the sofa. 'I'll budge up and you can sit in the middle, Betty,' she offered, moving along and patting the cushion in the centre.

Betty sank onto it. Her blue eyes were brimming. 'I knew it was going to happen. I shouldn't be upset...'

'Of course it's all right to be upset.' Sally angled herself to face Betty. 'None of us knew it was going to happen today.'

'They should have warned us!' Deborah declared.

Betty took out her hanky and dabbed her eyes. 'I'm sure they haven't done anything wrong. This is just the way the system works. The only reason we had little Bessie Beech at Star House this long was because of that sickness bug and then the snow.'

'Still,' Sally said, evidently making an effort to lighten the atmosphere, 'all being well, she won't be at the Foundling Hospital for all that long.'

'How long does the adoption process take?' Louise asked.

'They have to allow time for the mother to make herself known,' Betty explained, 'but we don't have to wait for that. We can start our application right away.'

'What do you have to do?' Mrs Beaumont asked.

'Adopting through a mother-and-baby home or an orphanage can be pretty straightforward,' said Betty, obviously happy to discuss the topic, 'but with little Bessie Beech being a foundling, the Town Hall has to be involved as well.'

'So, you'll have to jump through Corporation hoops as well as Foundling Hospital hoops,' said Deborah.

Betty nodded. 'That's right. It sounds like having to go through the same process twice, really, answering the same questions, providing the same information. And assuming we're considered suitable—'

'Of *course* you will be!' Sally exclaimed warmly and the others chimed in, voicing their sincere agreement.

'Thanks.' Betty gave the first real smile since she'd arrived. 'Because of Bessie being a foundling, a magistrate has to agree to the adoption, but if we get to that stage, then the agreement is really just a formality.'

'I'm sure it is,' said Mrs Beaumont. 'If you have the consent of both the Welfare Department and the Foundling Hospital, what magistrate is going to refuse? It wouldn't make sense.'

Betty looked around the room at all of them. 'Thank you for your kindness. It means a lot.'

'It isn't just kindness,' Sally told her. 'It's knowing what good parents you and Samuel will make.' She held Betty's hand in both her own, and raised it to drop a kiss on it before she said, 'I know it hurts to come here and find that little Bessie Beech has gone off to the Foundling Hospital, but there's a good side to it too. It means the snow's over, the thaw's over, the flu's coming to an end and life is getting back to normal – and *that* means your adoption application can go ahead.'

The scent of smoke and steam mingled together, creating a familiar sharp-sweet aroma loved by everyone who enjoyed travelling by train. Sally knew that for the rest of her life she would associate the smell with the joyful anticipation of waiting for Andrew's arrival after almost a year of separation.

At last, the train pulled in. Doors opened and people jumped out even before it halted. Sally stood on tiptoe beside a bench, bouncing from foot to foot, craning her neck. Suddenly consumed by the fear that she might miss Andrew in the crowd, she grasped the back of the bench and climbed up to stand on the seat. The heel of her shoe nearly went through the gap between the slats. Steadying herself, she looked over everyone's heads, her eyes peeled.

A hand raised above the crowd had her homing in on Andrew right away. All concerns and worries fleeing, she jumped down and started pushing her way through to meet her husband.

They each burst from different sections of the crowd into a gap. For a long moment, they stood still, simply gazing at one another, before they moved at the same time and threw themselves into each other's arms and clung together. Sally held her husband close, pressing herself to him as if to meld them together. She tilted back her head, and his mouth covered hers, sending delight shimmering through her. Oh, she had missed this. She hadn't known how much until this very moment.

She gazed hungrily at him, taking in every detail of his face, his warm, intelligent brown eyes, his narrow, firm jawline and straight nose. He was the same man she had seen off at the station last spring, yet there were also subtle differences: a new toughness about his chin, perhaps less boyishness in his smile.

When the kiss ended, Andrew held her so tightly that her hat got knocked off. They stepped apart, laughing, still holding hands, both of them stooping to reach for the hat, which brought their faces close together again. There was another kiss, and a laugh and a sigh, then Sally scooped up her hat and, as they both stood up, she stuffed it onto her head, laughing again because it was a way of diverting a gush of happy tears.

Andrew repositioned his kitbag over his shoulder. Holding hands, they walked down the platform. Andrew handed in his train ticket and Sally gave up her platform ticket. They walked through the barrier onto the busy concourse and headed for the exit.

When they left the vast building, Andrew asked, 'Bus to Chorlton?'

Sally smiled up at him. 'No. I've booked us a room in a hotel. There wouldn't be a lot of privacy at Star House.'

'I like the sound of privacy. Have you booked us into the Claremont?' Andrew asked teasingly.

'Chance would be a fine thing,' Sally retorted. The Claremont was one of the smartest hotels in Manchester. 'I tried to get us a room in Dunbar's on Lily Street, but it isn't a hotel any more.'

'That's a shame. They always had a good reputation.'

'I know. Dad used to take Mum and me there for afternoon tea as a special treat for our birthdays. Anyway, they're shut now, but they sent me over the road to a hotel called the Grove, so I've got a room for us there. And don't worry,' Sally added. 'I'm not going to keep you all to myself, no matter how much I'd like to. We'll have the evenings and nights at the Grove, and the days with family and friends. Your mother is dying to see you.'

'I'm looking forward to seeing her too,' Andrew replied, 'but mostly I'm looking forward to being with my beautiful wife.'

'That's a coincidence.' Stopping, Sally swung him round to face her. 'I'm looking forward to spending time with my handsome husband.'

'Come along,' he said. 'Let's go and start using some of that *privacy*.'

TWELVE

Deborah enjoyed her job in the Food Office. It was interesting and varied, including getting out and about regularly, and she loved the company of the girls from the other departments when they ate their midday meals together in the canteen.

Probably the other girls' company was what she liked best. Not like Sally, who had always thrown herself into whatever work the pair of them had done. Friends all their lives, they had left school together and started as shopgirls the next day. At Sally's instigation, they had gone to night-school to learn how to type, and that had resulted in positions in the Town Hall typing pool. At the start of the war, they had been moved from there into the Food Office.

It was here that Sally had come into her own, gathering recipes to hand out to women, even though that wasn't part of the job. That was just like Sally. She was always on the lookout for ways to do something extra. Deborah admired her friend and was proud of her, but she had never felt like making the same effort herself. She fulfilled all her duties to the best of her ability and that was good enough for her.

The snow and subsequent thaw hadn't put the brakes on the introduction of yet more alterations to the rationing rules. When she went out to staff an advice desk, Deborah made sure that all the housewives who came to her with a query were up to date with the changes. The cooking fat ration, which had been temporarily increased, had come down again; and the sugar and cheese rations had also been reduced.

As well as personal rations, there was also the points system, which was a separate way of rationing in which you had to hand over coupons with a points value each time you bought certain items. In March, the points value of fish and tinned meat had both gone up.

'It's so that housewives can't buy as much of them,' Deborah said to Mrs Beaumont at home. 'If less is eaten, the stocks will last longer.'

But it was the clothing ration that was of the most interest to Deborah and her chums in the Town Hall. It was St Patrick's Day when the announcement was made.

Deborah met up with her usual crowd in the canteen and it was their first topic of conversation.

'They've brought down the number of clothing coupons from sixty-six to sixty,' mourned Miss Jameson, a dark-haired clerk from the Welfare Department. 'Sixty!'

'I know,' said Miss Greening, her normally bubbly personality subdued. 'It was hard enough having to manage with sixty-six.'

'They've got to last longer too,' Deborah added.

'No!' Miss Brelland from Transport jerked her chin in surprise and dismay, making her reddish-gold hair shimmer. 'I hadn't heard that bit. How much longer?'

'Two extra months,' Deborah said glumly. '*Fourteen* instead of twelve.'

'I thought things were going to get easier now that America

has joined the war,' said Miss Hill. She was a colleague of Miss Brelland's in Transport.

'My dad says it'll be a long time before things get easier,' said Miss Jameson.

'That's enough gloom,' said Miss Brelland. 'We haven't been out dancing together for ages, not least because of the frightful weather.'

'It's high time we went out again.' Deborah said eagerly.

They all lived in different parts of Manchester and had social lives in their own neighbourhoods, but, like all young people, they also loved to spend an evening in the centre of Manchester at one of the famous dance halls.

After some discussion, they decided to go to the Ritz together on Friday night. At home that evening, Deborah invited Sally and Louise to come too. She knew Sally, as a married woman, would say no, but she asked her anyway rather than leave her out.

'Thanks for asking,' said Louise, 'but I'm on the late shift on Friday. Ask me next time, though, won't you?'

'Of course!' Deborah said willingly.

She was looking forward to the night out. She'd been to the Ritz many times. On Friday evening she put on a rose-pink dress that looked good with her dark hair. The dress was made of rayon and had a silky feel.

When she entered the ballroom, having left her coat and hat in the cloakroom, she stood for a moment to enjoy the atmosphere and the spectacle of the couples on the dancefloor, those sitting out this dance, the pillars, the art deco features and the balcony. Then some people wanted to get past her, so she headed to where Amy, Josephine and Rosemary were seated together at a table.

Amy was Miss Brelland, Josephine was Miss Hill and Rosemary was Miss Greening. They all called one another Miss So-

and-So at work because the formality was expected, but when they went out together it was first names all round.

Before Deborah reached the table, a chap in RAF blue approached and bent towards Amy, who nodded and rose. A moment later, the two of them were twirling around the floor.

Deborah was asked to dance several times. She was nimble and all the steps were second nature to her because she'd learned them at an early age. She was sitting at the table, sipping lemonade, watching the dancers quickstepping past, when a man appeared in front of her.

'We meet again,' he said with a smile. 'Would you like to dance?'

It was Constable Timms, looking smart in a grey suit with a navy tie.

Amy, who was sitting beside Deborah, leaned toward her, murmuring, 'Good-looking…'

Deborah already knew that. The young policeman had dark eyes in a squarish face, and dark, slicked-back hair.

She quickly stood up, embarrassed in case he had overheard Amy's comment. With a smile, he offered his hand. Such a simple gesture, a completely ordinary thing to do, but for some reason Deborah's heart bumped. She placed her fingertips on the edge of his hand, feeling oddly breathless. The next moment she was in his arms, and they were on the floor. He was a good dancer, easy to follow. When the music ended, she wondered if he would ask her for a second dance. What was she thinking? She didn't want a second one. Yes, she did. No, she didn't. Yes, she—

He escorted her back to the table. With a smile and a 'Thank you', he disappeared into the crowd.

Her Town Hall friends knew all about the man who had twice made her look like a twerp – three times if you included the time he corrected her when she talked about the thaw. They squealed when Deborah told them that was who her handsome partner was.

'And you *danced* with him?' Josephine exclaimed.

'Don't forget,' said Amy, 'he's also the copper who took charge when that UXB destroyed that house in the snow. I think our Deborah might have changed her mind about him.'

'Maybe,' Deborah admitted. 'A bit...'

That made the others laugh in pure delight.

'For a chap who looks like that,' said Josephine, 'I'd change my mind more than just a bit!'

As always, Deborah spent Saturday morning at work, finished at one o'clock and went home on the bus. The snow and slush were long gone and it was good to look out of the window and see everything back to normal. Normal! Bomb sites, buildings reduced to rubble, craters in the road – what sort of normal was that? But everyone was used to it by now.

Two women in headscarves sat on the seat in front of Deborah.

'It's the twenty-first today,' one of them said. 'Isn't that the first day of spring?'

'About time too, if it is,' her friend replied. 'I'm not sorry to see the back end of the winter we've just had.'

When she alighted at the terminus in Chorlton, Deborah walked along Beech Road, sniffing the air and acknowledging the bright scent of new growth.

At Star House, Mrs Beaumont served up macaroni cheese. Deborah was on her own in the dining room. It was Betty's Saturday for opening the depot and normally Sally would have waited for Deborah so they could have a late meal together, not only for the company but also to make Mrs Beaumont's life a little easier.

'It's one of those days,' Mrs Beaumont told Deborah. 'Sally

wanted to go to Withington this afternoon, so she asked to have her dinner early. You worked until one and Louise's shift doesn't finish until two. I swear there are times when all I do is provide dinner at different times all day long.'

But she smiled as she said it. She wasn't complaining. She took great pride in her status as a professional landlady, and nothing was too much trouble for her.

'I'm due at MacFadyen's at three,' Deborah said, 'but only for a couple of hours. We're having a toy-making afternoon.'

'A lady at my knitting circle sent off to the Craft Council for some toy patterns,' said Mrs Beaumont, sticking a cigarette in the end of her holder. 'Next time, we're all going to take the leftovers from our fabric boxes and cut out animal patterns to put together at home.'

Pudding was semolina with a little grated nutmeg on top. Afterwards, Deborah went upstairs to Marie Lloyd – instead of being numbered, the bedrooms were named after the greats of the music hall – to change into her WVS uniform.

She set off up Beech Road, went past the terminus and crossed over to MacFadyen's. Inside, as well as all the usual tasks that were undertaken every day, a long trestle-table had been set up for the toy-making session, which was in progress.

Mrs Oakley was in charge. She was an elderly lady whom everyone admired because her energy was boundless. She showed Deborah what had been made so far. Rattles for babies made from painted matchboxes with buttons inside. Yo-yos made from doorknobs glued together, with string wound between them. Teddies made from a worn-out blanket. Broken toys that had been repaired.

'Very impressive,' Deborah observed. And it was, but it was heartbreaking, too, to think that children relied on make-do-and-mend instead of having proper toys and games like they would have had before the war.

She felt a pang, also, on Sally's behalf. When Andrew had

still been at home in his reserved occupation, he used to make wooden toys to donate.

Deborah took a seat and was given a fabric rabbit to finish sewing. She joined in with the chat going on around her. After an hour or so, she looked up from stuffing the toy to see that the women on the opposite side of the table were looking at her – no, not at her, behind her. She turned to glance over her shoulder – and there was Constable Timms. Her heart gave a little bump. He was dressed in a tweed jacket, so he couldn't be on duty.

Mrs Oakley and came round the table to him. 'What brings you here, young man?'

'I was hoping to speak to Miss Grant, if I may,' he replied politely.

Heat flooded Deborah's cheeks. Talk about *embarrassing!* Everyone was looking their way, their interest unmistakable. Deborah felt as if her rapid pulse must be obvious to the whole of Chorlton WVS.

Constable Timms was saying, 'She and I were involved in a rescue when a UXB went off and I've come to tell her about the report into what happened.'

'I believe you,' Mrs Oakley answered drily. 'Thousands wouldn't.'

Deborah couldn't get away from the audience round the table fast enough. She headed outside, then turned to face her visitor. It was as if all her previous reservations and annoyance had been stripped away from her, and she was left seeing him as the ladies indoors had seen him. Handsome. Slim but strong. And – yes – with a certain shy charm.

Before she could utter a word, he said, 'I'm sorry if you feel I've landed you in it, but after seeing you last night... well, I was keen to see you again as soon as I could.'

Deborah hoped he didn't hear her little intake of breath. 'How did you know where to find me?'

'I didn't. I went to the WVS in Stretford. Fortunately for me, Mrs Carter was there. She was at Longford Hall that day, if you remember.'

Deborah nodded.

'She told me to try Chorlton WVS. I came along this morning, but you weren't here. So I came back this afternoon and here you are.' He smiled at her, warmth flooding his dark eyes. 'Lucky me. Just so you know, I was going to keep coming back until I found you.'

Deborah felt fluttery. She couldn't think what to say.

'And also just so you know,' he went on. 'I know we came across one another before that day with the UXB. It took me a moment to recognise you at Longford Hall, but I know that – well, that I threw a bucket of water all over you.'

Somewhat to her surprise, Deborah found she was enjoying herself. She tilted her head to one side. 'Aren't you forgetting something?'

'Am I?'

'Mistaking me for a *man*.'

'Oh... that.' He flushed. 'That was unfortunate.'

'*Unfortunate?*' She kept her face straight. He deserved a little teasing. 'It was very upsetting.'

'I'm sure it was. I tried to apologise at the time. I can only say I'm sorry all over again. Can we please make a fresh start?' he asked. 'I'm Patrick Timms and I'm with the police in Stretford. When I danced with you yesterday – well, I could happily have carried on dancing with you all night, but I didn't dare ask for another dance in case you said no. Then I spent the rest of the evening kicking myself for not having asked. I know we didn't get off to the best of starts, but please don't hold it against me. I've gone to a lot of trouble to find you because I want to ask you if you'll come out with me. We can go to a dance or to the flicks, anything you like. Just please say you'll let me take you out.'

Deborah's breathing caught and she felt tingles all over. She looked at Patrick Timms as if searching for clues. His gaze was directly on hers and, overwhelmed, she had to glance away.

She had to push her reply past the pulse in her throat.

'*Yes.*'

THIRTEEN

The end of March was in sight and there had been no air raids over Manchester since early January. Hitler was too busy with Russia.

'If there keep on being no raids,' Betty said to Sally one night on fire-watching duty, 'do you think we'll be stood down?'

'It's too soon to know,' Sally answered. 'After all, it hasn't been three months so far. I can't imagine it, myself. It's such an important job.'

Memories popped into Betty's head. First and foremost, of course, the devastating Christmas Blitz. Other images too: dashing downstairs and out of the depot yard when incendiaries were dropped on Beech Road; the night an incendiary fell down the depot chimney. That same night, a flat-bed lorry loaded with paper had caught fire in the yard.

'Are you thinking what I'm thinking?' Betty asked.

'Without a doubt,' Sally answered soberly.

'Just think,' said Betty. 'What if all that kind of thing is over and finished with now? As much as I want that to be the case, it's difficult to imagine.

'It's unsafe to imagine,' Sally cautioned. 'Not until the war is over will it truly be safe to set aside the fear of possible raids.'

The night went on. Sally and Betty, great friends that they were, were never short of things to talk about, even though they spent so much time together. They ended up talking about the tightening of clothes rationing.

'Actually, I don't mind that so much as I mind soap being put on the ration,' said Betty. 'I can make-do-and-mend clothing, but there's nothing you can do about soap.'

'There are one or two small things,' said Sally.

'Go on, then, Mrs Salvage,' Betty said with a grin. 'Tell me how to make a cake of soap stretch further.'

'They aren't my ideas,' said Sally. 'I got them from an advertisement for Lifebuoy. It said not to work up a lather by wetting the soap but to wet your skin and apply the dry soap to it.'

'I'll give it a try,' said Betty. 'All I've been doing so far is sticking the end of the old tablet onto the new one.'

Sally went down to make tea. Betty duly received the mugs through the skylight and then Sally climbed through.

'Have you made arrangements to go over to Salford yet?' she asked as they sipped their hot drinks.

Betty shook her head. 'Dad and Grace still don't know about little Bessie Beech. I keep wondering if I ought to tell them by letter, but I very much want to do it in person.'

'Of course you do.' Sally was quick to reinforce her wish.

'The trouble is, Dad is having to work lots of extra shifts since the snow,' Betty explained. 'It seems that half the coppers in Salford have gone down with the flu.'

'Your poor dad,' Sally sympathised. 'He must be worn out.'

'If he is, he'll never admit it,' Betty replied.

'My dad's the same,' said Sally.

'I just hope that, when I finally do see him and tell him, he won't mind having been kept in the dark for so long.'

'He'll understand,' Sally reassured her. 'He'll know it was because of the snow and the thaw.'

'And the flu,' Betty added, cheering up.

'Try not to worry about it,' Sally advised. 'That dreadful snow threw everything out of kilter. Your dad knows that. Just concentrate on how happy he's going to be.'

Betty smiled. 'You're right.'

Sally hesitated, then said in an eager rush, 'I've got to tell you. I heard from Andrew yesterday. I didn't say anything before, because I really ought to tell his mother first, but I can't keep it to myself a moment longer. You're my friend and you're Andrew's friend too.'

'What is it?' Betty asked.

'He's being shipped out tomorrow – and he's going to... *North Africa*.'

Betty caught her breath. 'Such a long way away.'

'He wasn't allowed to say it in so many words,' Sally told her, 'but when he was here on leave, we agreed on a code. "Somewhere hot" meant North Africa, and that's what he put in his letter.'

Although Sally spoke in a matter-of-fact voice, Betty knew she must be worried sick. She caught hold of her friend's hand and gave it a quick squeeze that said more than words could.

'I'll say special prayers for him,' Betty whispered.

'Thank you,' Sally said emotionally. 'That means a lot. I wish I could say he won't need them, but he will.'

'All our boys in the forces do,' Betty said soberly.

The news in recent weeks had often been hard to stomach. Singapore had fallen – a great blow. In the Channel, three German battleships had evaded attack by both the RAF and the Royal Navy, and had got away. According to a letter from Lorna, the *Illustrated London News* had described their escape as a 'spectacular dash'. And as for the appalling news from Hong Kong about the treatment of British officers and men by the Japanese... well, that had sent a wave of horror across the entire country – across the Empire.

And now Andrew, Sally's *dear* Andrew, was to be deployed overseas. With tears clogging her throat, Betty wrapped her arms round her friend and cuddled her close.

April brought warmer days and cool evenings. From her bedroom window at the front of Star House, Deborah saw folk in the allotments over the road planting out onions that had been raised under glass, and spraying fruit trees. Mrs Beaumont didn't have much garden, but what she did have was put to good use, and the girls were ready to prepare the ground for broad beans, carrots, parsley, swede and celery, to go with the early potatoes they had planted in March.

To Deborah's delight, Patrick helped turn over the soil.

'You're not allowed to take him home to meet your parents, Deborah,' Mrs Beaumont joked, 'or he might end up doing their garden instead of mine.'

Deborah loved every moment of having a boyfriend. She hadn't had one before and it gave her a new status among her friends. She was constantly aware of how lucky she was that Patrick was in a reserved occupation.

'I'll never take it for granted,' she said privately to Sally, 'not after what happened to you.'

'Andrew followed his conscience,' Sally replied. 'I assumed he would stay in his reserved occupation for ever, but after the Christmas Blitz he felt he had to join up, and I understood that.'

The girls at work teased Deborah about her early meetings with Patrick and how he'd made a chump out of her, but Deborah didn't mind in the slightest, because those unfortunate incidents were all part of what had made her end up with a handsome boyfriend. Her chums were pleased for her and maybe a little envious too.

Because Patrick wasn't just handsome. He was also good-natured and considerate, and he wanted to please her. When she mentioned liking Cary Grant, he took her to see *Penny Serenade* and *Suspicion*; and even though he didn't like screwball comedy, he sat through *Mr & Mrs Smith* twice because she loved it so much.

And they told one another about their families.

'I've got my mum and dad in Withington,' said Deborah, 'and my older brother Rod lives up in Barrow. He was sent there to work on shipbuilding. He used to work on the Manchester Ship Canal. He's married to a girl called Dulcie. We've never met her, but we write and she seems really nice.'

'How come you've never met?' Patrick asked.

'Rod met her up there. It was a whirlwind romance. That was, not last autumn, the autumn before that, and Rod hasn't been back down here since. It's a fair old journey from Barrow.'

Patrick grinned. 'You make it sound like the Outer Hebrides.'

'Well, you know what travelling is like these days.'

Deborah wondered whether to mention that Rod had once been Sally's boyfriend, and he had met and married Dulcie in a rush after Sally ditched him. But that had been quite a while ago now and she didn't want to sound gossipy. Maybe she'd tell Patrick one day, but not yet.

'Have you got brothers and sisters?' she asked, eager to find out all she could about him.

'Two of each. I'm in the middle. My parents had boy, girl, boy, girl, boy. Very tidy.'

The Timms family hailed from Stretford.

'I know you've had it bad over that way,' said Deborah.

'It's been bad everywhere,' Patrick replied. 'Chorlton and Withington have taken their fair share.'

'Being near to the Trafford Park factories must have made Stretford a particular target,' Deborah remarked.

He nodded. 'I think, for me, the worst night we had was in the Christmas Blitz when the police station on East Union Street as destroyed. Six coppers lost their lives. The trouble is, when these things happen, you don't have time to be shocked. You don't have the chance to get over it and get to grips with it. You have to get on with whatever needs doing.'

'I know what you mean,' Deborah said sympathetically.

'What needed doing that night was getting new police premises set up, not to mention all the work the messenger-boys had to do because all the telephone lines had been blown to kingdom come and we'd lost contact with the rescue party depot, the ambulance depot, you name it.' Patrick gave her a rueful smile. 'The Christmas Blitz was tough on everyone, not just us in Stretford. I don't mean to make it sound as if I'm competing for whose local area had it worst.'

'It doesn't sound like that at all,' Deborah reassured him. 'We can all understand what it's been like for other people and other places. That's the point. It's happened to all of us. Let's just be grateful the raids seem to have stopped for the time being.'

Patrick folded her into his arms and gave her a hug. 'Long may it last.'

And long may this relationship last, thought Deborah.

She loved the feeling of closeness that was growing between her and Patrick. When they were in one another's company, she felt fluttery in her chest and her tummy; and when they were apart, she enjoyed nothing more than daydreaming about him.

At other times she found herself smiling for no reason at all – except that there was a reason, and she was in the arms of that reason right now.

FOURTEEN

It was Samuel and Betty's first wedding anniversary. As well as sharing fond memories of last year, they were also full of anticipation, as today was the day when they were going to travel over to Salford and tell Dad and Grace about little Bessie Beech.

'Imagine,' Betty said with a sigh. 'We'll spend our first anniversary telling Dad he's going to be a *grandfather*! What could be better?'

She put on her royal-blue dress. Made of jersey wool, it had a collarless neckline and patch pockets, and the buttoned bodice nipped in at the waist above the skirt's slight flare. It was actually a cast-off of Lorna's, but it was still better than any garment Betty had ever possessed, because Lorna's father was a wealthy man, and Lorna's clothes were all tailor-made.

Betty's hand nestled in the crook of Samuel's elbow as they walked from the bus stop to Dad's house. Samuel rang the bell and Grace let them in. This time last year, after the showdown with Dad when he'd found out the real way Grace had previously treated Betty, Grace's light-brown eyes had been wary for quite some time, as Dad had gradually put his vexation behind him. But then her confidence had returned.

Grace was a good-looking woman with conker-brown hair and good cheekbones. She presented a cheek first to Betty and then to Samuel to be kissed, and helped them off with their coats, which she then gave to Betty to hang up.

They went into the parlour. Dad stood up. He was a tall man, well-built even though he didn't have especially broad shoulders. His serious features softened when his gaze settled on Betty. He gave her a kiss, his moustache brushing her cheek, and then he shook hands with Samuel.

'Happy anniversary!' he said sincerely. 'This is a great treat for us, having the two of you here today – isn't it, Grace?'

'Of course,' Grace said in a pleasant voice. 'I've prepared us a special tea of sandwiches, savoury leek fritters, pilchard tartlets, and fruit fool for afters.'

'It's nice of you to take the trouble,' said Betty.

'You can help me warm the fritters and the tartlets and serve everything,' said Grace.

They sat and chatted for a few minutes, then Grace stood up.

'I'll put the kettle on,' she said and left the room.

Times were when she would have more or less dragged Betty with her rather than let her have time alone with her father, but she hadn't done that since the showdown. But Betty would have felt bad if she hadn't followed and helped. Soon the two of them brought in the tray of tea.

Dad was talking to Samuel about an arrest he had made. Betty tried to contain her impatience. She and Samuel had agreed to introduce their important topic as early in the afternoon as they could.

Presently, Samuel said, 'Betty and I have s-something to tell you.'

Betty told her father and stepmother all about little Bessie Beech, how she was found and named, and how she was looked after to start with at Star House before being moved to the Foundling Hospital.

'That was a very special thing you did, Betty, finding that little baby,' Dad said. 'To think all this has been happening in your life.'

'There's more,' said Betty, feeling excitement stirring.

'Oh aye?' Dad chuckled. 'Don't tell me. It's given you ideas about leaving salvage and working with children. I think you'd be very good at it, Betty.'

Betty was too surprised to answer.

'W-we want to adopt little Bessie Beech,' said Samuel.

'You what?' Grace exclaimed.

'You should see her,' Betty burst out. 'She's so tiny and she needs a family.'

'It's to your credit that you feel strongly,' said Dad, 'but this isn't something to rush into...'

'We're not rushing,' Betty answered, her heart beating fast. 'It's what we both want.'

Dad blew out a breath. 'I'm sorry if you think I'm speaking out of turn, but you have to admit this has come right out of the blue—'

'The last thing your father wants is to upset you,' Grace put in. 'You know that, don't you?'

'Of course we do – don't we, Samuel?' said Betty. 'I know this must be a shock to you both, especially since you hadn't even heard of Bessie Beech before this.'

'Go back to the start and tell us again,' said Grace.

'It's a lot f-for you to take in,' said Samuel. 'I c-can understand that.'

They went through the story again, with Dad and Grace asking questions, especially Grace.

When it was time to prepare the tea, Betty accompanied Grace into the kitchen.

'Thank you for supporting us by asking all those questions.'

In that moment, Betty was almost tearful with gratitude, but to her astonishment Grace snapped the door shut and rounded on her.

'I didn't do it to support *you*,' Grace said sharply. 'I was trying to help *Samuel*.'

'Samuel? What d'you mean?'

'The one thing that's really obvious about all this,' said Grace, 'is that it's all *your* idea, Betty. *You* started it. *You're* the one who wants to have this baby for yourself. Samuel's just going along with it.'

Betty could hardly breathe. 'You're wrong.' Her breath hitched on a sudden gasp.

'No, I'm not,' said Grace.

After tea, the four of them went for a walk.

'It's such a fine day,' said Dad. 'We ought to take advantage of it.'

'Poor old Dad,' Betty said with a smile. 'Have we forced you to stop indoors when you could have been seeing to your vegetable patch?'

'Very funny,' Dad answered good-naturedly.

To start with, Dad and Samuel walked together, leaving Grace and Betty to pair off. As a rule, Betty loved to see her two special men side by side, listening to one another, getting along well. The regard they had for one another meant the world to her. But today she felt hurt that Dad hadn't instantly fallen in with her and Samuel's plans to adopt little Bessie Beech. It had never occurred to her that he wouldn't immediately and whole-heartedly see things their way. She loved Dad dearly, all the more so since losing Mum. Feeling that she and Dad were close was important to her, and now that closeness felt as if it had sustained a direct hit.

On top of that, she was stuck with Grace. As well as

feeling vulnerable because of Dad's reaction, Betty was also smarting after Grace's sharp, judgemental words. Would she want to talk about little Bessie Beech again? But no, Grace settled for an ordinary wartime conversation about how breakfast cereals and tinned milk had been added to the points system.

'And the extra four points a month we've all been given is very welcome,' she said, 'though I wish we could have kept white bread.'

'The National Loaf is a poor substitute,' Betty agreed. Were they really discussing *bread* when all that mattered was little Bessie Beech?

When they waited to cross the road, they changed partners. Betty noticed it was Dad who orchestrated this. Now she was with Dad, and Samuel was with Grace. Betty slipped her arm through her dad's.

He let the others take the lead as the two pairs walked along the road. Betty thought nothing of it, but then Dad slowed his pace, allowing the gap between them and the two in front to grow.

'I'll tell you what worries me about all this, Betty,' he said without preamble. 'Well, perhaps "worries" is a strong word, but it's a concern I have. It's about the real mothers of children and the children who don't have real mothers.'

Betty couldn't believe her ears. 'Are you suggesting I wouldn't be a... *real* mother?'

'Well, you wouldn't, would you? Not to *this* child. I'm not saying you don't have feelings for her or that you wouldn't do your best, but what would happen when your own children come along?'

'She would be one of our own children,' Betty said in a fierce undertone.

'Would she? Fully?' Dad asked. 'Can you honestly say there would be no difference?'

'I can't believe you're saying this.' Betty was close to tears. 'I can't believe you think of me like that.'

'I know you have the very best intentions,' said Dad, 'but – well, it might not be so simple. Think how much your mum loved you, God rest her soul. And then – well, then think of how Grace treated you. It astonished me to find out that my wife, my lovely girl's stepmother, didn't love you the way I thought she did.'

'This is different. Grace had no choice about me. I was just foisted onto her.'

'What about having little ones of your own, Betty? You can't imagine how much you're going to love them. It hits you like a sledgehammer. The feeling you have for your own child, the child that is born to you, is overwhelming.' Dad had to cough to clear his throat. 'Why not hang on and wait for that, eh?'

'Maybe me and Samuel will have both,' Betty said obstinately. 'An adopted daughter and then children of our own on top. You can't compare me to Grace. It won't be like that for us and little Bessie Beech.'

Dad sighed. 'I never thought it would be like that for Grace, but it was.'

'Well, you couldn't be more wrong,' Betty said fiercely. She felt fierce too – fierce and frustrated. She felt like dashing her hat to the ground and dragging her fingers through her hair. She felt like stalking away and not looking back. 'We *love* little Bessie Beech and we want her to be our first child. We're going to love her with all our hearts – we already do!'

FIFTEEN

As April went on, Sally didn't feel well, though not in a morning sickness kind of way, which was bitterly disappointing. It was difficult to put her finger on what was the matter. She just didn't feel *herself*. One thing she was sure of, though, was that she was suffering from bad heads, but they weren't headaches as such. The only thing that relieved the discomfort was to lie down. When the bad heads turned into one long, never-ending bad head, she made an appointment to see Dr Mullen.

'Tell me what it's like,' he directed her. 'Describe it as clearly as you can.'

'It's like the inside of the top of my skull is on fire.' Did that sound ridiculous? Dramatic? 'And there's a... dull throb.'

Dr Mullen nodded, though he didn't say anything. To Sally's surprise, he reached for the blood-pressure cuff.

'Take off your jacket and roll up your sleeve.' He wrapped the cuff round her upper arm and pressed the rubber bulb several times while watching the dial. 'Thought so.' He let the cuff deflate before he removed it. 'High blood pressure. Any history of it in your family?'

'Not that I know of.'

'Might be a good idea to find out. Not that there's anything you can do about having it. Are things more difficult at work than usual?'

'No,' Sally answered, 'and certainly not enough to make this happen.'

'Well, if it's not an inherited condition, and you can't account for it in your everyday life, there is another possibility. Some women get it as a side-effect of pregnancy. Might you be in the family way, Mrs Henshaw? When did you last see your husband?'

'Last month. He had embarkation leave.'

'Hm. This early in a possible pregnancy I'd normally advise the lady to wait and see, but in this case, with the high blood pressure and also with your history, I recommend a test. Are you happy to pay for that?'

Sally experienced a small lurch of excitement as she said, 'Yes.'

'Personally, I think there's little doubt,' said the doctor, 'but, with the blood pressure question, it's as well to know for sure.'

Sally could barely believe it. After the trauma of her miscarriage, she'd had to face the possibility of perhaps never becoming a mother. Her own mum had been lucky to have her.

And now, was she to be given another precious chance? Should she be thrilled – or should she be afraid?

Sally returned to Dr Mullen's surgery at the beginning of the following week. Although she held herself firmly under control on the outside, inside she was trembling with a potent mixture of anxiety and hope. When she sat in front of the doctor's desk, she leaned forward, holding her breath and gazing enquiringly at him as she clutched her handbag with rigid fingers and her skin flashed from hot to cold and back again.

'Congratulations, Mrs Henshaw,' said Dr Mullen. 'I'm pleased to...'

Sally didn't hear the rest. Shutting her eyes, she drew in a deep breath of pure longing for her child. All her thoughts turned inwards as her fears drained away. The fear would return, she knew, probably in spades, but for now she felt calm and strong, deeply grateful too as her bodily tension melted away.

After that, things happened with extraordinary speed. When she had been pregnant the previous year, Sally had tied herself in knots trying to tell people in the right order. She had written to Andrew but hadn't been able to wait for his reply before she'd felt obliged to confide in the prospective grandparents. They'd had to be told sharpish because her condition couldn't be kept secret from the other girls in Star House once the extra milk pregnant women were entitled to started to be left on the doorstep.

This time round, Sally had no option but to inform Mr Merivale and Mr Pratt, her bosses at the Town Hall, because Dr Mullen said she wasn't allowed to work while her blood pressure remained high.

'I've got to stop *working*?' She had been incredulous.

'Stay at home, put your feet up, and your blood pressure will come down.'

'And then I can go back to work?'

'You can try, but, if this hypertension is pregnancy-related, returning to work will send your BP soaring again. Don't be surprised if you have to spend the next few months resting.'

'*Months?*' Sally had repeated.

'If you don't follow my instructions, I'll have you admitted to hospital.'

Crikey. Sally went to the depot to ring the Town Hall. The mere thought of having the necessary conversation with one of her bosses brought heat to her face and she was certain they would find it every bit as embarrassing as she would.

Instead, she explained the situation to Mr Merivale's secretary and left it to Mrs Fordyce to deal with.

'May I offer my congratulations?' Mrs Fordyce said in a formal voice. Then a note of excitement burst through. 'That really is happy news. Please ask your doctor to confirm everything in a letter. And I hope you feel better soon, Mrs Henshaw.'

After hanging up, Sally continued to sit at her desk. She would do anything to have a healthy pregnancy, of course she would – but to give up her beloved job for months...? She couldn't take it in.

She couldn't allow herself time to absorb it before she told Betty. Her friend was entitled to know about this major change at the salvage depot, and the sooner the better.

After the formalities of the telephone call, joy bubbled up inside Sally as she drew her friend into the staffroom and shut the door.

'What is it?' Betty asked.

Sally caught hold of her hands. 'I can't believe it. Oh, Betty, I'm expecting a baby.'

Betty's lips parted and her blue eyes widened. 'Sally, oh, *Sally*.'

Next moment they were hugging and weeping together.

'This is *wonderful*.' Betty dashed away her tears. 'Look at us. What a pair. I'm so happy for you.'

'Thank you,' Sally whispered emotionally. 'It's the best thing that could have happened.'

Betty giggled. 'You put that embarkation leave to good use.'

Sally laughed too, enjoying the moment with all her heart. Then it was time to get down to brass tacks, and she explained about her health while Betty frowned and swallowed visibly.

'I'm so sorry,' said Sally. 'I'll be leaving you high and dry.

Delaying replacing Lorna seemed like a good idea at the time, and then we had the snow... I ought to have found a new girl by now.'

'It doesn't matter,' Betty said loyally. 'I can get by on my own. When I started here, there was a girl called Pamela who had been on her own, and when she left I was alone until you came.'

'But not for long,' Sally replied. 'Unless my blood pressure sorts itself out, I could be off for months.'

'Well, there's nothing you can do about it,' Betty answered cheerfully. 'Forget the depot. It'll still be here when you're ready to come back. Just concentrate on the baby.'

'I know.' Sally shook her head. 'I've hardly had a moment to let it sink in.'

'You'll have plenty of time from now on,' said Betty, giving her a hug, 'which is just the way it should be.'

'That's what scares me,' Sally admitted, knowing she could tell her friend anything.

'I know,' Betty answered immediately 'You've got a lot to be scared of and, if you're going to be stuck at home, you're bound to dwell on it.'

Sally nodded, suddenly too overwhelmed to speak. She drew in a breath and heaved out a sigh so deep it seemed to come from the floor beneath her feet.

'What if... what if I *lose* it?' Her voice was the merest thread. 'It happened before, and I felt as healthy as a horse that time. And Andrew was stationed down south so, although I missed him like mad, I didn't have to worry about him.'

'Take each day as it comes,' was Betty's wise advice. 'That's all you can do. It's all anyone can do. And let the rest of us look after you as best we can.'

. . .

'I know you didn't want to come home to me to be taken care of when you left hospital after the miscarriage last summer,' said Mum, 'but this is different. This is going to last for months. You can't expect Mrs Beaumont to run around after you for that length of time.'

Sally was in Star House's sitting room with her parents. The vertical lines between Dad's bushy eyebrows looked deeper than usual and his blue eyes were clouded with anxiety. His cheeks looked more hollowed out too. Sally made a silent vow to keep herself in good health, not just for her own sake and her baby's, but also to remove that suggestion of gauntness from her darling dad's face.

'No one's going to be running around after anyone,' she told Mum. 'I'm not bed-bound. I just have to rest with my feet up, either lying on the sofa or else sitting in an armchair with a foot-stool. Mrs Beaumont understands my situation and she's adamant that it's fine for me to stay here.'

'All the same,' said Mum. 'You can't claim this is your home, Sally! It was different when Andrew lived here, but he's gone now and so has his mother. You ought to be at *home*, and that means in Withington with your dad and me.'

Sally's heart sank, but she kept her smile in place. As much as she loved her parents, she knew that moving back home would be a mistake, because Mum would be unable to stop fussing and telling her what to do.

'Mum, I appreciate the offer, I really do. You and Dad mean everything to me.'

'*But...?*' Mum frowned.

'There isn't a "but". It's an "and". You and Dad mean everything to me, *and* I know that staying at Star House is right for me. That doesn't reflect on you or on us as a family. All it means is that I'd like to stay here. Star House is five minutes from the depot so, even though I can't go back to work, I'll be close by and can hear all the news, and I can give advice if it's needed.'

As soon as she saw Mum's face, she knew she'd made a mistake.

'That's another reason why you should come home with us,' said Mum, 'so that you aren't tempted to pop along to the depot.'

'Mum,' Sally said gently, 'you of all people know how much this pregnancy means to me. I wouldn't do anything to jeopardise it.'

'Of course she wouldn't,' Dad said to Mum. 'This is where Sally will be the happiest and the most relaxed, and that's what the doctor wants for her.'

After that, Mum was more or less obliged to back down, though it was obvious she wasn't pleased about it, and Sally glimpsed once more the stroppy mother she had seen so often in the days before they had grown close after her miscarriage.

'I felt guilty about turning her down,' she told Deborah later on.

'Well, I for one am glad you didn't give in,' Deborah answered. 'I'd miss you dreadfully if you left Star House. I'm going to help look after you. If you want anything from the shops, or if there's an errand that needs running, leave it to me.'

'Thanks,' said Sally. 'There's one favour you can do me right away. When you go to see your parents, please don't repeat what I told you of the conversation I had with my mum. She'd be mortified.'

'Don't worry,' said Deborah. 'I won't say a word.'

'Talking of mothers,' Sally went on, 'Mrs Henshaw is coming to see me tomorrow, so I hope she isn't going to want me to move to Seymour Grove.'

'She can hardly expect it,' Deborah said, 'not after you've said no to your own mum.'

'That's true,' Sally agreed.

It helped her to look forward to the visit, and indeed she and Mrs Henshaw had a good old natter, the way they used to back when the three Henshaws had lived together in Andrew's childhood home before they were bombed out and moved into Star House.

'Are you knitting for the baby?' Mrs Henshaw's normally austere features softened as she posed her question. 'Or would that feel like jinxing it? That would be understandable.'

'I know there are people who are superstitious about not providing clothes for a baby until after it's been born safely,' said Sally, 'but I think that sounds highly inconvenient.' She hesitated before saying, 'I'll be honest. There's a big part of me that's terrified because of what happened last time. I don't dare think too much about the future in case, to use your words, I jinx it, but somehow knitting feels... well, like a safe thing to do. Don't ask me to explain it, because I can't. I'm knitting for the baby, the troops and the WVS clothing exchange, turn and turn about.'

'Good girl,' her mother-in-law said approvingly. 'I know this isn't easy for you – in all kinds of ways. How are you coping with the enforced rest? I imagine it doesn't come naturally to someone like you.'

'I've got over the surprise of having to do it,' said Sally. 'Obviously, what matters is the baby, but – well, the thought of being inactive until *December*...'

'You'll manage,' Mrs Henshaw said confidently. 'You're a strong person, Sally, and you know that what matters is the baby. But don't forget that you matter too. I know we haven't always seen eye to eye since Andrew left, but you matter very much to me.'

Tears sprang into Sally's eyes. 'You matter so much to me too, and you always will.'

Sally expected to be kept fully informed about what was going to happen now at the salvage depot. After all, her absence was far from being of her own choosing and had come completely out of the blue. Mr Merivale and Mr Pratt were certain to come to Star House to consult her. Nobody knew the depot and its day-to-day routines better than she did.

So, it was something of a slap in the face when news came to her via Betty, who turned up after work one evening.

'I wanted you to hear it right away,' she said. 'They're sending for Lorna. She's going to be ordered to come back to Manchester.'

'*Lorna!*' Sally exclaimed.

'They're going to make her the manager while you're off work,' said Betty.

'Well, that's... good news,' Sally forced herself to say through the shock.

'Are you sure you don't mind?' Betty asked, her blue eyes full of concern. 'Only, you don't sound exactly thrilled...'

Sally couldn't admit to feeling hurt and excluded because Messrs Pratt and Merivale hadn't extended her the courtesy of a visit. Presumably they saw no need to. She pulled herself together.

'Of course I'm pleased. Who better than Lorna? The main question is, do *you* mind? You're the one who's worked there the longest.'

'Oh, I'm not manager material,' Betty said with character-istic cheerfulness. 'I feel bad for Lorna, though. It'll be hard for her to leave George behind in London.'

'But it'll be wonderful for us to have her back again.' Sally was warming to the idea. 'She can come back to Star House. Her old room is still empty.'

Betty said, 'There's one more thing,' and then she stopped.

Sally sensed trouble. 'What is it?'

'Mr Merivale and Mr Pratt weren't best pleased that Lorna's old job at the depot hasn't been filled. I didn't know what to say to them. I said something about the snow holding things up, but they said you ought to have done something before that. I couldn't tell them that you were giving Mrs Lockwood time to vanish off the scene, could I?'

Sally berated herself mentally. She ought to have found a new member of staff, but she hadn't and now the matter had been taken firmly out of her hands. So much for her professional reputation. Well, she'd just have to— no, wait. She wasn't in a position to do anything to make amends and wouldn't be for some considerable time to come.

A feeling of surprise coursed through her. She had always put such a lot of effort into her work, but her life was different now, and she'd better start getting used to it.

SIXTEEN

Lorna was deeply involved in voluntary work in Grosvenor Crescent, which was where the Red Cross had one of their two sets of headquarters in London.

The other HQ was responsible for training and Grosvenor Crescent covered everything else. Lorna's job was to liaise with the Invalid Children's Aid Association, finding opportunities for physically incapacitated and sickly children to be evacuated since they weren't covered by the government's evacuation scheme. There was a great deal of to-ing and fro-ing of letters, providing information about the children's physical needs and making appropriate arrangements for transport.

She arrived home at the same time as a couple of ARP wardens got there. They stood aside to allow her to enter the house first, and she exchanged a few pleasantries with them before they disappeared into the room that was now the ARP station.

Lorna picked up the Broughtons' letters from the hall table and headed upstairs. There were letters for George and Sir Jolyon and two for her, one from her mother in Lancaster, the other in a typewritten envelope.

She took off the jacket she was wearing over a turquoise linen dress, and removed her hat. She liked hats. This one had an upswept brim at the front. George liked it because it showed off her face.

Sitting on the gold-and-red-striped sofa, she put Mummy's letter on the side table to enjoy later, and turned her attention to the official-looking letter.

It was from Mr Merivale at Manchester Town Hall, and she read it with increasing surprise. It was short and to the point. Her work in London, though valuable, was voluntary and therefore she could resign from it. Now she was being ordered back to Manchester to run Chorlton Salvage Depot.

'I can't understand it,' she told George and his father later, while they ate their evening meal. Because of the two men working long and often irregular hours, it was something of a novelty for the three of them to sit down to a meal together. 'Something must have happened to Sally, which is an awful worry. I'll have to telephone the depot first thing in the morning.'

Before she could do that, however, a letter arrived by the first post from Sally herself.

Lorna caught her breath as she read it at the breakfast table.

'She's expecting a baby. Oh, my goodness,' she added as memories assaulted her of that terrifying drive through the air raid to get Sally to hospital last summer. 'I hope she'll be all right this time. Oh, poor girl. Listen, George. *My blood pressure has shot up and the only way to control it is for me to have complete rest.* Poor Sally. She's such an active person.'

'What else does she say?' George asked.

Lorna raced through the rest of the letter. She would read it properly later – many times, trying to extract every possible nuance from it – but for now she simply scanned the lines.

She looked at George. 'Well, we wondered last night why I'd been sent for. This explains it. Sally has to stay at home for as long as the high blood pressure lasts, which the doctor expects to be for the *entire* pregnancy. Mr Merivale and Mr Pratt want me to run the depot for her.'

'Not for her,' George said gently. 'For the war effort.'

'It'll feel as if I'm running it for her,' Lorna replied. 'She takes her job so seriously.' She sighed, feeling a wave of sympathy for her friend. 'The most important thing is that she's able to have this baby. Heavens, it doesn't seem five minutes since Betty wrote to say that she and Samuel wanted to adopt that foundling baby.'

'You'll be there to support both of them,' said George.

'I feel torn,' said Lorna. 'I want to go – and in any case, I don't have a choice in the matter. But I don't want to leave *you*.'

'And I don't want you to go.' George's grey-blue eyes were tender as he reached across the table to take her hand. 'I'll miss you every single day. But you've been called upon to do your duty, and that trumps everything else. It's not just your wartime duty either, my love. It's your duty to your dearest friends.'

Vesta Victoria, Lorna's former bedroom on the first floor of Star House, was still empty, and she was delighted to be able to move back in. When Mrs Beaumont met her at the front door, Lorna dumped her suitcase and gave her a hug.

'Thanks for having me back, Mrs Beaumont.'

'It's a great pleasure,' the landlady replied, 'though there's nothing pleasurable about the circumstances.'

'How is Sally?' Lorna asked, hanging up her things on the pegs in the hallway.

'Ask her yourself. She's in the sitting room.'

Lorna opened the door and walked in. Sally was lying on the sofa. Her skin was paler than usual, making her hazel eyes appear darker. At the sight of Lorna, she was all smiles. She swung her feet to the floor and rose.

Laughing as if Lorna had made a joke, Sally gave her a hug. 'It's so good to see you.'

'Likewise. Now sit down and tell me *everything*. I thought you'd be bed-bound! I'm glad to see you aren't.'

Sally sat down. Lorna started to lower herself to the place next to her, but Mrs Beaumont said, 'Feet, please, Sally,' and Sally lifted her legs onto the sofa cushions. Lorna quickly moved to one of the armchairs.

'How are you?' she asked. 'Really?'

'I'm all right as long as I don't overdo it – and you'd be surprised how little it takes for me to overdo it,' Sally added with a rueful chuckle. 'I can go for a gentle stroll, but I couldn't go striding off across the meadows. I can do a little light pottering in the garden, but I'm not allowed to dig or bend down. Actually, my head tells me quickly if it doesn't like what I'm doing.'

'And mostly it keeps her resting indoors with her feet up,' said Mrs Beaumont.

'What rotten luck,' Lorna commiserated, 'though for the nicest possible reason. Congratulations, and I hope – well, you know what I hope.'

'We *all* hope it,' said Mrs Beaumont.

'Does Andrew know yet?' Lorna asked gently.

'I honestly don't know,' Sally answered. 'I was spoiled last year having him on home soil. We wrote all the time, knowing that letters would arrive quickly. I write every other day, and he does the same, but everybody knows that letters to or from places overseas take ages. You receive none for ages and ages, then several arrive all at once. So far, I've had one batch, and I'm waiting for my next.'

'I hope you don't have to wait too much longer,' said Lorna, thinking how lucky she was to have George down in London.

'I'm glad you're the one they've chosen to be in charge of the depot,' said Sally. 'I'll give you all the help I can – by which I mean all the advice I can, since I'm no use in other ways.'

'I'm depending on it,' Lorna replied truthfully. She had always admired how efficiently Sally ran things. 'You've given me a lot to live up to.'

'Take your things upstairs, Lorna,' said Mrs Beaumont. 'Your room's waiting for you. I've aired the bed.'

'You're a darling, Mrs B,' Lorna said, rising to her feet, 'but if you don't mind I think I'll nip along to the depot and see Betty.'

She shrugged back into her jacket and popped her hat on, sliding her bag and her gas-mask box up her arm onto her shoulder. As she walked along to the corner of Wilton Road, the bright tang of the privet hedge surrounding the rec filled her nostrils, adding to her sense of well-being. Yes, she was going to miss George dreadfully, but it was splendid to be back. Returning after a five-month absence made her realise afresh how dear this place and its people were to her.

She turned the corner onto Beech Road and made her way to the depot, smiling to herself as she walked through the open gates. Hearing a sharp tapping sound, she looked up, and there was Betty, banging on an upstairs window to get her attention.

Betty disappeared and Lorna strode across the yard. She met Betty as she came hurrying out of the door, her blue eyes bright and her dimple showing her excitement.

They hugged, both talking at once, then they stopped at the same time and laughed.

'I want to hear all about little Bessie Beech!' said Lorna.

Betty smiled. 'I told you everything in my letters.'

'And now I want to hear it from your lips. She'll be so very lucky to have you and Samuel as her parents.'

'I'm trying to hold back from wanting it too much,' Betty confessed, 'but I just can't. Anyroad, never mind that now. You're my new *boss*!'

'I know.' Lorna laughed. 'Who'd have thought it?'

'I'm glad you've come back,' Betty said enthusiastically. 'I mean, I'm sorry you've had to say goodbye to George for the time being, but I can't think of anybody else I'd rather have running the depot.'

'Thanks,' Lorna replied. 'I value your support, and I know I'm going to be picking Sally's brains for all kinds of help and information.'

'Oh.' Betty looked flustered. 'Haven't you been told yet?'

'Told what?' Lorna was puzzled.

'I assumed you would already know,' said Betty.

Before she could say anything else, another voice broke in – a booming voice Lorna remembered only too well.

'*Mrs Broughton!*'

Lorna turned round to face Mrs Lockwood. Dressed in the herringbone tweed suit of the WVS, with a salvage officer armband on her sleeve, she was a buxom, keen-eyed, middle-aged woman with a broad forehead and an air of energy and supreme confidence.

'I'm pleased you have arrived,' she said, her tone conveying the words *at last* even though she didn't actually utter them. 'I'm looking forward to having you working for me.'

'For *you?*' Lorna couldn't disguise her surprise. 'I thought I was going to be responsible to Mrs Henshaw.'

'Of course not. What a *preposterous* idea! She is on long-term sick leave. From now on, you'll be answerable to *me*, Mrs Broughton. I went to see Mr Merivale and Mr Pratt and offered my services, and they have placed me in charge of the depot.'

'Oh.' Did she look as taken aback as she felt? Remembering her manners, she added, 'Congratulations,' and stuck out her right hand.

Mrs Lockwood gave it a hearty shake. 'Thank you. I'm sure we shall do very well together.' Then she surprised Lorna by adding, 'I'm well aware of the friendship between you and Mrs

Henshaw, and I know how she has devoted herself to the depot. You will now be running the depot on a day-to-day basis, and I'll provide you with all the support I can.'

Such a supportive attitude was the very last thing Lorna would have expected from the bombastic Mrs Lockwood, who had in the past done her level best to undermine Sally's position. But now it seemed that, presumably because of Sally's medical situation, she had come round. Lorna felt optimistic. Maybe being responsible to Mrs Lockwood wouldn't be such a bad thing after all.

'And the first thing we have to do,' Mrs Lockwood said, 'is appoint a new member of staff.'

Deborah was pleased Lorna had returned to Star House. She knew it would be easier for Sally to hand over her beloved job to a valued friend rather than being replaced by a stranger.

'Especially as Mrs Lockwood is going to be overseeing everything,' Sally confided when she and Deborah were together in the sitting room, Sally lying up on the sofa and Deborah perched beside her feet. 'I couldn't believe it when Lorna told me. I think she was worried about upsetting me, bless her, so I decided that, for her sake, I'd take it on the chin even though I did feel distinctly iffy about it.'

'I know Mrs Lockwood used to make your life tricky...' Deborah said sympathetically.

'And then some!' Sally answered. 'On one occasion, she gave me the chance to attend a meeting at the Town Hall. I was chuffed to bits. I thought she'd finally accepted that I was in charge – more fool me. When I came back from the meeting, all gingered up because I'd had such a good morning, it turned out that she'd made use of my absence so she could be the one to show the men from the ministry round the depot. She'd deliberately hidden it from me that they were due to visit.'

'Careful.' Deborah gave her a cheeky grin. 'Thinking about things like that will send your blood pressure up again.'

Sally rolled her eyes, but then she looked rueful. 'You're right. And, honestly, Mrs Lockwood and her imperious behaviour are the least of my problems from now on. I have to put that behind me. All that matters is staying healthy for my baby's sake.'

'Of course it is,' Deborah agreed.

'Which isn't to say I don't care about the depot any more. I *do*.'

'And always will,' Deborah said, smiling. 'Whatever job you've had has always been important to you, because that's the kind of person you are. But now, all of that has been forced into the background because of the baby. Having this baby is your new job.'

'You're right,' said Sally. 'It is, but...'

'But?' Deborah prompted. She looked in concern at her oldest friend. 'Come on. You can tell me.'

'I can't help feeling I've been... shoved aside,' Sally confessed. 'Don't get me wrong. I couldn't be more delighted to have Lorna back and I know she'll do a champion job at the depot, but no one consulted me beforehand, and I'm well aware of how mean and *petulant* that makes me sound—'

'It doesn't make you sound like that at all,' Deborah said at once, anxious to reassure her. 'It's no reflection on your abilities as manager that you weren't asked what you thought. They probably thought they couldn't ask you, in your state of health.'

'I'd like to believe that,' said Sally, 'but the men from the Town Hall put Betty on the spot over the fact that I never got round to replacing Lorna after she left – and, before you try, there's nothing you can say to excuse the way I let that situation ride. As it is, the responsibility has been taken out of my hands.'

'It's a shame,' said Deborah. 'You'd have enjoyed interviewing for a new recruit. You'd have been good at it too. I can imagine you drawing up a list of questions and making notes after each interview.'

'I feel I let Betty down – and Lorna as well now – by not finding a new girl,' Sally confided. 'The interviews wouldn't just have been about finding someone reliable and capable, who'd take an interest. I'd have had the chance to decide if each girl would fit in on a personal level. When there are only three of you working somewhere, that's important.'

'I can see that,' said Deborah. 'You and Betty became such good friends through working together that you had her as one of your bridesmaids.'

She'd never said so, but Deborah had always felt intrigued by that. She had known ever since she was a little girl that she was going to be Sally's bridesmaid, and it had come as a surprise that a friend as new as Betty had been at that time was worthy of having the same honour conferred on her. It had been a bit of a blow, to be honest. Deborah had wondered at the time if it was her own fault. Had Sally been in the market for a new chum because of the way Deborah had been nasty to her after Sally had rejected Rod?

'And then we got Lorna,' Sally went on. 'I wasn't given any choice in the matter. I was just told to expect a new girl. We're great friends now, of course, but it wasn't anything like that to begin with. That's how come I know how essential it is for a recruit to fit in on a personal level.'

Deborah nodded, understanding. 'Look at how you and I loved working together at the Food Office. It's a different atmosphere now that I've got Rosalind Rushton with me.'

'I thought the two of you got along all right,' Sally remarked.

'We do, in a working-together kind of way,' said Deborah, 'but we aren't proper friends. I miss that. I miss what you and I had.'

'You've got other chums in the Town Hall,' Sally pointed out.

'And they're lovely, but they're in other departments. I'm talking about what it's like working alongside *real* friends.'

'Lorna, Betty and I were very lucky in the respect at the depot,' Sally answered with a smile.

'Yes, you were – just like you and I were at the Food Office,' said Deborah.

And that was when the idea popped into her head.

Why not go and work at the salvage depot? The more she thought about it, the more it seemed like a good idea.

'Well, much of the time, anyway,' she confided in Patrick.

It was the afternoon of Easter Sunday. Easter was late that year; it would be the beginning of May next Friday. The two of them were walking hand in hand on the meadows that ran alongside the Mersey. It was a warm, sunny day, which made spring feel further along than it really was, though one glance at the wildflowers showed how early in the season it was. Yellow cowslips drooped in sweet-scented clusters, and the tight flower-heads of ribwort grew tall in the grass, while here and there the delicate pink of the cuckoo flower wafted gently in the light breeze. It would be a while yet before other wildflowers – lady's mantle, white clover and wild marjoram – appeared.

'Much of the time?' Patrick repeated. 'Going to work at the salvage depot seems like a good idea *much* of the time, but not all the time?'

Deborah couldn't hold back a sigh. 'Truthfully, I wonder if I'm being a bit mad. After all, it isn't as though I don't *like* my current job.'

'Let's talk it through together,' Patrick offered. 'Tell me the reasons why you working at the salvage depot is a good idea.'

Deborah thought about it. She could say, 'Because, through Sally, I've learned how important salvage work is.' She could say, 'Because collecting salvage is a never-ending job but Sally has brought new life to it. Look how keen all the local Scout troops and Girl Guide groups are now.' She could even say, 'It would be hugely convenient to work five minutes away from where I live.'

And all those things would be true, but none of them was the real reason, and she didn't want to lie to Patrick or even mislead him a little bit. He mattered too much to her for that. It took only one glance at his dark eyes to remind her how much he mattered. As well as feeling attracted to him, she also admired him, and she wanted him to admire her too.

'I know how shallow this is going to sound,' she admitted, 'but I want the camaraderie.'

Patrick nodded. 'As a copper, I can understand that. Don't you get it at the Town Hall?'

'Yes and no. I have pals I meet up with in the canteen most days, and sometimes we all go out together in the evening, but in the office itself it's just me and Miss Rushton...'

'Where it used to be you and Sally,' Patrick finished for her.

'We didn't spend our time larking around,' Deborah said quickly. 'But there's a specific pleasure in having your friend as a colleague.'

'And Miss Rushton isn't a friend?'

'She's civil and pleasant and she works hard. There's nothing to object to in her, but we've never hit it off and become friends.'

To her surprise, Patrick threw back his head and let out a roar of laughter. When he regained the power of speech, he said, 'I think that's what is called damning with faint praise. "Nothing to object to in her," indeed! Poor Miss Rushton. What would she think?'

'I didn't mean to sound lukewarm.' Deborah couldn't help feeling miffed. 'I just mean we aren't pally.'

'But you would be pally with Betty and Lorna,' said Patrick.

'I said it would sound shallow.'

'Getting along well with your workmates is important at any time,' Patrick answered, 'but it matters even more in wartime.'

'So, you don't think I'm being daft?' Deborah asked, looking up at him.

Patrick stopped walking. Turning to face her, he put his hands on her shoulders. Deborah's insides responded with a little quiver. Patrick wore a tweed flat cap, beneath which his dark hair was slicked back, showing off the broad forehead that balanced the sweep of his strong jawline. His gaze held hers before he lowered his face and gently, tenderly, covered her lips with his, coaxing a response from her. Deborah slid her arms round his neck, happily surrendering to the pleasure of the moment.

When the kiss ended, she took a moment to catch her breath before she smiled up at him to ask, 'Is that your way of avoiding telling me I'm daft?'

His dark eyes were warm. 'Maybe a bit, but only a bit. All that matters to me, Deborah Grant, is that you're happy. If this is the right thing for you, then you should do it.'

EIGHTEEN

Deborah didn't waste any time. That same evening at Star House, she joined Sally and Lorna in the sitting room, where she found them playing cards. Sally had a tray across her lap and the two of them were slapping cards down at top speed in a giggly game of beggar my neighbour.

When the round ended with Sally scooping up all the cards, Lorna turned to Deborah. 'Do you fancy joining in? You can stop Sally cheating,' she added with a twinkle in her green eyes.

'I don't cheat!' Sally retorted.

'Actually,' Deborah said, sitting down, 'could you leave off playing cards for a bit? I've got something to ask you both. Ask you, tell you. I'm not sure which.'

Lorna gathered the cards into a neat bundle and placed it on the tray. 'I'm officially intrigued. Fire away.'

Deborah took a breath. 'It's the job at the salvage depot. What would you think if I applied for it?'

They both stared at her, which brought a flush of heat to her cheeks.

'I thought you were happy where you are?' Sally asked.

'I am,' Deborah told her, 'but that doesn't mean I'm not open to something different.' She tried not to sound anxious as she asked her lifelong friend, 'Does that mean you think I shouldn't apply?'

'Not at all,' Sally assured her at once. 'I'd love it if you worked there – but it isn't up to me now.' She looked at Lorna.

'It isn't up to me either,' Lorna stated.

'Don't tell me Mrs Lockwood has nabbed the application and interview process for herself!' Sally sounded indignant.

Lorna shook her head. 'Mr Pratt and Mr Merivale have taken it on. They said that, with the post having been empty for so long, they want to fill it quickly, so they're going to arrange for someone from the Town Hall to be transferred.'

Sally reached for Deborah's hand. 'It could be you. Oh, Deborah, that would be champion.'

Deborah squeezed Sally's hand. 'If I do get it, I'll work hard, I promise.'

Sally laughed. 'Don't tell *me* that. Tell Lorna. She's in charge now.'

Happiness and excitement radiated through Deborah, and she couldn't contain her smile.

This was her chance.

Deborah couldn't believe how well it had worked out for her. The fact that outsiders wouldn't have the opportunity to apply went in her favour, as did having Mr Merivale and Mr Pratt in charge of the process.

Had it been left to Lorna to deal with, Mrs Lockwood would undoubtedly have stuck her oar in, and Lorna would probably have been obliged to excuse herself from the process because of being Deborah's fellow billetee. That would have left Deborah to be interviewed by the fearsome Mrs Lockwood. As things stood, not only was she spared that possibility, but Mr Pratt and Mr Merivale wanted the matter settled quickly.

It was all Deborah could do to hold in her happy laughter as she sat at her desk. She wasn't the sort to believe in fate and things happening for a reason, but this really did feel like it was meant to be.

Her pulse quickened with nerves when she told her boss, Mr Morland, that she intended to apply for the post at Chorlton Salvage Depot.

'I'm not sure that Mr Merivale and Mr Pratt have invited applications,' he replied. He was what Deborah's mum would have called a fine figure of a man, and he always looked his best, in pinstripes and a watch-chain. He had a kindly demeanour but, as Sally and Deborah had soon learned when they started working for him, nothing got past his sharp eyes.

At first Deborah was downcast to think that formal applications weren't being sought, but then it occurred to her that this could work to her advantage.

'If no one else submits a letter of application, and I do,' she explained to Mum when she visited Withington one evening, 'it'll prove how keen I am.'

'It's bound to show you in a favourable light,' Mum agreed, her brown eyes glowing with pride.

'You won't mind, will you, if I go to work at the salvage depot?' Deborah asked. 'Not like Mrs White minded when Sally went there.'

'That was because she loved Sally being an *office* girl,' said Mum. 'She was distraught when Sally went off to work in salvage, but I shan't mind if you get your hands dirty doing war work, Deborah.'

'Thanks, Mum.'

'It's not as though you want to work in munitions,' Mum added with a little shudder. 'Now, that I really wouldn't be happy about. It's dangerous work. You hear such stories...'

It felt good to have her mother's approval. Last year Deborah had upset Mum badly by wanting to leave home and move into Star House. It had been Dulcie, the sister-in-law she'd never met, who had written the cheerful, sensible letter that had changed Mum's mind.

Now Deborah had an important letter of her own to write. It was tempting to seek Sally's help, because she was good with words, but it wouldn't be right to ask, not with Sally's close connection to the depot. This was something Deborah had to do for herself.

She composed the best letter she could, detailing her experience and explaining that she'd become interested in salvage work through her friendship with Mrs Henshaw, Mrs Atkinson and Mrs Broughton. At that point, she paused to mull something over. Would it be appropriate to mention that, by working in the depot, she would be supporting Mrs Henshaw through her time of sickness? After some thought, she decided not to say that. She didn't want Mr Merivale and Mr Pratt to imagine she was acting out of sentiment.

She delivered the letter in person to Mrs Fordyce, feeling energised as she handed it over. Would it create a good impression that she had gone to the trouble of writing a letter that she hadn't needed to write? Surely that was bound to go in her favour. She almost skipped back to the Food Office.

She'd left home and moved to Star House. She'd got a boyfriend. And now – *fingers crossed* – she could look forward to a new job.

Everything was going her way.

'Miss Rushton,' said Mr Morland, 'would you please take these papers over to the Accounts Department and hand them to Mr Overton personally? Thank you.'

Deborah felt a flicker of excitement. A couple of days had

gone by since she had handed in her letter, and now it looked like something was about to happen. There was no earthly reason for Miss Rushton to be sent over to Accounts. It had never happened before. Mr Morland was clearly just getting rid of her so he could have a private word with Deborah – and that could mean only one thing.

A smile sprang to her lips, and she had to suck in her cheeks to smother it. It wouldn't do to look triumphant, even if that was the way she felt. Deborah bent her head over her work as if she'd barely noticed Miss Rushton's departure, so that when Mr Morland said, 'Miss Grant, a word, if you please,' she was able to look up innocently as if she had no notion what was coming next.

'Yes, Mr Morland?'

'You have expressed a wish, have you not, to be transferred to the salvage depot in Chorlton?'

'Yes, sir.' She couldn't hold in her smile any longer.

'It is my duty to tell you that you have been unsuccessful.'

'*What?*' The word burst out before Deborah could stop it. The smile dropped off her face.

'I have recommended Miss Rushton for the position.'

'Miss *Rushton?*'

'Indeed. She is highly capable and will do a splendid job. That's what the salvage depot needs, with Mrs Henshaw off sick.'

Deborah felt winded. 'I – I didn't know Miss Rushton was interested in the job...'

'This is wartime, young lady. It isn't a question of who wants what. It's about putting the best people in the right places. To be blunt, Miss Grant, you are not one of the... *best* people.'

Deborah's mouth fell open. Had he really said that? 'Mr Morland, I...' Her words shrivelled. She couldn't dredge up anything to say.

'I know you believe Miss Rushton is just another Food Office clerk, but she was assigned here to investigate a serious case of food coupon theft in the Fallowfield area. Thanks to her, two men are going to stand trial for being in possession of thousands of stolen coupons.'

'She never said anything to me,' Deborah whispered.

'Of course not. It was a secret investigation.'

'So... that's why she's being sent to the depot – because she's someone who takes on work in special circumstances?'

'It's one reason,' Mr Morland replied, 'but you should know, Miss Grant, that in any case I shouldn't have put your name forward.'

Deborah gasped. 'But—'

Mr Morland held up a hand to stop her. 'You're a good enough worker, Miss Grant, and you get your job done – but that's as much as I can say about you. You have *never* given your all. For example, when Mrs Henshaw was here, she collected recipes and distributed them to housewives.'

Deborah seemed to hear a ringing in her ears. Her posture stiffened and she stared incredulously. Mr Morland had *loathed* it when Sally had done that. He hadn't wanted her to work beyond her remit. Now he was praising her for it.

'And Miss Rushton was appointed to the post in this office specifically to undertake the Fallowfield investigation, which was a piece of work I would never have entrusted to you,' Mr Morland continued. 'You have always coasted along, Miss Grant. You're good enough at what you do and you don't make mistakes, but at the same time I don't believe you have worked to your full capacity. That's what bosses need in wartime, workers who give their all.'

Tears rose in Deborah's eyes, and she blinked them away fiercely. Her brow furrowed and she had to swallow hard, her face flushing. She had never felt more humiliated in her life. And after she'd shared her hopes with Patrick, Sally, Lorna and

Mum too! What a comedown. The worst thing was that, as much as she wanted to rage against Mr Morland's harsh judgement, she knew in her heart of hearts that he was right; she had always coasted along – but what was wrong with that? She'd always got her work done. She wasn't slipshod or unreliable. But now, because she'd done her job to the letter, she was being punished for not going the extra mile.

And *Rosalind flaming Rushton* had got the job Deborah had set her heart on.

A dull ache took up residence in her heart. She kneaded her chest with the heel of her hand to make the pain go away. She could almost feel her body shrinking.

How could she put on a brave face after this?

NINETEEN

Betty spent the morning collapsing cigarette boxes. All she had to do was carefully flatten them and drop them into a sack, but for her own satisfaction she first put them into piles of sixty. Sally had pinned lists on the noticeboard of the things salvage could be turned into, and sixty large cigarette boxes could become the outer container of a shell. Likewise, half a dozen shop-bills might end up as a washer for the same shell.

She hummed 'I, Yi, Yi, Yi, Yi (I Like You Very Much)' as she performed the simple task.

'And *who* is it you like very much?' Lorna asked, coming over to her. 'Don't tell me. A certain bookseller.'

Betty pretended to think about it. 'Maybe.'

'And maybe also a certain little baby?' Lorna asked, tucking a lock of dark-brown hair back under her silk headscarf. 'What stage are things at now?'

'It's all settled – well, as good as. We're waiting to be seen by the magistrate. After that we'll be allowed to take little Bessie Beech home with us.'

A ripple of joy mixed with sheer wonderment passed through her. That darling little baby would officially be theirs.

Their daughter. It was unbelievable, yet at the same time completely right and natural.

'We've done all we can to get ready,' said Betty, launching happily into her favourite topic. 'Some of the neighbours have passed on baby clothes and we'll be given a bottle and teat and the usual allocation of clothes coupons.' Subduing her excitement, she said seriously, 'I want you to know I shan't leave you in the lurch. I've arranged with a young mother up the road that she'll have Bessie during the day for the time being, just until things are more settled here. After that – well, let's wait and see.' Not wanting to have that discussion just yet, she went on, 'Grace has been knitting, and so have her neighbours.'

Lorna hitched one hip onto the edge of the table. 'Your dad and Grace must be thrilled at the prospect of being grandparents.'

'Actually, they both have reservations,' Betty admitted, feeling hurt well up inside her, making it painful to breathe. Her mouth went dry. 'Dad says, "*Why adopt when you should be having children of your own?*" – children he thinks we're bound to love more because they'll be our "real" children.'

'Little Bessie Beech will be your real child,' Lorna said at once.

'I wish Dad could be as sure as you are,' said Betty, 'but, oh Lorna, he sees it in terms of how much my mum loved me—'

'And how Grace didn't,' Lorna finished, catching on immediately. 'That's fiddlesticks. You're nothing like Grace. From what you've said about her, it sounds like all she wanted from her marriage was a husband, and a grown-up stepdaughter was always going to be a nuisance. It's completely different for you and Samuel. You're both longing to adopt little Bessie Beech.'

Betty's heart swelled. 'Thank you for saying, "and Samuel" automatically,' she said gratefully.

'Why wouldn't I?' Lorna asked, puzzled.

'You've heard my dad's worry over the adoption. Now listen

to Grace's objection. She's convinced it's all *me*, and that Samuel is just going along with it.'

'That's more than fiddlesticks,' Lorna replied frankly. 'That's pure codswallop. Grace needs to get her eyes tested.'

'This looks cosy,' came a new voice.

Mrs Lockwood.

She walked in, dressed in her smart WVS uniform with the Salvage Officer armband. Betty was used to her sounding loud and hectoring. She was still loud – she had what Sally called a parade-ground voice – but the bossy note wasn't there any longer. As unlikely as it sounded, the formidable Mrs Lockwood seemed to have mellowed.

Lorna slipped from the table. 'We were just having a chat while Mrs Atkinson finishes her job.'

'Just so long as all the work gets done,' Mrs Lockwood replied in a gracious voice that Betty had never heard from her before. 'Mrs Broughton, now that we're in May, I have come to assemble the monthly statistics for April. I'll talk you through all the figures that are required, but compiling the statistics and delivering them to the Town Hall will be something I will do each month, not *you*.'

Betty and Lorna exchanged a glance. They knew full well that this had previously been Sally's job. Mrs Lockwood left the room. Lorna gave Betty a wink before following her. Betty hurried to get her task finished and then spent some time sorting out a huge tangle of string and twine, separating the two types. She had finished doing this and was about to put the kettle on when Lorna came to seek her out.

'All well?' Betty asked softly. 'She didn't haul you over the coals for chatting, did she?'

'No, she didn't – which is very different to the Mrs Lockwood we all know and loathe.'

'She must have softened because of Sally and her medical condition,' Betty suggested.

'As long as she's being nice to us, who cares about the reason?' Lorna leaned forward. 'Listen. She wasn't here about the statistics. I mean, yes, she was here about that, but she had news as well, about our new girl.'

'Really?' asked Betty. Lorna had told her about Deborah's idea. She felt a little flutter of anticipation.

Lorna held up a hand. 'Before you get excited, it isn't Deborah. I know,' she added when Betty stared at her.

'She's going to be so disappointed,' breathed Betty.

'It's worse than that,' said Lorna. 'The girl who has been given the job is Deborah's colleague.'

Betty winced. 'That's going to make it uncomfortable in the office while this girl works out her notice.'

Lorna huffed out a breath. 'Not for long it won't. Miss Rosalind Rushton starts here on Monday.'

'So soon?' Betty asked. 'Well! I don't know quite what to make of it. Oh, but poor Deborah...'

Lorna glanced through the window. 'Here's something that might cheer you up.'

Betty moved to stand beside her – and moments later she was hurrying outside to meet her husband. She just had time to register that his gentle hazel eyes were gleaming and his lean, usually serious face was bright with excitement before he caught her up in his arms and swung her round in a circle.

She laughed, breathless and startled. 'Samuel! What is it?'

He set her on her feet. 'W-we've had a letter from the magistrates' court. I meant to bring it here f-for us to open together, but I couldn't w-wait to read it. Do you mind?'

'Of course I don't. When is our appointment?'

'F-Friday of next week – the f-fifteenth.'

Betty was torn between tears and laughter. 'I can't wait!'

Behind her, Lorna said, 'This looks like good news.'

Holding Samuel's hand, Betty spun round to beam at her

friend. 'The appointment I told you about, where the magistrate gives us his approval – it's next week.'

'How wonderful!' Lorna responded. 'Congratulations.'

'Thanks,' said Samuel.

'Which day?' Lorna asked.

'Friday,' said Betty. Belatedly it occurred to her to ask, 'Please may I have the time off?'

'Of course,' said Lorna. 'And I'll square it with Mrs Lockwood, so don't give her a thought. Just look forward to becoming a *mum*!'

Betty felt like dancing around the yard. She gazed up into Samuel's eyes, which were glowing. Betty took a deep breath, savouring this very special moment.

'It's happening,' she whispered to Samuel. 'It's really happening.'

TWENTY

Although she did her best to hide it, Sally was dreadfully bored. They were into May now. Was she really going to have to rest up all the way through to December? Her brain would have dribbled out of her ears long before then.

But she couldn't say so, because she didn't want to look as if she wasn't doing her very best for her baby. And she was, she really was. Keeping her baby safe was the most important thing in her life. Sometimes beads of sweat bloomed on her forehead at the memory of how her first pregnancy had ended and she had to hold her breath to prevent sobs of the deepest fear. It was exhausting swinging between her darkest dread and desperate boredom.

The closest she came to admitting her feelings was when she said to Mum, who was a regular visitor, 'It's as if I don't have a life of my own any more. I just get to hear about other people's.'

'Well, I've got plenty of news from Withington,' said Mum.

Imagine if, instead of saying that, she'd said, 'Lying there on that sofa every day must feel like it will last for ever.'

Then Sally could have told her how hard she worked to

keep herself occupied. She read library books and the newspaper; she tackled the crossword every day. Then there was her knitting and the minor repairs she did to clothes that had been donated to the WVS clothing exchange. She had started to make Thermos-flask covers with shoulder straps for land girls so they could carry their drinks to work more securely than by putting them in the baskets on the front of their bicycles. Oh, she did a hundred and one things to make the time go by... but it still wasn't enough to take away the feeling of dreariness that lay underneath.

After Mum had departed, Sally found herself doing what had become a habit she loathed herself for, yet which she couldn't resist. She'd become a clock-watcher. She had known several girls in her Town Hall days who had done this all the time, longing for their next break, desperate for six o'clock so they could go home. Sally had never been like that, but she was now. From about four o'clock every afternoon, her gaze kept straying to the clock on the mantelpiece, while she ached for her friends to come home.

Today, on top of the usual need for conversation, she had an additional interest – and an additional concern. Today was the day when Rosalind Rushton had started at the depot and Sally couldn't wait to hear all about it – but she was also aware of how difficult today must be for Deborah, who had been understandably upset not to get the job.

Lorna and Deborah finished work at the same time but, of course, Lorna got home far sooner. She came to say hello to Sally, who pushed herself up into a sitting position.

'Well?' Sally asked. 'What's she like?'

Lorna sat down. 'She's fine. Works hard, asks intelligent questions, and she's pleasant. I'm sure she'll fit in.' She smiled suddenly and her green eyes twinkled. 'I think the van drivers approve.'

'You mean she's pretty?'

'*Decidedly*. Red hair. Lovely complexion that looks like porcelain.'

'Perhaps she uses Radiance,' Sally said with a giggle, referring to the face cream that had featured their own Betty in two advertisements last year. 'How old is she?'

'Older than we are. The same sort of age as Louise, I'd say. I've told her that, in front of other people, we're all Miss or Mrs, but when it's just the three of us it's first names.'

'Is she called anything for short?' Sally asked, thinking how friendly Rosie sounded.

'Nope. She's Rosalind,' said Lorna. 'I'll bring her here to meet you once she's settled in – and when it won't bother Deborah, of course.'

'Deborah will be all right,' Sally said staunchly, wanting to stand by her lifelong friend. 'She just needs a little time, that's all.'

Sally was anxious for Deborah to come home so she could provide some support that she suspected was much needed. The moment she heard the front door open, Sally rose to her feet and went into the hallway. Deborah looked smart and trim in her office clothes, a white blouse and navy skirt with a coat that had front panels of leopard-patterned cloth, and a straw hat with a bow on the band.

'I remember you buying that coat!' Sally remarked.

'And you got your swing-jacket at the same time,' Deborah replied.

'It was our final splurge before war broke out,' said Sally.

'It seems strange now that we were ever that frivolous,' Deborah answered.

They went into the sitting room. Sally would have sat beside her friend, but Deborah gave her a little push.

'Put your feet up,' she said in a pretend-bossy voice.

Sally settled herself once more on the sofa. 'How was today at work?'

'On my own in the *office*, you mean?' Deborah replied, a touch of tartness in her tone.

'It can't have been easy,' Sally said sympathetically.

'I didn't sigh the day away, if that's what you're worried about. Even if I'd felt like it, I couldn't have because Mr Morland was at his desk all day, so I kept my head down and got on with it – especially after what he said about my attitude to work.'

'That was unfair of him.' Sally spoke not just out of loyalty but also because she truly meant it. 'When I used to collect and give out recipes, he didn't like it. Now he's criticising you for simply doing what's required.'

'Bless you for that,' said Deborah. 'I can always count on you to stand by me.' Dropping her voice, she added, 'I didn't tell you before, but what Mr Morland actually said about me was that I don't give *my all* at work. He said I *cruise along*... and you're not saying anything, which means you think so, too.'

'Well, you've never been one for taking on extra responsibilities,' Sally said carefully.

'Maybe it's time for me to buck my ideas up,' Deborah said firmly.

Sally reached for her hand. 'Good for you,' she said warmly. 'A lot of people would have been crushed and resentful after what's happened to you, but you've taken it on the chin. I admire that.'

'Thanks,' Deborah answered, 'but it doesn't feel very admirable. I do feel rather crushed, since you mention it. It would have been easier to lose out on the depot job if it had been given to anyone other than Rosalind Rushton.'

This obviously wasn't the moment to mention that Rosalind had made a promising start at the depot, but Sally was proud of her friend for being able to accept what Mr Morland had said about her.

'Thanks for helping me through this,' said Deborah.

'I'm glad to do it,' Sally told her. 'Everyone is being so kind to me and it's good to think I can give something back.'

It was true. She was aware that to an extent she was living life vicariously through other people, but that didn't mean she was using her friends as entertainment. They meant the world to her, and she cared about them dearly.

They were the best friends she could possibly hope for. What would she do without them?

The following evening, Louise sat with Sally and shared an idea she'd had.

'I haven't mentioned this to anyone else,' she said, her brown eyes serious. 'I thought I'd ask you first since you know everyone better than I do.'

'Who is everyone?' Sally asked, intrigued.

'Betty, Lorna – but mainly Deborah.'

'I've known Deborah all our lives, but you probably know Betty or Lorna as well as I do now. You've lived here since this time last year.'

Sally smiled. Louise had fitted right in, even though she was a few years older than the others. Although there was something self-sufficient about her, she wasn't at all stand-offish. She was good-natured and kind. She could also keep a cool head in a crisis. Most of what had happened on the night of her miscarriage was a blur, but Sally was able to recall the calm determination Louise had displayed.

'Anyway, I think you're the right person to ask,' said Louise. 'It's a way of helping Deborah. At least I hope it is.'

Sally wriggled her way into a more upright position. 'What is it?'

'It's to do with the new girl at the depot.'

'Rosalind Rushton,' said Sally.

'I know Lorna wants to bring her here to meet you,' said

Louise. 'She still sees you as the real manager, even though you're laid up.'

'But bringing Rosalind here is tricky because of the way Deborah was passed over for the job,' Sally finished.

'It's only going to get trickier the longer it's allowed to go on,' said Louise, 'so we need to do something about it sharpish.'

'What's your idea?' Sally asked her.

'Betty and Samuel have got their meeting with the magistrate this coming Friday,' said Louise. 'What if we asked Betty round tomorrow evening or Thursday evening to talk about little Bessie Beech? We could get Rosalind here as well. A situation where Betty is the centre of attention is bound to make it easier for Deborah.'

Sally nodded, pleased. 'I can't think of a better icebreaker than little Bessie Beech.'

TWENTY-ONE

Betty loved visiting Star House. She had been very happy living here. It had been a huge wrench to leave Dad behind, especially knowing that Grace had manipulated her into moving several miles away from where she'd grown up, but Mrs Beaumont and the three munitions girls had made her feel welcome, and she had soon settled into her new home.

Instead of walking all the way down the main road, Betty cut through and walked down Wilton Road from the other end. Before she was halfway along, Rosalind Rushton turned in from the Beech Road end.

Betty gave a friendly wave and quickened her pace. She had taken a liking to Rosalind. Her fair-skinned beauty endowed her with a rather fragile look, but that was misleading because she had mucked in with all the physical work without any trouble; and she showed no sign of minding that Lorna, who was younger than she was, was in charge.

The two girls met at the garden gate.

'You found your way here all right?' Betty asked.

'I could hardly miss it,' Rosalind answered. 'It's no more than a stone's throw from the depot.'

Lorna already had the front door open. Betty and Rosalind hung up their things and entered the sitting room.

Betty drew Rosalind across to Sally.

'Come and meet Sally Henshaw. Sally, this is our new girl, Rosalind Rushton.'

'We've met before, briefly,' Sally said with a smile.

'Yes, you popped into the Food Office one day,' Rosalind replied, 'on your way to a Town Hall meeting.'

'It's nice to see you again,' Sally told her.

Mrs Beaumont walked in with Deborah. Did Rosalind's light-blue eyes widen just a fraction at the sight of Mrs Beaumont's glossy, jet-black hair, ruby-coloured blouse and long cigarette-holder? If so, it didn't stop her greeting her hostess politely as they were introduced.

Deborah and Rosalind exchanged nods.

'How's the new job?' Deborah asked.

'Fine, thanks. Lorna and Betty are helping me settle in.'

'Now where is everyone going to sit?' Mrs Beaumont asked.

'I really don't need all this space—' Sally began to say.

'Yes, you do,' Lorna interrupted with a grin. 'Deborah, come and sit with me on the hearthrug.'

'Plonk yourself in an armchair, Rosalind,' said Louise. 'No, not that one – that's Mrs Beaumont's. This one. And I'll perch on the arm, if that's all right with you.'

'Betty, you sit on the end of the sofa,' said Mrs Beaumont.

'You can put your feet on my lap, if you want,' Betty said to Sally.

'Louise and Betty,' said Mrs Beaumont, 'before you settle yourselves, come and give me a hand. I've made some nibbles.'

'You shouldn't ask Betty,' said Lorna. 'She's the guest of honour.'

'Not when I'm here,' Betty said at once. 'Here, I'm just one of the Star House girls.'

In the kitchen was a plate of apple fritters, another of bread triangles covered in leek spread, and a third plate of home-made peppermint sticks. There was also a pretty bowl filled with fairy toast – wafer-thin pieces of bread baked to a golden-brown crispness.

'You always spoil us, Mrs B,' said Louise.

'A professional landlady takes care of her guests.' Mrs Beaumont handed Betty a plate and the bowl and picked up the other two plates herself. 'Put the kettle on while we take these in,' she told Louise.

As she walked into the sitting room, Betty was pleased to hear Deborah finishing a funny story about something that had happened at the Town Hall.

Soon everyone was settled. There was some general chat to begin with, and everyone complimented Mrs Beaumont on the tasty snacks.

'The real reason we're here,' said Louise, 'is to talk about little Bessie Beech. This time tomorrow, Betty, it'll all be done and dusted.'

Betty couldn't hold in a gasp of excitement. 'I can't quite believe it. Tomorrow we'll be given official permission to adopt her.'

'It's a wonderful thing you're doing,' said Deborah.

'What arrangements have you made?' Mrs Beaumont asked.

'A mum up the road is going to help out. Lorna has agreed that I can have half-days at home for the first week or so. I don't want to let the depot down by leaving, but at the same time I want to be at home with the baby. We'll have to see how things go.'

'Soon little Bessie Beech will be Bessie Atkinson,' said Lorna.

'Elizabeth Atkinson,' said Rosalind. 'That's a fine name.'

'It's a pity she wasn't given a middle name,' said Sally.

'It doesn't work like that,' Betty told them. 'When you adopt a baby, you're allowed to give him or her a new name.'

'To go with the new surname,' said Lorna.

Betty nodded. She pressed her lips together. The next bit was private, and she didn't want it to burst out by accident.

'Have you chosen a new name?' Deborah asked, her bright-blue eyes alight with interest.

'We have,' Betty said carefully, 'but we don't want to announce it yet. Not until everything is official.'

'I don't blame you,' Mrs Beaumont said before anyone else could chip in. 'Is adopting a foundling different from adopting a baby whose mother is known?'

Betty was happy for the conversation to move on from baby names. 'I don't think so.'

Distress flickered across Sally's face. 'I can't imagine a mother being able to abandon her new baby.'

'It's hard to comprehend,' said Louise. 'She must have been desperate.'

'That's no excuse,' said Lorna. 'She might at least have left Bessie in a place where she'd have been found sooner – like the steps of the police station. The police are coming and going day and night.'

'Do you think she knew we were on duty on the depot roof?' Betty asked Sally. Had the mother in a manner of speaking chosen her to be the baby's new mother?

Sally sighed. 'We'll never know. Even if she did know we were up there, she still took a risk. I never heard the baby whimper. I was all set to go home. You were the one who heard her.'

Betty was thrown back to that scene. 'I thought it was a cat. I might so easily have ignored it. Just imagine if we'd left—'

'But you didn't leave,' Louise put in. 'You *did* go to look, and you *did* find her.'

'Even if you had gone home and had breakfast,' Deborah added, 'you'd still have found her later on.'

Sally placed a hand on her tummy. 'I wonder what the

mother's doing now. I wonder what she's been thinking these past few weeks.'

'Imagine carrying that secret with you until your dying day.' Rosalind's shoulders gave a little shudder.

'My mum says the mother doesn't deserve to have a child after what she did,' Deborah added.

'It's a very messy situation,' said Mrs Beaumont, 'but it will all be cleared up tomorrow when Samuel and Betty are given the permission they've been waiting for.'

'The perfect happy ending,' said Louise, smiling warmly at Betty.

There was one more thing that Betty wanted to talk about. Not her dad's concern about an adopted child playing second fiddle when another baby came along, not Grace's ridiculous idea that Samuel was only doing this to please her, but what Warden Everett had suggested.

'The first time we went to the Foundling Hospital,' she said, 'the warden talked about children inheriting their mothers' morals.'

'Can you inherit morals?' Louise asked, looking around at everyone.

'Apparently, there's a common belief that you can,' said Betty. 'Mrs Fitch, the lady from Welfare, told me and Samuel. She said that there are some mother-and-baby homes that will only accept a girl if it's her first illegitimate baby, because that way they can tell prospective parents that she's only made one mistake and she's a decent girl really.'

'I can see why prospective parents would prefer that,' said Mrs Beaumont.

'But it's *wrong*, isn't it?' Betty asked. 'Suggesting that a baby is less worthy of adoption, less worthy of having a loving family, because the mother was less than perfect – well, it's heartless, if you ask me. It's not the baby's fault!'

'You're right,' said Rosalind. 'It isn't the baby's fault. But if the prospective parents are given a choice between a baby whose morals are more likely to be questionable, or less likely, you can't blame them for taking the safer option.'

'I still think it's wrong.' Tears filled Betty's eyes. 'Samuel and I don't know anything about little Bessie Beech, other than that she's a baby in need of parents to love her and take care of her. Actually,' she went on, fierceness entering her heart as well as her voice, 'we do know something. We know that in official adoption terms we're taking on the child of an unfit mother, and plenty of folk will think that means we're storing up trouble for ourselves.'

'D'you know what I think?' said Mrs Beaumont. 'I think it's very easy for people to make those judgements about innocent babies. That's the way of the world. But maybe they should pay more attention to the beliefs and values of the adoptive parents instead of scaring them off with tales of immoral mothers.'

'Hear, hear.' Sally sat up and reached for Betty's hand. 'Little Bessie Beech is going to have devoted parents who will set her a wonderful example in every way. You know what that means, don't you, Betty? It means she'll grow up to be happy and warm-hearted and utterly gorgeous – just like you.'

TWENTY-TWO

The next morning, Betty and Samuel ate breakfast in their dressing gowns before heading upstairs to get dressed.

Betty dithered over what to wear. Her best dress was the royal-blue one Lorna had given her. She loved wearing it, but what if it made her look *too* smart, *too* elegant? What if the magistrate looked her up and down and said, 'If you've got that sort of money, you're too good to take on a foundling'?

Oh, she was being ridiculous. Of course the magistrate wouldn't say any such thing. The royal blue was her best dress and if this wasn't a best-dress occasion she didn't know what was. Samuel, who wore his tweed jacket with elbow-patches for everyday, had put on his suit this morning, so they would wear their Sunday best together.

When she went downstairs, Samuel turned round to look at her. His gentle nature always made his lean, good-looking face look modest, even shy, but all Betty could see now in his features was the love and pride he felt for her.

'Are you ready to go and make it off-ficial?' he asked.

Betty nodded, too full of emotion to speak. She put on her jacket and her film-star hat. Samuel checked his pockets before he ushered her out of their living quarters and through the shop, in which the smells of wooden floorboards and paper mingled with the faint scent of furniture cream because Betty polished the bookcases regularly.

The shop was to be shut all morning and Samuel had left a note to that effect on the windowpane in the upper half of the door. Betty stepped outside into the May sunshine and Samuel locked up behind them.

'Not that w-way,' he said when Betty turned to go to the bus stop. 'On a d-day like today, we travel in style.'

He placed his hand on the back of her waist, took her to where a taxi was parked at the kerb, and helped her in.

They held hands all the way to town. The driver dropped them off outside the magistrates' court. While Samuel paid him, Betty looked up at the building, remembering the other time she had been here. What a day that had been! Coming up for two years ago now, when Sally had still been working in the Food Office and Betty had worked in Mr Tucker's grocery shop, Sally had duped Betty into letting her buy some butter she wasn't entitled to since she wasn't registered with Tucker's. Betty had been summoned to appear at the magistrates' court, as had Mr Tucker. He might not have been the one to sell the butter, but it was sold in his shop, which made it his responsibility.

'You look like you're miles away,' said Samuel.

Betty looked at him with a smile. 'I was. I was remembering when I was fined for selling that butter to Sally.'

'I think that w-was a good thing,' said Samuel, his hazel eyes crinkling behind his glasses. 'If you hadn't lost your job at Tucker's, you'd never have gone to work at the salvage depot, and I'd never have met you. I c-can't imagine my life without you.'

'And I can't imagine mine without *you*,' Betty answered.

'Pretty s-soon we w-won't be able to imagine our lives w-without our baby daughter.'

They walked up the steps and went inside. Samuel announced their arrival at the reception desk.

Ushering Betty to one side, he explained, 'We have to w- wait over here.'

After a minute or two, a tall, good-looking man appeared. He was around fifty and his hairline had receded right over the top of his head, leaving a thin quantity of hair around his dome. Betty caught a whiff of pipe tobacco.

'Mr and Mrs Atkinson? Good morning. I'm Mr Shires and I'm one of the magistrates' clerks. My job is to ensure that there are no breaches of the law. As a rule, I am inside the courtroom, but your meeting today will take place in a private room. Allow me to show you the way.'

Mr Shires escorted them across the foyer and up the stairs, then along a couple of corridors lined with doors, all of them closed, some of them with a couple of chairs outside. A few of the chairs were occupied by nervous-looking people. Betty could understand just how they felt. Even though she and Samuel were here for the happiest of reasons, she still had butterflies.

Then they turned a corner and further down this corridor someone stood up, and then another person did too – a woman. *Grace!* And the first person was *Dad!*

They came forward to greet Betty and Samuel.

'You've got a few minutes before your appointment,' Mr Shires said. 'Excuse me,' he added, then opened a door and disappeared inside.

Dad shook hands with Samuel, then he put his hands on Betty's shoulders and kissed her cheek, his moustache gently rasping against her smooth skin. When he let her go, Betty turned to Grace, who was elegance personified in a caramel- coloured hip-length jacket with a buckled belt, and a matching skirt with a pleated panel down the front. Atop her conker- brown hair she wore a dainty hat with ribbon-and-bow trimming, and her shoes were two-tone leather. Crikey, she was even carrying a muff.

Betty immediately felt glad she'd chosen her royal-blue dress – and if that was a shallow thought to have on such a momentous occasion, well, there it was. It couldn't be helped.

'We're here to show our support,' said Dad. Drawing Betty aside, he said quietly, 'I've been thinking about what I said to you that time about not loving little Bessie Beech as much as you'll love your own children—'

'She will be our own child,' Betty put in. *Why couldn't Dad see that?*

'You know what I mean,' he said.

'I do, and I wish you wouldn't differentiate between her and any children we might have in the future,' Betty said. 'To us, they'll all be the same.'

'And to me an' all, love.' Dad's brown eyes were tender. 'I was so busy thinking about you and your mum, and you and Grace, that I forgot to think about what I should have been thinking about – namely, you and Samuel. Little Bessie Beech will never be second best to the two of you, and she won't be to Grace and me either. I want you to know that before you go inside that room.'

Betty had to blink away tears, her heart overflowing with gratitude. She laid a hand on Dad's arm and stepped nearer to him. 'Thanks so much, Dad. That means the world to me.'

Mr Shires reappeared. He glanced questioningly at the little group.

'This is my father and stepmother,' said Betty. 'May they come in with us?'

Mr Shires addressed Dad and Grace. 'You will have to sit behind Mr and Mrs Atkinson. Please don't say anything unless you are invited to.' His tone suggested this was most unlikely to happen.

They all went in. The back wall was lined with shelves of

books on either side of an interior door. In front, a big table with two shield-backed chairs faced the room. Over to one side were two desks, side by side.

Positioned in front of the big table was a pair of ordinary chairs. With a look at Betty and Samuel, Mr Shires indicated them. As she took her place, Betty looked round to see Dad and Grace taking seats. They weren't simply behind her and Samuel. They were at the back of the room.

Samuel was looking at the pair of shield-backed seats.

'I thought there w-would be just one magistrate.'

'Mr Brent-Williams is in charge of this matter,' Mr Shires explained. 'He believes that issues involving children should be held in the presence of a lady magistrate, and so Mrs Ames will be here too.'

Mr Shires took his place at one of the desks to the side of the room, where he was joined by a clerk. Then the door in between the bookcases opened and the two men stood up. Mr Shires motioned to Betty and her family to do likewise.

A craggy-faced, dark-eyed man entered. So much for ladies first! This had to be Mr Brent-Williams. He was followed by a stout lady with a pair of reading glasses dangling from a silver chain round her plump neck.

The magistrates took their places.

'Mr Shires, if you please,' said Mr Brent-Williams. He couldn't have sounded grander if he had had been entertaining the King to tea.

Mr Shires was still on his feet. 'The magistrates are convened on this fifteenth day of May in the matter of the proposed adoption of the foundling known as Bessie Beech.' He sat down.

Mr Brent-Williams looked at Betty and Samuel. 'I have read the report submitted by Mrs Fitch of the Welfare Department.'

'As have I,' Mrs Ames put in. Betty had the feeling that if

she didn't stick her oar in she wouldn't get the chance to say anything.

Mr Brent-Williams ploughed on. 'I have also read the recommendation submitted by Warden Everett of the Foundling Hospital – as has Mrs Ames,' when that lady stirred as if about to speak. 'Everything appears to be in order.'

The breath caught in Betty's throat. Was this the moment when they were given permission to become parents to little Bessie Beech? She had to control her breathing so as not to laugh in sheer joy.

But Mr Brent-Williams said, 'Mr Atkinson, I have seen the details of your financial situation, but I should like you to tell me in your own words how you intend to provide for your family.'

Before Samuel could stand up and speak, the door between the bookshelves opened and a clerk hurried inside on silent feet. He bent to speak to Mr Shires, who looked startled for a moment before his face became a polite mask. Rising, he went to the magistrates. Mr Brent-Williams turned to speak to him, but Mr Shires moved on a couple of paces so that he was in between the two magistrates, and Mr Brent-Williams's conscious or unconscious move to exclude Mrs Ames was foiled.

Mr Shires spoke in a low voice that, no matter how much Betty strained her ears, she couldn't make out. The magistrates looked at one another with widened eyes before they too schooled their expressions. Betty felt a strange dropping sensation in her stomach. Instinctively she reached for Samuel's hand.

Mr Brent-Williams stood up. 'Please excuse us, Mr and Mrs Atkinson. We shall return presently.'

And the magistrates and the clerks all vanished through the rear door. Betty swivelled on her seat to face Samuel, her heart hammering.

'What was that about?' she asked.

He shook his head. 'I've no idea.'

'Well!' Grace said in an offended voice. 'It's a pretty poor show, if you ask me.'

The four of them sat and waited, with Grace emitting the occasional huff of annoyance. Betty wasn't far from tears by the time the door opened again. She half-expected someone to rush in and explain, but instead the magistrates and clerks walked in sedately and took their places in no hurry at all. Betty tried to read their faces, but all four expressions were blank.

Mr Brent-Williams put his elbows on the table and leaned forward. 'Mr and Mrs Atkinson, I apologise for the interruption, but something most unexpected has occurred. A... person arrived at the magistrates' court this morning, claiming to be the mother of the foundling child known as—'

Betty shot to her feet. '*No!*'

Mr Brent-Williams looked, not at her, but at Samuel. 'Kindly restrain your wife, Mr Atkinson.'

Samuel laid a gentle hand on Betty's arm, encouraging her to sit down. She sank down, and not a moment too soon. Her insides had turned to slush.

Mr Brent-Williams dealt her a hard look before he continued. 'The... *person* was able to describe how the foundling was dressed, and exactly whereabouts in Chorlton Salvage Depot she was left. Mrs Fitch is satisfied that the person is indeed the mother.'

'But sh-she abandoned her baby!' cried Samuel, clasping Betty's hand.

'And now she wants her back,' said Mrs Ames, giving them a sympathetic look.

Mr Brent-Williams jiggled his shoulders as if he would gladly have shoved his colleague off her chair if he could have got away with it.

'The situation is this,' he declared. 'You are not entitled to know who this... person is.' He made *person* sound like an insult. 'She is married, but the father of the baby is not her husband. The husband is overseas fighting for his country and knows nothing of the child. I have instructed the mother that she must write and inform him. She was most reluctant to consent, but I told her that, if she declined, I would immediately hand over the foundling to its prospective adoptive parents. Therefore, she has agreed to write. We will wait and see what the husband has to say on the subject. If he agrees to accept the cuckoo in the nest, it might – I repeat, might – be possible for her to have the baby returned to her.'

'*Might* be?' Samuel questioned.

'She abandoned the child and there's a strong case for refusing to let her have it back at all,' Mr Brent-Williams declared. 'Let's see what the father says. That's the starting point. I'll also require a letter from his commanding officer about what sort of fellow he is. Will he be able to keep his wife on the straight and narrow in future?'

Betty's voice quivered as she asked, 'What about us, sir?'

'You've found yourselves in the centre of a fine old pickle,' the magistrate replied. 'You might do better to look for another child to adopt, one whose mother has been to a mother-and-baby home and has made the necessary arrangements to surrender it. I don't know why you took it into your heads to go after a foundling in the first place.'

Betty's eyes widened and then somehow got stuck, leaving her unable to blink. Her chin quivered. She wanted to cry out in frustration, but her pain was too great. She felt cold all over, her body quaking with the power of held-in sobs.

Were they truly going to have little Bessie Beech wrenched from them?

TWENTY-THREE

On her way home from work, Deborah got off the bus a few stops early to see Betty and Samuel and offer her congratulations.

But when she arrived she was startled to see how strained Betty appeared. Instead of glowing with happiness, her normally creamy complexion was pale, almost colourless; and Samuel's shoulders were slightly hunched. The smile faded from Deborah's face.

'What's happened?'

What she really wanted to ask was, 'Has something bad happened to little Bessie Beech?' But just imagine asking a question like that!

Betty invited Deborah to sit in one of the armchairs and she and Samuel sat together on the sofa, holding hands, while, between them, they told the story – or not so much their story as that of little Bessie Beech's mother.

'And now you have to wait for the husband to write back,' Deborah summed up, shocked, 'but even if he says yes to having the baby, the mother might not be allowed to have Bessie Beech back. The whole tale is extraordinary.'

'The magistrate said w-we ought to find another baby to adopt,' said Samuel with a frustrated shake of his head, 'one whose mother has officially handed it over for adoption.'

'He made it sound as if any baby will do,' Betty burst out, tears sparkling in her blue eyes, 'but it's not like that. We don't want just any baby. We want little Bessie Beech. We *love* her.'

Deborah was stumped for what to say. She'd come here expecting celebrations and instead her friends were in a state of shock and grief. She slipped from the armchair and knelt in front of Betty, taking her free hand.

'I'm very sorry that this has happened to you – to the pair of you. You don't deserve it. You were all set to be parents and now...'

Her voice faded and she sat back on her heels as Betty slumped against Samuel, unable to contain her sobs any longer.

With Betty and Samuel anxiously awaiting word of little Bessie Beech's mother's husband's response, and with Sally always hoping for letters from Andrew, and Lorna being separated from her new husband, it was brought home forcefully to Deborah how very lucky she was to be able to be with Patrick regularly.

Having a handsome boyfriend made her feel differently about herself. Silly as it sounded, it made her feel successful. With almost all the young men away fighting, there were plenty of girls without boyfriends. Deborah hadn't realised how much being unattached had mattered to her until she'd started going out with Patrick.

Lots of girls of her age had spinster aunties who had lost their sweethearts in the last war, or who had never had the chance of a sweetheart because of the terrible loss of life in the trenches. Now that she had Patrick by her side, Deborah could finally admit to herself that she'd been worried that the lists of those who had fallen in action this time around would mean she would never have a man of her own.

But she did have Patrick and that meant that life was wonderful. It was a shame he worked shifts, but she could cope with that. Betty's dad was in the police force as well and Deborah longed to ask her chum what it was like living with a policeman, but she didn't dare in case it sounded as though she was planning her future. She also itched to ask Sally what it felt like to be pregnant, but she didn't want to tempt fate, or stress her friend.

Was she planning her future? She was and she wasn't. When the girls at work pressed for information, Deborah laughed and said, 'Good heavens, no. We're just enjoying being together, that's all,' which was true – up to a point. Didn't every girl with a boyfriend indulge in secret daydreams about the future? Surely it was only natural.

The one person Deborah fully trusted to have a conversation about Patrick was Sally. With years behind them of sharing everything, Deborah knew Sally would understand without leaping to conclusions and making arch remarks about a new hat.

Sally had received three letters all in one go from Andrew and had become uncharacteristically tearful.

'Don't mind me,' she told Deborah. 'My emotions are liable to run riot. I'm delighted to get three letters – but I miss him all the time. I wish he could be here because of the baby, but then I feel selfish because every wife has umpteen reasons to want her husband to come home.'

'It isn't selfish,' Deborah assured her. 'Being a soldier's wife is hard. You have so much to worry about for his sake, and at the same time there are all the extra responsibilities of keeping life ticking over at home. It's just that you, Mrs High Blood Pressure, have more time than most to think about it.'

'You can't imagine how much I'm longing to get back to normal,' said Sally.

'It'll be a new sort of normal when it happens,' Deborah answered with a smile. 'You'll have little Master or Miss Henshaw.'

'You saying "little" makes me think of Bessie Beech,' Sally remarked.

'I know.' Deborah sighed. 'Poor Betty – and poor Samuel too. Betty says they're going to carry on visiting little Bessie Beech at the Foundling Hospital while they wait for news. It must be such a strain on them.'

Sally touched her tummy. 'However ropey I feel, I'm glad I have my baby safe in here.'

'You have to look after yourself.'

Sally laughed. 'There are plenty of you watching like hawks to make sure I don't take any risks. Not that I could take any even if I wanted to, not with my blood pressure permanently poised ready to leap sky-high.' Her tone had turned serious, even glum. She switched on the light-heartedness again as she said, 'It's up to the rest of you to keep me entertained, so you can now fulfil your obligation by telling me all the latest about you and Patrick.'

A glow of happiness filled Deborah's chest. 'He's *gorgeous*. It's funny to remember that I didn't like him at all to start with.'

'But the way he conducted himself when the UXB went off made you see him differently,' Sally prompted.

'I never thought I'd say I'm glad a bomb went off, but I'm glad that one did. It changed my life.'

'Is it getting serious between you?' Sally asked.

'I really like him,' Deborah confided. 'I go all tingly when he's near and I love it when we walk along holding hands. I love to think of other people seeing us together.'

'Does that matter to you?' Sally asked her. 'The way you appear to the rest of the world?'

'Oh yes,' Deborah answered at once. 'Being seen to be a couple is part of the excitement.' She lowered her voice, feeling very daring as she added, 'But the most exciting bit is that spark of feeling when our eyes meet, especially if it happens unexpectedly.' She shivered. It was a delicious sensation and all the hairs on her arms stood up.

'It all sounds very promising,' Sally commented, her hazel eyes warm.

'He's not the sort to push things along too quickly,' said Deborah, wanting to make this clear. 'You hear stories of men on leave wanting their girls to give them something to remember them by, as the saying goes. Patrick's not like that – and don't say it's because he isn't about to be sent to the battlefront.'

'I wasn't going to.'

'Even if he were a soldier on leave, he wouldn't try to take advantage. He was brought up to have more respect than that for girls.'

'That must make you feel safe,' Sally suggested.

'I don't want to make him sound boring,' Deborah said at once. 'It's funny how something can feel safe and exciting at the same time. He's good fun and all he wants is for me to be happy.'

'There's a lot to be said for that,' Sally replied. 'He sounds ideal.'

'It isn't like it was for you and Andrew,' said Deborah. 'As soon as you met, something happened between you, even though you didn't act on it right away.'

'A bit different to you and Patrick, and him mistaking you for a man,' Sally said with a chuckle. 'But that doesn't matter. All that matters is that, after a couple of mishaps, things fell into place for you. What more can anyone ask for?'

. . .

May came to an end. At the beginning of June, the news broke of the huge raid carried out by the RAF on Cologne that had taken place at the very end of May.

'Did you hear about it on the news?' Deborah's dad asked her when she called round. 'The RAF sent over a thousand planes.'

Deborah felt proud of their boys, but she also felt a thrill of fear. *What reprisals might follow?*

Early in June came the government announcement that it was going to take over all the coal mines. On the domestic front, opinion was divided over the prospect of dried eggs, which were due to go on sale towards the end of the month.

'Each person will be allowed the dried-egg equivalent of a dozen eggs every four weeks,' Deborah told her housemates.

'I wonder what they'll taste like,' Lorna said. 'I have to say dried egg doesn't sound appetising.'

'We'll have to wait and see,' said Mrs Beaumont. 'I'll do the best I can with them.'

'And your best will knock spots off everybody else's,' said Louise.

'I'll bring home copies of every dried-egg recipe I come across,' Deborah promised.

She had started gathering recipes the way Sally used to, to hand out as necessary. After the dressing-down she'd received from Mr Morland, she had privately vowed to buck her ideas up. She kept the recipes in a shoebox in the office. Whenever she finished her work, she would type up a few additional copies to give out. Her collection was growing nicely, and she was pleased with it.

Miss Greening from Housing had promised to bring a variety of recipes for stuffing from her mother – mint stuffing, rhubarb-and-raisin and apple-and-celery. Deborah picked up her handbag and headed downstairs to the canteen.

As she walked inside, she immediately saw her friends

sitting around a table on the far side. Miss Brelland caught sight of her. Deborah was about to wave, but Miss Brelland glanced away. Did she murmur something to the others? Miss Jameson looked embarrassed and Miss Greening, normally so bubbly, looked serious.

What on earth could they be talking about? All Deborah knew beyond any doubt was that it was about her. With a thumping heart, she made her way across the room. Her friends looked at one another, their discomfort obvious. Deborah was all too aware of a flush creeping across her cheeks. She gritted her teeth, then realised what she was doing and forced a smile instead. It was impossible to know what to do for the best, how to react. It felt as if everybody was looking at her and she had to swallow a massive obstruction in her throat.

Miss Greening stood up and came to meet her.

'Come with me,' she said, and her kindly tone nearly made Deborah burst into tears. 'You don't want to hear this in public.'

Deborah didn't know how she managed to get through the afternoon. She had to type up some letters for Mr Morland, but tears kept welling up, turning the words of the handwritten copy into a messy blur. Worse, each time the tears bloomed her nose threatened to drip, so she had to take what she hoped were dainty little sniffs.

'Are you all right, Miss Grant?' asked Miss Duggan. 'Are you starting a cold?'

Deborah faked a cheery tone. 'No, I'm fine, thank you. It must be the pollen.'

Miss Duggan was the girl who had been brought in to replace Rosalind Rushton. She was younger than Deborah, only sixteen, which Deborah had found unsettling at first. After the way she'd been passed over in favour of Rosalind, coupled with Mr Morland reading the riot act, she had conceived a fear that young Miss Duggan might also outstrip her and be promoted. That really would be a kick in the teeth.

'Have you finished that filing yet?' Deborah asked.

'Almost.'

Deborah wasn't officially in charge of Miss Duggan, but, after the huge blow to her pride, it felt important to assert herself. She wasn't bossy about it. On the contrary, she was kind and cheerful. But she made a point of watching over her young colleague, providing guidance and generally helping her and, yes, giving her reason to be grateful. And if that made her feel better, that was her own business. There was nothing wrong with wanting Miss Duggan to look up to her.

But what was going to happen when Miss Duggan heard the gossip on the grapevine? She wouldn't look up to Deborah after that. Quite the reverse. She'd look down on her. Worst of all, she might *pity* her. Deborah knew this because it was how she would feel if it had happened to somebody else.

But it hadn't happened to somebody else. It had happened to *her*.

She was the girl whose boyfriend had only gone out with her to win a bet.

TWENTY-FOUR

Deborah got ready to go out with Patrick that evening.

Was it a good thing or a bad one that she was seeing him so soon? Part of her felt the need for more time to get used to it – but how could anyone ever get used to something like this? The other part of her simply wanted to get it over with.

She stood in front of her hanging-cupboard, not knowing what to wear. She wanted to look like the bee's knees just to make Patrick sorry, but she also felt like wearing an old rag, just to show him he wasn't worth the effort.

There was a light tap on the door. When Deborah called, 'Come in!' Lorna entered, holding a magazine.

'Here's the film mag you said you were interested in, with the piece about James Stewart. What are you going to wear this evening?'

'Haven't decided.'

'Patrick will think you look lovely in whatever you choose.'

Deborah couldn't think what to say, but Lorna's next words made her wonder if something had showed in her face.

'You aren't just dressing to please Patrick, though obvi-ously you want to look nice for him. You have to dress for yourself as well. Betty said that to me once and I've never forgotten it.'

That made Deborah straighten her backbone. Yes, she would dress up and she'd feel good about herself for doing it.

'Here. What do you think of this?'

Removing a dress from the cupboard, she held it up for inspection. Often, with her dark-brown hair and bright-blue eyes, she favoured strong colours, but this rayon-crape dress in lavender and cream stripes had surprised her the first time she tried it on by being very flattering. The style suited her too. Short-sleeved, it had lightly padded shoulders, a narrow belt and a gently flared skirt that Mrs Beaumont had helped her to take up an inch or two in accordance with the current fashion.

Normally, Patrick would collect her from Star House, and she had loved drawing him into the sitting room to say hello and have a chat. But not today. This evening, she bade the others a hasty goodbye and set off to meet him on the corner.

She saw him coming towards her, his jacket sitting smartly on his broad shoulders. Seeing her, he put on a spurt.

'I'm not late, am I?' he asked.

'No,' said Deborah. 'You're never late. I felt like a bit of fresh air, that's all.'

The fib brought a twinge of guilt with it. *She* hadn't done anything wrong, yet circumstances had made her tell a lie.

Patrick offered her his arm. 'Shall we? Have you chosen a film?'

'Actually, I'd rather go somewhere where we can talk. There are still some park benches in the rec. We can have a sit-down.'

Patrick frowned and his dark eyes clouded. 'I was about to say that sounds like the perfect way to spend an evening, but you look serious.'

'There's something I want to ask you.'

They went through the open gates into the old recreation ground. It was a warm evening of lingering sunshine. At the various allotments, men and women, helped by children, were thinning out carrots, lettuce, parsnips and beet. Others picked broad beans or checked for blackfly. The rich tang of earth hung in the air.

Deborah looked around for an unoccupied bench. There were three. She chose the one furthest away from the gardeners.

'Well, if I didn't think you were serious before, I certainly do now,' Patrick said in a dry voice that didn't conceal a note of anxiety. 'Talk about wanting privacy.'

Deborah sat down. Patrick took his place beside her. He moved his hand as if to take hers, then didn't. But then he changed his mind and did. Deborah caught her breath. Should she pull away?

'Why do the words "innocent until proven guilty" spring to mind?' Patrick asked. 'Tell me what's going on, Deborah, because I don't have a clue.'

After the shock, distress and sheer humiliation she'd battled against all afternoon, Deborah felt her temper stir.

'That first time you asked me to go out with you, was it so that you could... win a *bet*?'

Now it was Patrick's turn to catch his breath. He had been looking at her, but now he jerked his head round to face forwards before ducking it as if he wanted to examine his hands. The fingers round hers uncurled and let go.

'You know about that?'

'So, it's true?' Something inside Deborah collapsed in on itself as a fresh wave of humiliation poured through her. Her shoulders lifted instinctively as if to shake off the burden of shame and distress.

Patrick angled himself to face her. 'It's not how it sounds.'

'Really?' She faked a laugh. 'Let me tell you how it sounds, and you can tell me where I've gone wrong. The first time we met – I use the word "met" in the loosest possible sense – you mistook me for a *man*, something your friend Roy Knowles found hilarious. The second time, you chucked a bucket of *water* all over me – again, much to Roy's delight. At least he wasn't there the third time,' she added bitterly, 'when I delivered soup to Longford Hall. You couldn't resist pulling me up for what I said about the thaw, could you? You just had to show you knew better. But then the UXB went off, and you took charge, and I saw a different side of you... a side I liked, a side I admired.'

'I felt very drawn to you as well,' Patrick said warmly, but Deborah wasn't interested in hearing that.

'After that, there was the dance at the Ritz, and then you sought me out at MacFadyen's and we started seeing one another,' she ploughed on, 'but what I didn't know then was that, at the Ritz, you and Roy had had a *bet* about whether I'd go out with you after our unfortunate meetings.'

'It wasn't like that—'

'Like *what*? Like two blokes having a joke at a girl's *expense*? Like two blokes seeing what one of them could get away with? How *could* you? And don't say it wasn't like that,' Deborah added on a surge of emotion that sent her heartbeat racing. 'Do you want to know how I found out? At work, that's how. All the girls know about it. As I learned this afternoon, Roy has a cousin called Maeve, and she was part of the group you were with on that night out at the Ritz. She overheard you. She overheard you and Roy making the *bet*.'

With a groan, Patrick leaned forward as if about to put his head between his knees. 'It was a joke. That's all it was – a joke.'

'Do you want to know the biggest *joke*?' Deborah demanded. 'Maeve Knowles has got a new job in the Town Hall. She saw me from a distance and recognised me, and guess what, it turns out that there's nothing Maeve likes better than a juicy bit of gossip. Now everybody at the Town Hall knows that my boyfriend is with me as a *bet*.'

'I know you're upset, but you're exaggerating. It can't possibly be everybody—'

'Oh, well, that's all right then,' Deborah flung back at him. She wanted to huddle in a corner and hide, but she was determined not to show how hurt she was. 'Just so long as it isn't *every*body. Just so long as the head porter and the postroom messenger and the Town Hall cat don't know!'

'You've every right to be hurt,' said Patrick. 'But it was a stupid joke, that's all. I'd never have joined in if I'd known someone else was listening.'

'So, you can make a stupid joke out of me as long as it's between you and Roy Knowles – is that it?'

'Please,' said Patrick, 'give me a chance to explain. Roy could see that I liked you and he said I didn't stand a chance because of thinking you were a man and then dousing you with cold water. That was how the bet started. "I bet she'd never go out with you after what you did." – "I bet she would." – "I bet she wouldn't." It didn't mean anything. It was a bit of messing about, that's all.' He huffed out a breath of pure frustration. 'And it wasn't a real bet. We didn't put money on it. It was a *joke*.'

'So you keep saying.'

'If I'd known anyone was listening—'

'So it was intended to be nothing more than a joke,' Deborah stated, leading him into a trap.

'*Exactly*,' said Patrick.

'A tasteless joke at *my expense*,' Deborah said bitterly as the trap snapped shut.

'Deborah – *please*. We didn't know one another at the time.'

'And we never would have done if I'd had any idea—'

'It was a *joke*. Not even a funny one.'

'On the contrary,' Deborah answered crisply, 'I'm sure there are numerous people at the Town Hall who are highly amused – and the ones who don't find it funny will be feeling sorry for me. They'll be *pitying* me.' Her eyes stung and her chest felt hollow. 'Can you imagine how that *feels?*'

'All I can do is apologise. I would never hurt you on purpose. You must know that. You're – well, you're important to me and I'm sorry if you've been hurt.'

Deborah raised an eyebrow. 'If?' *If?*

He thought there was an *if.*

'I never meant anything by it. Neither did Roy. We're mates. We were at school together and then we joined the police together. We muck about sometimes. That's what this was. It was nothing. Nothing.'

'Tell the girls at the Town Hall that,' snapped Deborah.

'I'll speak to Maeve—'

'You'll do no such thing. Don't you *dare* breathe a word to her. Do you want to make me look even more stupid than I do already?'

'I'm truly sorry. I can see how bothered you are and you've every right.'

'You've made a fool of me and what's worse is that everyone at the Town Hall knows.'

'And I'm sorry it happened. How many more times must I say it? I like you, Deborah. I like you a lot. I thought you felt the same. Surely you aren't going to let something as stupid as this come between us?'

'Are you calling *me* stupid for being upset?'

'Of course I'm not, and you know it.' He was starting to get vexed. 'I would never do such a thing. You're twisting my words.'

'And you're trying to turn this around and make it *my* fault.' She didn't really mean that. She knew she'd made her point and that it was time to rein in her feelings, but it was important to end up on top. *She* wasn't the one in the wrong. 'You're the one who caused this trouble, not me. You're the one who's made a monkey out of me!'

But instead of offering another apology, which was what she wanted, Patrick fought back.

'What is it that's really upset you, Deborah? A silly bet that wasn't even a real bet, just two pals having a laugh – or your work colleagues knowing about it? Is that what this is really about? You losing face at work?'

Deborah's eyes widened. It was horrible to be challenged like this – horrible and unexpected. She didn't deserve it. Until this moment, Patrick had always bent over backwards to please her. She was astounded that would go on the offensive like this. It made her feel even more injured.

Before she had time to think about what she was doing, she shot to her feet and walked away. Would he come hurrying after her? Did she want him to?

But it was a pointless question, because he didn't.

TWENTY-FIVE

Betty was as shocked as anyone when Deborah split up from
Patrick. Some girls had lots of casual boyfriends one after the
other, and all of it was just for fun, but Deborah hadn't had a
boyfriend before Patrick.

'I assumed it was serious,' Betty said to Lorna.

The two of them were sorting the daily sacks together.
Rosalind wasn't there, as Lorna had sent her out to collect the
bones from the bone-boxes that were tied to local lamp-posts,
generally one in each road. Housewives put out the bones left
over from the previous day's cooking, much to the interest of
any passing dogs.

Betty wouldn't have spoken so freely about Deborah in
front of Rosalind. Not because she and Lorna had any reservations about the new girl, whom they liked, but because Rosalind
was a new friend and discussing Deborah might have seemed
gossipy rather than compassionate.

'We *all* thought it was serious,' Lorna agreed. 'He certainly
seemed very set on her.'

Betty felt a faint flush rise in her cheeks. 'Mind you, who

am I to talk? It's not as though Samuel was my one and only boyfriend.'

'Eddie Markham set out to charm you,' Lorna replied. 'It was no wonder you liked him.'

'It was a lot more than just liking,' Betty admitted. She'd been mad about him – until she discovered he was a thief and a scoundrel whose sole interest in her had been to use her connection to the salvage depot for his own ends.

'The main thing is that the truth came out,' Lorna said, 'and Samuel was waiting in the wings.'

Betty's heart softened. *Darling Samuel.* She'd been so dazzled by Eddie that she hadn't been able to see what was right in front of her all along.

She smiled at Lorna. 'You and me both had a bumpy road, didn't we? And now Deborah is an' all. Poor lass. I hope she'll be all right. I don't know her as well as you do, because I've never lived with her.'

'She's had a tough time lately,' Lorna said, delving into the sack she was gradually emptying. 'First she didn't get the job here, and now this.'

They broke off from sorting the sacks as the paper-mill's collection van turned in through the gates and came to a halt. After it had been loaded and had gone on its way, Betty made to return to where they'd left the sacks.

'Sorry, but I'll have to leave you to it,' said Lorna. 'I've got to put together some figures.'

'No need to apologise,' Betty answered cheerfully. 'You've got a job to do. Rosalind can help me when she gets back, if I haven't finished. Anyroad, I thought Mrs Lockwood had taken on responsibility for the statistics and whatnot?'

'In a manner of speaking. She wants to be in charge of everything. You know what she's like. But I'm the manager, so the stats are my job, really.'

'Aren't you getting on with her?' Betty asked, concerned. 'I thought you were. She's stopped being such a harridan since Sally had to give up work.'

'That's true,' Lorna agreed. 'Believe me, I'm grateful that she's so much easier to work with, but at the same time I don't want her to take over and bulldoze me aside. I'm very conscious of being in Sally's place.'

'You're doing a good job,' Betty answered, happy to offer reassurance that was richly deserved, 'and I for one love having you here, though you must miss your George.'

'All the time,' Lorna agreed with a sigh.

'Does he still ring you on the office telephone after work?' Betty asked.

'No, I ring from the telephone box. Using the office telephone was something Sally let us do when we were organising the wedding. Now that I'm the manager, I appreciate what a big favour that was. Allowing staff to use the work telephone for personal calls, even if it's out of hours, isn't exactly on the manager's list of duties.'

'You're the manager now,' said Betty. 'You'd only be giving yourself permission to do what Sally let you do.'

'It doesn't feel that way,' Lorna replied. 'I wouldn't want to get caught out.'

'Caught out doing what?' And here was Mrs Lockwood.

The girls turned round quickly. Betty's skin felt tight, as though it had shrunk in the wash.

'I repeat,' said Mrs Lockwood. 'Caught out doing what?'

Lorna took a breath. 'Using the telephone for personal calls to my husband – after hours, naturally. Not that I've done it, of course.'

If Betty expected Mrs Lockwood's grey eyes to turn to flint with displeasure, and her more than ample bosom to swell, that didn't happen. Instead, she looked thoughtful, then she nodded.

'As a matter of fact, I consider that it would be quite in order, Mrs Broughton. You were after all required to come here as part of your war work, so it seems reasonable that this small concession should be made in your favour – as long as it is Mr Broughton who places each call and pays for it.'

'Of course,' said Lorna.

'In that case, I am pleased to offer my consent,' said Mrs Lockwood, with more than a little grandeur in her manner. 'Now, please accompany me to the office and show me the latest weights you have recorded for the various types of salvage.'

As the two of them walked across the yard and disappeared indoors, Betty lifted her face to the sunshine. She was delighted to think of it being easier for Lorna and George to stay in touch. It always gave her a lift when something went well for one of her chums. Other people's good news was especially welcome at present, when she and Samuel were so worried about the future of little Bessie Beech.

They visited her at the Foundling Hospital each Sunday. If she wasn't on duty at the depot, Betty also went on Saturdays while Samuel opened the bookshop; and he went alone on Wednesday afternoons during half-day closing. It was wonderful to see the baby's smile when she recognised them, and it was heartbreaking to have to leave her each time. Every time the Foundling Hospital's door shut behind her, heat flared behind Betty's eyelids and her muscles felt rigid enough to snap in two.

'Even if the mother's husband s-says he'll accept her,' Samuel had said a hundred times, 'it d-doesn't mean Mr Brent-Williams will automatically give little Bessie Beech back to her mother.'

'I don't want to feel sorry for the mother,' said Betty, 'but I do. She shouldn't have abandoned Bessie like that, but I can't help but understand why she wants to have her back. D'you think – d'you think she wants little Bessie Beech more than we do? Because she's the real mother, I mean.'

'I d-don't believe that giving birth makes her a *real* mother,'

Samuel answered staunchly. 'Being a real mother is to do with love and devotion and k-keeping the baby safe, not leaving it behind in the d-dead of night. Never let anyone tell you that you aren't a real mother, Betty.'

Betty moved closer to him, her heart brimming over with love for this dear, good man who made her feel cherished and valued. He was the best husband a girl could wish for. Given the chance, he would be the best sort of father too.

Would they ever be allowed to become a family with their little Bessie Beech?

Betty couldn't stop smiling. Usually when she and Samuel saw Dad and Grace, it was because they went over to Salford, but this time Dad and Grace were coming here to Chorlton. It was July now and Betty was going to hold a little tea-party on the first Sunday, not just for family but also for Mr and Mrs Kendall.

'You're as good as family,' she said to Mrs Kendall when she issued the invitation.

'You're a dear girl,' said Mrs Kendall, 'and we would love to come. Thank you.'

Betty had her menu all planned. On Sunday she made tomato sandwiches and meat-paste sandwiches, over the top of which she laid damp tea-towels so they wouldn't dry out, and buns with raspberry jam.

Samuel went to collect the Kendalls. Before they came, Dad and Grace arrived, and Betty let them in. As always, Dad's serious face softened at the sight of her. Grace removed her hat and shook her conker-brown hair, patting it not so much to check it was tidy as to draw attention to it. She was a good-looking woman, and she did elaborate facial exercises every day to prevent her chin from sagging. Other men probably thought Dad had done well for himself. But no matter how striking Grace was to look at, her appearance wasn't a patch on Mum's as far as Betty was concerned. Mum hadn't been a beauty, but her face had held kindness, common sense and good humour, which mattered far more to Betty than anything else.

Soon Samuel returned, escorting the Kendalls. After they had been introduced to Dad and Grace, Betty fussed over them a little, making sure they were comfortably settled.

'Now that w-we're all here,' Samuel said with a special smile for Betty, 'we c-can tell you our news.'

There was an audible gasp from Grace. 'You're expecting a *baby!*'

Colour flooded Betty's cheeks. Samuel looked flustered and his cheeks too went pink. Betty could have crowned Grace. Fancy saying that in public!

Samuel recovered quickly, or maybe embarrassment made him move on to stop others thinking about it. 'It's to do with little Bessie Beech, the child we d-dearly hope is going to be our d-daughter. W-we heard from Mr Brent-Williams, the magistrate, yesterday and we have an appointment to s-see him next F-Friday.'

'That's a long time to wait,' said Mr Kendall. 'You'll hardly sleep!'

'We're desperately hoping for good news,' said Betty. 'We're finally going to hear what the mother's husband has said.'

'But even if he says yes to accepting the baby,' said Dad, 'that doesn't guarantee the mother will get the baby back. That's what the magistrate said last time. If you ask me, she doesn't deserve to have a baby.'

'We just have to wait and see,' Betty said quietly.

'I agree with Sergeant Hughes,' Mrs Kendall said with a respectful glance at Dad. 'Fancy leaving a baby out in the cold all night for someone to find. That was cruel.'

'And don't forget this was a woman who carried on with

another man while her husband is away fighting for king and country,' Mr Kendall added.

Betty swallowed. All those criticisms were true, but she didn't dare take anything for granted. What if the husband had said yes to having little Bessie Beech and Mr Brent-Williams and Mrs Ames decided to give the mother another chance?

Samuel must have seen the distress in her expression because he said, 'Let's talk about s-something else.'

Pinning a smile on her face, Betty stood up. 'I'll bring the tea through.'

'Betty has made a lovely tea,' said Samuel.

'Can I do anything to help?' Grace asked, although she didn't back up her offer by rising to her feet.

'I can manage, thanks,' Betty answered, thinking of the many times Grace had all but dragged her into the kitchen in Dad's house. She might have felt miffed, but she chose to smile instead.

Soon the tea was on the table. Earlier, Samuel had moved their dining table away from the wall and extended the drop-down leaves, and Betty had proudly covered it with one of Mum's Irish linen tablecloths edged with masses of lace.

When the sandwiches were finished, Betty offered round the jammy buns.

'I made them from a basic cake recipe in a government leaflet,' she explained. 'You make the cake and then you add ginger or cocoa, or dried fruit if you can get hold of it. You can also use it for rock cakes or buns.'

'These are delicious,' said Mrs Kendall. 'Such a treat.'

'I formed the dough into buns,' Betty explained, 'made a hole in each one, put jam in and pulled the dough over the top.'

'Dried eggs?' Grace asked.

'No eggs of any description,' Betty told her. 'Diluted milk instead.'

'How are you getting on with dried eggs?' Grace asked. 'My

Yorkshire puddings are solid now and they used to be light as air.'

'My friend Deborah says that if you add a pinch of baking powder to dried egg, it makes omelettes and scrambled eggs lighter,' said Betty.

'I'll give it a try,' said Grace.

Handing out domestic advice made Betty feel like a real housewife. She was enjoying her tea-party and was proud of the compliments she had received, but underneath – oh, underneath all sorts of hopes and doubts were swarming. What was going to happen about little Bessie Beech? What decision had Mr Brent-Williams made?

And if she and Samuel weren't allowed to proceed with the adoption, would the rest of her life be like this afternoon? Normal on the surface, but all churned up underneath?

The following Wednesday morning, while Betty and Rosalind were using the handles of old forks to strip out the inner tubes from old bicycle tyres, Samuel walked in through the gates, his hazel eyes anxious behind his specs. Betty hurried over to him.

'What is it?' she asked.

'A c-clerk from the magistrates' court telephoned the sh-shop to ask if I can go and s-see Mr Brent-Williams this afternoon.'

Betty immediately leaped on the wording. 'Just you? Not me?'

'W-with this being half-day c-closing, the assumption is that I can go. I've c-come to see if you can get the time off too.'

'What's the meeting about?' Betty asked.

'No idea.'

Betty's shoulders tightened and she had to press her lips together to stop them from trembling. 'I've been hating the thought of having to wait until Friday, but now it's been brought forward, I'm terrified.'

Samuel gave her a hug and she felt her body mould itself to his of its own accord.

'I'm s-scared too,' he whispered, and Betty held him closer.

Lorna emerged from the building. Betty broke free and started to go towards her to ask for permission to have the time off, but she didn't have the chance to get a word out.

Lorna was already speaking. 'Go. Do what you have to do.'

'Thank you,' said Betty. 'They're having the meeting today instead of Friday.'

'I guessed as much.'

'We don't have to go until this afternoon. I can stay for the rest of the morning.'

'If you're sure,' said Lorna.

'It'll keep me busy,' said Betty, though she knew that nothing would distract her from what lay ahead... whatever it was.

All kinds of possibilities played through her mind. Had the mother changed her mind? Had the husband refused? Had Mr Brent-Williams decided to pay no heed to either of them and come down on Betty and Samuel's side?

There were all sorts of questions she couldn't hope to answer, but the biggest one of all was: why not wait until Friday?

She and Samuel talked about it all the way to town on the bus. It left Betty feeling even more fretful, but she couldn't possibly have talked about anything else.

At last they were at the Town Hall, waiting outside a different room to last time. The clerk who had brought them here had told them it was an ordinary office. Then he had knocked and signalled to them to stay put while he went inside. A moment later he reappeared, informed them that Mr Brent-Williams wouldn't keep them waiting, and walked away.

That had been nearly ten minutes ago, and Betty's nerves were reaching fever pitch and her mouth was dry as dust. At last, the door opened and Mr Brent-Williams asked them in, waving them in the direction of a pair of chairs, though he was back behind the desk and seated before they had time to sit down.

He placed his elbows on the arms of his chair, pressed his hands together and steepled his fingers.

'Mr and Mrs Atkinson, thank you for attending at such short notice.'

'Have you got news f-for us?' Samuel asked.

'Yes, indeed. The mother's husband wrote back to say he would not take on the child known as Bessie Beech, but that is immaterial as I decided soon after the last time I saw you *not* to hand over the baby to the real mother.'

Sheer relief had Betty covering her mouth with her hand for a moment. When her hand dropped away, she knew her mouth was pinched, her eyes narrow. He could have given them this news *weeks* ago!

'Thank you, sir,' said Samuel.

Mr Brent-Williams continued without acknowledging Samuel's words. 'It was my intention to inform you this Friday, but there has been a development that rendered it necessary to speak to you as soon as possible.'

Betty went cold and her hands slid loosely into her lap.

'The mother confided her troubles to her parents,' said the magistrate, 'and now they have come forward, wishing to adopt their grandchild.'

TWENTY-SIX

Deborah found it hard to believe that her wonderful springtime, full of romance and promise, had degenerated into such a lonely summer.

Sometimes her sense of loneliness was so intense it became a physical ache. Before she found out about the bet, she had loved being Patrick's girlfriend. Having a man to go about with was fun and special, and not just any man but *Patrick*. How many nights had she lain awake wishing he would come back so they could try again? But then she would remember the bet, and she knew she was better off without the man who would do something like that.

Announcing at work that she had dumped him had made her feel better... sort of. Briefly.

'Well, what else did you expect me to do?' she'd asked her friends in the canteen. She'd put on a bright and breezy voice, putting all her energy into not sounding brittle and betrayed.

'I hated having to tell you,' said Miss Greening.

'You did the right thing.' Deborah had aimed for sounding warm and reassuring. 'Honestly, I'm better off knowing.'

The others had all looked at her with sympathy and

concern. She felt as though she might drown in their pity and commiseration. She might have tried to smile except that even the smallest movement of her facial muscles would have brought the tears streaming out.

Since then, she'd put on a brave face every day, but she was still the girl whose boyfriend had only gone out with her for a bet. Being talked about, *gossiped* about, was humiliating. Whenever she found herself on the receiving end of a knowing glance, or she spotted a secret nudge between two clerks in the corridor, it was all she could do not to hang her head and hide her eyes, and then her anger at Patrick would come flaring up all over again.

Today she was out of the office – thank goodness. It was her afternoon for the advice session that was held regularly at the church hall near the big crossroads in Fallowfield.

Mrs Jasper came towards her. She wore the olive-green uniform of the WVS and was well-spoken with a calm manner. She had lost her husband in the last war and now her grown-up sons were in the merchant navy, braving the Atlantic crossing to help keep the country fed.

'Good afternoon,' Miss Grant,' said Mrs Jasper. 'I've put your table at the far end as usual.'

'Thank you.' Deborah had her leaflets and so on in a cloth shopping bag.

'What beautiful weather we're having,' Mrs Jasper remarked, walking beside her the length of the hall, heels tapping on the floorboards. 'I expect you've been for some lovely walks with your boyfriend.'

Deborah was so taken aback that she almost stumbled, but she caught herself in time. She went cold on the inside even while her cheeks betrayed her by flaring with heat.

'Oh dear,' said Mrs Jasper. 'Have I said the wrong thing?'

'Not at all.' Deborah had to unclench her teeth in order to force a smile. 'We aren't seeing one another any more.'

'I *have* said the wrong thing. I do apologise.'

Deborah dumped her bag on the trestle-table that had been erected for her and turned to Mrs Jasper with a smile that she sincerely hoped was dazzling. 'Think nothing of it – honestly. I'd better get set up. There are already a couple of people waiting for me.'

And what if they had overheard this exchange? Was she going to see sympathy or maybe curiosity in their eyes while they asked for advice or information?

It was a busy afternoon. The new food rationing year was due to begin later in the month, and if Deborah explained once she had to explain a dozen times that the number of food points each person was to receive each month was going to be reduced to twenty.

'And treacle and syrup are both coming off the preserves list and being put onto the points system,' she added each time.

'That's not fair,' one housewife remarked. 'Slashing the number of points—'

'It hasn't exactly been *slashed*—' Deborah put in.

'At the same time as adding new goods to the points list.'

Deborah wasn't going to get into an argument over it. 'The good news is that the cheese ration will go up to eight ounces per person per week as a short-term treat.'

'Not permanently, then?' the woman demanded.

'No.' Deborah pinned on her most professional smile. 'Unfortunately not.'

Honestly! Most folk took it on the chin when the rules and regs changed, but sometimes she came across one who was determined to look on the black side.

At least she had the chance to give out some of the recipes she had collected, pleased that she had taken the trouble. She also made a point of saying goodbye to Mrs Jasper before she left. That way, the WVS lady would have no reason to tell her colleagues that 'poor Miss Grant' was in a state because of a failed relationship.

Instead of going straight home to Chorlton, she went first to Withington to drop in on her mother. She loved her mum and dad and enjoyed seeing them, but she knew it continued to be a sore point with Mum that she'd chosen to live elsewhere. Mum would have kept her at home until the day she got married, if she'd had the choice.

Mum was peeling potatoes for cottage pie when Deborah arrived.

'You sit at the kitchen table and talk to me,' she said, her brown eyes warm with pleasure. 'How's Sally?'

'Fine, thanks for asking. She gets fed up with having to rest all the time, but she knows how much it matters so she wouldn't dream of doing anything else. Not that her blood pressure would let her.'

'I say a little prayer for her every night,' said Mum. 'It doesn't seem long since she was running in and out of this house as if she lived here.'

'You always said it was like having another daughter,' Deborah recalled with a smile.

Mum stopped peeling and looked pensive. 'It was – and I wanted her to feel the same way. I always felt sorry for her, truth be told, because of having such old parents. I wanted her to feel she had me as well, so that she had a mother-figure of the right age.' She pointed the knife at Deborah. 'Don't tell anyone I said that. Mrs White would be appalled.'

'I shan't breathe a word,' Deborah promised, delighted to have been confided in.

'And what about the salvage depot?' Mum asked, resuming her peeling. 'How is—' and a shiver went through Deborah in case the question was *How is Rosalind getting on?*, but Mum said, '—Lorna getting on? Does she like being the manager?'

Deborah considered. 'She seems to. She'd rather be in

London with George, obviously, and it's no secret how much she misses him, but I don't think she has any problems running the depot. To be honest, she doesn't really talk about it at Star House.'

'That's a shame,' said Mum. 'I bet Sally would love nothing better than to hear about it.'

'I think that's probably why Lorna keeps quiet,' Deborah answered. 'She doesn't want Sally worrying. None of us wants that. We want everything to be completely smooth and calm for her.'

'Has she heard from Andrew recently?'

'Not recently, but she'll probably get two or three letters at once. That's the way it happens.'

Mum chopped up the potatoes and put them in a pan of water, then joined Deborah at the table.

'And what about you? How are *you*, love?'

'I'm fine.'

'Are you sure?' Mum sighed and reached into the pocket of her apron for her cigarettes. 'Sally, Lorna and Betty are all married. I thought you were going to be next.'

'They're married,' Deborah said in as light a voice as she could, 'but my pals at the Town Hall aren't, so you don't have to worry about me being left on the shelf just yet.'

To her surprise, Mum said, 'I thought one of your Town Hall friends was engaged.'

'Rosemary Greening – yes,' said Deborah. 'She got engaged just before her chap joined up. Off he went and she hasn't seen him since. Fancy you remembering that.' Deborah felt a pang for her colleague. 'She isn't even in a position to start planning her wedding.'

If she hoped to steer her mother down a different path, she was disappointed. Mum clearly wasn't going to be diverted.

'Patrick was such a nice boy—'

'Mum!' Deborah pretended to make a joke out of it. 'He was hardly a boy.'

'Man, then,' said Mum, lighting up and blowing out smoke. 'And he had a good job. He'd have made a good provider—'

'Mum, please, that's all over.'

'All because of an argument—'

'It wasn't because of an argument.' Deborah's voice tightened. 'It was because of that stupid *bet*.'

'I know that, love, and I can understand why you're hurt, but the two of you got along so well.' Mum flicked her ciggie against the lip of the ashtray. 'Have you never thought of—?'

'*No*,' Deborah answered. 'I'm not the one who did something wrong.'

'You don't have to be the wrongdoer to be the one to make peace,' Mum said gently. She sighed. 'You've always had a stubborn streak.'

'And it seems I'm not the only one,' said Deborah. 'Patrick could have come to Star House at any point in the past few weeks if he'd felt so inclined.' She pushed back her chair and stood up. 'I'd better go.'

As Mum came to her feet, the chair-legs scraped on the tiled floor. 'You aren't running away because of what I said, are you?'

'Of course not. Mrs Beaumont likes us to be on time for meals, that's all.'

'If you're sure?'

Mum followed Deborah to the door and waved her off. Deborah was lucky with the bus. One came along just as she reached the stop. She was soon back in Chorlton, walking down Beech Road. Her thoughts had been on Patrick this whole time, but now she shoved them aside. Sally could sometimes read her thoughts, or at least that was how it seemed, and Deborah didn't want to have another conversation about Patrick so soon after the last one. She felt too unsettled. Her throat burned and there was a sour taste in her mouth.

She opened the garden gate. As she started up the path, the front door flew open, and Mrs Beaumont appeared.

'Oh – it's you,' she said, shaking her head. 'I heard the gate, and I thought it was the doctor.'

Deborah hurried towards her. 'Not Sally?'

Mrs Beaumont nodded, her blue eyes huge with distress.

'She's – I know I shouldn't say this to an unmarried girl, but you live here, so you have to know.'

'Know what?' Deborah asked urgently. She felt shaky and her skin prickled.

Mrs Beaumont's face was ashen beneath the powder. 'She's been *bleeding*.'

TWENTY-SEVEN

Sally lay against her pillows, feeling exhausted, as the doctor left her bedroom. Mrs Beaumont followed him out, turning her head to give Sally a sympathetic smile as she quietly closed the door.

Sally blew out a breath. Tears welled up, clogging her throat and making her vision blurry, but she forced herself not to cry. Suppose she wept and couldn't stop and then a sob gave her a sharp jolt that dislodged the baby? In her head, she knew it wouldn't happen like that, but her heart still quivered.

There was a soft tap on the door and Deborah popped her head in.

'Are you allowed visitors?' Her bright-blue eyes, usually so lively, were anxious.

Sally held out her hand and Deborah came over to the bed, picking up the chair Sally left her clothes on overnight and placing it beside the head of the bed. Sitting down, she took Sally's hand.

'I saw Mrs Beaumont showing the doctor out,' said Deborah. 'She says the baby is safe.'

Sally nodded, still too choked to speak.

'That's what matters,' Deborah said quietly. 'You must have been really scared.'

At last, the constriction in Sally's throat eased. Her voice came out as a whisper. 'I was *terrified*. I thought... well, you know what I thought.'

Deborah gave her hand a gentle squeeze. 'Are you staying here? Not going to hospital?'

'Apparently I don't need to. Did Mrs Beaumont tell you what was wrong?'

'She said you'd been bleeding.'

Sally nodded. 'But nothing like as much as last year when I lost the baby. It... it *flooded* out of me then.'

'How do you feel now?'

'Tired. Frightened... *Grateful*.'

'Are you definitely out of the woods?' Deborah asked.

'I hope so. I've just got to wait and see what happens.' How steady her voice sounded, even though she was trembling inside.

'If it isn't a stupid question,' said Deborah, 'is there anything I can do?'

Sally was all set to say no, but then an idea popped into her head. 'Actually, there is, if you don't mind. Could you pop round and tell Betty later on? I know Lorna would tell her tomorrow, but I'd rather she heard it at home than at work.'

'I'll let her know,' Deborah promised. 'Would you like me to go and tell your mum as well?'

'That's a kind offer, but she'd have kittens if an unmarried girl talked to her about something like that.' The thought made Sally give a chuckle. 'I shouldn't laugh. She'd be appalled. In any case, Mrs Beaumont has said she'll go and tell her. She's going to tell Andrew's mum as well.'

'Mrs B is more than a landlady,' Deborah said. 'She'd do anything to look after us. I'll just tell Betty for you.'

'Thanks,' said Sally. 'And please tell her I'm all right, and she's not to worry.'

'Some hope.' A smiled tugged at Deborah's mouth. 'We're all concerned about you, and we'll stay concerned until Master or Miss Henshaw puts in an appearance.'

Some of Sally's distress melted away. 'I'm lucky to have such good friends around me.'

'I wish I'd come straight home instead of going to see Mum,' said Deborah.

Sally seized on that. If all she did was talk about and think about her own health, she would drown in anxiety. 'How is she?' she asked.

'Same as always.' After a moment, Deborah added, 'She decided to chuck in her two penn'orth about Patrick. As far as she's concerned, it's my obstinacy that's keeping us apart. Never mind that he started it by taking that bet.'

'The two of you did seem to be a good match,' Sally ventured gently. Might she be able to nudge Deborah in Patrick's direction?

Deborah groaned, but it was a humorous sound, not a vexed one. 'Don't tell me you're siding with my *mum*.'

They looked at one another. It was a look that held a lifetime of closeness, knowledge and memories.

'You don't know how lucky you are that you met Andrew when you did,' Deborah said, 'at the same time that you decided Rod wasn't the man for you.'

'That isn't quite how it happened,' Sally answered. 'I already knew I needed to end my relationship with Rod.'

Deborah shrugged. 'Same difference. The point is that Andrew came into your life at just the right moment. That's what I need now – someone to come along at the right time for me.'

'If that's what you want,' Sally said warmly, 'then I hope it happens. I'd love to see you settled and happy.' She swallowed a soft sigh, schooling herself not to mention that she had thought Patrick was the right one.

'Me too!'

Deborah laughed and Sally, who knew her so well, could tell it wasn't entirely real. Had her friend done the right thing by not attempting to reconcile with Patrick? Yes, that bet had been hurtful and humiliating, but Mrs Grant was right about Deborah's stubborn streak. On the other hand, Patrick had shown he could be stubborn too, so maybe their relationship just wasn't meant to be.

'Patrick turned out to be for me what Rod was for you,' said Deborah.

Sally managed to hide her reaction. Rod had been a terrible mistake. He'd been a controlling bully. That was the truth. She couldn't believe for a single moment that Patrick was *that* kind of mistake.

'What I mean is,' Deborah went on, 'that Patrick started out seeming to be right for me, and then I found out I was wrong.'

Sally couldn't shake off the feeling that Patrick was right for Deborah, but at the same time she wanted to support her friend. It was all the more important because of the way Deborah *hadn't* supported her when she'd started seeing Andrew. She didn't want Deborah to experience the same disappointment and turmoil she herself had gone through when Deborah hadn't stood by her.

'What we need,' said Sally, 'is for your equivalent of Andrew to come on the scene. I couldn't wish for anything better than that for you. You deserve it.'

Sally had been ordered to stay in bed. Mrs Beaumont propped the door open, and her friends made sure she had plenty of company.

'It's made me realise how much I liked being downstairs on

the sofa,' Sally told Louise. 'At the time I thought it was dull and boring, but now I can appreciate how good it was. Sorry,' she added, 'I shouldn't moan.'

'You aren't moaning,' Louise answered at once. Her brown eyes were soft with concern. 'Of course it was better being downstairs, even if you were doomed to live on the sofa,' she added with a half-smile.

Sally returned the smile, wanting to show her agreement. It clearly worked, because Louise's smile widened.

'That's it exactly,' said Sally. 'All I can say is, when I'm allowed out of bed, I'll make the most of it.' Then, in the same way that she'd encouraged Deborah to talk about something other than the pregnancy and its ramifications, she steered Louise in a different conversational direction. 'What about you, Louise? How are things? Are you still looking for another job to move into?'

Before Louise had started working in the munitions factory, she had worked in a posh dress shop, a job that her mother had selected for her as being suitable for a young lady, but what Louise had yearned for was a job – a *career* – where the work was both interesting and challenging that she could stay in after the war was over.

'It's tricky,' said Louise, happy enough to accept the change of subject. 'There are heaps of war jobs that will only last for the duration. What I need is a civilian job, but I need to find one where I have a decent chance of being allowed to stay in it after the war. Recently I've been looking into applying to become a Post Office engineer. I think that after the war, when people get back on their feet, many more folk are going to want to have telephones in their own homes.'

'Really?' Sally asked, interested.

Louise nodded. 'I think so. Look at the way motorcar ownership was growing before the war. When I was little, nobody round our way had a motor, but then gradually a few appeared.

I think it's going to be like that with domestic telephones – the difference being that telephones will be a lot cheaper,' she added with a smile.

'There have certainly been times when it would have been handy for Star House to have its own telephone rather than us having to run round to the telephone box,' Sally remarked. 'Have lots of women become that kind of engineer?'

'Yes. I've met a couple of them. One of their tasks is to gather old telephones, cables, fittings and so forth to put together to make new telephones – I say "new" but of course the point is that new ones aren't being made these days and won't be for a long time. They also have to fit new switchboards, and repair broken lines.'

'Do you think you'll pursue that as a possibility?' Sally asked. 'If you do, I hope you'll be able to carry on living here at Star House. We'd all hate you to leave.'

'Thanks. That's nice to hear,' said Louise. 'To be honest, I think it's one of those jobs where, the minute the war ends and the first troops return, the women will be flung out and told to go back to being housewives.'

'Not for you, then?' Sally asked sympathetically.

'It's a shame, because it sounds interesting. I want to do something worthwhile with my life, something that makes me glad to get out of bed in the morning. I'm determined not to go back to working in a dress shop.'

There was a movement in the doorway. In the half-second before she looked, Sally assumed it would be Mrs Beaumont bringing her a cup of tea, but it was her mother.

'Mum!' Sally felt a little burst of pleasure.

As Mum entered the room, Louise stood up and moved away from the bedside chair. At the same time she invited Mum, with a wave of her hand, to take it.

Before she did so, Mum bent over to kiss Sally. 'Sally, dear, I'm so relieved you're all right – and the baby. What a scare.'

'I'll leave you to it,' Louise murmured, and she slipped from the room.

Mum sat down. She took Sally's hand and leaned towards her. 'Tell me how you're feeling.'

'I'm fine now, honestly. Like you say, it was just a scare.'

'There's no "just" about it,' said Mum, 'especially after what you went through last year. Dad sends his love.'

'Give him mine too,' said Sally. 'Is he going to come and see me?'

'Yes, of course. He'd have been here today if I'd let him.'

'If you'd *let* him?'

Mum shook her head. 'We've talked about this kind of thing before, Sally. There are certain things that are nothing to do with *men*.'

'Such as anything relating to having a baby,' Sally replied.

'Exactly. Now, I'll hear no more about it.'

Mum's expression, kind and anxious as it was right now, was in danger of returning to the critical, judgemental expression that Sally had been used to in the days before her tragic miscarriage had brought the two of them close together.

'Make sure Dad knows I'm looking forward to seeing him,' Sally said, her voice gentle but firm.

'Of course I will,' Mum answered. 'He'll come as soon as it's appropriate.'

'You mean, when it's clear there's going to be no more bleeding?'

Mum sat up straight. 'That's *precisely* what I mean.' After a moment, she angled herself forwards again. 'We both love you so very much, Sally.'

'I love you too,' Sally whispered.

Mum's hazel eyes went misty. 'You were my miracle child. All those babies I lost...' A sigh escaped her. 'I know how much you want this baby, because that's how much I wanted each one of mine. Now I find myself swamped by the same longing, but this time for my grandchild.'

'I'm doing everything the doctor wants me to,' Sally told her, seeking to reassure.

'Of course you are, darling.'

'Which mainly means keeping my feet up,' Sally added.

'It must be hard for you,' said Mum. 'You want more than anything to protect your baby, but all you can do is put your feet up. It must feel like you're doing nothing.'

'It does, in a way,' Sally answered, 'but at the same time I understand that, even if resting feels like nothing, it's very important. More than important – essential. It's the one thing I can do, even though it's... *passive.*'

Mum smiled. 'And that's the one thing you've never been, isn't it? Passive. That's why you went to night-school to learn typing when you were a shopgirl. It's why you collected all those recipes when you worked for the Food Office. Dad and I have always been so proud of you.'

Trust Mum to rewrite history. She had conveniently forgotten the things Sally had done that had *not* been a source of maternal pride, such as when she had rejected Rod Grant's proposal, and when she had started going out with Andrew, not to mention Mum's disapproval when her office-girl daughter had ended up in a job where she wore dungarees and a headscarf.

But none of that mattered now. Nothing mattered except the loving closeness brought about by last year's miscarriage.

'Mum, can I talk to you about something?' Sally asked. 'Can you close the door, please?'

Mum looked startled, but she complied.

'You're the only person I can say this to,' Sally said when Mum resumed her seat. 'I think the world of my friends and I trust them completely, but I couldn't tell them this. It's too sensitive.'

'Whatever it is, Sally, tell me.'

'It's little Bessie Beech. The process has come to a halt for the time being, because the grandparents have applied for permission to adopt.' Sally stopped. 'I'm ashamed of what I'm thinking, but I can't pretend the thoughts have never happened.'

'What thoughts?'

'I couldn't bear it if I lost this baby,' Sally whispered. She hadn't exactly meant to whisper, but her voice refused to come out any louder.

'I understand.' Mum's voice was soft as well. 'What's that got to do with little Bessie Beech?'

Sally had to force the words out. 'What if... what if Betty ends up with a baby and I don't?'

'Oh, my darling girl.' There was a hitch in Mum's voice. 'You mustn't think that way.'

'I can't help it. I spend so much time on my own and I can't help thinking. I'm so scared of another miscarriage. When I was bleeding...' She couldn't say anything further.

'Everything from last summer came rushing back,' Mum said gently.

Sally's gaze raked her mother's face. 'I want Betty to have little Bessie Beech, I honestly do. You have to believe that.'

'I know how much Betty means to you,' Mum said at once. 'Of course you want the best for her and Samuel. No one who knows you would ever imagine anything different.'

'I'd be heartbroken for them if they aren't allowed to adopt.'

'Would it help if I told you what it was like for me each time I was pregnant?' Mum asked. 'I've told you before that my miscarriages happened before I was three months along, which meant that, although *I* knew I was in an interesting condition, nobody else did. Whenever I saw a woman who was obviously expecting a happy event, I felt such *envy*, because she was far enough along to be certain of ending up with a bonny baby in her arms, while I... while I was scared witless of what might happen to me.'

'Oh, Mum...'

'I understand why you're having these thoughts about little Bessie Beech,' Mum went on. 'They're only natural. I used to despise myself for the thoughts I had when I saw a pregnant woman, for knowing she could look forward to her little bundle of joy while my own hopes were so fragile. I *knew* I'd be a good mother. I just wanted to be given the chance, but it seemed it was never going to happen.'

'But it did in the end,' Sally said. 'You had me.'

'When you think of the possibility of – God forbid – losing this child, while your friend might be allowed to adopt a baby, that isn't you being wicked or disloyal,' Mum said fiercely. 'It's you being an ordinary woman, a mother-to-be who has reason to fear things might not go well. You being laid up like this means you have masses of time for all these thoughts to plague you and wear you down.'

'I suppose so.'

'There's no "suppose" about it,' Mum insisted. 'It's all part of your worry about the baby. And don't forget that Betty must be worried sick that she won't end up adopting.'

'I hope she and Samuel get their happy ending,' Sally said sincerely.

'I do too,' said Mum, 'and I hope and pray that you and Andrew get yours as well. You deserve it.'

Sally's heart swelled. 'Thanks, Mum,' she said quietly, her eyes brimming. 'You've said all the things I needed to hear.'

'That's what mothers are for,' Mum answered in an emotion-packed voice.

Sally shut her eyes for a moment. This time, would she get the chance to be a mother? She longed for it more than anything.

Please let my baby be safe.

TWENTY-EIGHT

August brought scorching days and sticky nights.

Betty and Samuel were still making their regular visits to the Foundling Hospital. It tore Betty's heart in two each time they had to say goodbye to little Bessie Beech – and *say* goodbye was all they were allowed to do. There were no kisses, no snuggles. A member of staff was with them at all times to make sure.

'It's for your own good as well as little Bessie Beech's,' Warden Everett had told them. 'I can't allow closeness to develop. You'll thank me for it if you aren't allowed to adopt her.'

Betty hadn't known whether to burst into tears or stamp her foot in pure frustration. She ached with the need to hold little Bessie Beech and smother her sweet face with kisses. She and Samuel wouldn't have missed a single visit for the world, but each one was harder than the last when it came to leaving.

'How much longer do you think we'll be kept waiting for a decision from the magistrate?' Betty asked Samuel.

'I don't know,' he answered. 'I'll try telephoning Mrs Fitch in the W-Welfare Department again tomorrow. Maybe she c-can help.'

It was a couple of days before Samuel was able to get hold of Mrs Fitch. Betty feared that she was avoiding his calls, but then she arrived home from work to the news that Samuel had telephoned once more and this time he had spoken to her.

'What did she say?' Betty asked anxiously. 'Did she tell you anything?'

'That the adoption of a f-foundling child isn't exactly at the top of Mr Brent-Williams's list of priorities. Sh-she didn't use those w-words, but that w-as what she meant.'

Betty lowered her head with a sigh as disappointment trickled through her. 'So, there's no knowing how long the matter could take—'

'Mrs Fitch s-said she's had meetings w-with the grandparents. She had to look into their cir-circumstances.'

'You mean, their house and so on?'

Samuel nodded. He looked as if he was about to say something else, but then he didn't.

'Please, Samuel,' said Betty, 'if there's more, you have to tell me.'

He took her hand and raised it to his lips.

'I'm s-sorry, Betty. It isn't good news for us.'

The next morning, Betty could hardly wait to talk about the development with Lorna and Rosalind while they sorted through the daily sacks together.

'We've had some news about little Bessie Beech,' she told them.

'Good or bad?' Rosalind asked. 'Oh – bad, I think. You look... stricken.'

Betty felt wobbly, but she pulled herself together. 'It's about the grandparents. They – well, they're very *well-heeled*. Samuel spoke to the lady from Welfare yesterday and she gave him a few details. They live in a nice house in Cheshire – a detached house with a garden all the way round it – and we live above a bookshop.'

'It takes more than a nice house with a garden to make good parents,' said Lorna.

'And at the bottom of the garden, there's a paddock, and they've said little Bessie Beech can have a pony when she's old enough,' Betty went on. 'They'll pay for music lessons, and they've got their own piano.'

'Heaps of families have a piano,' Rosalind pointed out. 'You don't have to be rich to have one.'

'I'm not talking about an old upright that used to belong to Granny,' Betty answered, her heart heavy. 'They've got a *grand* piano. They can afford private school, art lessons, singing lessons, and heaven alone knows what else. They're... rolling in money.'

'It's like Lorna says,' Rosalind replied. 'Having money doesn't automatically mean they'll be the best parents.'

'But being well-off is a good start, you have to admit,' said Betty. 'They're related to Bessie an' all. It makes me feel we don't stand a chance.'

'Don't say that.' Lorna let go of her sack and it dropped to the ground with a muffled clatter. She gave Betty a hug. 'I can't think of anyone who'd make more loving, attentive parents than you and Samuel.'

Betty blinked back a few tears as she eased out of her friend's warm embrace. 'Thanks. I wish you were the magistrate.'

'If I were,' Lorna declared, 'you'd have been given little Bessie Beech weeks ago.'

'What happens next, if you don't mind my asking?' said Rosalind.

'We just have to wait and see,' said Betty. 'Magistrates aren't usually involved in adoptions. It's only happening this time because of little Bessie Beech being a foundling. Mrs Fitch said that Mr Brent-Williams has lots of other cases that are more pressing.'

'It surely can't drag on for much longer,' said Lorna. 'It's taken so long already.'

'I hope so with all my heart, for little Bessie Beech's sake,' Betty replied, 'but I'm scared – we're both scared – of what the outcome is going to be. When we think of what the grandparents can offer...'

'It's not a competition,' Rosalind said quietly. 'Being of modest means shouldn't go against you.'

'But wouldn't she be better off with all those advantages and privileges?' Betty asked, finally uttering the words that had kept her awake most of last night. 'Think of everything this couple can give her. If her going to live with them is the right thing, then Samuel and I have to accept that, and be glad for her.'

'Glad?' Lorna asked.

'We want what's best for her,' Betty said simply. 'That's what you want when you love someone. We know we can't compete with these people but, at the same time, all we want is to keep her. What will we do if we aren't allowed to?'

Emotion overwhelmed her and her vision blurred as the tears started. Distress sent a huge shudder all through her, jarring her.

Lorna and Rosalind stepped closer, and she fell into their arms.

TWENTY-NINE

Lorna walked home from the depot at the end of the day. It was one of those times when she missed George especially badly.

After keeping herself busy at work, the thought of going home *not* to be with her beloved George always gave her a feeling of being lost. It might sound silly, given that she loved living at Star House, but she quite simply wanted to be wherever George was. They had gone through so much to be together, and this separation was hard... but there was now the hope of a visit to cling to.

As always when she arrived home from work, Lorna went straight in to see Sally, who was now back in her position on the sitting room sofa. Apparently, the danger had passed, and the doctor had given permission for her to leave her bed. She'd also been told she could resume her short daily strolls.

It had been a scorcher of a day, the afternoon even hotter than the morning. When Lorna walked into the sitting room, Sally was lying on the sofa, using a concertina of paper as a fan.

'Good day?' she asked Lorna.

'The usual,' Lorna said with a smile. 'How about you?'

'My day definitely qualifies as the usual,' Sally answered

with a wry smile, 'given that I've spent most of it lying right here. I went out – as usual – for a stroll. No – wait – I did do something different.' She grinned. 'I sat at the kitchen table and shelled peas for Mrs Beaumont.'

Lorna chuckled. 'I hope you managed to contain your excitement.'

'Just about, though it wasn't easy,' Sally joked. After a moment, she said, 'What about the depot? What did you do today?'

'We sent off a large consignment to the paper-mill,' Lorna told her, 'and the metal went to the processing centre. Oh yes, and Mr Cox – you know, one of the Corporation van drivers – has become a grandfather.'

'That's lovely,' said Sally. 'Boy or girl?'

'A boy. No name yet.'

'Tell him congratulations from me next time you see him,' said Sally.

'I will,' Lorna promised.

'Lorna, I want to ask you something, but I don't want to put you on the spot. If I ask, will you give me an honest answer?'

Something fluttered inside Lorna. She rather thought she knew what was coming.

'You're never very forthcoming when I ask about the depot,' said Sally. 'Why is that?' Then she answered her own question. 'If it's because you're worried I'll get upset about not being able to work, and that it would affect my blood pressure, you needn't be afraid. Believe me, all I want is to do what's right for my baby – even more so after that scare I had.'

'I know,' said Lorna. 'To be truthful, there has been an element of that, certainly in the early days. You've been so devoted to your job that it was hard to imagine you letting go.'

'I didn't want to in the beginning,' Sally admitted. 'I miss working, but my job now is to think about the baby. You said you were careful what you said to start with, but what about now? You're still not exactly chatty when it comes to the depot.'

Lorna pressed her lips together for a moment. Well, why not tell the whole truth? Sally would understand.

'I've been avoiding talking about Mrs Lockwood, if you must know. You and she have a history of antagonism, but I'm getting along well with her and—'

'And you thought I wouldn't like that?' Sally finished.

'Sorry,' said Lorna. 'That makes it sound like I think you're a spoilt brat who has to be appeased and placated, and it isn't at all like that. It's because—' She stopped when the right words didn't appear.

'It's because you didn't want me to get vexed with Mrs Lockwood and send my blood pressure through the roof,' Sally said ruefully.

'Something along those lines,' said Lorna. 'You spent a lot of time asserting yourself and fending her off, and now she's, not exactly moved into the depot, but she's got her foot in the door – but in a good way. She's been a real help to me.'

A moment went by, then Sally nodded. 'She does know a great deal about salvage, I'll give her that.'

'Does it bother you that she's involved now in a way she didn't used to be?'

'It did in the beginning,' Sally told her. 'If I said anything back then that made you feel you had to watch your step with me, I'm sorry. However I felt then is beside the point. All I'm concentrating on now is the baby. He or she matters more than anything.'

'I know,' Lorna said gently. 'Do you forgive me for holding back and not speaking freely?'

'As long as you forgive me for making you feel you had to,' Sally answered with a sweet smile.

Lorna chuckled. 'What a pair we are! I'm glad we've cleared the air.'

'You won't mind if I tell Andrew in my next letter?' Sally asked. 'When you live your life on the sofa, it isn't always easy filling a letter.'

'Feel free,' Lorna said cheerfully. 'You can also tell him that I'm hoping George will be able to come up to Manchester for a day or two.'

'That would be champion,' Sally said warmly. 'I'm happy for you.'

'George says it isn't definite, but I can't stop myself from hoping,' said Lorna. 'I miss him, and that's putting it mildly.'

'I know you do,' said Sally.

'It's as if... as if my skin is hungry for him,' Lorna confessed quietly. 'I don't mean in a bedroom kind of way, though obviously there's that part of it. I mean in an ordinary everyday kind of way. It's this powerful feeling that we ought to be together while having to live with the stark fact that we're not.'

She had to stop speaking because a deep pang of longing threatened to chop her in two.

'When will you know about the visit?' Sally asked softly.

'Soon, I hope,' Lorna answered. Her eyes felt gritty with tears. 'Seeing him would make all the difference.'

The following evening after work Lorna stayed on at the depot to wait for a telephone call from George. They wrote to one another regularly and she loved receiving his letters, but the sound of his voice had the power to send tingles across her skin.

When the telephone rang, she lifted the black receiver and said in a formal voice, 'Good evening. Chorlton-cum-Hardy Salvage Depot' in case it was a work-related call. Such a thing shouldn't happen out of hours, but you never knew.

It was George. The operator connected them, and Lorna sat back in what she still thought of as Sally's chair to enjoy every moment of speaking to her husband. Her husband! It still thrilled her to use those words.

They were limited as to what they could talk about, just in case someone was listening in, so there was no discussion about work. Not that George could have confided in her about his job even if they had been alone together in the Broughtons' townhouse, because what he did was secret.

In any case, at the top of Lorna's list of topics was his possible visit.

'Darling, I'm so sorry,' he said. 'I've been told it isn't possible for me to get away, not even for a couple of nights.'

Disappointment chewed at her insides, but Lorna spoke cheerfully. 'Well, if that's the worst thing that happens to us in our married lives, we'll be doing pretty well.'

'Good girl,' George said approvingly. 'I knew you'd take it on the chin. I have a colleague whose wife played merry heck when they were in a similar situation.'

'I'd never do that,' Lorna declared. She kept her voice steady, but really it was a huge blow.

A little later at Star House, the other girls and Mrs Beaumont all sympathised.

'It's a great shame,' said Deborah.

'That's the war for you,' Louise said lightly.

Lorna consoled herself by writing a long letter to her husband. She had nothing new to say, but that didn't matter. She just wanted him to receive her letter and know that he was always in her heart and her thoughts.

It was as much as she could do.

THIRTY

Deborah was sorry that Lorna and George weren't going to be reunited. A little devil inside her made her want to say in a breezy voice, 'At least *I* don't have that problem!' Fortunately, she held her tongue, something she was glad of. It wouldn't have been kind. It wouldn't have been relevant. And, heaven help her, it might not have been true.

She and Patrick had split up three months ago, which was roughly the amount of time they'd gone out together, so he really shouldn't matter any more. Their relationship shouldn't matter. It was old news. She was over it – over him. Ask anybody at the Town Hall.

The gossip about her and that dratted bet had died down now, thank heavens. She still clocked the occasional glance coming her way, but essentially the gossip-mill had finished with her. Good. She'd been desperate for weeks for that to happen. Her romantic downfall had been followed by a flurry of engagements for other girls, which, instead of her being forgotten about, had had the effect of rekindling her humiliating position when she was compared to the lucky beggars who now had rings on their fingers.

It had been hard for Deborah to feign excitement for the newly engaged girls, but the certainty that she was being watched to see how she reacted had stiffened her backbone and enabled her to plaster a smile on her face as she squealed excitedly along with everyone else when each new sparkling ring was displayed.

It had taken a huge and protracted effort on her part to keep her chin up all this time. She had weathered the storm and now, finally, she was no longer the subject of pity and gossip.

She ought to be pleased. She *was* pleased. But it did leave her wondering what precisely she'd been left with. She had started off with a boyfriend she'd been very keen on, and now she had nothing.

No, not true. She had her pride. Patrick had made her look like a fool, but she had dumped him and had never once crumpled in the face of the talk about her in the corridors and offices of the Town Hall. So, yes, her pride was intact. She had shown everyone what she was made of. She had proved that she wasn't the sort of girl who could be messed around with by a chap, and her lofty indifference to the gossip had shown she had nothing to be ashamed of.

And if her tummy felt as though it was full of knots, and time dragged, and she sometimes wanted to howl with regret... well, that was her own private business, and there was no reason for anyone else to know.

She had coped with the situation very well, if she did say so herself. Not that she had ever actually said anything of the kind. She had never admitted to anybody, not even Sally, how shattered she had felt. She'd been too busy keeping her head above water.

Now, though, she wondered about Dulcie, who had been the one to write the letter that had convinced Deborah's mum to let her go and live in Star House.

I know it's the done thing for girls to stay at home until they get married but times have changed, and I can understand Deborah's wish to move in with her friends. It would be a shame for her to miss out. After all, she won't be far away, and you know the people. Just imagine if she'd joined the Wrens!

That was what Dulcie had written, and it had changed the course of Deborah's life, and no, that wasn't her being dramatic. It was true. Without that perfectly calibrated intervention from Dulcie, she would still be living with Mum and Dad in Withington.

So far, she hadn't confided fully in Dulcie about the Patrick debacle. All she had said was that the relationship hadn't worked out and she'd decided it was for the best that she didn't see him again. Dulcie had sympathised. She had also given her approval.

If he isn't the right man for you, then you've done the right thing. Lots of girls like to imagine that the first man they meet will turn out to be their future husband – and even if the girls don't hope that, their parents certainly do – and that's lovely and romantic, but it doesn't happen that way for everyone, and it's best to be honest about it.

Now, after considerable thought, Deborah decided to tell Dulcie the full truth of what she'd gone through, so she wrote about the bet and the gossip, and how difficult it had all been for her. She also admitted that, in spite of everything, she still thought about Patrick... *though I don't know why I should*, she wrote. *He doesn't deserve it.*

Dulcie's answer came by return.

I'm shocked to hear about the bet, and so is Rod. I hope you didn't intend me not to tell him, but when I read your letter, I couldn't help exclaiming out loud, so of course he wanted to know why. Anyway, the bet – I'm shocked. I can see why you wanted to end things with him, but what matters now is what you want to do next. If he is still in your thoughts, why not go and see him? It wouldn't commit you to anything and it might help clarify your thoughts. Either you'll think he's worth a second chance – or you'll never want to see him again.

It was exactly what Deborah had wanted to be told. Dulcie had in a manner of speaking given her permission to see Patrick. Not that she needed permission, but it felt good to have her wish backed up and to know that the sister-in-law she thought so well of was thinking along the same lines as she was herself.

After working in the Food Office on Saturday morning, Deborah spent the afternoon at MacFadyen's, helping to staff the WVS clothing exchange.

Mostly she loved doing this, as it was satisfying for everyone when someone was thrilled to bits to acquire exactly what they had dreamed of finding. The clothing exchange operated by giving second-hand garments a points value. People who donated could then use these points to 'pay' for something else, and any left-over points could be saved up for next time. But there were occasions when Deborah frankly loathed clothing exchange duty, and this was one of those times.

She had just finished explaining to a disappointed mum that, no, she couldn't ask for football boots for her football-mad son, as boots were only ever handed over in exchange for other boots because they were in such short supply these days, when a shabby-looking woman walked in, clutching a cloth bag under her arm.

Knowing what was very likely going to happen next, Deborah deliberately carried on talking to the young footballer's mum. It might be cowardly of her, but she wanted to avoid what was going to be an awkward situation.

'You do understand our position, don't you? It's the same with wellington boots. They're also extremely difficult to get hold of, so we have to apply the same rule to them.'

The mother gave her a look that said she wasn't in the slightest bit interested in the national shortage of wellies.

'Maybe I'll try the market,' she said without much hope.

As she turned to leave, Deborah could see that Mrs Callaghan, the branch organiser, had stepped forward to speak to the shabby woman, who was clearly from a poor background.

'Have you brought something for the exchange?' she asked. Her voice held a kind note, Deborah was pleased to hear. 'Would you like to show me?'

Deborah couldn't help but watch as the down-at-heel woman produced a worn-out dress. Poor creature.

To give her credit, Mrs Callaghan was polite about it. She drew the woman aside and spoke quietly, but Deborah knew what was being said. The branch organiser was explaining that the worn-out dress wasn't of sufficiently good quality to be accepted for the clothing exchange.

Deborah made a dive for the kitchen and put the kettle on so that she wouldn't be obliged to witness the woman's shame as she crept from the premises.

Mrs Callaghan entered the kitchen behind Deborah.

'Did you see?' She shook her head sadly. 'I'll find another way to help her. Are you making tea?'

Not long afterwards, the clothing exchange shut up shop and Deborah's shift was over. She went home for tea. For those whose main meal it was, Mrs Beaumont had prepared mince-in-the-hole, while for those who'd eaten their main meal in the middle of the day, she'd made pea soup and salad sandwiches. All the girls had fruit flan for pudding.

Afterwards Deborah excused herself. Lorna had an evening

WVS shift, but Louise would be at home because her chums, Stella, Mary and Lottie, the munitions girls who used to live at Star House, were coming to see Sally.

Deborah stuck her head round the sitting room door to say goodbye to Sally. 'I've got to run an errand. I shan't be long. Have a good time!'

She left the house. Although she tried not to feel excited, she couldn't prevent herself from tipping back her head and shutting her eyes for a moment. She was shocked at her own audacity. Was she really on her way to see Patrick? It hardly seemed possible that she would want to but, once the idea had got into her brain, it had got lodged there and, ever since reading Dulcie's letter, Deborah had given up trying to ignore it or fight against it.

She caught the bus to Stretford. The distance was walkable, but she wanted to arrive looking cool and as if she hadn't made an effort of any description.

She walked along Patrick's road and knocked on the door. Her heart bumped and her mouth went dry.

The door was opened by his mother. Her faded brown hair was rolled neatly at the back of her neck. She wore a shirt-waister dress in stripes of plain green and green floral with a buckled belt. She had answered the door with a smile, but it dropped off her face when she saw who it was.

'Oh! It's you. I wasn't expecting to see you again.'

A tingle appeared in Deborah's cheeks. 'Hello, Mrs Timms. I hope it's all right for me to turn up unannounced. Is – is Patrick in, please?' She had prepared those words in her head, and she managed to say them in a normal voice.

'He's not here at the moment.'

Deborah was ready for this. 'When he gets in from work, could you tell him I came round?'

Mrs Timms gave her a steely look. Curiosity, sharpness and a touch of sympathy mingled in her face.

'When I say he's not here, it isn't because he's at work – well, it is, but not the way you mean. He got himself transferred after you *ditched* him.' All at once she thrust her head forward. Curiosity and sympathy had been obliterated. All that remained was sharpness. 'And if he doesn't come back again, it'll be all thanks to *you*.'

Mrs Lockwood walked into the depot yard and stood looking around with an assessing expression in her cool grey eyes.

'How does she do it?' Betty whispered. 'If I wore the full WVS uniform in this weather, I'd faint clean away.'

Lorna had to smother a giggle. '*Shh!*'

She, Betty and Rosalind were in dungarees as usual, although, instead of the sweaters they wore in chilly weather or the warm shirts they wore when it was mild, they had all teamed the sturdy dungarees with lightweight blouses.

'Good morning, girls,' Mrs Lockwood greeted them in her booming voice. 'Mrs Broughton, would you care to show me what has been done since my last visit?'

Lorna spent the next few minutes showing her around, with Mrs Lockwood nodding and approving. She certainly enjoyed having Lorna being responsible to her!

They chatted as they went. When she had first come to Manchester, Lorna had lodged with the Lockwoods, which made a slight personal connection between them, a connection that had ended on a cool note after the Lockwoods had realised that the supposed Miss Sadler was the notorious Miss West-

Sadler who had been comprehensively dragged through the mud by the press.

When this new arrangement at the depot had begun, Lorna had felt she oughtn't to be on friendly terms with Sally's arch-enemy, but that was just barmy. She and Mrs Lockwood had settled into a pleasant relationship. Lorna often asked after Mr Lockwood, whom she had grown fond of while living under his roof, and Mrs Lockwood returned the compliment by asking after Lorna's parents and George.

Last time Mrs Lockwood was here, Lorna had mentioned the possibility that George might be coming up to Manchester.

'Are the arrangements finalised yet?' Mrs Lockwood asked now. 'It would help me to know in advance so I can be here on any days you need to be absent.'

'It's all fallen through, I'm afraid.' Lorna experienced the disappointment all over again, though she hid it behind a smile.

'I'm sorry to hear it,' Mrs Lockwood replied. 'What a shame.'

'Yes, it is,' said Lorna.

They ended the tour in the office. When the telephone rang, Lorna more than half-expected Mrs Lockwood to make a dive across the room so she could answer it. Lorna, closer to the desk, lifted the receiver. Mrs Lockwood, she noted, didn't appear at all put out. She had seen something or someone through the window, and went swanning off. As she spoke on the telephone, Lorna glanced through the window to see Mrs Lockwood marching purposefully towards the post-lady, reaching her before Betty or Rosalind could.

The telephone call was from the Town Hall to confirm the dates for sending the collection van to pick up various types of salvage, and it lasted a few minutes. During it, Mrs Lockwood returned to the office and sat down to open and read the letters. Lorna couldn't suppress a flicker of annoyance. *She* was the manager here. On the other hand, she was answerable to Mrs

Lockwood, so presumably it didn't really matter which of them opened the mail.

By the time Lorna hung up, Mrs Lockwood had placed the letters on the blotter and was rummaging in her trusty handbag.

She fastened the clasp and looked at Lorna. 'All done? Good. I've had a thought. If your husband can't spare the time to come here, why don't you go down to London? Even if he has work commitments, you'll still be able to snatch some time together.'

Lorna's heartbeat picked up. 'Would I be allowed to have the time off?'

'I fail to see why not. You're here for several months, after all. You aren't on duty this Saturday, are you? Why not travel down then?'

'I'd come back early next week,' Lorna offered, not wanting to take advantage.

'Nonsense. You haven't seen your husband since – when? May?'

'Late April,' said Lorna.

'And Mrs Henshaw's baby isn't due until December. That's a long time for you and Mr Broughton to be separated.'

'Yes, it is,' Lorna murmured. All at once, she longed for George most dreadfully. Her insides fluttered and she longed for his touch. 'Yes,' she declared in a stronger voice. 'I'll go down on Saturday—'

'—which will very likely take all day, given the way travelling is these days,' Mrs Lockwood broke in, 'and you'll lose an entire day coming back as well. Don't forget that.'

Lorna made up her mind. 'I'll go on Saturday and come back next Thursday, then I'll be back at work on Friday – if it's all right with you?' she added.

'Then it's settled,' said Mrs Lockwood. 'Now then, I must be getting along.'

Waving aside Lorna's thanks, she bustled out, leaving Lorna

standing in the office feeling as if she was bathed in a golden glow of joy and excitement.

She was going to be reunited with George!

First thing on Saturday morning at Star House, there was a bit of a flurry, what with Lorna going away at short notice.

After breakfast, as she got her things together to go to the office for the morning, Deborah smiled to herself. The flurry was nothing to do with lack of organisation, because Lorna had packed her suitcase last night. No, it was purely an emotional thing, a feeling of excitement. Lorna's happy anticipation was infectious, though Deborah's pleasure on her friend's behalf was tempered by a swelling of sorrow for her own situation when she recalled how she used to look forward to being with Patrick — no, she would *not* dwell on that. It was over. It had been over for weeks, but it felt even more over now that she knew he had gone away without feeling any need to tell her. How could he have done that? Well, at least it was clear now where she stood — though there was precious little comfort in that.

There was a knock on her bedroom door and Lorna stuck her head in.

'I've booked a taxi. You'll come with me, of course?'

'Thanks,' said Deborah. 'That'll be a treat compared to going on the bus.'

Lorna was so down to earth that it was easy to forget that she came from a world where taxis, not buses, were the normal mode of transport. They set off together and the driver dropped Deborah close to the Town Hall. She stood on the pavement waving as Lorna was driven away, then she walked into the building.

She had always thought working on Saturdays until one o'clock to be rather a bind. Yes, there were times when the morning flew by, but mostly it dragged. Today was one of those days, but, instead of complaining to Miss Duggan the way she would have cheerfully complained to Sally in the old days, Deborah wanted to set a good example to her younger colleague. Consequently, she neither counted down the minutes to their tea break nor kept looking longingly through the window at the glorious sunshine.

At long last the morning was over. Deborah and Miss Duggan tidied their desks and put everything away before they ran downstairs and said goodbye at the imposing front doors. Deborah didn't hang about. She hurried to the bus stop and was soon on her way to Chorlton.

On Saturdays, Sally had a late meal so she could eat with Deborah. Sally always came through to the dining room. Mrs Beaumont would have been happy to serve her meals on a tray, and she would have done the same for Deborah on Saturdays, but Sally insisted.

Today, Mrs Beaumont gave them baked herrings with salad from the garden, together with bread and a scrape of butter. For afters, there were slices of steamed jam pud. Mrs Beaumont sat with the girls, smoking, while they ate.

After the meal, they all had a cup of tea together, then the girls went into the sitting room while their landlady washed up.

Deborah's instinct was to help Sally settle herself, but she knew Sally wouldn't want that. While Sally made herself comfy, Deborah was drawn to the framed photograph taken on Betty's wedding day. She picked it up. Inspired by Mrs Beaumont's array of photographs of the music hall stars on the walls in the hallway and up the stairs, Sally, Betty and Lorna had decided to have a wedding picture taken of them with Mrs Beaumont so that they could present her with a framed copy as a token of their appreciation and affection, for her to remember them by after the war.

Deborah noticed how Betty had angled herself slightly

towards Mrs Beaumont, so that, even though she was the bride, it was Mrs Beaumont who was the focal point.

At the time the photograph was taken, Sally had been married to her beloved Andrew for about six months; Betty had been married for about half an hour; and Lorna had just got back together with George. Now the two of them were married as well.

Deborah drew in a breath and released it.

'Big sigh,' Sally commented.

Deborah put down the picture and went to sit beside her.

'I was just wondering. You, Betty and Lorna are all married. I wonder if it's ever going to happen to *me*.'

'Your turn will come,' Sally said gently.

'Will it? I hope so.' Knowing herself to be on the verge of confiding, Deborah felt emotion ballooning inside her. 'I don't want to end up like Louise. How old is she? Twenty-six or thereabouts, and without so much as an engagement ring.'

'To be fair,' said Sally, 'her main aim is to look for an interesting job she'll be happy to stay in when the war ends. But we aren't talking about her. You'll meet someone else.'

'Do you think so?'

'I *know* so,' was the firm reply.

'After the Patrick fiasco...' Deborah began, and then had to stop because her throat had closed up.

'If you and Patrick were supposed to be together,' Sally said gently, 'I'm sure you'd have reconciled by now. One of you would have sought out the other one—'

'I did,' Deborah blurted out.

Sally's eyes widened. '*When?*'

'Last weekend. I went to his house, and he wasn't there. He got transferred. That's how much he wanted to see me again.'

'He *got* transferred, or he *was* transferred?' Sally asked.

'*Got*,' Deborah said crisply. 'He got himself transferred, or so his mother says.'

'Oh, Deborah, I'm sorry – and you went to see him?'

Deborah shrugged. 'I shouldn't have wasted my time, should I? Still, it's better to know. If you want to know, it was... humiliating. Just like the humiliation I went through every day for weeks at work. Please don't tell anyone what I did.'

'Of course not,' Sally reassured her. She took Deborah's hand. 'Listen. Getting your first boyfriend is romantic and exciting, but not every relationship is the right one.'

'That's what Dulcie said,' Deborah told her. 'I poured it all out in a letter, and now I wish I hadn't.' She felt hollowed out with desperation.

'Second chances do come along,' Sally insisted. 'Betty and I are living proof. And believe me, if your second boyfriend is the right one, then it'll be as if the first chap never existed.'

'Really?' This was what Deborah's sore heart needed to hope for.

'Really,' Sally stated. 'Stop looking back. Just get out and enjoy yourself. You never know when something's about to happen.'

'You mean you never know when you're going to trip on the stairs and go flying into the arms of your future husband?' Deborah asked with a grin, her spirits starting to pick up.

Sally grinned back. 'You never know your luck,' she quipped.

They both looked round as the door opened and Mrs Beaumont came in.

'The afternoon post has just come,' she said. 'There's one for you, Deborah.'

She held it out and Deborah took it and looked at the handwriting on the envelope.

'It's from Dulcie,' she said, pleased.

Mrs Beaumont smiled and withdrew.

Deborah looked at Sally. 'I told her about Patrick having gone away. D'you mind if I...?'

'Go ahead,' said Sally.

Deborah opened the envelope with care so that it could be used again, and drew out the letter. She skimmed through it, then her lips twitched into a smile as she reread part of it with greater attention.

'What are you smiling at?' Sally asked.

'Because Dulcie says the same as you,' Deborah answered. 'Listen. *You've had an unhappy experience, but you mustn't give up on your social life. I hope a better man comes along soon.*'

'Oh well, if we *both* think it,' Sally said, smiling, 'then it *must* be the right advice.'

There was a little flutter in Deborah's tummy.

It took her a moment to realise it was hope.

Lorna's train journey to London that Saturday was long and taxing. The carriages were packed solid and on two separate occasions the train, which was so long it had to be pulled by two engines, drew into the sidings, where it remained for almost an hour both times to wait for goods trains to go past. Troop trains and goods trains were always given precedence over passenger trains in these days of wartime.

By the time Lorna left the train at Euston station, she felt exhausted and rumpled, but then, as she approached the ticket barrier, she saw George waiting for her. Instantly, her heart lifted, and she felt excited and beautiful. That was the effect he had on her. He was so very attractive, tall and lean with a narrow face and intense grey-blue eyes.

She rushed into his arms, dropping her suitcase at their feet and clinging to him. After being apart for all these weeks, it was only now that she could finally allow herself to realise just how desperately hard it had been

She lifted her face for his kiss, her lips parting willingly beneath his.

'Let's go home,' he said.

He bent to pick up her case, then took her hand and kept her close as they made their way through the crowded station. Outside, they queued at the taxi rank, and didn't have to wait long before they were on their way. Lorna's heart raced as they sat close together all the way to the townhouse.

They were still holding hands when they walked through the front door. Upstairs, George dumped the suitcase on the landing and threw open the drawing room door.

Lorna gazed around the room.

'You look happy,' said George.

'A feeling of homecoming,' she replied.

'You're supposed to get that from looking at me,' George said, pretending to be offended, 'not from looking at the furniture.'

Lorna faced him and slipped her arms round his waist. 'It's pretty good furniture, you must admit.'

'And I'm a pretty good husband,' he replied, 'as *you* must admit.'

Lorna tilted her head, giving him a cheeky smile. 'Could be a lot worse, I suppose.'

'Which suggests there's room for improvement.' George's grey-blue eyes, which were so often grey with thought, were now blue with delight. 'Now, let's go to the bedroom and I'll show you how much better things can get...'

THIRTY-TWO

When Lorna returned to Manchester on the long train journey, nearly everyone was wearing a black armband in honour of the Duke of Kent, who had died when his plane came down on a hillside in Scotland. It was a loss keenly felt by the public, among whom he had been a popular and respected figure.

Lorna arrived at Star House in time for the evening meal of vegetable soup followed by corned beef salad with mustard sauce. It was one of those meals when all four girls were present. Louise often ate at different times because of her shifts.

'When someone comes home,' said Louise, 'it's normal to ask if it's good to be back, but I'm sure you'd rather still be in London with your husband.'

'Obviously,' Lorna agreed, 'but this is a good place to be, too. This is my *other* home,' she added with a smile for Mrs Beaumont.

'Were you able to spend much time with George?' Sally asked. 'You said before you went that he wouldn't be able to take any time off work.'

'D'you know what?' Lorna answered. 'After not seeing one another for all that time, the small amounts of time we had together were pure bliss. Yes, we'd have loved to have more of it, but we both have our war work to do, and that takes precedence over everything.'

A little later, Lorna got Sally on her own for a private word.

'I want to make sure you aren't feeling guilty about me being dragged back here to run the depot for you.'

'I'm aware you'd rather be in London,' Sally answered.

'If anything had to take me away from George,' said Lorna, 'this is what I'd choose.'

'Bless you for that,' Sally said gratefully.

Lorna whiled away the evening writing a long love letter to George for posting the next morning on her way to the salvage depot. She was looking forward to seeing Betty and Rosalind again.

But the next morning when she arrived at work, even though she was prompt the other two were already there. She saw the looks on their faces and immediately thought it must be bad news about little Bessie Beech.

It wasn't that at all, though.

'We got here early so we could tell you right away,' Rosalind explained.

Lorna went hot and cold. 'What's happened?'

'Mrs Lockwood happened,' said Betty. 'I'm sorry, Lorna. There was nothing we could do to stop her.'

'To stop her doing what?' Lorna demanded, but in her heart she already knew.

'She's made changes,' said Rosalind, 'and she's had Mr Pratt and Mr Merivale here agreeing to everything.'

'What kind of changes?' Lorna asked, feeling chilled.

'Just to the general routines and how we do things,' said Rosalind. 'She called it "putting her own stamp on things". I'm sorry, Lorna.'

'You couldn't have prevented it,' Lorna acknowledged, 'especially if she brought in the gentlemen from the Town Hall to back her up.' She shook her head, indignation flaring. 'I can see it now. She knew perfectly well that they would agree to anything sooner than get on her wrong side. They've always been scared of her.'

'She must have been waiting for you to go away,' said Betty, 'so she could get started.'

'But I didn't just go away,' Lorna replied, vexed. 'She was the one who was keen for me to go – and now I know why!' She looked at the other two. 'I can see why you feel bad about it, but it wasn't your fault. If it's anyone's, it's mine for believing Mrs Lockwood when she talked about us working well together. *Ha!*'

'This isn't your fault,' Rosalind stated firmly.

Betty sighed. 'This is what Mrs Lockwood did to Sally – do you remember, Lorna?' To Rosalind, she explained, 'She packed Sally off to attend a course at the Town Hall. Sally was thrilled because it seemed she was receiving proper acknowledgement at last.'

'What she didn't know,' Lorna continued, 'was that the men from the ministry were coming that day to do an inspection of the depot, and Mrs Lockwood had got rid of her so that she could be the one to show them round and answer their questions and generally look important.'

'And you and me had to tell Sally when she came back,' Betty finished.

'Now Mrs Lockwood has done something similar to me,' said Lorna. 'Talk about pulling a fast one!'

'Watch out,' Rosalind murmured with a glance over Lorna's shoulder.

Lorna swung round to see Mrs Lockwood herself swanning in her usual confident fashion into the yard.

'Good morning, Mrs Broughton,' Mrs Lockwood boomed cheerfully before Lorna could so much as draw breath, let alone utter a word. 'I trust you enjoyed your trip to London. I'd like a word in the office, if you please.'

'Good – because I'd like a word with you too,' Lorna answered, trying to snatch back at least some of the initiative.

Mrs Lockwood was already on her way towards the building. Lorna managed to dodge past her and get through the door before her so that she could enter the office first, but of course she had to pause for a moment to remove her jacket and hat and put down her handbag and gas-mask box. When she turned round, Mrs Lockwood was seated squarely behind the desk.

Lorna's blood boiled. Then she hauled her temper under control. She needed to be careful. Did sitting at the desk mean Mrs Lockwood was now in charge on a *daily* basis?

'Please have a seat, Mrs Broughton,' said Mrs Lockwood. 'I shan't waste time on pleasantries as I can see from your expression that they wouldn't be welcome. No doubt the other girls have filled you in on the changes I have instituted in your absence—'

'You had no business doing any such thing!' Lorna interrupted.

'On the contrary,' Mrs Lockwood replied loftily, 'in my capacity as your supervisor, it was unquestionably my business. The depot must work at maximum efficiency, and I have taken steps to ensure that. Shall I run through the improvements I have made? Here's what I have done...'

Mrs Lockwood's changes included altering the use of a couple of the depot's rooms, reorganising the yard – which must have been a massive undertaking for Rosalind and Betty – and even altering the collections schedules. Lorna's hands locked into fists as she battled to control her indignation.

'I explained to Mr Merivale and Mr Pratt that my new timetable will be far more efficient,' said Mrs Lockwood, 'and they were in full agreement.'

I bet they were, Lorna thought. Those two gentlemen would have agreed to eat their own feet if it would have saved them from having to face Mrs Lockwood's wrath.

Determined to stand up for herself, she said politely, 'I wish you hadn't done this in my absence. I'm the depot manager, after all.'

'And I'm the person to whom *you* are responsible,' Mrs Lockwood replied complacently. 'I have now made you responsible for doing things in a slightly different way. I assume you are capable of this?'

Lorna set her jaw. 'Yes, Mrs Lockwood. Of course.'

'Good.' Mrs Lockwood pushed back her chair – *Lorna's* chair – and rose to her feet. 'Then I'll leave you to get on.' At the door she glanced back, and was that a gleam in her flint-grey eyes? 'By the way, Mrs Broughton. Welcome back.'

When the door shut behind Mrs Lockwood, Lorna felt like hurling something heavy at it, but what good would that do? She shook her head slowly in a way that might have appeared disbelieving – but it was all too easy to believe what that dratted woman had done.

She'd pulled a fast one on Sally some time back, and now, just when Lorna was taking care of the depot for Sally, she'd had the gall to pull a fast one on Lorna, too.

THIRTY-THREE

On Friday evening, Deborah was in the sitting room with Sally when Lorna walked in, looking serious.

'Fed up being back at work instead of with George?' Deborah asked, then instantly regretted it when Lorna's lips formed a straight line.

'Sally, there's something I need to tell you,' Lorna said, her green eyes serious.

'Do you want me to skedaddle?' Deborah asked.

'No need,' said Lorna. She sank onto an armchair, perched on the edge and leaned forward, her elegant hands lightly clasped. 'Sally, I've spent all today asking myself if I should keep this from you because of your health.'

Sally's eyes widened. 'What on earth is it?'

Deborah shifted in her seat. 'Lorna, you aren't supposed to upset Sally.'

Sally looked directly at Lorna. 'Just tell me.'

Lorna released a breath, and her shoulders dropped. 'It's Mrs Lockwood. While I was away, she stepped in and made changes.'

'*No...*' breathed Sally.

Deborah bridled, protective of her lifelong friend. 'Couldn't you have kept quiet about it?' she challenged Lorna.

'Not without swearing Betty and Rosalind to secrecy,' Lorna answered, 'and that would have been hard on Betty. Not to mention the fact that I live here, and I don't want to keep secrets.'

A gentle pressure on Deborah's arm made her turn to Sally.

'It's all right,' she said softly. She looked at Lorna. 'Tell me all of it.'

Lorna rattled off a list of changes Mrs Lockwood had made at the depot, then she and Deborah waited.

Sally puffed out a breath. 'Oh my.' Annoyance glittered in her hazel eyes. 'The cheek of the woman.'

Lorna shrugged. 'She's in overall charge, so I suppose she thinks that makes her entitled. At any rate, Mr Merivale and Mr Pratt agreed to everything.'

'Of course they did!' Sally exclaimed. 'They'd be too scared not to. Honestly, if she was here right now, I'd throttle her – so it's a good job she isn't,' she added, clearly reining herself in. 'I've got more important things to think about.'

'Like your blood pressure,' said Deborah.

'And the baby,' Lorna added. 'I'm so sorry this has happened, Sally. If I hadn't gone away—'

'Don't be daft,' Sally answered. 'It's wonderful that you could be with George. None of this is your responsibility. She'd obviously been biding her time.'

Just when Deborah feared Sally might be about to get riled up again, her face softened and her eyes warmed as she smiled at Lorna.

'Don't blame yourself. I know better than anybody what Mrs Lockwood is like. You were right to tell me.'

'Thanks,' said Lorna. 'I just wish I could promise you it won't happen again, but... I can't.'

· · ·

Deborah's dad looked pleased with himself. His brown eyes were bright, and his moustache was freshly trimmed. It was the first Saturday in September and Deborah had called round to see her parents that afternoon. She and Mum had been chatting for a while over a cuppa when Dad had arrived home from his allotment, bringing the aromas of fresh air and rich soil into the house.

He had a small sack in his hand.

'What have you got in there?' Mum asked him before Deborah could even stand up for a kiss. 'Don't put it down in the house. I don't want the place getting dirty.'

Dad held the sack open for them to see inside. 'My onion crop. Not bad, if I do say so myself.'

'Put them in the bottom of the vegetable rack,' said Mum.

'They need to go in the garden shed,' Dad told her. 'They have to be hung up, four to a rope, to dry out and keep aired.'

Deborah laughed. 'I can just see you with ropes of onions slung round your neck, Dad, like a French onion-seller.'

'Before the war, most of the country's onions used to come from France and Spain,' Dad reminded her. 'That's why there were almost no onions to be had to start with.'

'Last year, an onion was the top prize in a summer raffle at the WVS,' said Mum.

Dad winked at Deborah. 'Does that mean I get a hug for growing our own little crop?' he asked Mum.

'Not while you've got that filthy sack in your hands,' Mum retorted.

Laughing, Dad disappeared, leaving Mum and Deborah smiling at one another.

'I must be going soon,' Deborah said.

'Wait for Dad to finish in the shed and wash his hands,' said Mum.

Deborah nodded. Mum often found a reason for her to stay a little longer. She had never quite come to terms with Deborah's decision not to live at home any more. Even though Deborah had never once wanted to give up her room in Star House, there were still times when she felt a pang of guilt.

When Dad returned, Mum made a fresh pot of tea and the three of them passed the time of day.

Deborah was once again beginning to think of leaving when the doorbell sounded. Mum got up to answer it. The moment she left the room, Deborah stood up, bending over to kiss her father.

'I'd better be making tracks,' she said.

'It's lovely to see you,' said Dad.

Mum walked back in, looking surprised but pleased.

'Deborah's going now,' said Dad.

'That's a shame,' said Mum. 'Do you have to go? We've got a visitor.' She glanced over her shoulder. 'Come in.'

Into the room walked a handsome young man.

'He's a friend of Rod's from when he worked on the Manchester Ship Canal,' Deborah said later that afternoon to Sally. 'He's another caulker.'

'Why didn't he get sent to work at the Barrow shipyard when Rod went?' Sally wanted to know.

'Not all of them went,' Deborah explained. 'They still need caulkers here.'

That was the shipbuilding job her brother Rod did. The caulkers were the men who ensured the ships were watertight. Caulkers on the Manchester Ship Canal, where Rod had worked before the war, did repairs, whereas now, up in Barrow, his work was part of the shipbuilding process.

'What's his name?' Sally asked.

'Len Fordham.'

Sally thought for a moment. 'I don't remember him. Not

that Rod introduced me to his friends. He was more interested in us having time together.'

'I don't know him either,' said Deborah, 'though he said he'd seen me from a distance a couple of times at the same dance as Rod.'

'So, you had a bit of a chat, then?' Sally asked.

'Not really,' said Deborah. 'Dad had just announced I was leaving, so it would have looked a bit odd if I'd hung on. There was just time for introductions and a few words, and that was it.'

'I wonder why he went to see your parents,' Sally mused, 'when he's never been there before?'

'Don't know,' said Deborah.

Sally giggled. 'He's a man of *mystery*.'

'Idiot,' Deborah said affectionately.

'What does he look like?' Sally asked.

Deborah couldn't help grinning. 'You should have seen him! Talk about good-looking.'

'Did you swoon?' Sally teased.

'Very funny,' Deborah retorted.

'What does he look like?' Sally asked again.

Deborah took a moment to compose herself. She didn't want to look swoony. 'Tall and... muscular.' She felt oddly embarrassed using the word, and she was right to, because Sally immediately pounced.

'Ooh, you noticed his muscles, did you?'

'Well, he's bound to be fit and strong, working at the shipyard.'

'True,' Sally conceded. 'The question is, would you like to see him again?'

'Do you think it's too soon after Patrick?' Deborah asked.

'No,' Sally answered without hesitation. 'Does that mean you'd like to see him again? Come on, Deborah. This is me you're talking to.'

'It's immaterial, really, isn't it?' Deborah replied, deftly evading a direct reply. 'I'm hardly likely to have the chance.'

But... would she like the chance? She still felt bruised from her experience with Patrick, but were Sally and Dulcie right? Was it time to move on?

And if so, was she ready?

The mystery was soon solved. Mum turned up at Star House the very next afternoon, much to Deborah's surprise. Sally's parents, especially her mother, had always called at Star House to see her, and all the more so now, but Deborah's mum was keen on having Deborah at their house in Withington.

But, today, here she was. Her Sunday best of a dark-blue jacket and skirt with a pillbox hat looked a bit faded, as so many people's clothes did these days, but she had enhanced her jacket with new buttons and a silky scarf.

Mum chatted with Mrs Beaumont and the girls for a while. Then Mrs Beaumont accompanied Sally on a short stroll, leaving Deborah and her mother together.

'It's nice of you to come here,' said Deborah.

'I'd have come yesterday, only your father wouldn't let me. He said it would look *desperate*.'

Deborah raised her eyebrows. 'Desperate?'

'To get you fixed up with a boyfriend.'

'*Mum!*' Deborah exclaimed, but at the same time her heart began to thump. She couldn't prevent herself from asking, 'What are you talking about?'

'Len Fordham, of course.' Mum's tone said, *Isn't it obvious?* 'The reason he came to see us yesterday was because he wanted us to pass on a message to Rod. He'd got our address from the shipyard office. He wants us to tell Rod about a mutual friend of theirs who copped it in North Africa, poor blighter.'

'I'm sorry to hear that,' Deborah said. A friend of Rod and

Len would presumably be in his late twenties. What a waste. She spared a moment to think of Andrew. Poor Sally, living with that worry hanging over her.

'This Len fellow *likes* you,' Mum said with a smile.

'Don't be ridiculous.' Surprise made Deborah laugh, but she was pleased too, and her pulse gave a little jump. 'We weren't in the same room for more than two minutes.'

'That's plenty long enough,' Mum replied as if her word was law. 'It's less time than it took me to make up my mind when I met your father. You should have seen the way Len's eyes followed you as you left the room. Anyway,' she went on breezily, 'after me and your dad had commiserated about his friend, he stopped for a bit and we chatted about this and that, and I asked him if he liked dancing, and I mentioned that you and your work pals sometimes go to the Ritz on a Friday evening.'

'Mum, you *didn't.*'

'Deborah, I *did.*'

'*Mum.*'

Deborah poured all the indignation at her disposal into the word, but at the same time her mind buzzed with the plans she intended to make with her Town Hall chums tomorrow.

On Monday evening, Deborah couldn't wait to get home from work to tell Sally about going to the Ritz on Friday.

Everybody loved the Ritz, which was famous for its revolving stage. The ballroom had two dance bands and, when the performing band came to the end of their set, the stage would start to turn while they continued to play. Meanwhile, on the far side of the revolving stage, the second band would be playing along in perfect time. The music carried on as the first band slowly disappeared from view, and the dancing never stopped.

Deborah didn't even bother to take off her outdoor things before she waltzed into the sitting room to share her news with Sally, only to come to a sudden halt as Sally and Betty both looked at her.

Not so long ago, she would have felt a bit miffed – more than a bit – to see this evidence of the closeness between Sally and Betty. Truth be told, she had been somewhat jealous of Betty, who had so quickly become such a dear and close friend to Sally, close enough to be one of her bridesmaids, sharing the role that Deborah had been looking forward to since girlhood. This jealousy had sometimes burned inside Deborah's chest, something she had hated herself for.

But seeing how Betty and Samuel had conducted themselves in the matter of little Bessie Beech, and seeing how much love Betty had for the baby, had eased Deborah's feelings considerably as her admiration for the Atkinsons had grown. By now, her resentment of Betty had dissipated and been replaced by genuine warmth, and she wanted to give her and Samuel as much support as she could.

'Sorry,' she said. 'Shall I come back later?'

'No,' Betty answered. 'Come in. I've just been telling Sally my news.'

'Little Bessie Beech?' Deborah asked.

Betty nodded. Her peaches-and-cream cheeks went pink, making her look a little flustered. 'I don't know whether to be excited or scared. Samuel and I have to go to the magistrates' court next week.'

'Has Mr Whatsit made a decision?' Deborah asked anxiously.

Betty shook her head, and her golden curls swayed and bounced. 'Not yet. Since we last heard anything, the grandparents have been putting together all the reasons why they should be allowed to have little Bessie Beech.' She dropped her voice as she added, 'They've employed a *solicitor*. Now we're worried that we should have done that too, but it never crossed our minds. The grandparents have had this solicitor working for them for *weeks* now, and I'm sure we couldn't have afforded that, except that we'd have paid *any*thing if it would have helped us adopt little Bessie Beech. We'd have sold everything, if we'd had to.'

'If you'd sold everything, they'd never have let you have little Bessie Beech,' Sally said affectionately. 'Did Mrs Fitch ever say you had to be rolling in money? Did Warden Everett ever say it?'

'Of course not,' Betty agreed. 'I'm overreacting.' She huffed out a sigh. 'I can't stop thinking about everything the grandparents have to offer, and all we have is a bookshop—'

'—and a reasonable standard of living, and two dear, *loving* people who are eager to be little Bessie Beech's mummy and daddy,' Deborah finished. 'I'm sure the magistrate knows that from Mrs Fitch.'

'That's why we have to go in next week,' said Betty. 'Mr Brent-Williams wants to hear evidence from the Welfare Department.'

'That means Mrs Fitch is going to stand up for you,' Sally said earnestly.

'I hope Mr Brent-Williams listens to her,' Betty said fervently.

'Of course he will,' said Deborah. 'Don't forget, little Bessie Beech's adoption was all set to be rubber-stamped until the mother threw a spanner in the works. And didn't Mr Brent-Williams say later that he wouldn't have given her little Bessie Beech even if her husband had said yes? That means he was happy to give little Bessie Beech to you – until the grandparents came along.'

'They haven't just chucked a spanner in the works,' Betty said gloomily. 'They've thrown in a bloomin' great crane.'

'The only "crane" is that they're well-heeled,' said Sally.

'Nothing else has changed. You still have Mrs Fitch and Warden Everett on your side.'

Deborah went to Betty and knelt down beside her, taking one of her hands as she looked into her blue eyes.

'It doesn't matter what Sally or I or anyone else says, does it?' she asked gently. 'Nothing is going to stop you worrying. Just remember you have friends who care about you and Samuel, and who want you to adopt little Bessie Beech.'

'I know.' Betty's eyes were swimming with tears, but she managed to smile. 'That means everything.'

THIRTY-FOUR

On Friday evening, Deborah dressed with just the right amount of care. She wanted to look nice, but at the same time she didn't want her chums thinking she'd made a special effort and quizzing her as to why.

She hadn't mentioned Len in the Town Hall canteen, and she wasn't entirely sure why not. After the way the gossips had made her life miserable over the summer, shouldn't she be keen to provide proof that she had moved on from her relationship with Patrick? Especially after he had upped sticks and disappeared without making any attempt to see her first.

She chose her rayon-crape dress. It was blue, with short sleeves, lightly padded shoulders and a narrow belt. She wore it with her blue-and-white court shoes and her linen jacket. Mrs Beaumont had steamed out some creases for her.

Deborah met up with her friends outside the Ritz and they went in together, handing in their outdoor things and gas-mask boxes to the cloakroom attendant and receiving tickets in exchange. They walked into the ballroom. Most people stayed downstairs, where the dancefloor was, but there were some upstairs, watching from the balcony.

The girls found a free table and sat down – Deborah, Amy Brelland, Josephine Hill, Rosemary Greening and Katie Jameson. It wasn't long before men, most of them in uniform, began approaching them to ask for dances. Deborah appreciated a man in uniform as much as the next girl, but this evening she was far more interested in looking at the chaps in civvies.

Would Len Fordham have taken Mum's not-so-subtle hint about the Ritz?

Deborah accepted invitations to dance from a few men, and sat at the table sipping lemonade in between times. Usually, she liked to watch the other couples on the dance-floor, but tonight she made a point of joining in with the conversation at the table as if it was of consuming interest. She absolutely was not going to allow her gaze to rake the ballroom.

'Excuse me?'

Deborah, Amy and Katie, who had been busy talking about the ban on new garments being made with pleats so as to save fabric, all looked up – and there he was, dressed in flannels and a tweed jacket, his light-brown hair slicked back. There was a smile on his full-lipped mouth, but it wasn't wide and confident. There was something hesitant about it.

Len looked at Deborah and cleared his throat. 'Do you remember me? I was at your parents' house.'

Amy and Katie's interest was so intense it was practically oozing out of their pores.

'Of course.' Deborah turned to her friends. 'This is Len Fordham. He used to work with my brother.' She performed the introductions, then said to Len, 'My mother told me about your friend getting killed. I was sorry to hear it.'

It was the polite thing to say, of course, but it also had the effect of making Amy and Katie stop shooting her sparkling-eyed looks as they murmured their condolences.

'Thanks,' said Len. 'He was a good bloke.'

'It's just horrible to think of all the boys who've been lost,' said Katie.

The music ended and there was warm applause on the dancefloor. Some couples stayed put, ready to have the next dance together, while others separated, the men escorting the girls back to their seats before they headed off in search of a pint, or another partner.

Deborah looked at Len. It was as if she was seeing him through everyone else's eyes – handsome, broad-shouldered. She sensed the stirring of interest from the other girls and knew they were thinking how lucky she was to have attracted Len's interest.

Her heart ought to be beating faster, but it wasn't. She wished it was, but it just wasn't. It wouldn't – not for Len, no matter how good-looking he was, no matter how much her friends' eyes shone with encouragement, no matter how energetically her mum had done her matchmaking.

Deborah wanted to feel the spark, she really did, but it just wasn't there.

And then – and then another man stepped in between her and Len.

'Excuse me for pushing in,' said Patrick, 'but I don't want you to do this, Deborah. I can see this chap has his eye on you, and I completely understand why – but I hope with all my heart that you'll tell him you can't dance with him. Because you're going to dance with *me*.'

In spite of everything going on around her – the music, the couples, the voices – Deborah felt as though she and Patrick were the only two people in the ballroom, the only two in the world. She couldn't tear her eyes away from him. His tall, athletic frame carried his suit well. Most young men in civvies were at a disadvantage when nearly all the others were in uniform, but not Patrick.

He didn't move, didn't shift uncomfortably, even though she was making him wait. No, not *making* him wait, not on purpose. She was too overwhelmed to respond. She was entranced. She had spent the whole summer telling herself that she didn't want this, but she did, oh she did.

When he held out his hand to her, she took it. Of course she did. This was right and perfect and natural. His touch made her bones turn to wax. Did her touch do the same to him?

They went onto the dancefloor and turned to one another. Deborah melted into his arms, and they began to dance. The music played a dreamy waltz, but Deborah wouldn't have cared if it was the quickest of quicksteps or even a mad polka. Simply being with Patrick, their steps fitting together easily, made it romantic.

At the end of the dance he led her from the floor, but not towards her table. Deborah caught her friends watching, but she didn't care. Let them make of it what they would. Let anyone. She didn't care what anybody thought. These moments were for her and Patrick and nobody else had the right to comment or wonder or talk about them.

Patrick took her to a corner where there was an empty table, and they sat down.

They both started speaking at the same moment.

'You first,' said Patrick.

'I thought you'd left Stretford,' said Deborah. 'Your mother said you'd transferred somewhere else.'

'She stretched the truth, I'm afraid. I'm sorry about that,' said Patrick, 'but she was angry with you.'

'You *weren't* transferred?'

'I was, but not permanently and not through my own choice – though I must admit that it did seem like the best thing at the time. I was utterly miserable after we split up and so working elsewhere for a few weeks seemed like a good idea. I thought it would help me to get over you.' Patrick shook his head. 'Imagine me thinking I could ever get over you.'

Deborah reached for his hand and he immediately laid his other one on top of hers. 'Does that mean you still...?' Shyness swept over her and she couldn't bring herself to finish the question.

He smiled and his eyes crinkled. 'Yes, it does mean,' he told her. 'It very much means.'

'I'm sorry I was so horrible to you,' Deborah burst out. 'I was upset and hurt over that bet.'

'I know, and I don't blame you. It was stupid of me, but it wasn't serious. I've been kicking myself ever since and wishing I'd kept my mouth shut.'

'It made it so much worse when everybody at work knew about it. It made me feel I had to brush it off, brush *you* off, so that I could claw back some of my dignity. The gossip went on for ages and it hurt me every single time I was made aware of it. I know now,' she added, 'that I shouldn't have let myself be swayed like that, shouldn't have let myself be *controlled*. But at the time... I thought I was doing the right thing.'

'You aren't the only one who set store by what the proverbial "everyone" thought,' said Patrick. 'I had plenty of "everyone" around me too. And then I was sent away at very short notice. I agonised over whether to write to you, but then I reminded myself that you hadn't made any attempt to see me, and so I didn't.'

'Well, I for one shan't pay attention to what others think after this,' said Deborah. 'Well, I shall, but it depends who the person is and if it's someone I should take notice of. But I certainly shan't let the dreaded "everyone" take over and tell me what to think.' Although she spoke the words in a light tone, she had never felt more serious. What a twit she'd been. 'There was something else too,' she admitted. 'All the time that we were going out together, I simply loved having a boyfriend.'

'That sounds like a good thing,' said Patrick, his dark eyes crinkling as he smiled.

'What I mean is that, as well as caring about you and wanting to be with you, I also absolutely loved the simple fact of having a boyfriend. It made me feel good about myself. It made me feel…' She could hardly say it made her feel she could dream about the future. She settled for, 'It was what I'd wanted for ages. I don't think I showed off about it – about you – but I certainly felt showy-offy.'

Patrick grinned. 'Went around boasting about me, did you?' Wiping the smile from his face, and pretending to be serious, he said, 'I can understand that. I'm worth a boast or two.'

'No, I felt showy-offy when perhaps I ought to have concentrated on feeling happy and – and lucky.'

Patrick took a deep breath and let it out slowly. 'I felt lucky every day when we were a couple. Every single day. Some chaps like to play the field, but not me. You were the only girl for me. You still are. During the weeks when I was away working elsewhere, I spent hours planning how I was going to persuade you to come back to me.'

'You could have written,' Deborah said mildly, but he shook his head.

'I wanted it to be more special than that. I wanted to do it in person.'

'Like you did tonight. You certainly made an impression.'

'We have your father to thank for it,' said Patrick.

'My *dad*?'

He nodded. 'I've got another week to go in Leeds before I'm officially transferred back to Stretford. I had a letter from your father at the start of this week. He'd been round to my parents' house wanting to see me. My dad explained about my secondment and gave him my address.'

'I had no idea...' breathed Deborah.

'Your dad told me by letter that your mother was busy matchmaking between you and a new fellow and, if I still cared for you, then I should come home and do something about it.'

'Dad said that? *Dad* did?'

'Yep. So, I'm here tonight on special leave to boot the other man out of the door and sweep you into my arms... if you'll have me?'

'Yes,' she said, and leaned across to kiss him.

And everything in Deborah's world slotted back into the right place.

THIRTY-FIVE

Betty and Samuel talked endlessly about what might happen at the meeting with Mr Brent-Williams. Not knowing what to expect was both frustrating and frightening.

'She will be ours in the end, won't she?' Betty asked, biting her lip anxiously.

'I hope s-so with all my heart.' Behind his glasses, Samuel's hazel eyes were worried.

'I'm sorry,' said Betty. 'It wasn't fair of me to say that.'

'Who else sh-should you turn to for reassurance but y-your husband?'

'It wasn't reassurance, though, was it? Not really,' said Betty. 'You can't make promises like that, and I shouldn't ask it of you. Neither of us can possibly know what's going to happen. All we can do is hope.'

The days dragged by. Betty's feelings of anxiety grew as Wednesday approached. Their appointment was for that after-noon. Was it possible that Mr Brent-Williams had selected then because it was half-day closing and he knew it would be straightforward for Samuel to attend? No, not a hope. The magistrate wouldn't have taken their best interests into account.

With Mrs Lockwood's consent, Lorna had given Betty the afternoon off from the depot. She hurried home to the bookshop and made a light meal for her and Samuel.

'I'm not sure I can eat anything...' She made to push her plate away.

Samuel placed gentle fingers over hers, staying her hand. 'I f-feel all knotted up too, but w-we must try to eat.'

They did their best, then Betty covered the leftovers and put the plates on the marble slab in the pantry to keep them cool.

After that, they went upstairs to get changed into their Sunday best, and soon they were on their way. Betty clung to Samuel's hand as they sat together on the bus, hanging on to him so determinedly that he had to murmur to her when he wanted her to let go so he could offer his seat to a lady when the bus filled up.

At last, they were outside the court building. Betty drew a deep breath before they went in, and the movement of Samuel's shoulders told her he was doing the same. Betty wished Grace could be there to witness it, so she would see with her own eyes that this hoped-for adoption meant as much to Samuel as it did to her.

Inside, a clerk showed them to a room they hadn't been in before. As they walked inside, he stayed for a moment in the corridor to speak to someone. The room had a long, polished table down the centre, with three chairs on each of the long sides and two at each end. At the end that was furthest from the door were a pair of blotters and a small wooden tray with a bottle of ink.

'That must be w-where the magistrates are going to s-sit,' Samuel whispered.

'Mrs Ames must be on duty as well,' Betty said softly before asking, 'Why are we whispering?'

But she knew the answer. It was because they were nervous.

The clerk followed them into the room.

'Please sit on that side,' he said.

'Not here?' Betty asked, indicating the pair of chairs at the opposite end from the magistrates' seats.

'No, the welfare lady will sit there,' said the clerk. 'If the two of you will sit on the far side, Mr and Mrs Prescott and their solicitor will sit opposite you on this side.'

'Mr and Mrs Prescott?' Betty replied, startled. 'Are they the baby's grandparents?'

'I believe so,' the clerk answered, his neutral tone and expression giving nothing away.

'We haven't met them before.' Betty's heart beat quickly.

'W-we didn't even know their name,' Samuel added.

The clerk didn't meet their eyes. 'Excuse me.'

He left the room, closing the door behind him.

Betty and Samuel stared at one another. There was a flush of colour in Samuel's cheeks that showed how troubled he felt.

'I w-wasn't expecting this,' he said.

'Me neither,' Betty agreed She reached for Samuel's hand and their fingers tangled together. 'D'you think – d'you think the grandparents are here because Mr Brent-Williams has made up his mind?'

Samuel shook his head. 'I d-don't know what to think at this point.'

The door opened to admit a well-dressed older lady, who walked in followed by two gentlemen. The lady wore a wool coat with a fur collar and deep fur cuffs. Her hat had a froth of net on the crown, some of which tumbled forward and hung as low as her eyes. Inside her gloves were certain lumps and bumps that suggested rings with stones of significant size.

Her husband, also dressed in an expensive overcoat, removed his homburg and dropped it on the table, revealing a head of silver hair, though his eyebrows were dark, as were his eyes. He drew out a chair for his wife to be seated before he took the place next to her.

The second man was younger, though still somewhat older than Betty and Samuel. He too placed his hat on the table. His sober suit and leather briefcase proclaimed him to be the Prescotts' solicitor.

Betty's insides turned to mush. These people were so *grand*. Who in their right mind would hand over little Bessie Beech to the likes of her and Samuel? They were so *ordinary* in comparison.

Betty and Samuel were still on their feet, too taken aback to move. Then Betty felt a small movement beside her and saw that Samuel had pulled out a chair for her. She sat, not sorry to do so, because her knees had turned to blancmange. Would the posh Prescotts think Samuel had only pulled out her chair for her because he was copying Mr Prescott? If so, that wasn't fair. Samuel was the perfect gentleman. You didn't have to be rolling in money to be a gentleman.

The Prescotts looked across the table at them, their expressions frankly appraising. Betty bristled but smiled politely.

'You must be the people who want to adopt our grandchild.' Mr Prescott was as well-spoken as he was well-dressed.

'I'm sure it's very commendable of you to offer to take in an abandoned baby,' said Mrs Prescott, 'but you can stand aside now.'

The door opened again. Mr Brent-Williams stepped inside – trust him to be first onto the stage – but, having done that, he politely waited for Mrs Ames to overtake him. They headed for the top of the table and sat down. A pair of clerks followed them in and sat at a table to one side.

Mr Brent-Williams fussed with his blotter and removed an expensive fountain pen from his inside pocket before lifting his chin and looking at the others seated around the table. Was it significant that he looked at the Prescotts first?

'Good afternoon,' he said solemnly, lapping up the respect accorded to him. 'I have summoned you here to hear the professional opinion of a highly experienced lady from the Corporation's Welfare Department. She is waiting outside, and I will invite her to join us in a moment. I believe we shall all benefit from hearing what she has to say.'

Betty took her eyes off the magistrate for long enough to glance at Samuel. They shared a brief, warm smile. Betty's confidence rose and she started to feel positive.

'I take it there are no objections?' Mr Brent-Williams enquired.

'None at all,' replied the Prescotts' solicitor. 'We welcome her opinion.'

'S-so do we,' Samuel added.

'Mrs Fitch has been a great help to us,' Betty added.

'Mrs Fitch?' Mrs Ames repeated. 'No, she wasn't available—'

Mr Brent-Williams quickly took over. '—and so we shall have the benefit of Miss Brewster's experience.' He lifted a finger to summon one of the clerks. 'Ask Miss Brewster to join us, if you please.'

'Miss Brewster?' Betty whispered to Samuel. 'Who's she when she's at home? She doesn't know us. We need Mrs Fitch.'

Samuel squeezed her hand, but didn't get the chance to answer, because Mr Brent-Williams cleared his throat.

'Is there something you wish to say, Mrs Atkinson?'

Heat poured into Betty's face. 'No, sir.'

The clerk opened the door and in walked a middle-aged lady in a navy coat and grey hat. For a moment – just for a moment – Betty thought her plain and insignificant, but then she realised her mistake. Miss Brewster might be no bobby dazzler, but she exuded competence and authority, and her face was shrewd.

Betty's heart dipped. Those sharp eyes and narrow lips didn't appear kindly. Then again, did that matter? She and Samuel didn't need Miss Brewster to be soft-hearted. They needed her to be professional, just like Mrs Fitch.

Miss Brewster was followed by another woman – probably in her mid-forties, her clothes clean and pressed but far from new. Her brown eyes were compassionate, and Betty warmed to her. Maybe the first lady wasn't Miss Brewster after all. Maybe *this* was Miss Brewster. She hoped so.

No such luck.

The first woman said, addressing the two magistrates, 'This is Miss Inkerman. She is a junior colleague, and I am responsible for her training.'

Miss Inkerman was being trained? How odd. At her age, she ought to have worked in welfare for donkey's years. But no further explanation was forthcoming. Realising she had sat forward, as attentive as a child at school, Betty deliberately sat back, then made sure she was sitting up straight. She didn't want to look like she didn't care.

The clerk held a chair for Miss Brewster. Before she sat down, she nudged Miss Inkerman, who was about to take the seat beside her.

'Over there, if you please, Miss Inkerman. I'm the one giving the evidence.'

Poor Miss Inkerman's face coloured. Samuel, ever the gentleman and always alert to the feelings of others, immediately rose to his feet and drew out the chair next to his. Miss Inkerman subsided into it.

'Miss Brewster,' said Mr Brent-Williams, 'thank you for attending this meeting. I understand you have acquainted yourself with the facts of this case. These are the child's grandparents, and these are the child's former prospective adoptive parents.'

Betty gasped. '*Former—?*'

Mr Brent-Williams flicked a glance in her direction. 'I cannot in good conscience refer to you in any other way, Mrs Atkinson, not with matters as they stand.' To Miss Brewster, he said, 'I have read the reports provided by your colleague Mrs Fitch and by Warden Everett about the Atkinsons; and I have read the report compiled on behalf of Mr and Mrs Prescott by their legal representative. I would now be glad to hear your opinion on the subject of natural family versus adoptive family.'

Miss Brewster waited a moment, as if allowing time for everyone to turn their attention her way.

'I am not the welfare officer for this case,' she said, 'but I am happy to provide my professional opinion, which is based upon years of experience on the question of the two sorts of family.'

She then embarked on a description of her experience with the Corporation. Betty listened attentively to start with, but she'd soon heard enough – more than enough. She wanted to jump up, shake Miss Brewster by the shoulders and say, 'I know you're qualified to have an opinion. Just tell us what it is!'

She didn't dare stop listening, though, for fear of missing the crucial bit.

Finally, it came.

'It is my professional opinion, based upon years of working in the Welfare Department, that a child is almost always better off in its natural home, by which I mean the home of the people he or she belongs to by birth.'

Betty stopped breathing. Beside her, Samuel stirred. Before he could speak, Mr Brent-Williams raised a hand to stop him.

'You are not here to comment or ask questions, Mr Atkinson.' Looking down the long table at Miss Brewster, he said, 'You said, "almost always". Tell me what you mean by "almost", if you please.'

'Obviously there are exceptions,' Miss Brewster replied. 'Some families are so objectionable that there can be no question as to their suitability. I am a great believer in certain things. One is that small children are better off in the home with their mothers rather than in a nursery – unless the mother is completely unsatisfactory, of course. Another belief I hold is that a child should, where possible, grow up in its family home with its blood relatives. I cannot speak more plainly than that.'

THIRTY-SIX

October brought a blaze of colour. On the trees that grew round the edges of the rec, the leaves became a glorious mixture of gold, crimson and burgundy, and berries gleamed in the bushes, attracting sparrows.

Lorna had spent recent weeks thinking hard about the situation at the depot. She was also full of exciting new thoughts about changes she was aware of in her own body. She wasn't *completely* sure yet, and she didn't want to say anything until she was. If she and George had been living together, it might have been different – in fact, it undoubtedly would have been – but with their living arrangements the way they were, she needed to know for certain before she breathed a word, no matter the temptation.

So, she held her tongue about the possibility of a new generation of Broughtons and concentrated on what had taken place at the depot while she was in London.

'The truth is,' she told George during one of their telephone calls, 'that the changes Mrs Lockwood made are perfectly all right.'

'They were a good idea?' he asked.

Lorna took a moment simply to enjoy the sound of her husband's deep voice before she answered. 'But the way Sally ran things was perfectly all right as well. Mrs Lockwood made her changes just for the sake of it – to prove she could, I suppose.'

'What for?' said George.

'She's always wanted to run the depot. This long absence of Sally's has given her the opportunity to make her mark in a way she never could before.'

'Maybe she hopes Sally won't return to work after she has the baby,' George suggested.

'I don't think Sally has a choice,' Lorna replied. 'Everyone works these days – wives, mothers. The country can't afford to let anybody off the hook. It's the only way we're going to win the war. Everyone has to pull together.'

'If Sally is going to return as the manager,' said George, 'she can change everything back again, if she sees fit.' Before Lorna could comment, he added, 'Of course, you know what I regard as the best thing about Sally going back to work, don't you?'

Something inside Lorna wriggled in delight. 'Tell me.'

'You'll be free to come home to London,' he replied. 'I can't think of anything better than that – can you?'

Remembering her all-too-brief trip to London, and the possibility of pregnancy, Lorna tingled all over. 'All I want is to be with you, George.'

'Does that mean being with me is better than being up there with your friends?' he teased.

'Well, it's a close-run thing, of course,' she teased back, 'but I think you might just about have the edge. Just about,' she added, unable to keep the smile out of her voice.

'Then you'd better get more leave as soon as you can, and come down here again,' George said with a hint of challenge in his voice.

'And why would I want to do that?' Lorna asked archly.

'In order for me to find ways to tip the balance in my favour,' said George. 'Why else?'

Lorna had yet to talk to Sally about the future. She had avoided it so far – everyone had. The memory of her miscarriage had affected them all. As happy as they were for her now, there was also a strong shared feeling that no one should take anything for granted.

Sally seemed to feel the same.

'I'm excited about the baby,' she'd told Lorna a while back, 'but I'm terrified too in case something goes wrong, like it did last time.'

'You look well,' Lorna had replied, anxious to make her feel better. 'I know you'd feel awful if you stopped resting, but because you're taking good care of yourself, you look good.' She smiled. 'You're glowing.'

Sally had lowered her voice to a whisper, real fear haunting her hazel eyes and her smooth complexion turning pale. 'In the here and now, right this moment, I feel all right. But I dare not, simply dare not, look to the future.'

'Scared of jinxing it,' Lorna had said, understanding.

'Exactly,' Sally confirmed.

That was why the future had never really been discussed in detail. They all felt protective towards Sally and her unborn child, and didn't want to place her under additional pressure.

But now it was October and surely, if anything bad had been going to happen, it would have happened by this time? Even so, Lorna was reluctant to broach a subject that Sally never raised.

In the end, it was through Betty's situation that they ended up talking about it.

'How do you think Betty is – really and truly, I mean?' Sally asked Lorna. 'It worries me that she might not want to speak freely in front of me because she's concerned about my health.'

Lorna measured her words carefully, because she too was concerned for Sally. 'She and Samuel are both scared that the magistrate will come down on the side of the grandparents after what that Miss Brewster said.'

Sally nodded and pressed her lips together so firmly that little wrinkles appeared in her chin. 'They really have set their hearts on having little Bessie Beech as their daughter. They'll be devastated if it doesn't happen, especially Betty.'

Sally let a silence develop. The thoughtful look in her eyes prompted Lorna to stay quiet and wait.

At last Sally said, 'Can I tell you something that's going to make me sound totally selfish?'

'I can't imagine you being selfish, but go ahead.'

'It's to do with my baby,' Sally said quietly. 'The midwife says that, even if something goes wrong and it comes into the world now instead of waiting for December, it should still be all right. It wouldn't be so premature that it could be... *damaged*.'

Tears of pure relief welled up behind Lorna's eyes. 'Sally, that's *won*derful. I'm happy for you.'

'Thanks,' said Sally. 'Yes, it is wonderful. I'm finally starting to let myself believe...'

'That you'll have your baby in your arms,' Lorna finished, feeling a powerful tug of emotion.

Sally's eyes sparkled as she nodded.

'I don't see what's selfish about that,' Lorna said, mystified.

'That isn't the selfish bit,' Sally answered. 'I'm wondering about who will take care of my baby when I go back to the depot. I can't ask Mrs Beaumont. It was one thing for her to look after little Bessie Beech temporarily, but she's too busy to take on a baby permanently. My mother will want me to move in with her and Dad so she can be the childminder. Have you heard of childminders? It's a new word. And Andrew's mother will no doubt want me to go to Seymour Grove and live with her and Auntie Vera.'

'And you'd rather stay here,' Lorna finished for her.

'Star House is my home,' Sally said simply. 'I've lived in two places with Andrew, the house that got bombed, and here. If I can't have him here with me, then at the very least I want to be in a home we lived in together, however briefly. I want our baby to be in the home where his or her daddy used to live.'

'I can see that,' Lorna agreed. 'But I'm still waiting for the selfish bit.'

'Well, here it is,' said Sally. 'I was hoping Betty would act as my childminder. She fell in love with little Bessie Beech right away and it came as no surprise to me when she wanted to adopt her. I've never been able to imagine her carrying on working at the depot, though she has said she's going to stay on in the first instance so as not to leave you in the lurch. All young mums work these days – either in war work or else as childminders so that other women can go out to work.'

'Have you ever asked her about childminding for you?' Lorna asked.

'I've never really had the chance,' Sally explained. 'First of all, of course, I've held back from jinxing my pregnancy by making plans. Then little Bessie Beech's real mother popped out of the woodwork, followed by the grandparents. Samuel and Betty still have no idea what the future holds for them, but it doesn't look like things are going in their favour. It's not as though I can say to Betty, "If you end up at home with little Bessie Beech, please will you look after my baby as well?", is it?'

Lorna smiled. 'And this is you being selfish, is it? Wanting to make plans for your baby to be taken care of?'

'In the context of Betty's anguish over little Bessie Beech, it *is* selfish.'

'Fiddlesticks,' Lorna retorted. 'It's your duty to make plans for your baby. Betty would be the first to agree with me on that.'

Sally looked troubled. 'She would be the perfect childminder. I can't think of anybody I would trust more. But with little Bessie Beech's future hanging in the balance, I can't picture what I'm going to do. There,' she added, with a heavy sigh, 'I told you it was selfish...'

Lorna stayed on after work the following evening to await a scheduled telephone call from George.

The arrangement they had was that he would place the call between six and half past if he was able to. If she hadn't heard from him by six thirty, it meant he was tied up at work. She hated it when that happened, as it made her miss him even more. Their telephone calls meant so much to her, and it was all very well reminding herself that war work came first, but that didn't make it any easier.

For half an hour, Lorna sat beside the telephone, hands clasped under her chin, elbows on the desk, willing the instrument to ring. She kept holding still in expectation, her breath bottling up in her chest. Something fluttered in her tummy a dozen times as hope flared afresh. At last, the clock showed half past six, and she lowered her head in disappointment, but she pushed the feeling away. It was no use giving in. Things were the way they were.

With a soft sigh, she shrugged on her coat, picked up her things and headed for the door. She had just switched off the light when the telephone rang. Quickly she put the light on again and hurried to the desk to grab the receiver.

'You're still there,' George said when the call had been connected. 'Thank heavens. I was sure I'd miss you.'

'You almost did!' Lorna answered with both tears and laughter in her voice. 'It's so good to hear your voice.'

'And yours, my love. I miss you all the time.'

'I miss you too.'

'It's October now,' said George. 'Not too many more weeks.'

'I know,' said Lorna. 'I can't wait.' She was desperate to tell him about the possibility of her being pregnant, but she forced herself not to. 'But there's something I'm worried about – well, two things, actually.'

'Tell me,' George responded at once. 'I expect it's about Sally. Her husband is in North Africa, isn't he?'

'Yes,' Lorna answered. 'He's with the 44th Infantry. We listen to the news every day and things are tough over there. Well,' she added, 'I don't need to tell you that.'

'Don't forget that, after the setbacks in the summer, we've now prevented the enemy from advancing further into Egypt,' said George.

'I know, but it isn't over yet, is it?' said Lorna.

'Not by a long chalk.'

'Sally says Andrew thinks the world of General Montgomery. They all do.'

'He's a superb strategist,' George replied. On a wry note, he added, 'He needs to be, now that Rommel is back in the field. Listen, darling. Tell Sally from me that Monty is the man for the job. It won't stop her being scared on her husband's account, but it might give her some confidence.'

'I'll tell her,' Lorna promised.

'Now, what's the other thing you're worried about?'

'It might sound rather trifling after talking about El Alamein, but it's Mrs Lockwood. I've told you about her before.'

'Yes, you said how helpful she was… until she made those changes in your absence.'

'I think she's making sure she has her feet well and truly under the table before Sally comes back,' said Lorna. 'I feel awful about it, because it seems like it's my fault.'

'If anybody has conducted themselves in an inappropriate manner, it most certainly isn't you,' George said in a no-nonsense voice that put Lorna in mind of his mother, which made her lips twitch into a smile in spite of her anxiety for Sally and the future of the depot.

'All along, ever since I took over as the depot manager,' said Lorna, 'Mrs Lockwood has been supportive, or at least has seemed to be, but I'm sure now that she saw Sally's long absence as an opportunity for herself. She's always wanted to run the depot. It isn't enough for her to be the WVS salvage officer. She wants to run the whole show.'

'It sounds like you'll be leaving Sally with a handful to cope with,' George commented. Before she could speak, he added, 'I know that's the last thing you would wish to do.'

'With bells on,' Lorna agreed, glad of his understanding.

'I'm sorry you're in this position. I know how much you care about Sally. You must hate the thought of her walking into hot water when she returns to work – and even though it isn't your fault, I can appreciate why you feel that it is. It happened while you were in charge.'

'Mrs Lockwood has been very clever,' said Lorna. 'I didn't see it happening.'

'She sounds like a very clever woman,' George said thoughtfully.

'In a sneaky and manipulative sort of way,' Lorna added. 'I just don't know what I can do about it.'

She could hear the smile in George's voice when he replied, 'Fortunately for you, my lovely wife, I know another very clever woman – and one I'm prepared to bet is even cleverer than your Mrs Lockwood.' The smile now became an audible grin as he said, 'I think we should let my mother loose on the problem.'

THIRTY-SEVEN

Towards the end of October, owing to the fall in the production of milk, the milk ration had to be reduced by half a pint per person each week, though as compensation every household received a tin of dried milk every eight weeks.

'This dried milk puts me in mind of our tea-party,' Betty told Samuel, 'when Grace and I talked about dried eggs.' Her voice fell flat as she added with a heavy heart, 'That was just after we'd heard from the magistrates' court and we were so excited to tell everyone because we thought the appointment would end up with us getting permission to adopt little Bessie Beech.'

'I know,' Samuel answered with a sigh. 'It's w-what would have happened, too, only that was the d-day the mother turned up. If sh-she hadn't done that...'

'Or if she'd been a day *later*,' Betty added. She turned to Samuel and looked up into his dear, kind face. 'I never thought that something could happen that would be worse than the war, but this... *this* is worse. It hurts more than all the air raids. It hurts more than the Christmas Blitz, more than the lists of dead servicemen. Our situation with little Bessie Beech matters more to us than any of that.'

'Of c-course it does,' Samuel agreed.

'We live, think and breathe her,' said Betty. 'I feel guilty sometimes. It's as if we're in our own world.'

'Everyone must f-feel like that for their own various reasons,' said Samuel. 'We all w-want to know everything that's going on in North Africa, but it means even more to Sally because that's w-where Andrew is. Everybody has d-different things they concentrate on.'

Betty considered that. 'Just think of all those Australian and New Zealander wives and mothers and sweethearts who feel as close to the news from Egypt as Sally does, not to mention all the women over here.'

'W-war connects people in sh-shocking ways,' said Samuel.

'But also in good ways,' Betty reminded him. 'Think of how everyone has helped one another. Do you remember after the Christmas Blitz when hundreds upon hundreds of people got together in various places on Christmas Eve to prepare thousands of Christmas dinners for the people whose homes had been destroyed?'

'I remember,' Samuel said softly. 'S-such a tragic reason for all those people to work together to help others – but s-so much pride and satisfaction afterwards.'

Betty couldn't hold back a chuckle. 'It was at one of those Christmas Eve kitchens that George sought out Lorna to say he wanted to see her again.'

'They're not the only ones brought together by the w-war,' said Samuel.

Betty pretended not to catch on. 'Yes – Andrew and Sally were as well. He would never have been at the Town Hall that day if he hadn't been running that youth club in the school holidays. That was a wartime commitment he'd taken on.'

Samuel tilted his head, his lips twitching into a smile. 'It w-wasn't them I had in mind.'

'You mean Deborah and Patrick? I know. If it hadn't been for that UXB going off—'

He pulled her into his arms. 'I d-don't mean any of them, Mrs Atkinson.'

'Is that so, Mr Atkinson?' she answered saucily. 'In that case, I can't imagine *who* you're talking about!'

'Then I'd better remind you,' he replied, and he bent his head to kiss her.

It was here at last, the day they had waited for, dreading it and longing for it.

With the nation triumphant, relieved and proud at the news of victory at El Alamein, Betty and Samuel were once more deep inside their own little world, wrapped up in all their hopes for their future with little Bessie Beech – and their fear of the future without her.

Yesterday evening Betty had gone round to see Sally, to hug her and make sure she knew that she and Samuel hadn't forgotten about her and Andrew.

'You must be so happy and relieved that the battle has been won,' Betty had said, 'but at the same time you must be worried sick about whether Andrew is all right.'

Tears shone in Sally's hazel eyes, but she lifted her chin. 'I haven't had one of the dreaded telegrams, but even so I won't know for certain until I hear from him.'

'I know,' Betty had said, injecting all the sympathy she could into her tone. 'This is hard for you – so hard for everyone with a husband or son or boyfriend in the Eighth Army.'

She had badly wanted to say, 'He'll be all right, you'll see,' but she knew she mustn't. People so often gave that kind of assurance without any way of knowing if it was justified – and in many cases, it wasn't.

She had hugged Sally, and they had both laughed because Sally's baby bump was quite large now. The baby had kicked during the embrace, much to Betty's delight. She wanted Samuel and her to make a baby of their own, but first she wanted little Bessie Beech.

And now, today, at long last, they were going to find out if it was going to happen. Betty was too choked up with nerves to be able to speak as – yet again – they made their way to town and entered the magistrates' court.

On this occasion, they were shown to the room they had been in the first time – back when they had assumed they were about to be given permission to adopt. It seemed impossible now that the process had ever seemed straightforward. Looking back, Betty thought they must have been very naive. She felt she'd learned a lot in recent months – and it wasn't a good feeling.

The big table with two shield-backed chairs for the magistrates faced the room, while over to one side were two desks, side by side, for the clerks. But this time, instead of there being just a pair of chairs facing the magistrates' places, there was a total of five, two on one side, obviously for Samuel and Betty, and three on the other, for Mr and Mrs Prescott and their solicitor.

Even now, when it was far too late to change anything or make any sort of a difference, Betty found herself agonising over whether she and Samuel ought to have employed a solicitor to put forward their own case.

After they'd been sitting for a few minutes, the door opened again. Betty didn't want to look, because she knew it was going to be the Prescotts and she didn't want to be caught gawping. All the same, her gaze swung in that direction of its own accord – and there stood Dad and Grace.

With a small cry, Betty jumped up and ran to her father. He hugged her hard. When he let her go, she had to straighten her hat.

'I didn't know you were coming,' she said, a catch in her voice.

'On a day like this?' Dad said in a gruff voice. 'Of course we came. We know how much today means to you.'

He shook hands with Samuel before escorting Grace to the seats at the back of the room.

This time when she sat down, Betty's heart was singing. The door opened once more and this time she looked round, ready to say, 'Good morning' to the Prescotts in a civil voice.

In came Mrs Beaumont and Lorna. Betty and Samuel hurried to greet them.

'I hope you don't mind?' said Lorna. 'We felt we had to come.'

'We wanted you to have our support,' said Mrs Beaumont, squeezing Betty's hand. 'We don't expect we'll be allowed to remain once the hearing starts, because that will be private, but we wanted to be here all the same.'

'That's very k-kind of you,' Samuel said appreciatively.

'You know that Sally would have been here if she possibly could,' said Lorna.

'I know,' said Betty.

'Rosalind is keeping the depot open for me,' said Lorna.

The door opened again and this time it really was the Prescotts, followed by their legal man.

Mrs Prescott paused to look around. In a pretend-undertone that was clearly designed to be heard, she remarked, 'Well, this looks like quite the party. How... *inappropriate.*'

With a toss of her head, she moved towards the set of three seats and sat down.

'Don't leave unless you're asked to,' Betty whispered to

Lorna and Mrs Beaumont. 'Sit at the back and we'll see what happens.'

When the clock struck the half-hour, the door at the back of the room opened and the two magistrates walked in and headed for the shield-backed chairs. Mrs Ames took her place, but Mr Brent-Williams made a show of freezing with his hand on the back of his chair, his gaze aiming at the other end of the room.

'Who are these people?' he enquired in a lofty voice. 'Not members of the press, I hope?'

One of the clerks murmured something to him.

He breathed in through his nose. 'Friends and family? Of whom? The Atkinsons?' His gaze landed squarely on Samuel and Betty. 'This isn't a charabanc trip.' Lifting his chin and giving the distinct impression of looking down his nose even though he was looking straight ahead, he addressed Dad and Grace, Lorna and Mrs Beaumont. 'Your presence is not required. Wait outside if you must, but I do not want you in here.'

'Mr Brent-Williams, sir,' said Dad, 'I am Police Sergeant Hughes, Mrs Atkinson's father.' He and Betty exchanged a look, and he gave her an encouraging smile. 'My wife and I were allowed to sit in last time we came here.'

'But not *this* time, sir,' barked the magistrate. He offered no explanation, only a craggy-faced glare.

One of the clerks opened the door. Betty's cheeks flamed as the darling people who had come to support her and Samuel filed out.

Mr Brent-Williams dragged back his chair and sat down. He fussed about before finally settling and looking at the two couples in front of him.

Without preamble he said, 'I have taken into account all the evidence and made my decision, and Mrs Ames is in agreement with me.' He didn't so much as acknowledge her with a glance. 'Mr Atkinson and his wife are decent, hard-working people of good character. Mr Atkinson is a man of modest means, but I have no doubt he will do his best in the coming years to provide for his wife and any family they may have.'

This sounded promising... A tiny opening appeared in Betty's heart and hope dripped out.

'Mr Prescott is a gentleman of substantial means,' Mr Brent-Williams continued. 'He owns – owns, mark you, not rents – a four-bedroomed detached house in the Cheshire countryside, with gardens, a tennis court and an orchard, and with a splendid golf course at the other end of the village. Mr Prescott and his wife are in a position to offer their grandchild the very best of everything. They may be somewhat... ah, *mature* to take on a baby, but, as Mr Prescott has the wherewithal to provide a qualified nanny, I do not view that as a problem in and of itself. Mr Prescott has also assured me that the estrangement between himself and his wife, and their errant daughter, the mother of the baby known as Bessie Beech, is complete and permanent. In his care, the child would grow up to believe that both her parents are dead. As well as these considerations, there is the evidence given by Miss Brewster from the Welfare Department, who is an advocate of keeping children within their natural families.'

He stopped, making sure that all eyes were upon him. Betty felt as if her stomach had dropped through the floor.

'Taking all this into account,' said the magistrate, 'I have decided to award the care and upbringing of the child known as Bessie Beech to her grandparents, Mr and Mrs Aldwyn Prescott.'

'*No!*' A great gasp burned Betty's throat.

Beside her, there was a loud scrape of chair-legs and, through a blur of distress, she saw Samuel had risen to his feet.

'Sir, I *must* protest—'

'Kindly resume your seat, Mr Atkinson,' Mr Brent-Williams ordered.

'I w-will not, sir, until I have s-said my piece – said what is in my heart. Yes, I am a man of modest means and I c-can't promise any child of mine a private education or a nanny or a tennis c-court, but I have a w-wonderful, beautiful, loving wife, who w-will dedicate herself to the baby in a w-way that no nanny, no matter how *professional*, can possibly reproduce.'

'No one is suggesting—' the magistrate began.

'Let him speak,' said Mrs Ames, leaning forward, elbows on the table.

'D-does it matter that our piano is an upright instead of a grand?' Samuel asked, his voice full of emotion. 'D-does it matter that our children w-will be taken to Chorlton Park to play ball instead of having their own tennis court? We are young and healthy and can be parents to little Bessie Beech in a w-way you clearly believe the Prescotts, being older, c-cannot.'

'Mr Atkinson—' began Mr Brent-Williams testily.

'Please go on, Mr Atkinson,' Mrs Ames said, with a vexed glance sideways at her colleague.

'Let me tell you another w-way in which we w-would make more appropriate parents,' said Samuel. 'Because we would never, no matter w-what the cir-cirumstances, *never* disown a child of ours. We w-would love and s-support him or her no matter what, and w-we would do everything in our power to put them back on the right path if s-something bad happened that made them stray from c-correct behaviour. Mr and Mrs Prescott might have money and a gracious home and c-comfortable circumstances. They might have a sw-swimming pool filled with milk from Jersey cows for all I know. But they c-cannot, they *cannot* promise never to turn their backs on little Bessie Beech – because they have already turned their backs on her mother.'

'She's a *fallen woman*!' Mrs Prescott declared.

'She's your *daughter*!' Samuel retorted.

'Well said!' piped up the lady magistrate.

'Mrs Ames!' thundered Mr Brent-Williams. 'Kindly know your place.'

Her chin jerked back, and her mouth dropped open. She swivelled in her chair to face him. 'Know my place?' she demanded. 'Know my *place*?'

'Now, see here, my good woman—'

'No, *you* see here, Mr Brent-Williams. I've read every single document that pertains to this matter, and I've listened to all the evidence. Now that I've heard Mr Atkinson speak so eloquently—'

'*Eloquently?*' scoffed Mr Brent-Williams. 'The man has a *stammer*, for crying out loud!'

'The man has a *sound heart*,' she retorted, 'and if Bessie Beech's mother hadn't come blundering in when she did, you would never have questioned the Atkinsons' suitability.'

'I am the senior magistrate in this matter,' stated Mr Brent-Williams. 'You are here, at my invitation, purely because you are a woman.'

'And as a *woman*, I offer it as my opinion that Mr and Mrs Atkinson are the better prospective parents. And as a *magistrate*, I give you notice that I will contest your decision if I have to.'

'*Contest* it? You've agreed with me from day one.'

'I've been looked down on and bulldozed, Mr Brent-Williams, and I've had enough. I would remind you that Warden Everett and Mrs Fitch are both perfectly happy to hand over the child to the Atkinsons. They visit the child regularly at the Foundling Hospital.' Mrs Ames's head snapped round and she eyed the Prescotts. 'Tell me, Mr and Mrs Prescott, have you visited Bessie Beech?'

'Of course we have,' Mrs Prescott said, looking offended.

'How many times?' Mrs Ames fired back at her.

'Well... once or twice. The Foundling Hospital is not somewhere we wish to go to.'

'We *love* going there,' Betty couldn't resist saying, 'because it's where little Bessie Beech is, but at the same time it hurts us to think of her having to live there. All we want is to take her back home with us.'

Mrs Prescott stuck her nose in the air, not looking at Betty. 'As do we.'

Mr Prescott surged to his feet. '*We're* the best people to be in charge of that child, and I'll tell you why. Because we won't let her grow up to be like her mother, that's why. I spared the rod with her, and I shan't make that mistake a second time. There will be proper discipline right from the start. She'll learn what's what, believe you me.'

After all those loud voices, Samuel's tone was quiet and measured. He made no attempt to drag attention to himself, yet somehow that made his words all the more compelling.

'Little Bessie Beech is a real live person, not a s-second chance for Mr Prescott to refine his discipline techniques. Over the weeks, a lot has been s-said about the child inheriting its mother's morals and patterns of behaviour, but I c-can't believe it happens that way. I think a child absorbs its morals and behaviour from the parents who bring it up, and I'll tell you this. There is no better person to be the mother of little Bessie Beech than my w-wife. From her, Bessie Beech would learn to be k-kind, polite, loving, good-humoured, helpful, honest and eager to please, and this w-would happen simply by being in my wife's presence and learning f-from example. And there w-would be no need at all for *learning what's what.*'

After this, there was a long silence. Betty drew in a deep, satisfied breath that filled her lungs with pride. There was no man better than her Samuel, no man kinder or more generous or considerate. He might not be in tip-top physical condition and able to fight for his country, but he was her hero in every way that mattered, and she was the luckiest girl in the world.

Mrs Ames pinned down Mr Brent-Williams with her eyes,

though her tone was conciliatory. 'May I remind you – *again* – that, before the mother muddied the waters, you were content for the Atkinsons to adopt?'

Mr Brent-Williams made a show of shooting out his cuff and examining his wristwatch. His shoulders rose and fell as he sighed.

'This matter has already taken up more time than it ought. Very well, Mrs Ames. I amend the original order—'

'You can't do that!' Mr Prescott bellowed.

'On the contrary, I can, and I have,' the magistrate replied. 'The child known as Bessie Beech is to be handed over to Mr and Mrs Samuel Atkinson for them to adopt. So ordered.'

He shoved back his chair and stalked out of the room, leaving Betty and Samuel staring at one another. Tears sparkled behind Samuel's glasses and Betty felt dampness on her cheeks. They hugged one another, then they left the room, half-stumbling in their eagerness, to share their news with their well-wishers in the corridor.

Four pairs of eyes swung anxiously in their direction as they stepped into the corridor. The air vibrated with tension so potent that Betty felt it hit her in the face. Immediately wanting to allay everyone's fears, she exclaimed in a trembling voice, 'She's ours! Mr Brent-Williams says she's ours!'

The atmosphere changed instantly. The tension vanished, replaced by a moment of profound stillness. Mrs Beaumont clapped her hand over her mouth and Lorna pressed hers to her heart, her green eyes shining with tears, before laughter spurted from her lips.

Dad's face, initially rigid with apprehension, crumpled into an expression of gratitude and joy. He caught Betty to him and hugged her. She could tell from the way his breath hitched that he was struggling not to give in to tears.

'Oh, Betty,' he mumbled. 'Oh, Betty, I'm so pleased for you. She's a very lucky little girl to have you and Samuel.'

'Thank you... *thank you*,' Betty whispered back. Her darling dad's approval was the cherry on the cake. His initial reservations had hurt her deeply, but now he was completely on her side and that meant the world to her. 'You'll be a wonderful grandfather,' she told him, drawing out of his embrace slightly so as to look up into his brown eyes, which swam with tears all over again.

He delved in his jacket pocket, produced a handkerchief and honked into it before clearing his throat and trying to look as if he'd never shed a tear in his life.

Betty handed him over to Samuel and the two men pumped one another's hands while clapping each other heartily on the shoulder. Betty gazed lovingly at the two special men in her life, but only for a few moments, because then Lorna and Mrs Beaumont both tried to embrace her at the same time.

Betty laughed and pulled them to her, all three of them weeping freely.

'Thank you for being here,' Betty managed to say.

'We wanted to support you if you had bad news,' Lorna told her, 'but of course what we hoped for was to be here to celebrate the good news.'

'The *best* possible news,' Mrs Beaumont added. 'Congratulations, Betty. This is the start of a new life for you.'

'It's little Bessie Beech who deserves to be congratulated,' broke in a new voice – Grace's – and the three women split apart and turned to her. 'She's the one who's going to benefit from this, by becoming Betty and Samuel's little girl – and a very lucky little girl she's going to be.'

'Thank you, Grace,' Betty said warmly. 'And thank you for being here.'

'It meant a lot to your dad to be here today,' Grace replied. After a pause she added, 'It means a lot to me too. You were gracious enough to let me be your mother of the bride, and I hope you'll let me be a grandmother as well.'

'Of course we will!' Betty exclaimed. 'We'd never exclude you. It would never occur to us.'

Grace put her arms gently round Betty and kissed her cheek. 'You're a good girl, Betty. You're all heart.'

Grace let go as Samuel appeared at Betty's side and slipped his arm round her. Betty leaned against him, filled with happiness.

'You were wonderful in there, Samuel,' she told him admiringly. 'You spoke so well and knew exactly the right things to say. I was so proud.' To Grace she added, 'I wish you could have heard him. Then you'd be in no doubt as to how much he wants to be little Bessie Beech's father.'

For once in her life, Grace had the decency to blush. 'It was wrong of me to say the adoption was all your idea, Betty. I can see that now – and I believe the two of you will be the best possible parents. I think I could learn a thing or two from you about being a mum... if you'll let me.'

Betty looked frankly at her stepmother, the woman her darling mum had always had reservations about. Betty had shared those reservations, and still did, but it was time to put them behind her once and for all.

She and her lovely Samuel were about to become a family of three with little Bessie Beech. It was essential that everything was as perfect for her as they could possibly make it, and that included having no coolness whatsoever within the wider family.

Betty smiled at Grace. 'There's more than enough love to go round.'

THIRTY-EIGHT

That evening after work, as Lorna went into town to meet Lady Broughton off the train, she still felt emotional about the happy outcome of the adoption case.

As well as being glad and grateful on behalf of her friends, she also felt a surge of protective love for her own baby, and vowed to provide him or her with the best life she possibly could. She knew that the temptation to share her special news with the mother-in-law she admired and valued so highly would be great, but she was determined not to breathe a word to anybody until she had told George.

Lady Broughton was a good-looking woman with deep-blue eyes and once-dark hair now liberally threaded through with silver. There was elegance and dignity in every line of her body. She and Lorna had had a very rocky start, to say the least. In her ladyship's eyes, Lorna's father had been a gold-digger, determined to push his daughter into a highly advantageous marriage complete with a title in the offing. It wasn't until Lorna had proved herself without even realising she was doing any such thing that things had changed and Lady Broughton had come to see her for the person she truly was. Since then, they had become staunch allies.

After George had suggested that Lorna should confide in his mother about the Mrs Lockwood problem, things had happened quickly.

'Hm. Leave it with me,' Lady Broughton had said when Lorna had rung her from a public telephone box, 'and I'll think about it.'

Now, without Lorna having any clue as to what her mother-in-law had in mind to solve the problem, her ladyship had come across the Pennines for a couple of days.

She had booked a suite at the Claremont, where the Broughtons always stayed, and she and Lorna enjoyed a meal together in the hotel's dining room, which was on the first floor with a balcony overlooking the ballroom. They both had soup of the day, which was spinach. Lorna followed hers with a fillet of pork – in reality sausage meat mixed with mashed potato – while Lady Broughton asked for vegetable casserole.

'I'm sure you would far rather have had a visit from George,' said her ladyship, 'but I'm afraid you'll have to make do with me – on your wedding anniversary weekend too.'

'I can't believe it's been a whole year,' said Lorna.

'I remember you sneaking out and breaking all the rules by seeing George before the wedding,' Lady Broughton said in a mock-severe voice.

Lorna laughed. 'I simply couldn't wait another moment to see him!' She shivered. 'Those weeks while he was away – the thought of him making the Atlantic crossing.' Her voice dropped to a whisper as she added, 'I was so relieved and grateful when he came home safely.'

'As were we all,' Lady Broughton concurred. 'And your actual anniversary is on Sunday, when the church bells will peal out to celebrate the victory at El Alamein. I feel quite emotional just thinking of it. This will be the first time the church bells have been permitted to ring out since the war began.'

Lorna nodded. 'It's going to be very special. The church bells were silenced because ringing them was going to be the signal we were being invaded. Now they're going to ring because of victory in an important battle that has changed things for the Allies in North Africa.'

They ate in silence for a short time, each thinking her own thoughts, then they started chatting again. Lorna told Lady Broughton all about Betty and Samuel's joy earlier that day when they had, after months of waiting and hoping and fearing, finally received permission to become the parents of little Bessie Beech.

'They're going to collect her from the Foundling Hospital tomorrow,' said Lorna. 'It was marvellous to see them so happy after the hearing. Betty was laughing and crying at the same time. She's wanted this ever since she found the baby all the way back at the beginning of the year.'

'I'm pleased they've had good news,' said Lady Broughton. 'I assume Betty will carry on with her war work?'

'Certainly, for the time being,' said Lorna, 'but I wouldn't be surprised if she packs it in and becomes a childminder. I'd understand if she wants to do that, but it would still be a great shame. I'd miss her at the depot.'

Lady Broughton lifted one eyebrow. 'You shan't be there to miss her. Once your other friend...'

'Sally.'

'Once Sally has had her baby, she'll be back at the depot running things, and you'll be back in London... which brings me very nicely to why I'm here this weekend.'

'I only wanted advice when I rang you,' Lorna put in. 'I never imagined you would actually come here.'

Lady Broughton gave her a wicked smile. 'All part of the

plan, my dear Lorna. It's your Saturday to work at the depot – is that correct?'

'Yes,' Lorna confirmed.

'Good. And you've asked Mrs Lockwood to come along and meet me and show me round?'

Lorna nodded. 'She doesn't know you've been there before.'

'It wouldn't matter if she did,' Lady Broughton answered. 'She'll be flattered that I have asked for her by name. People generally are flattered to be singled out by a person with a title – as you will find out for yourself one day.'

'Don't say that!' Lorna begged her. 'I don't want to think of you and Sir Jolyon not being here any more.'

'That's just as well,' her mother-in-law replied in a wry voice, 'as we intend to be around for a long time to come.'

'What exactly do you intend to do with Mrs Lockwood?' Lorna asked, intrigued.

'Why, get her out of your hair, of course,' Lady Broughton replied serenely, 'and in so doing get her out of your friend Sally's hair too, so that you can hand the depot back to her just the way she wants it to be.'

'If you can make that happen,' said Lorna, 'I'll admire you for ever.'

Her ladyship chuckled. 'Admiration is very nice, my dear Lorna, but I'd prefer to have your *friendship*.'

'You've already got that,' Lorna answered truthfully. 'And the admiration, for that matter.'

Lady Broughton nodded, looking satisfied. 'Shall I tell you what I look forward to once this war is finally over? You and I living together at Platt House. Because I think we'll make a *formidable* team.'

'What a day it's going to be!' Mrs Beaumont said on Saturday morning as she served the breakfast, 'with Samuel and Betty bringing home little Bessie Beech. *Fancy!* Who would have thought, when Betty found that baby at the depot, that she'd end up becoming her *mother?*'

Sally laughed. 'It didn't take me long to see which way the wind was blowing. She was smitten from the start!'

'Fortunately, it wasn't long before Samuel was too,' Deborah added. 'I'm surprised they're being allowed to take little Bessie Beech home so quickly. I would have expected them to have to wait for the formal adoption to go through.'

'It's because they've been made to wait such a long time already,' said Lorna, 'through no fault of their own.'

She headed off to work as usual. Her breath fogged in the chilly air. There had been a frost last night and sparkling crystals coated the ground, shimmering in the milky sunlight. Halfway through the morning, just after she had finished sorting through the daily sacks, Mrs Lockwood arrived. She always carried herself well and looked smart, but somehow today she managed to stand up even straighter and appear even more polished.

Lady Broughton walked through the gates a few minutes later and Lorna performed the introductions.

'Mrs Lockwood,' said her ladyship, 'I've heard so much about you and your dedication to your war work here in the salvage depot. Would you kindly show me round? I should appreciate hearing the views of an expert.'

Lorna gave a small gasp. Would Mrs Lockwood fall for that? But evidently she did, and the two women disappeared. Lorna got on with her work, wanting to look busy when they returned.

When the tour was at an end, Lady Broughton said to Lorna, 'Mrs Lockwood has invited me to her house for a bite to eat with her and Mr Lockwood. So very good of her. We have so much to discuss. I'll see you later on, Lorna dear.'

And off they went, leaving Lorna staring after them. As

they walked through the gates onto Beech Road, Lady Broughton glanced back and winked, actually *winked*!

Lorna counted the minutes until her mother-in-law returned. What could be happening? What precisely was the 'so much' the two ladies had to talk about?

At last Lady Broughton came back. Seeing she was on her own, Lorna flew to her.

'What happened?' she asked.

'Let's go into your office,' said Lady Broughton. 'This isn't something to be discussed outside.'

Lorna led the way, opening the doors. When they were both seated, Lady Broughton smiled at her.

'I believe I have solved your problem.'

'How?' Lorna exclaimed.

'It was the voluntary work you did in London that gave me the idea.'

Lorna nodded, intrigued but still none the wiser. She remembered her duties in Grosvenor Crescent, working for the Red Cross, liaising with the Invalid Children's Aid Association in order to find opportunities for sickly and physically incapacitated children to be evacuated. It had involved a great deal of decision-making and letter-writing, not to mention patience, resolve and knowledge of red tape.

'After you telephoned me seeking assistance,' Lady Broughton went on, 'I started making enquiries. I have been able to find a suitable voluntary position for your Mrs Lockwood. I told her how easily I could see her in the post, making a splendid job of it, and I *almost* offered it to her – but then I pulled back and said that, of course, it would take up so much of her time, and she might prefer to stick with the salvage depot, where she has done, and continues to do, such valuable work.'

'And?' Lorna asked breathlessly.

'She practically snatched my hand off,' Lady Broughton replied. 'She is going to work for the Invalid Children's Aid

Association and she will, with deep regret, give up her important work at Chorlton Salvage Depot.'

Lorna burst out laughing. 'Oh, that's *marvellous*! Thank you, thank you, thank you. And thank you on Sally's behalf as well. I can't wait to go home and tell her.'

'Run along to Star House now,' said Lady Broughton. 'I can wait here for a while. I'm sure things will tick over in your absence.'

Lorna planted a kiss on her cheek. 'Thank you,' she said again and dashed off, not bothering to fetch her coat.

She was nearly home when she realised she hadn't brought her key. She rang the bell, and beamed at Mrs Beaumont when she answered it.

Lorna darted inside. 'I've only got five minutes. I've come to see Sally.'

'I'm afraid she's otherwise engaged,' said Mrs Beaumont. 'She's gone into labour.'

THIRTY-NINE

Deborah had spent Saturday afternoon at MacFadyen's on WVS duty. She had loved working for the WVS right from her very first shift in the spring of last year, and she still loved it.

The wide variety of tasks appealed to her, and she enjoyed the company and the strong sense of women working together to get things done. She hadn't realised before she started that a great deal of what the WVS tackled was welfare work. How would the government manage without them? How would the *country* manage without them?

She smiled to herself now, as she walked home along Beech Road after her shift. She was due to go out with Patrick this evening and she could hardly wait. After her lonely weeks without him, she couldn't think of anything better than having him back in her life once more.

She had barely set her hand on the garden gate when the front door opened and Lorna came out, wrapped up warmly in her plum-coloured coat and brimless fur hat.

'Off out?' Deborah asked, then she remembered. 'You're seeing Lady Broughton again this evening, aren't you?'

'I am,' said Lorna, 'but that isn't why I'm setting off now. I'm going to Withington first to see Sally's parents.'

Deborah experienced a little thrill of alarm. 'Why?'

Lorna laughed. 'To tell them their grandchild is in the process of making an unexpectedly early appearance.'

Deborah gasped. '*Never!*'

'The midwife has been here, but she's gone again. Everything is in the early stages, apparently, and she's going to come back later.'

'*Blimey,*' said Deborah. Her pulse had picked up speed. 'It's all happening today. Betty and Samuel will have brought little Bessie Beech home by this time, and now Sally's baby is coming. *Two* babies in one day!'

'I must dash,' said Lorna. 'But do go in and see Sally.'

'Is that allowed?' Deborah asked.

Lorna grinned. 'Nothing scary is going on at the moment. She's in bed. Toodle-oo!'

She hurried on her way, leaving Deborah feeling winded. Then excitement poured through her and she went indoors, threw off her outdoor clobber and rushed up the stairs to the second floor to see her friend.

'Crikey,' Deborah said as she walked in through the open doorway to find Sally in bed and Mrs Beaumont sitting on a chair beside her.

'I know,' said Sally. 'It's not how I thought I'd be spending Saturday night.'

'The midwife says she has delivered babies that are more premature than this,' said Mrs Beaumont, 'and all has gone well.'

'Is there anything I can do?' Deborah asked.

'No, thank you, dear,' said Mrs Beaumont. 'I've got everything ready. You're going out with Patrick this evening, aren't you?'

'I feel I ought to stay here,' Deborah said with an anxious glance at her friend.

'No,' Sally answered at once. 'Go out. Enjoy yourself. I mean it. Nothing much is going to happen for ages yet.'

'First babies take a long time,' Mrs Beaumont added, standing up. 'Patrick will be along soon, so you'd better go and get ready, Deborah. Would you like a cup of tea, Sally?'

'Yes, please,' said Sally.

A cup of tea? How casual that sounded! It didn't fit in at all with Deborah's admittedly vague ideas of childbirth.

She went to get changed. Her room was downstairs from Sally's double room. From the hanging-cupboard she took a dark-red dress with a V-neck and long sleeves. She had been lucky enough to get it from the WVS clothing exchange and Mrs Beaumont had helped her to alter it so that it was a perfect fit.

She hung it from the front of the cupboard door and stood for a moment admiring it before she went to the bathroom to freshen up.

When she was ready, she popped in to say goodbye to Sally.

'Are you sure you don't need me to stay? I'll sit downstairs and wait for as long as it takes, if you want me to.'

Sally shook her head. 'Go and have a lovely time. You and Patrick have got a lot of catching up to do.'

Deborah gave her friend a kiss and skipped downstairs, eager now for Patrick to arrive. Would there be a new baby in the house when she returned? What a lovely thought!

When Patrick rang the doorbell, she opened the door a crack for him to slip inside without breaking the blackout. She already had her hat on. When she turned her back for him to help her on with her coat, she told him about Sally's baby being on its way.

'But you're still happy to come out tonight?' Patrick asked. 'If you'd prefer to stay here, I'd understand.'

'That could be useful,' Deborah said, deadpan. 'Policemen are supposed to be able to deliver babies, aren't they?'

'I've never been called upon to do it, and I don't fancy using your best friend as my guinea pig,' Patrick retorted with a grin.

They left the house. It was a cold evening with clouds scudding across the skies. Patrick had told Deborah he was taking her to a small restaurant near Chorlton station, and it promised to be a chilly walk.

She was surprised to see a taxi at the kerb.

'Is that for us?' she asked.

'I don't want you getting cold,' he answered.

But when the taxi reached the big crossroads where it should have turned right to head towards the station, it carried straight on instead.

Deborah was about to say something, but Patrick shushed her.

'I asked him to take the scenic route.'

She raised her eyebrows. 'Scenic? In the *blackout*?'

It didn't take her long to realise they were on their way to the city centre, but Patrick smilingly refused to divulge their destination no matter how she tried to tease it out of him. She started to feel excited.

The taxi pulled up outside a large blacked-out building. Deborah could hardly believe it. Patrick had brought her to the Claremont Hotel.

When they were inside, she turned to him in delight. 'There I was, expecting to go to the little place on Wilbraham Road – and here we are in the Claremont.'

'I wanted it to be a surprise.'

'It's certainly that.'

He helped her off with her coat and handed it in at the cloakroom, where the cloakroom girl gave him a ticket. Then he escorted Deborah up the gracefully curving staircase to the dining room, where he had booked a table. Deborah's heart pitter-pattered at the thought that he had taken this trouble to please her.

'Starter and main course?' Deborah suggested, knowing it was what Patrick would prefer.

'Main and pud,' he replied. 'I can't bring you here and expect you *not* to want the chocolate whip.'

He gave their orders to the waiter, and they chatted about this and that until his mock duck and Deborah's vegetable goulash were brought to the table.

'I'm looking forward to hearing all the church bells tomorrow,' said Deborah. 'There's going to be a special programme on the wireless. The sound of the bells is going to be broadcast all over the world.'

'It shows how significant the El Alamein victory is for us,' said Patrick. 'Did you hear Mr Churchill's speech? He called it "not the beginning of the end, but possibly the end of the beginning". He wouldn't say anything he didn't mean. He wouldn't mislead us. That shows we have hope at last, *real* hope of eventual victory.'

Their main courses arrived. Deborah's goulash was delicious, thanks to its blend of herbs. Patrick had mock duck, made from sausage meat, leeks, sage and mash.

'Are you looking forward to your chocolate whip?' he teased. 'Should I order one as well so you can have both?'

When the meal was over, Deborah said, 'This has been a wonderful treat. Thank you.'

'My pleasure,' he told her. 'And... there's something more.'

'Dancing?' she asked at once.

'Maybe later, if you want to, but that's not what I meant.'

'What did you mean, then?' Deborah asked, feeling happy and relaxed. 'Another chocolate whip to take home?'

'Something better than that, I hope.'

'Better than a chocolate whip?' Deborah teased. 'Is there any such thing?'

'Let's find out, shall we?'

Before she had time to realise what was going on, Patrick had removed something from his pocket, and, leaving his seat, he dropped to one knee in front of her. Above the sound of her own gasp, Deborah was vaguely aware of quiet exclamations of delight from other diners as a ripple of interest ran around the room.

Looking nervous but resolute, Patrick opened the box and held it out for her to see. The sight of a sparkling blue stone was enough to bring forth another gasp from Deborah.

'Deborah, you are the most special girl in the world. I was so happy when you came into my life and then, when I lost you, I lost the most important part of myself. When you came back to me, my life began all over again, and I want us to be together for always. Will you marry me?'

'Yes,' Deborah whispered, and then, more loudly, '*Yes!*'

She held out her left hand and he slid the ring into place.

'A sapphire,' he murmured. 'It had to be a sapphire to go with your beautiful blue eyes.'

Deborah gazed at her ring, then lifted her eyes to meet Patrick's. She leaned forward to kiss him as the other diners burst into applause.

FORTY
SUNDAY, 15 NOVEMBER

Sally's little girl was born in her bedroom in Star House on Sunday, a month early, while the church bells rang to celebrate the important victory at El Alamein.

'Your daddy fought there,' Sally whispered, bending her face to drop a kiss on her daughter's head, 'and now they're ringing the church bells for him, and all the other brave soldiers.'

Fear clutched painfully at her heart. Had Andrew survived? Was he safe? Uninjured? How long would it be before she knew? He *had* to come home. Being a father meant he was needed here even more.

Seated beside the bed, Sally's mother made a slight movement. Sally was aware of it and knew Mum was dying to hold the baby again, but she couldn't bear to let go of her. The birth had been arduous, and Mum had enjoyed lots of cuddles with her brand-new granddaughter while an exhausted Sally had lain flaked out. But she was stronger now, and instinct, wonderment and overwhelming love made her want to keep her baby safe in her arms for ever.

'You'll have to choose a name now,' said Mum.

Although Sally had, naturally, thought about names during her pregnancy, and she and Andrew had done their best to hold a discussion by letter, she had never talked about names to anyone else. It had been another example of not wanting to jinx things.

And the possible names from pregnancy were beside the point now, in any case.

'Bella,' she said, tearing her gaze away from her baby to smile mistily at her mother, 'because she was born while the church bells rang for El Alamein. Short for Isabella, but always to be known as Bella.'

'Isabella Henshaw,' Mum said emotionally. 'That's *lovely*.'

'Isabella Sarah,' Sally added.

There was a light tap on the door at the same moment as it opened, and Andrew's mother came hurrying in. Sally's dad had gone over to Seymour Grove to share the news and bring her here to meet the new member of the Henshaw family.

'Come and see Isabella Sarah,' said Sally.

Mrs Henshaw – strong, austere-looking Mrs Henshaw – stopped dead and pressed her fingers to her mouth.

'Oh my goodness! Oh my goodness!'

Then she hurried forward, her features melting into an expression of adoration as she gazed at her little granddaughter.

'Oh, Sally,' she breathed, a crack in her voice. 'Thank you. Thank you for having her. I wish Andrew could be here.' And she burst into tears.

Sally's mum hastened to comfort her. By nature, she was very much a keep-your-hands-to-yourself sort of person, but today she put her arms round Mrs Henshaw and patted her gently on the back.

'There now, Mrs Henshaw,' she murmured. 'There now.'

Mrs Henshaw extricated herself and performed a hasty

mopping-up operation. 'I mustn't upset the baby. Let me look at her. Isabella Sarah Henshaw.'

'To be known as Bella,' Sally told her.

'Bella – Bella Henshaw. It has a nice ring to it.'

'I'm pleased you like it,' said Sally.

'Did Andrew choose it?' her mother-in-law asked.

'No,' Mum said at once. 'Sally did.'

'It's because she came into the world while the church bells were ringing for El Alamein,' Sally explained.

Mrs Henshaw nodded. 'The battle where Andrew fought.'

'It feels appropriate,' said Sally. 'As soon as the idea came to me, I knew she couldn't possibly have any other name.'

Mrs Henshaw brushed a gentle finger across the baby's soft cheek. 'Andrew will love it – and he'll love her. He'll be so proud. I wish he could be here now to see her, to see the two of you.'

'One day.' Sally spoke lightly but her heart was full to bursting. 'One day.'

'She's beautiful,' said Deborah, gazing at Bella. Then she glanced at Sally, her lips twitching. 'Even more beautiful than my engagement ring, and that's saying something.'

Sally widened her eyes, turning herself into the picture of innocence. 'Oh, you're engaged? I must have missed that, though, in fairness, I was busy having a baby at the time.'

'That's no excuse!' Deborah teased, straight-faced.

'It's the best I can offer. So – you're getting hitched? Fancy that! I assume the lucky man is Patrick?'

'You assume correctly,' said Deborah.

'Seriously,' said Sally, 'I do think it's *wonderful*.' She couldn't be happier for her friend. 'Tell me again.'

'I've already told you three times,' said Deborah.

'So what?' Sally replied, laughing. 'Who's counting? There's no such thing as too many times when it comes to reliving a romantic proposal.'

To Sally's delight, Deborah blushed.

'It *was* romantic,' she agreed, and a happy little sigh escaped her.

'Especially when everyone clapped,' Sally suggested.

'To be honest, I barely noticed that bit. I was too busy being happier than I've ever been in my whole life.'

Sally smiled warmly at her lifelong friend. 'I'm so glad that you and Patrick found your way back to one another, and it makes it even more special that your getting engaged coincides with Bella being born.'

'And it's Lorna and George's first wedding anniversary today,' Deborah added.

'I want everybody to be happy,' said Sally. Her sense of happiness and fulfilment after the birth had only been increased by Deborah's news.

'Well, you can certainly put Patrick and me on your happy list,' Deborah said with a smile.

'Did you really have no idea what was coming?' Sally asked.

'Not a clue,' Deborah replied.

'Which made it all the more romantic,' Sally confirmed. 'Can I see the ring again?'

Deborah grinned. 'Tell you what. I'll show you my ring and you can show me your baby.'

'Oh, that's a good idea,' Sally answered, playing along. 'Haven't you seen my little girl yet? Isn't she beautiful?'

'Such tiny fingers,' Deborah observed in the same wondering tone in which everyone so far had made this enchanting observation. 'And, yes, she is beautiful. I'm a very lucky auntie.'

'Bella is a very lucky niece,' Sally replied. 'She's got you and

Betty, Lorna and Louise, and Rosalind as well, I hope, though I don't know her as well as the rest of you.'

'Once she's set eyes on Bella,' Deborah said confidently, 'she'll be round here at Star House all the time. You wait and see. No one could resist your little Bella.'

Sally knew full well that all mothers probably thought that of their own babies, but all the same it struck her as the simple truth where her darling daughter was concerned.

Deborah laughed. 'Now we've got little Bella and little Bessie Beech. All those names beginning with B. Isn't it lovely?'

Yes, it was. Sally loved Betty dearly and valued the friendship that had grown between them and helped keep them both strong in wartime. She wanted her Bella and Betty's little Bessie Beech to grow up being great friends, chums for life – like herself and Deborah.

What could be better than that?

'Goodness me!' Betty exclaimed and burst out laughing. 'How *tiny* Bella is! I'd forgotten how small new babies are...'

'It takes you back, doesn't it?' Sally said. 'To that early morning in the depot and thinking you could hear a cat meowing.'

Old feelings squeezed Betty's heart. She and Samuel had been dragged from pillar to post emotionally these past ten months. Seeing baby Bella made her remember just how tiny and vulnerable little Bessie Beech had been when she had found her in the depot yard last March.

'Bella makes our baby seem very big and sturdy in comparison,' Betty told Sally. How wonderful it was to be able to say 'our baby' like that.

They were in the sitting room in Star House. Betty and Samuel had come to meet Bella on Sunday afternoon. Deborah was out with Patrick, telling her parents about their engagement – or maybe by this time they were on their way to Stretford to share their news with Patrick's family.

Louise was here and so was Mrs Beaumont. Lorna had gone into town to see Lady Broughton onto the train. Sally's parents and her mother-in-law had all been here earlier, but they had gone home just before Betty and Samuel had arrived. Although Betty was fond of Mr and Mrs White and Mrs Henshaw, privately she was glad they weren't here now, because she didn't want her own child to be overwhelmed by lots of new faces.

Her own child. *Their* own child. She was sitting up on Samuel's lap now. Betty had never seen a baby on a man's knee before, but Samuel was unselfconscious about showing his affection for his new daughter. Betty sighed softly. Life didn't get any better than this.

'I d-do like the name Bella,' said Samuel, 'and all the more because of the reason behind it.'

'Bessie and Bella,' Mrs Beaumont said complacently. 'They sound like sisters.'

'I hope they'll grow up to be as close as sisters,' said Sally.

'Actually,' Betty said, with a happy smile for her husband, 'we have some baby-name news for you. We're allowed to choose a new name for her when we adopt her formally, and she isn't going to be Bessie any more.'

'Oh.' Mrs Beaumont sounded disappointed. 'It's such a sweet name.'

'Yes, it is,' Betty said warmly, 'and I'm so glad you thought of it for her back in January, but Samuel and I thought long and hard about what we want to call her, and we've made our decision.'

'She's been little Bessie Beech for so long,' said Louise. 'It'll be strange getting used to her being something else. What have you chosen?'

'You're right about Bessie Beech having been her name for a

long time,' said Betty. 'Ten whole months, in fact.' She looked lovingly at Samuel and their daughter. 'Do you want to tell them or shall I?'

'You d-do it,' said Samuel.

'Bella,' said Betty, 'I'd like you to meet your new friend – *Bebe*.'

'Like Bebe Daniels the film star?' Mrs Beaumont asked.

'No – like Bessie Beech's initials,' Betty told her proudly. 'You're right, Louise. She's been Bessie Beech for ages – her whole life, in fact. Bebe just feels right.'

'Bebe Atkinson,' said Sally, sounding pleased. 'Is she having a middle name?'

'Elizabeth, after you?' Mrs Beaumont asked.

'Bebe Mary,' said Betty, a lump suddenly filling her throat, 'after my mother.'

'Oh, Betty, that's perfect,' said Sally. 'I know how much you miss her. That's a lovely thing to do.'

'Thank you,' Betty whispered. She hoped with all her heart that darling Mum was somewhere close by, watching over them all and approving. Betty made a silent vow to be the best, most devoted mother she could possibly be to Bebe – just like Mum had been to her.

'W-we want you to know w-what we're going to tell Bebe when she's older,' said Samuel. 'Apparently, plenty of adopted children never know that they're adopted, because their parents choose not to tell them, but w-we're going to tell Bebe.'

'We'll say that her mother was killed in an air raid and her father died in battle,' Betty continued. 'That's quite a common story to tell adopted children, apparently.'

'What about the grandparents?' Mrs Beaumont asked.

'At the point where the adoption becomes formal,' said Betty, 'Bebe ceases to have any connection to them. That's how it works with adoption.'

'Good,' said Mrs Beaumont. 'I remember you telling us after

the hearing what the grandfather had said behind closed doors about wanting to discipline Bebe. She's better off with him well and truly out of her life. And she couldn't have better parents than the two of you.'

'We'll be the very best parents we can possibly be,' said Betty. 'That's what Bebe deserves.'

FORTY-ONE

Deborah and Patrick caught the bus to Withington to give Deborah's mum and dad their news.

'I don't know if you're more excited about us getting engaged or Sally having a baby,' Patrick said with a smile, squeezing her hand as they sat side by side on the bus.

Deborah could hardly contain her smiles. *What a weekend!*

'Mum and Dad are going to be chuffed to bits about Sally's baby,' she said.

That made Patrick laugh. 'I thought you were going to say they're going to be chuffed about us.'

'They will be,' Deborah promised, 'but would you mind if I tell them about Sally first? She's always been like a second daughter to my mum.'

'If you like,' said Patrick. A slight frown said he was a bit befuddled by her wish, though he seemed willing enough to go along with it.

Deborah smiled ruefully. 'I'll be honest. If we announce our engagement first, I'm not sure I'll want to break off from that to talk about the baby, so I'd rather share the baby news first.' She chewed her lip. 'Does that make me sound rotten?'

'Not a bit,' said Patrick.

'Here's our stop,' said Deborah.

They stood up and moved along the aisle between the seats, ready to get off when the bus pulled in at the kerb. Patrick alighted first from the wooden platform. He turned and took Deborah's hand to help her down, a sweet gesture that she loved.

It was a chilly day, although it was excitement, not the temperature, that made Deborah set off at a brisk pace for her parents' house. She couldn't help beaming her head off when she saw folk she knew.

'In the next day or two,' she whispered to Patrick, 'when the news gets around about us, they'll realise why I looked so happy today.'

'You'd better get used to being this happy,' Patrick answered, 'because from now on it's going to be my job to make sure you're happy every single day.'

Elation coursed through Deborah's bloodstream. How lucky she was that everything had turned out well for her and Patrick.

'Do you mind if I take off my ring?' she asked. 'Mum has a sixth sense where engagement rings are concerned. I don't want her homing in on it before I'm ready for us to make our announcement.'

Patrick chuckled.

'What are you laughing at?' Deborah asked.

'I think I'm starting to get an idea of what our wedding preparations are going to be like,' he told her.

At the house, Dad let them in and called to Mum.

'Come and see who it is, Edith. Deborah and Patrick.'

Mum was surprised, but pleased as well, of course. She immediately decided that she knew why they'd come round.

'You're here because of El Alamein and the church bells,' she said, not asking but stating it as a fact. 'Everyone wants to be with family today. It's only natural on such a special occasion.'

'Actually, we're here to tell you about Sally,' said Deborah. 'She had her baby early this morning and, even though the due date wasn't until December, all's well.'

Mum gasped. 'What did she have?'

'A girl. Isabella Sarah.'

'Pretty name,' Dad commented.

'Yes, it is,' Deborah agreed. 'She's going to be known as Bella.'

'Bella Henshaw,' said Mum, trying it out. 'Any news on Andrew yet?'

'Not yet,' Deborah told her.

'No news is good news, as the saying goes,' Dad remarked. 'The most important thing is that there hasn't been a telegram. That's a good sign.'

'Yes, it is,' said Patrick.

'And how is Sally?' Mum asked.

'Tired but happy,' said Deborah, 'and Bella is adorable.'

'I've knitted a baby blanket for her,' said Mum. 'I'll take it round after Sally has had a few days to recover.' She smiled and her brown eyes shone. 'Mr and Mrs White must be beside themselves with joy!'

'And you came all the way over here to tell us,' said Dad.

'You make it sound like we had to cross a stormy sea,' Patrick joked.

Secretly Deborah slid her ring back on, before saying, 'We have another reason for coming.' Her heart thumped as she looked at Patrick – her *fiancé*! 'You tell them.'

Pushing back his shoulders, Patrick proudly announced, 'I asked Deborah to be my wife, and she said yes.'

Mum's mouth fell open and she slapped her hands to her cheeks. '*Deborah!*' she squealed and hugged Deborah, before pushing her away and snatching her hand to see the ring. 'How beautiful. It suits you. Is it a sapphire? When are you thinking of getting married?'

Deborah felt breathless. '*Mum!* Slow down. We only got engaged last night.'

'I want to hear all about it,' Mum insisted. 'But first let me go and put the kettle on. You can come and help, Deborah.'

They went into the kitchen and Mum shut the door. Anticipating wedding talk, Deborah smiled widely, filled with a mixture of excitement and well-being.

But, to her surprise, Mum said, 'I'm so sorry, Deborah.'

Deborah blinked. 'What for?'

'For Len Fordham. For trying to... *foist* you onto him.'

'Well, you were rather obvious about it,' Deborah said with a smile.

'You seemed so sure about never seeing Patrick again,' said Mum.

'I was sure – or I thought I was – but I was wrong,' Deborah replied. 'When Len Fordham came long, I tried to like him. I *wanted* to like him, but I just couldn't, not in that way.'

'Thank goodness Patrick came back, that's all I can say.'

'Dad told him to,' said Deborah.

'*Dad* did? What are you talking about?'

'He knew you were pushing me at Len, so he found out Patrick's address and wrote to him. Basically, he told Patrick that, if he wanted me back, it was time to stop playing silly beggars and do something about it. Or words to that effect.'

'*Dad* did?' Mum said again. The stunned look on her face made Deborah laugh.

'It looks like you aren't the only matchmaker in the family,' she teased.

'I can't believe Dad did something like that,' said Mum.

'It's a good job he did or heaven knows what might have happened,' Deborah replied.

'Would you have gone off with Len if Patrick hadn't seen sense?' Mum asked.

'No, I think I'd have ended up on my own,' Deborah

answered. 'I can't imagine ever feeling about anyone else the way I do about Patrick.'

Mum took her hands and looked into her eyes. 'That's good to know. I'm glad things have sorted themselves out. I always said what a perfect chap Patrick is. He's handsome and easy to get along with, and he obviously thinks the world of you. And he's in a good, steady job. He'll make a good provider for you and your children.'

'Steady on!' Deborah laughed. '*Children?* We aren't even married yet.'

'You don't want to wait too long,' said Mum. 'Couples aren't going in for long engagements these days, and who can blame them?'

'Well, I'm not going to race straight round to the registry office like Rod did.'

'It was the biggest disappointment of my life, not attending my own son's wedding,' said Mum, looking upset. 'You're having a proper wedding, my girl, do you hear? The best sort of do that can be had in wartime – that's what I want for you – and for me. I don't mind admitting I want it for me as well. I was *distraught* when Rod got in touch to say he'd got married, and we didn't even know he'd met a new girl.'

'It was a huge shock all round,' Deborah recalled. 'I'm going to have a proper wedding, like Sally.'

'No,' said Mum, 'not like Sally. She went to the registry office, and if that was what she wanted, then that's fine, but I want a church for you.'

'Good,' said Deborah, 'because that's what I want too. And I want to be able to give the guests plenty of notice of the date. I want Dulcie to be there.'

'And Rod,' Mum added.

'Obviously,' said Deborah. 'But won't it be wonderful to meet Dulcie at last?'

'Oh, it will,' Mum said emotionally, 'and what better occasion could there be for it?'

Deborah felt a fresh surge of joy. Imagine meeting Dulcie at last, the girl Rod had swept off her feet, the sister-in-law whose friendly letters and sound advice had made her seem like a real sister.

'Mrs Patrick Timms,' said Mum, leaning forward to kiss Deborah's cheek. 'Congratulations, my darling.'

FORTY-TWO

After seeing Lady Broughton off at the station, Lorna headed back to Star House, feeling pleased all over again at what her mother-in-law had done to help her. It seemed to have set the seal on their friendship.

But no matter how glad she was, she couldn't help being aware that today was her first wedding anniversary and she was spending it alone. Her wedding day had been so happy and romantic, perfect in every way. When she had moved to London to be with George, she hadn't pictured long months of separation; and it felt even harder now that she was keeping her special news to herself.

When she got back to Star House, she was delighted to find Betty and Samuel there with little Bessie Beech.

'Except that she isn't little Bessie Beech now,' said Betty. 'We're calling her Bebe. Bebe Mary.'

'Bebe Mary Atkinson,' said Lorna, smiling. 'That's charming!'

Betty beamed and her dimple popped. 'I'm glad you like it.'

'We've got babies Bella and Bebe,' said Lorna, 'and one of the mums is Betty.' She chuckled. 'All those Bs.'

'And Mrs Beaumont is an honorary grandmother,' said Samuel.

'*Oh*,' breathed the landlady, pressing a palm to her bosom.

'W-well, we've got to use up every B we can f-find, haven't we?' Samuel replied, not with his usual sweet smile, but with a fully-fledged grin. It did Lorna's heart good to see it.

'I'm sorry to drag everybody away from all this baby talk,' she said, 'but I've been sitting on some good news since Friday. You're going to be pleased about this, Sally.'

'How intriguing,' Sally said, gently rocking her baby.

'It's about the depot.' Lorna went on to explain how Lady Broughton had charmed the formidable Mrs Lockwood into accepting a different voluntary position. 'That means, when you come back to work, you'll be safe from Mrs Lockwood's ambitions and machinations for ever.'

'Sally, that sounds splendid,' Louise exclaimed.

'With bells on,' Betty added. 'I can't describe how awful Rosalind and I felt when Mrs Lockwood barged in and took over when Lorna was in London—'

'And I felt awful having to tell Sally afterwards,' Lorna added.

'But you've fixed the problem now,' said Mrs Beaumont, 'or rather Lady Broughton has.'

'Who cares who fixed it?' Louise said with a laugh. 'It's sorted out. That's what matters. Congratulations, Sally. Your depot really is going to be all yours.'

'Thanks, Lorna,' said Sally. 'To think of George's mother going to all that trouble. If you let me have the address, I'll drop her a line.'

'She'll appreciate that,' said Lorna, pleased, though she couldn't help thinking that Sally was less thrilled than she'd expected her to be. Mind you, she could hardly rip her gaze away from Bella, so it was understandable if the news about the depot hadn't quite sunk in yet.

The doorbell rang. Mrs Beaumont stood up and went to answer it. She returned with a big smile on her face.

'Look who's here!'

George.

He walked in, still in his overcoat, and with his hat in his hand. For a moment Lorna was too shocked to move, then, with a cry, she jumped up and hurried to him. She threw her arms round him and leaned against him. He smelled of tobacco and frosty air, and his coat was chilly to the touch.

Lorna's cheeks were damp as she lifted her face to her husband's. His grey-blue eyes were tender as he removed his gloves and gently knuckled away her tears.

'I hope those are happy tears!' he said.

'They're *ecstatic* tears,' she answered with a sniff.

'Take your coat off and warm yourself by the fire,' Mrs Beaumont invited him.

'I will, just for a minute, if you don't mind,' George said, jamming his gloves in his pockets and divesting himself of the coat. 'Or for as long as it takes my wife to pack an overnight bag. I've booked us a suite at the Claremont, darling. I'd have been here a lot sooner if the train hadn't had to give way to I don't know how many goods trains. I thought I'd never get here.'

'I'm sure it was worth all the inconvenience,' said Betty.

'Without a doubt,' George concurred. 'I wanted to give my beautiful wife a second honeymoon, no matter how brief it had to be.' He raised Lorna's hand to his lips and kissed it, his eyes on hers. 'You didn't honestly think I wouldn't move heaven and earth to be with you on our wedding anniversary, did you?'

Lorna sat in the back of the taxi, leaning against George, his arm round her.

'This is what they mean when they talk about a girl being

swept off her feet,' she said. 'You should have told me you were coming.'

'Ah, but didn't you like feeling swept off your feet?' George asked, amusement in his deep voice.

'Yes, I did,' Lorna said happily. She tilted her head to look at him and caught a whiff of his cologne. 'You're forgiven for not telling me. But you do realise it places you under an obligation to do something special on every other wedding anniversary, don't you?'

'You can count on it,' George promised.

As the motor pulled in at the kerb, he removed his arm from round her. He got out of the vehicle and walked round to her side to open the door, offering her his hand to help her out. The driver placed the two small suitcases on the pavement and George paid him. The appreciative tone in the driver's voice as he said, 'Thank you,' reminded Lorna that her husband was a generous tipper.

The doorman came down the steps to pick up their cases. Soon they were in the gracious foyer and George had signed them in. A porter took their luggage up to their suite. A coin changed hands, and the sitting room door closed softly.

Lorna barely had a chance to glance at the Adam-style fireplace, the armchairs arranged for conversation and the floor-length curtains of heavy velvet before she was in her husband's arms, being thoroughly kissed.

When the kiss ended, she giggled. 'Shouldn't we at least take our hats and coats off first?'

'Would it be ungentlemanly to say that I'd prefer to remove a lot more than that?'

'You can be as ungentlemanly as you like,' Lorna replied, 'but not until I've told you my news.'

'I've got news as well,' said George.

'You first,' said Lorna, not wanting anything to distract from her own news when she told it. Joy bubbled up inside her at the thought of telling him.

She turned her back so he could take her coat. There was no sofa in the room, so George chucked some cushions on the bed and they lay up against them, snuggled in one another's arms.

'What's your news?' Lorna asked.

George's broad chest rose and fell as he took a deep breath, and Lorna's head and shoulders moved with it.

'It's a matter of bad timing, I'm afraid, my love. The War Office needs a man to head up a new office in this neck of the woods, and it's going to be me.'

'You're coming up north? George, that's wonder—*oh*.' Delight drained out of her as she thought it through. 'You're coming north just as I'm about to go back down south.' She twisted her head to look at him with a feeling of urgency. 'Do I have to go back? My work in London was voluntary, and I could find a new voluntary position here, couldn't I?'

'It doesn't work that way,' said George. 'People don't get to choose these days. Listen, darling. Let's not dwell on it just now. Tell me your news.'

Lorna's heart expanded and she gave a breathy little laugh. 'I'm so glad you've come here today, George. Otherwise, I'd have had to tell you over the telephone, and it wouldn't have been the same. But you're here, and that's perfect. Darling, you're going to be a *father*.'

There was a moment of profound silence, then George moved. Still holding her close, he shifted so that he was leaning over her, looking in her face.

'Are you sure?' he asked.

She nodded. 'I've had a couple of appointments at the doctor's. I told Betty and Rosalind I had to go to the Town Hall, and I sneaked off. It's all thanks to that break I had in London with you.'

'That was August,' said George, and Lorna could tell he was working out the months, which made her laugh.

'Next May,' she told him. 'A springtime baby.'

George clasped her tightly to him. When his embrace relaxed, there were tears in his eyes.

'I hope it's a girl,' he announced.

'Aren't you supposed to want a boy to inherit the title one day?'

'We can get round to him another time. For starters, I'd like a girl with dark-brown hair and exquisite green eyes – just like her mother.'

'I don't mind whether we have a girl or a boy,' said Lorna, 'but I do want dark hair and grey-blue eyes, like the father.'

'We're agreed on the dark hair, at any rate,' said George. He kissed her lingeringly. 'You couldn't have given me a better anniversary gift. Thank you, my darling.'

'Happy anniversary, Mr Broughton,' Lorna whispered.

'Here's to lots more of them,' he replied.

'Are you talking about anniversaries or children?'

'Both,' said George, and kissed her.

FORTY-THREE

Sally was thrilled when Lorna announced her pregnancy at Star House. 'Many, many congratulations!' she cried, hugging her friend. 'This makes three of us – you, me and Betty.'

'It's another little friend for Bella and Bebe,' said Mrs Beaumont.

Lorna laughed. 'Well, that's what George and I had in mind, of course! After Betty, Sally and I are such friends, we thought we ought to make it a trio for the next generation as well.'

'Lots more salvage girls to add to my collection,' Mrs Beaumont said with a chuckle, 'even if Lorna's child will grow up a long way away.'

A day or two later, Sally, Betty and Lorna spent a happy evening together, chatting. Deborah had gone out with Patrick, Louise was at work and Mrs Beaumont had gone to her knitting circle.

'How far along are you?' Sally asked Lorna. Then she smiled. 'Not that I need ask. You were in London towards the end of August, so you're on your way to three months.'

'I haven't known for certain for all that long,' said Lorna, 'and of course I wanted to tell George first. Being able to tell him in person was a dream come true.'

'I can understand that,' Sally said quietly. She hadn't had the opportunity to do that on either occasion, but she wasn't going to spoil Lorna's pleasure. 'I think it's champion. George must have been thrilled to bits, and so proud!'

'You could say that.' Lorna's green eyes softened at the memory. 'He's hoping for a girl.'

'And who can blame him?' Betty asked with a laugh. 'Girls are best. You have to choose a name that starts with B.'

'Belinda?' Sally said at once.

'Briony?' Betty suggested. 'I read that in a book.'

'There are loads to choose from,' said Sally.

'Then the baby will be B-first-name Broughton,' said Betty. 'You'll have your very own BB.'

Laughing, Lorna put her hands over her ears. 'Stop! George might not like any of those names.'

'George isn't the one having the baby,' said Sally.

'He might want a name that's been in his family for generations,' Betty suggested.

'Or he might simply want me to be happy with the name,' Lorna said with the quiet confidence of a wife who knew how deeply important she was to her husband. 'Maybe I'll be like you, Sally, and have a special reason for choosing a name when the baby's born. Bella and Bebe are such meaningful names.'

'Yes, they are,' said Betty. 'Maybe your baby will have a meaningful name, or maybe they'll have a name you and George simply like the sound of. Either way, it'll be the perfect choice.'

'Yes, it will,' said Lorna.

Sally felt sorry and concerned for Betty. As a new mother, Sally was allowed time off to recover from the birth, but Betty wasn't given any time at all because she was 'only' an adoptive mother.

'Don't go fretting yourself over Betty,' said Mrs Beaumont. 'She knew what she was getting into – and have you heard her complaining? No, you haven't.'

'I can't help feeling worried,' said Sally.

'That says more about your kind heart than it does about our Betty,' Mrs Beaumont replied.

Sally knew she was right. Betty was indeed knuckling down to her new life. She was still at the depot, though at present, thanks to Lorna's willing support, she was working half-days and relying on a close neighbour, who was also the mother of a little one, to childmind for her.

When Sally had a go at talking to Betty about her new arrangements, she found that Betty was also concerned about someone – Lorna.

'It's all happened the wrong way round for her,' Betty told Sally. 'If George had been given this job move back in the spring, they could both have come here and at least they'd have had that much time together. As things stand, George is being sent up here just as Lorna is about to be sent back down to London. It feels horribly unfair.'

'I know,' Sally agreed. 'Poor Lorna...'

'She isn't going to be here with us for much longer,' said Betty. 'You'll be back at the depot soon, won't you? So she won't be needed any more.'

'We're going to miss her,' said Sally.

'Very much,' Betty agreed. 'Look, I've been meaning to ask you about your childminding arrangements. I never said anything before because we were all waiting for little Miss Bella to be born in December, only she took us all by surprise.'

'Especially me,' Sally answered with a smile.

'I'm working half-time at the depot,' said Betty, 'but what I really want is to give that up and stay at home. That means setting up as a childminder. I'd love to take care of Bella for you, and it would mean Bebe and Bella can spend heaps of time together. Wouldn't that be grand?'

'Yes, it would,' Sally agreed. 'I'd love them to grow up being an important part of one another's lives.'

Betty sat back, looking pleased. Her blue eyes were bright. 'Good. That's settled, then.'

'But...' Sally's voice trailed away. She took a breath.

'What?' Betty asked.

'I've always loved my work, ever since my very first day after I left school.'

'I know,' said Betty. 'I've only known you for two and a bit years, but it was clear from the start that you take your job seriously and always do your best – and your best is streets ahead of everybody else's.'

'Thanks,' Sally answered, flattered, 'but things are different now. All along, all the time I was resting up because of my dratted blood pressure, I pictured myself going back to the depot after I had the baby. I never had to ask myself what I wanted, because, as far as I was concerned, I already knew. Everyone knew.'

Betty frowned. 'What are you saying?'

'I don't want to spend all day Monday to Friday, and every third Saturday, at the depot. I want to be with my little girl. All the energy and commitment I've always felt for my work – I want to put that into looking after Bella and bringing her up. She's so precious to me.'

'So is Bebe,' said Betty. 'That's why I wanted to be at home with her, and have Bella with us too.' She smiled ruefully. 'I want what's best for you, and I want you to have what you want, but I'm also very disappointed for myself. I was looking forward to taking care of our two little girls.'

'You still can,' said Sally, 'just not in the way you pictured. I think we can both have what we want – well, if Mr Pratt and Mr Merivale agree, then we can.'

'You're talking in riddles,' Betty said, mystified.

'What if you and I *both* went part-time at the depot? You're already half-time, sharing each day between work and home. My idea is that one week you work full-time at the depot while I look after our babies, and the next week we swap over, and I go to the depot while you stay at home.'

Betty didn't answer right away, but Sally could practically see the thoughts flashing across her mind.

After a minute Betty said, 'We'd both have lots of time to be mums, and the girls would grow up together.'

'They'd have *two* mums,' Sally added. 'My mother and Deborah's mother have always said it's like having two daughters.'

'But what about being the depot manager?' Betty asked, looking alarmed. 'Does it mean there would only be a manager during your weeks? I certainly wouldn't want to run the place in my weeks. I wouldn't know where to start.'

'I'd have to step down,' Sally told her.

Betty was shocked. 'Wouldn't you mind?'

'Not when I think of what I'd be getting instead.'

'So, in work terms, you and I would be the equivalent of one worker?' Betty asked, sorting it out in her mind.

'That's right,' Sally confirmed. 'What do you think?'

'I need to talk about it with Samuel,' said Betty, 'but I'm sure he'll agree with me. It sounds just right – not only for you and me, but also for our daughters. That's what matters more than anything.'

FORTY-FOUR

When Mr Pratt and Mr Merivale came to the depot to tell
Lorna about the new working arrangements that had been
agreed for Sally and Betty, she sat politely through the long
explanation as they went at great length through all the ins and
outs. *Honestly!* Did they really think she didn't already know?
Did they imagine that Betty had never mentioned it during the
working day? Didn't they realise Lorna and Sally lived under
the same roof and they talked about everything?

'Thank you for explaining so comprehensively,' Lorna said
in her politest voice when they had finished.

'It's important that you understand,' Mr Pratt replied, 'so
that you can appreciate the knock-on effect.'

'Which is, of course, that you will have to remain here as the
depot manager,' said Mr Merivale, 'since we cannot entertain
the notion of Mrs Henshaw returning to that role on a part-time
basis.'

'You want me to *stay* at the depot?' Lorna exclaimed.

'To be accurate, Mrs Broughton,' said Mr Pratt, 'we *require*
you to stay on. You do not have a choice in the matter.'

'We realise you must have been looking forward to

returning to London,' said Mr Merivale, 'but the needs of the war effort take precedence over all else.'

'Naturally,' Lorna murmured.

She managed to keep a straight face, but her heart was singing. After the gentlemen had departed, she rushed to tell Betty and Rosalind.

'I'm getting exactly what I dreamed of!' She laughed in pure happiness. 'I'll be able to live with George when he moves up here. I'm being ordered to stay. I'll still be with my friends as well. Things couldn't have worked out better for me.'

The icing on the cake was that she had arranged to have a telephone call with George that very evening, so she would be able to share her news at once. George was every bit as delighted as she was, and Lorna wafted around on a cloud of happiness for a day or two.

Then reality hit.

'The men from the Town Hall have no idea I'm expecting a baby,' she told Sally.

'That needn't stop you continuing as manager,' Sally pointed out. 'You haven't collapsed in a heap like I did. Far from it. You're *glowing* with health.'

'To tell the truth,' Lorna confided, 'I don't think I've ever felt healthier.'

'Then what's the problem?' Sally asked.

'I'm looking to the future,' said Lorna. 'I think you and Betty have the right idea. You've found the perfect balance between war work and motherhood, and how many mothers have any hope of achieving that these days? It's going to work beautifully for the two of you, as well as for Bebe and Bella, and I've decided it's what I would like for myself and my own baby.'

'But who would you share the job with?' Sally asked.

'There must be any number of women who would jump at the chance to work part-time,' said Lorna. 'Think of all the women in the WVS. They work tirelessly for no pay. Some of them are hard up but they don't let that stop them, because it's for the war effort.'

'True,' Sally agreed. 'But if you can get permission to work half-time, you won't be able to be the depot manager. The whole point of bringing you back from London was because you're familiar with the depot. Mr Merivale and Mr Pratt aren't going to want a newcomer as manager.'

'No, they aren't,' Lorna agreed. 'That's why I'm going to come clean with them as soon as I can about what I'd like to do – so that they can bring in a new bod for you and me to train up before she takes over as manager. If I can present them with the right person, they're more likely to agree. And I know just who I'm going to ask.'

'Think about it, Louise,' said Lorna. 'You've said all along that you want to find a good job you'll be able to stay in after the war is over.'

'I don't think being the manager of the salvage depot comes into that category,' said Louise.

Lorna thought carefully about what to say next. Louise hadn't said an outright no. In fact, she was clearly intrigued, and that augured well for Lorna's plan.

'You're right,' she said. 'Once the need for collecting and processing salvage has gone, the depot will shut down. How long will the war go on? Think how long the last one dragged on for. This one will be the same. If you become the depot manager now, you'll have been a Corporation employee for a considerable time when the depot shuts its gates for the final time, and the Corporation always wants good workers.'

A thoughtful expression appeared in Louise's brown eyes.

'The Corporation has always employed women,' Lorna added. 'After the war, the married ones will lose their jobs, but the single ones won't. You'll be in a strong position to get a new job. Isn't that what you want? And with the Corporation, you'd be in line for a pension. That's worth thinking about.'

'I would need permission to leave the munitions factory...' said Louise.

That was the moment when Lorna knew she'd won her friend round. She wanted to give three hearty cheers.

'And there's nothing to say that Mr Pratt and Mr Merivale would actually want me,' Louise added.

Lorna chuckled. 'They will, Louise! Believe me, they will.'

'How can you be so sure?'

'Because you and I aren't going to put forward the suggestion.'

Louise frowned. 'Then who will?'

'Mrs Lockwood, of course. She isn't finishing at the depot until Christmas. If she barges into the Town Hall and announces that she's made all the necessary plans for the future of the depot, I promise you that Messrs Pratt and Merivale will fall over themselves in their eagerness to agree to everything. They're frightened silly of her, always have been.'

'But would she do that?' Louise asked.

'Try and stop her,' Lorna replied confidently. 'There's nothing she loves more than chucking her weight around. This way, she gets to leave the depot in a blaze of glory, free to declare to all and sundry that the depot owes its future success entirely to her. Trust me. There's nothing she'd enjoy better. It'll be her last hoorah for Chorlton Salvage Depot.'

FORTY-FIVE

SUNDAY, 6 DECEMBER

It was Stir-Up Sunday, the traditional day for making the Christmas pudding.

For Sally, it was one of those days in which happiness mingled poignantly with sadness, because her beloved Andrew wasn't there with her. With an effort, she set aside those feelings, not wanting to lower anyone else's spirits, and determined to make this a special day for little Bella, even though the baby wouldn't have a clue.

Star House was filled with the delicious aromas of apples and pudding spice. The girls took turns to stir the pudding, as tradition required. Betty and Samuel had brought Bebe round to join in with the festivities, and Rosalind was here too, as were Stella, Lottie and Mary, Mrs Beaumont's original munitions girls. Patrick was here with Deborah. Patrick and Samuel had made jokes about being the only men in a houseful of women when they shook hands.

'It smells *gorgeous* in here, Mrs B,' said Lorna. 'You've done us proud, as always.'

'It's my first Christmas pud with dried eggs, so I hope it turns out all right,' said Mrs Beaumont. 'There were no lemons to be had at the greengrocer's, so I've had to make do with lime cordial.'

'I'm sure it's going to be fine,' said Sally.

Mrs Beaumont gave a wicked little smile. 'Mrs Dawson up the road gave me half a bottle of her husband's home-made wine to use instead of milk in the recipe, so I'm pretty sure it'll turn out very fine indeed one way or another!'

Everyone crowded into the kitchen and had a go at stirring the pudding.

'Don't forget to make a wish!' said Mrs Beaumont.

'Are you meant to make wishes over the Christmas pudding?' Stella, a tall redhead, asked.

'In this house you do,' Mrs Beaumont replied.

Holding Bella in one arm, Sally stirred the pudding mixture with her free hand.

'No prizes for guessing your wish,' Betty murmured, standing beside her, jiggling Bebe, who was watching, blue eyes wide.

The two girls – the two mums! – left the kitchen and returned to the sitting room. Everyone else followed in dribs and drabs. They made quite a crowd. Samuel and Patrick had brought the dining chairs through but there were still those who had to lounge on the floor. It all felt cosy and chummy. Betty put Bebe down and the little one clung to the furniture, wobbling and longing to take a step but not ready quite yet to do so.

'It won't be long before she starts walking,' Mrs Beaumont said admiringly. 'You'll be run off your feet when that happens, Betty.'

'She'll be into everything,' Louise added.

Bebe waved one chubby arm towards her daddy and he obliged at once, picking her up and settling her on his lap, where she sat up, looking confidently all around at the grown-ups filling the room.

Sally's heart clenched. How long would it be before Andrew met Bella? Babies had been born early in the war whose fathers still hadn't seen them. Those children were little ones aged three now.

Mrs Beaumont had made some treats for them all to enjoy. The celery rolls in particular were a big hit.

'Real shortcrust pastry instead of potato pastry,' said sandy-haired Lottie, closing her eyes all the better to relish the taste.

'The landlady where we are now is very nice,' Mary added, 'but her cooking isn't a patch on yours, Mrs Beaumont.'

'Are you going to give Deborah cooking lessons ready for when she's married?' Rosalind asked, and everyone looked at the engaged couple. Deborah blushed and Patrick looked proud.

'I'm happy to teach anyone if they like,' said Mrs Beaumont, 'but I don't imagine Deborah and Patrick will have a place of their own where Deborah can do her own cooking.'

'Not until long after the war,' Patrick confirmed. 'There's so much rebuilding to do.'

'My parents want us to live with them,' said Deborah, 'but it's too far away from Patrick's work.'

'My parents are happy to have us,' said Patrick. 'It'll be an awful squeeze, but we have no other option.'

Inspiration struck Sally. Why hadn't she thought of it before?

'Yes, you do,' she said clearly, making all the attention swing in her direction. 'With Mrs Beaumont's agreement, of course.'

'Agreement to what?' asked the landlady.

Sally turned to her. 'You gave Vesta Tilley to Andrew and me because it's the double bedroom. Andrew will be away until the end of the war, so why not let Deborah and Patrick have Vesta Tilley after they get married, and I'll move into Marie Lloyd with Bella?'

Deborah gasped and her bright-blue eyes widened. 'Are you sure?'

Sally felt a warm glow spreading through her at the thought of being able to make such a difference to her dear friend's life. 'Of course I'm sure. Bella and I can manage perfectly well in a single.' She looked at Mrs Beaumont. 'What do you think?'

'It's fine by me,' said Mrs Beaumont.

Deborah jumped up with a squeal. 'I don't know who to hug first – you or Sally.'

'I think you should hug your fiancé first,' Louise said with a grin.

Patrick rose to his feet and he and Deborah hugged one another, to a smattering of applause. Then they kissed Mrs Beaumont and Sally.

'Thank you!' Deborah whispered in Sally's ear. 'You've no idea how much this means.'

'You're welcome,' Sally murmured. 'We've got to keep the Star House family together, haven't we?'

'Speaking of which...' Deborah said softly. Raising her voice to normal speaking pitch, she addressed Mrs Beaumont. 'You'll need someone new in Vesta Victoria when Lorna leaves to live with George.'

'Unless George wants to move in here?' Louise joked.

Lorna laughed. 'As much as I love it here, I have to tell you I shan't be staying after George moves north. But I'll visit *all* the time. You don't get rid of me that easily.'

'That's true,' Sally said with a laugh. 'You moved out when you got married and look what happened. A few weeks later, back you came.'

'We'll still need a new girl for Vesta Victoria,' said Deborah. 'Maybe... Rosalind?'

Sally was proud of her friend. It hadn't been easy for Deborah when Rosalind was given the depot job – in fact, it had been darned hard – but this generous suggestion showed that she had well and truly moved on from that upset.

Rosalind laughed a little self-consciously. 'It isn't really fair to say that in public when it's Mrs Beaumont's decision.'

'Don't fret on that score,' Mrs Beaumont answered. 'I know you well enough to know that you'll fit in here, so the room is yours, if you'd like it.'

Rosalind paused before saying, 'I wasn't going to say anything until after Christmas, but... I'll be moving on next year.'

'From the depot?' said Betty.

'Is it because Louise is going to be trained up as the new manager and you weren't asked if you'd be interested?' Deborah asked. Patrick gave her a little nudge and she looked sheepish. 'Sorry. That wasn't exactly tactful.'

'Don't worry,' said Rosalind. 'It's nothing to do with hurt feelings, I promise.'

'Why, then?' Lorna asked.

'When I worked in the Food Office, I wasn't there as an ordinary clerk – well, I was, but I was also there to undertake a secret investigation into a food coupon racket.'

'Mr Morland told me about it when I didn't get the depot job,' Deborah put in.

'Before I was sent to Manchester Corporation to do that,' Rosalind went on, 'I worked in the Food Office in Rochdale, doing something similar, and before that I was in Wiltshire.'

'You get sent to different places to do these investigations?' asked Lottie. 'And the colleagues you're put with think you're just one of them?'

'I once had to investigate a Food Office clerk.' A little shiver passed across Rosalind's slender shoulders. 'That was a horrid thing to have to do – but necessary,' she added.

'What happened?' Stella asked. 'Or aren't you allowed to say?'

'It was to do with the tests Food Office clerks carry out on shopkeepers,' said Rosalind.

It didn't escape Sally's notice that now it was Betty's turn to shudder. She had been caught out in just such a test. It was how she and Sally had met.

Deborah took it upon herself to explain to anyone who was unaware. 'Doing a test means turning up as a stranger in a shop and trying to persuade the shopkeeper to bend the rationing rules for you. If he does, he ends up in court.'

'The clerk I had to investigate would catch out a shopkeeper,' Rosalind explained, 'and then give him the chance to avoid the court appearance and the inevitable fine and the possibility of a prison sentence by slipping her a few bob. It wasn't easy to prove, and of course I had to work alongside her in the office every day, pretending everything was normal and taking turns to put the kettle on.'

There was a short silence while everyone digested this.

'Sorry to put a damper on things,' said Rosalind, 'but you did ask.'

'When you came to the depot,' said Lorna, 'were you investigating *us*?'

'No, I swear.' Rosalind's light-blue eyes were sincere. 'They sent me simply because my investigative work was over.'

'And now you're moving on,' said Sally, feeling sorry to think of Rosalind leaving them.

'To do another investigation?' Louise asked.

Rosalind smiled. 'Sorry, I'm afraid I can't say. You understand.'

Yes, they did. Everyone was always being reminded to keep mum and that *loose lips sink ships*.

Sally and Lorna exchanged a private glance. They knew better than anyone about secret war work, because George had himself been involved in an important and dangerous investigation at the time when he and Lorna had found one another again after their separation.

'Best of British luck to you,' said Patrick, 'wherever you go and whatever you do.'

Everyone else echoed his sentiment.

'Thanks,' said Rosalind. 'It's a relief to have told you.'

'So, we're going to need a new girl in Vesta Victoria when Lorna goes to live with George,' said Louise, '*and* a new girl at the depot when Rosalind leaves.'

'It'll be all change,' said Lottie.

'No, it won't,' said Mrs Beaumont. 'It will all work out very nicely. These things do, in my experience. The Vesta Victoria girl and the depot girl might be the same person. Let's wait and see. Whatever happens, Star House will continue to be the homely, comfortable place it's always been, that I can promise you.'

'What will you do after the war, Mrs Beaumont?' Betty asked. 'I suppose you'll go back to taking in theatrical people.'

'Well... I don't know,' said Mrs Beaumont.

'But we all know how much you loved being a theatrical landlady,' said Sally.

'I did – and I will be again one day,' Mrs Beaumont told them, 'but I'm not going to ask anyone to leave who has lived with me throughout the war years. I especially want you to know, Sally, that there'll be a home here for you and Andrew for as long as you need it. Ever so many folk are going to need to find a home after the war, but you won't have that worry, I promise. The same goes for you two, Deborah and Patrick – and you, Louise.'

'And the new girl in Vesta Victoria,' Lorna added with a smile.

'Exactly so,' Mrs Beaumont confirmed, 'because she'll be one of us.'

Sally sighed. She had caught herself sighing a lot recently, mostly little huffs of joy and gratitude when she held Bella in her arms. But this sigh was different. It encompassed everything that Star House and dear Mrs Beaumont meant to her.

'If I'm ever lucky enough to have another daughter,' she said, 'I'm going to call her Seren, because it means "star". Star House is my place of refuge. Bella will grow up here knowing how brave her daddy was at El Alamein, and Seren, if I have her, will know all about the friendship and wonderful support I found here at Star House.'

'What a lovely thing to say,' Mrs Beaumont murmured, dashing away a tear.

'There goes the letter box,' said Patrick. 'I'll go and see what the Sunday post has brought.'

He returned moments later with a couple of letters, one for Mrs Beaumont and one for Sally – an overseas envelope, but with handwriting she had never seen before. She breathed in and then couldn't breathe out again. She adjusted Bella's position so she could handle the letter, but her fingers trembled so much she couldn't open it. Lorna gently took it from her and unsealed it.

Sally removed the flimsy sheet of paper, aware of the profound silence all around her. Anxiety vibrated in the air. She knew she was surrounded by love, but there was fear too. Was the letter from a comrade sending condolences? But there hadn't been a telegram—

Through a painful mist of frightened tears, Sally made herself read the opening words.

'*Oh...*' she breathed. 'It's from Andrew – only it's written by a nurse. He was injured at El Alamein – nothing serious, but it's his right arm.'

'Is he all right?' Betty asked.

Sally nodded. 'He's... he's copped a blighty. They're sending him home on a troop ship to recuperate.' She laughed. 'He'll be on his way right now. This letter must have come via the previous ship.' She could hardly believe she was about to say the words, 'He'll have to go back again once he's better, but... he's *coming home!*'

Delight and relief erupted all around her, and Bebe burst into tears at the sudden noise. Bella didn't. She slept on.

'Isn't she good?' Lorna said when the fuss had subsided. 'She slept through all that.'

Sally bent to kiss her baby's downy head. 'Sleep well, little Bella, and dream of Daddy coming back to us. He's going to love you so much.'

'Yes, he is,' Samuel confirmed, with a doting look at his own little girl.

'Bebe is going to have her daddy well and truly wrapped around her little finger,' Lorna murmured to Sally.

'She already has,' Sally replied, amused. 'It's sweet to see Samuel so enraptured.'

Her heart was light because it wouldn't be too much longer before Andrew was equally smitten with his own daughter. She inhaled a breath of deepest satisfaction, closing her eyes as she slowly released it.

'Do you think Andrew might be home in time for Christmas?' Mary asked Sally.

'Now, Mary, that isn't a fair question,' Mrs Beaumont chided gently before Sally could frame a reply. 'None of us can possibly know the answer to that – but we can all have our hopes,' she added, smiling kindly at Sally.

'It would be wonderful if he could be here by then,' said Sally. 'It would make it the best Christmas ever, but just knowing he's on his way is more than enough. I can't begin to tell you what a relief it is.'

'You've missed him so much,' Betty said sympathetically.

'Yes, I have,' Sally said simply. 'But all the other wives and sweethearts feel the same, and virtually all of them won't have their boys at home with them for Christmas.' After a moment she added honestly, 'It's a strange thing to feel grateful that my husband has been injured, but I do.'

'Some of the gratitude is that he is going to make a full recovery,' Lorna pointed out.

'Yes,' Sally agreed. 'That's a big part of it.'

'How is your blood pressure these days?' Lottie asked her.

'Fine, thanks,' Sally was pleased to assure her. 'Back to normal.' She snuggled Bella close to her body. 'It was all to do with carrying this one, and it went back to normal after I'd had her.'

'I bet she was worth all the discomfort, though,' Stella commented.

'Definitely,' Sally confirmed. 'I can hardly remember what life was like without her.'

'W-we feel the same way about Bebe,' Samuel said with a loving glance at Betty.

Sally smiled warmly at Betty. She and Samuel had been through so much this year, but now their future was rosy, and they couldn't be happier.

Sally turned her gaze upon Deborah and Patrick. They too had had their troubles, but everything had worked out for them, and Deborah and her mum were already planning the wedding. Sally, Lorna and Betty were all going to be matrons of honour, and Deborah had invited Louise to be her bridesmaid.

'Isn't it meant to be the other way round?' Louise had asked with a chuckle when Deborah had made her request. 'One matron of honour and three bridesmaids, not three matrons of honour and one solitary bridesmaid bringing up the rear?'

'Not for a Star House wedding,' Sally had assured her. 'We have our own style – don't we, Mrs Beaumont?'

'Besides, you won't be the only bridesmaid,' Deborah had added, smiling all over her face, 'because I'm going to have a couple of girls from work as well. And I hope there will be a fourth matron of honour too, because I want to ask Dulcie.'

'Your parents are really pushing the boat out, aren't they?' Mrs Beaumont had remarked, sounding as if she approved.

'Well, Mum is,' Deborah had answered with a chuckle. 'She says Dad's job is to put his hand in his pocket and pay for it.'

'And he doesn't mind one bit,' Sally had commented with the confidence of a friend who had known the Grant family all her life.

'No, he doesn't,' Deborah had confirmed, looking happy and proud. 'I am his only daughter, after all.'

Sally couldn't have been more thrilled for her lifelong friend.

Now, her attention moved on and settled on Lorna, someone else who, in Sally's view, very much deserved her happy ending. She and George, instead of living together in London, would shortly be living together up here instead.

'Which works out perfectly for all of us, not just for you two,' Betty had told Lorna, 'because we hated it when you went off to London.'

'This way,' Sally had added, 'you'll be here to watch Bebe and Bella growing up, and before you know it, your own little one will be here as well.'

'You know that you and George will be welcome to drop in at Star House at any time,' Mrs Beaumont had added. 'You'll always be one of my girls.'

'And you'll always be the lovely landlady who looked after us so beautifully during the war,' Lorna had replied, giving Mrs Beaumont a hug.

From Lorna, Sally's gaze now travelled to Louise – the depot's future manager! She had liked Louise from the start and knew that the depot would be in good hands. Sally had no qualms about officially handing over the reins to Lorna and returning to work part-time. Her priorities had changed, and she was profoundly grateful that she and Betty would have the chance to do their war work *and* share the care and upbringing of their darling little girls.

Bebe and Bella. Sally's dearest wish for them was that they would grow up to be friends for life.

The doorbell rang, interrupting her train of thought. Mrs Beaumont left everyone chatting in the sitting room. Moments later the landlady gave a cry of shock, and the talking stopped. Everybody looked at one another. Patrick and Lorna both stood up.

Lorna opened the door and stepped out into the hallway – then she too exclaimed aloud.

'Who is it?' Stella called. 'What's happened?'

Lorna came back into the sitting room, followed by Mrs Beaumont. The landlady's face was pale with shock, making her eyes appear more blue and her hair more black, but she was smiling broadly and her eyes were shining. She focused her gaze on Sally and the sweetly slumbering Bella.

Sally felt a flutter of alarm mixed with confusion. Those exclamations had dismayed her, even scared her, but the big smile on Mrs Beaumont's face, and now also on Lorna's, left her not knowing what to think.

'Sally, my dear—' Mrs Beaumont began, and then couldn't say any more. Her hand flew to her chest as though to contain her emotions.

'Sally,' Lorna chimed in. 'The most wonderful thing has happened. You said Andrew would be coming home – well, he's here—'

'*What?*' Sally cried. She wanted to spring to her feet, but her limbs had drained of strength. 'Andrew—? *Here*—?'

And Andrew walked in, his left arm in the sleeve of his army greatcoat, his right arm nothing more than a bulge across his front, showing where the arm was cradled in a sling. His face was drawn, his brown eyes exhausted, but the moment he saw Sally, his expression lit up with an inner glow and his eyes filled with love. A second later, when he realised what she was holding in her arms, his mouth dropped open.

Sally felt a prickling across the back of her neck and down her spine. Heat rushed into her face and then poured out again. Her pulse stuttered and then raced.

Nobody moved, nobody breathed, as Andrew stood frozen. Then he flung himself across the room and dropped to his knees in front of Sally. His army coat had parted company with the shoulder holding the sling and lay half-strewn behind him. Seeing the sling made Sally realise how close she had come to losing her husband.

She stared at him for a long moment. His face was filled with wonderment at the sight of his child, but beneath that Sally could make out the strain, the bone-deep tiredness... as well as the lines that had been scraped out in his face, the new resolve in an already determined chin. The effects of war on her husband tore at her heart, but his brown eyes were still full of love, just as she remembered, still kind and intelligent, just as she remembered; and that smile, oh that smile, when he lifted his gaze from their baby to meet her eyes, was sweet and vulnerable and proud and filled with awe.

Sally nodded, tears trickling down her cheeks. 'Yes, she's ours. She came early. Bella – her name is Bella.'

'Bella...' Andrew murmured, his voice cracking with emotion.

'Isabella Sarah Henshaw,' Sally whispered. 'Your daughter. *Our* daughter. Our precious baby girl.'

Andrew gave a short laugh and then had to dash away a tear. 'I thought I was coming home to you, but I've come home to a family... my family.'

'I can't believe you're here,' Sally told him emotionally. 'Your letter, the one the nurse wrote for you, only arrived today. We thought you'd be on the next ship.'

'I must have been put on the boat with the mail,' said Andrew, his gaze once more glued to his daughter.

'Would you like to hold her?' Sally asked.

By way of reply, Andrew glanced down at his injured arm. Mrs Beaumont, Lorna and Betty all immediately swooped on him. Next moment, he was seated on the sofa. Sally got up and placed their slumbering daughter into the crook of his good arm and Lorna slid a cushion under his elbow to help him hold Bella safely.

'There,' Mrs Beaumont said in a tone of great satisfaction. 'Doesn't that feel good?'

Without lifting his eyes, Andrew nodded, evidently too overcome to utter a word. Sally slipped into the place beside him and sat as close as she could to her husband and their beautiful daughter.

'Thank you for coming home,' she said softly. 'Thank you for being here.'

'I wish I could put my other arm round you,' he replied, 'and hold all my family.'

'If you were able-bodied enough to do that,' Sally answered lightly, 'they wouldn't have sent you back to Blighty. But if you want us all to be held together, I can do that for you.'

She put her arm round Andrew's shoulders, not tightly for fear of jolting his injured arm, but warmly and securely. Shutting her eyes against a fresh rush of tears, she drew in an expansive breath, her chin quivering slightly. Opening her eyes once more, she shared a nod and a meaningful look with Betty, seated close to Samuel, who was still holding little Bebe.

'This is what it's all about,' Sally said, a quaver in her voice. 'Family and home. Children. This is what we're all fighting for. Our future. Our freedom.'

'El Alamein marked a turning point,' said Lorna.

'Thank you to all the brave men who fought there,' said Mrs Beaumont.

'Including our own Andrew,' Deborah added.

'We have reason now to hope for victory,' Louise stated. 'It will still take a long time and will undoubtedly cost many more lives, but we've turned a corner.'

Andrew dropped a kiss on Sally's temple. 'Thank you for Bella. Thank you for my beautiful daughter. I love you. I love both of you.'

'We love you too,' Sally answered softly.

As Andrew looked back at Bella once more, the baby opened her eyes and gazed up at her adoring daddy for the first time.

A LETTER FROM SUSANNA

Dear Reader,

I want to say a huge thank-you for choosing to read *A Baby for the Home Front Girls*. If you loved finding out what happened next to the Star House girls, and want to keep up to date with all my latest releases, I'd like to invite you to sign up at the following link. You can do so knowing that your email address will never be shared; and you can, of course, unsubscribe at any time.

www.bookouture.com/susanna-bavin

I sometimes get asked about Star House, and I can tell you that the name comes from a real house – though the Star House of the Home Front Girls books, with its bedrooms named after the greats of the music hall, and signed photographs of Florrie Forde, Vesta Tilley and others lining the walls in the hallway and up the staircase, is my own invention. After the war, my gran was for some years a theatrical landlady in Windsor Road in Levenshulme in the south of Manchester. Her boarding house wasn't called Star House, but she had a friend nearby who was also a theatrical landlady – and *her* boarding house was Star House.

And, no, Mrs Beaumont isn't based on Gran – although Gran did dye her hair black for some years instead of gracefully going grey!

Wartime Britain couldn't have managed without women. With able-bodied men away fighting for King and country, women also served their country – by taking over the jobs that had been vacated, as well as tackling specific roles that had come about because of the war. Many women and girls worked long shifts round the clock, plus compulsory overtime, in munitions factories – like Stella, Lottie, Mary and Louise in my stories. They churned out bombs and ammunition that were needed urgently.

My mother worked in a munitions factory in Farnborough, though she wasn't on the production line. She was a bright girl who had gone to grammar school, where she'd gained a distinction in mathematics in her School Certificate. The bombs and missiles in the munitions factory were designed by experienced engineers and my mother's job was to double-check their maths and measurements. (If you've read my Railway Girls books written as Maisie Thomas, the job done by Joan's sister Letitia was my mother's job.) Mum thought nothing of it at the time, but in later life she realised how galling it must have been to these skilled professional men to have their work checked over by an inexperienced young woman – and she *was* young. She was only fifteen when war broke out.

A Baby for the Home Front Girls marks the end of the Home Front Girls series and I hope you were delighted with the girls' happy endings, which I think they very much deserved. It has been a huge pleasure to write these stories for you and to know that you regard the girls as your friends.

Salvage was a massive part of the war effort on the home front. Everything was in increasingly short supply as items vanished from the shops, never to be seen again until after the war – ordinary things like hairpins, paper-clips (a bag of paper-clips was once offered as a prize in a raffle), needles, pencils, coat-hooks... My grandfather described finding a coat-hook in the soil when he was digging for victory. Did he chuck it away? Absolutely not. It was given a good clean and put to use.

During the war, reusing was essential. Many items were redirected into another purpose. Three or four layers of wool fabric for the soles, with a piece of old curtain, tapestry or even old carpet for the tops, and hey presto – a pair of slippers. The shirt-tails could be cut off a man's shirt and made into a new collar and cuffs when the old ones wore out. Old shirts and blouses were turned into baby clothes, and many a blanket found a new life as a winter coat. The WVS ran clothing exchanges, where you could choose something 'new' in return for a good-quality donation. Women's magazines were full of clever ideas for giving clothes a new lease of life, such as turning a full-length coat that was past its best into a hip-length coat and using the left-over fabric to make a smart new collar, cuffs and pocket-flaps.

And let's not forget the part that children played on the home front. I have dedicated this book to all the wartime Brownies, because salvage soon became a job for children. Hundreds of thousands of children joined the 'cog' scheme, each of them becoming a small cog in the mighty war machine. Schools, Guides and Brownies, Scouts and Cubs all competed with one another to collect the most salvage in their local neighbourhoods. Newspapers ran a 'cog' page each week for children, and a special song was written called 'There'll Always Be a Dustbin', which was sung to the tune of 'There'll Always Be an England'. Working towards earning their 'cog' badges was an important part of wartime life for many youngsters.

So, the next time you're sorting through your own recycling, preparing to put it out for collection in the various boxes, spare a thought for our salvage-minded wartime generation, who by the time D-Day came round had provided 1.1 million tons of waste paper, 1.3 tons of metal and more than 80,000 tons of rags to help fight – and win – the Second World War.

I hope you loved reading *A Baby for the Home Front Girls*, that you felt wrapped up in the story and that you were with the girls every step of the way. If you enjoyed the book, I would be very grateful if you could write a review. I'd love to hear what you think, and it makes such a difference helping new readers to discover one of my books for the first time.

I always enjoy hearing from my readers – you can get in touch on my Facebook page, through Twitter, Goodreads or my website.

Much love

Susanna xx

www.susannabavin.co.uk

 facebook.com/MaisieThomasAuthor
 x.com/SusannaBavin

ACKNOWLEDGEMENTS

One of the greatest joys of being an author is that, when the book is written, it's everyone else's job to make it into the best possible version of itself and launch it into the world, and I am enormously lucky to have the Bookouture team behind me. Jess Whitlum-Cooper, whose insightful editing made the story stronger. Jess Readett, for her work on publicity. Ria Clare, for overseeing production. Occy Carr, for marketing. Jacqui Lewis, the series copyeditor, and Anne O'Brien, the series proofreader. Thanks also to Imogen Allport, Nina Winters and Nadia Michael. If you love the covers of the Home Front Girls books, it's Nick Castle you have to thank.

I am fortunate to have my agent, Camilla Shestopal, in my corner. Love and thanks to my writing chums Jen Gilroy and Jane Cable. My tech elf, Kevin, always knows how to make the computer behave itself. Thanks also to Beverley Ann Hopper, Helen Hopwood, Meena Kumari and Vicki Eddison.

I am proud to be part of the Ulverscroft family. Magna Large Print and Magna Story Sound, divisions of Ulverscroft, produce the Home Front Girls books in large print and as audiobooks. I want to send a huge thank you and lots of love to the hugely talented Julia Franklin, who narrates this series. Every book that I have had published under all three of my names – Susanna Bavin, Polly Heron and Maisie Thomas – has been narrated by Julia, with the intuitive understanding of character, atmosphere and timing that characterises all her narrations. Of all my professional relationships in the world of publishing, the one I have with Julia dates back the longest: to the very beginning. Many thanks for bringing my stories to life, Julia. You're a star.

Proofreader
Anne O'Brien

Marketing
Alex Crow
Melanie Price
Occy Carr
Cíara Rosney
Martyna Młynarska

Operations and distribution
Marina Valles
Stephanie Straub
Joe Morris

Production
Hannah Snetsinger
Mandy Kullar
Ria Clare
Nadia Michael

Publicity
Kim Nash
Noelle Holten
Jess Readett
Sarah Hardy

Dear Reader,

We'd love your attention for one more page to tell you about the crisis in children's reading, and what we can all do.

Studies have shown that reading for fun is the **single biggest predictor of a child's future life chances** – more than family circumstance, parents' educational background or income. It improves academic results, mental health, wealth, communication skills, ambition and happiness.

The number of children reading for fun is in rapid decline. Young people have a lot of competition for their time, and a worryingly high number do not have a single book at home.

Hachette works extensively with schools, libraries and literacy charities, but here are some ways we can all raise more readers:

- Reading to children for just 10 minutes a day makes a difference
- Don't give up if children aren't regular readers – there will be books for them!

- Visit bookshops and libraries to get recommendations
- Encourage them to listen to audiobooks
- Support school libraries
- Give books as gifts

There's a lot more information about how to encourage children to read on our websites: **www.RaisingReaders.co.uk** and **www.JoinRaisingReaders.com**.

Thank you for reading.